THE
SPACE
BETWEEN
THE
STARS

Anne Corlett has an MA in Creative Writing from Bath Spa University and has won a number of awards for her short stories, including the H. E. Bates Award. She works as a criminal solicitor and freelance writer, and lives with her partner and two young boys in Somerset. *The Space Between the Stars* is her first novel.

THE
SPACE
BETWEEN
THE
STARS

ANNE CORLETT

PAN BOOKS

First published 2017 by Macmillan

First published in paperback 2017 by Macmillan

This paperback edition published 2018 by Pan Books
an imprint of Pan Macmillan
20 New Wharf Road, London N1 9RR
Associated companies throughout the world
www.panmacmillan.com

ISBN 978-1-5098-3355-9

1 3 5 7 9 8 6 4 2

A CIP catalogue record for this book is available from the British Library.

Printed and bound by CPI Group (UK) Ltd, Croydon, CR0 4YY

To Simon, for never telling me to stop arsing about on the laptop and get a proper job.

Well, almost never.

Acknowledgements

Like lots of other writers, I have spent many a happy hour mentally composing the acknowledgements for my debut novel, deciding which artist would perform the theme tune for the film, and drafting imaginary acceptance speeches for major literary awards. The one for the Nobel Prize is an absolute corker – really profound and moving. Particularly the bit about world peace.

Unfortunately, when I came to *actually* write the acknowledgements for my debut novel, I couldn't remember any of the interesting and witty things I'd come up with, so I'm afraid I'm going to have to fall back on the tried-and-tested 'wow, that Oscars speech went on for a long time' format.

There are many, many people who deserve my thanks. Some have had a specific role in bringing this book to life, while others have helped and supported me throughout the whole of my writing journey. It is probably inevitable that I will miss someone out. If I do, please take it as a lapse at the moment of drafting this list, and rest assured that your contribution is not otherwise forgotten.

First on this long list is my wonderful agent, Lisa Eveleigh, who believed in me from the first, and always went above and beyond. Thank you for everything.

My heartfelt thanks also go to my equally wonderful editors, Bella Pagan and Cindy Hwang, and the rest of the Pan Macmillan and Berkley teams.

Thank you to my MA tutor, Maggie Gee, for telling me I

could do it, and also how to do it in considerably fewer words. Also to Fay Weldon, for all her support and some lovely lunches. I consider myself very lucky to have had the opportunity to learn from two such great writers.

I've been fortunate enough to have had the support and encouragement of many other writers, as well as of others involved in the creative industries. I cannot name them all, but some deserve a specific mention. The Intensive Critique group on the Writewords forum for giving me my first ever feedback, as well as my 'real-life' writing group, The Beermat of Silence, for shouting at me loudly whenever a sentence went on for so long that it was in danger of rivalling *War and Peace*. Particular thanks go to Roger Barnes, for shouting about long sentences *and* correcting some of my spectacularly incorrect sailing terminology. Last, but not least, Jen Faulkner and Kate Simants, fellow writers and fellow child-wranglers, for support, encouragement and friendship.

Thanks must also go to everyone at The Little Coffee Shop in Saltford and the Waterstones cafe in Bath for endless cups of tea while I wrote and edited this book.

Finally, thank you to my family, for their unwavering love, support and gentle mockery. To Margaret, for babysitting above and beyond the call of duty, Simon, without whom this book could never, ever have been written, and Thomas, Ben and Sam, who all did their level best to make sure it wasn't.

Actually, scratch that 'finally' – there's another one.

Tony and Steve, builders and decorators extraordinaire. Because I promised I would, and I'll never hear the end of it if I don't.

THE
SPACE
BETWEEN
THE
STARS

CHAPTER ONE

She knew it was the third day when she woke. Even in the twists and tangles of the fever, her sense of time had remained unbroken. More than unbroken. Whetted into a measure of such devastating accuracy that she'd wanted nothing more than to die quickly and be done with that merciless death-watch count of her last hours. And dying *was* quicker, according to the infomercials that spiralled out from the central planets when the virus first took hold there. Most people were gone by halfway through the second day. If you were still lingering beyond that midpoint, chances were you'd still be there after the fever had burned itself out in a last vicious surge on the third day.

Jamie could taste blood in her mouth, bitter as old coins, and her back was aching with a dull, bed-bound creak of pain. But her bones were no longer splintering in some unseen vice, and there was none of the twisting vertigo that had flung her about inside relentless nightmares. In the throes of the fever, skeletal horses had leered at her, and an organ-grinder who was nothing but teeth and hands had turned the handle faster and faster until it all blurred into nothingness.

Her senses were slowly coming back online. She could hear her own ragged, uneven breathing, and she could smell the reek of sweat-stained sheets.

She was alive. That realisation brought no leap of joy or relief. There was a nag of unease working its way around the edges of her thoughts.

Survival was something she'd never dared hope for in those interminable days before the virus took hold on Soltaire, when there'd been nothing to do but wait for the inevitable to hit their planet too. The disease's long incubation period meant that it had already reached every corner of settled space before the first symptoms appeared on the capital, Alegria. The messages from Alegria and the central worlds stopped a week or so before the sickness hit Soltaire. The infomercials had already given way to blunt emergency transmissions. As the days passed, the silences between them grew longer, the messages shorter, less coherent, as though the airwaves were fraying. But by then they knew what was coming. The virus was terminal in almost all cases.

Ninety-nine point nine nine nine nine per cent, one of the ranch hands had said. Jamie didn't know where he'd got that figure, but it spread and became fact. The day he said that was the day they all stopped looking at each other. How many of them could hope to make it into a minority so staggeringly small? The odds were akin to launching a paper plane off the planet's surface and hoping to hit a target back on Earth.

Nought point nought nought nought one per cent.

She felt stiff and brittle, like she'd snap if she moved. Her senses had turned on her. She could hear all the noises that her home wasn't making. The generator at the main house was temperamental, and it wasn't unusual for it not to be running. But she should have been able to hear the distant hum of machinery from the logging station over at the lake, or the farmhands calling to one another and swearing at the cattle. Instead, all she could hear was the soft, barely-there swish of the station's turbine, and the squabbling of the immigrant sparrows in the trees behind the croft.

That was it. No human sound.

Survival was a one in a million chance. The virus was a

near-perfect killing machine. Contagious as hell, it had a vicious little sting in its tail. It mutated with every reinfection. A single exposure was survivable – with luck – but it was as though it knew us. As the disease spread, people did what people always do. They clung and grabbed and mauled one another. They queued at the hospitals. They died in the waiting rooms. They clutched at their lovers and held on to their children. And the disease rampaged joyously, burning through thought and will, then flesh, and, at the very last, through bone – until there was nothing but dust, and no one left to mourn over it.

Dust to dust, Jamie thought, rising slowly onto one elbow. The sun was slanting under the top edge of the window, illuminating the interior of the single-roomed croft that had been her home for the last three months. It was a standard settler's dwelling, flat-packed as part of some colonist family's baggage allowance when the first ships made their way through the void.

Jamie's head was aching, and her mouth was so dry that she might as well have been dust herself.

Had she breathed them in? The dead? Were they inside her now, clinging to her throat, hoping for some chance word that might carry them back to an echo of life?

Ninety-nine point nine nine nine nine per cent.

She yanked herself back from the fall that lay beyond that thought. It might be different here. They'd had some warning. And they didn't live crushed up close against each other, like on the central worlds.

But . . . the silence.

Something snagged in her throat, and she coughed, and then retched, doubling over.

Water.

The thought instantly became an urgent need, with enough

force to tip her over the edge of the bed and into a sprawled half-crouch on the stone floor. She pushed herself upright, leaning hard on the bed, and then crossed the floor, moving with a club-footed awkwardness. When she reached the sink, she clung to it with both hands. The mirror in front of her was clouded and warped. The distortion had always unsettled her, with the way it caught her features and twisted them if she turned too quickly. But today the clouded surface was a relief. She didn't need a reflection to know how reduced she was. She felt shrunken, stretched too tight over her bones, her dark hair hanging lank and lifeless on her shoulders, her olive skin bleached to a sallow hue.

The tap sputtered, kicking out a little spurt that grew into a steady stream. She splashed at her face, the cold water forcing the shadows back to the edges of her mind, leaving nothing to hide that pitiless statistic.

Ninety-nine point nine nine nine nine per cent dead.

Ten billion people scattered across space.

Nought point nought nought nought one per cent of ten billion.

Ten thousand people should have survived.

Spread across how many populated worlds? Three hundred, or thereabouts. Thirty-three survivors per world. And a few left over.

She had a nagging sense that her maths was wrong. But then she was weak, reduced by her illness. It was making it hard to think clearly.

When the answer struck her, she initially felt only a little snick of satisfaction at figuring it out. All worlds were not created equal. Almost half the total human population lived on Earth and the capital planet cluster. There must be a couple of billion people on Alegria alone.

That meant two thousand survivors. Set against the omin-

4

ous silence outside the croft, that seemed like a vast number, and she felt a flicker of relief.

But then there were all the fledgling colonies, right out on the edges of civilisation, some of them numbering only a few hundred people.

Soltaire fell somewhere between those two extremes. Its single land mass was sizeable enough – about the size of Russia, she'd been told – but settlement had been slow. There were ten thousand people, or thereabouts, most of them clustered around the port, or over in Laketown. Then a few smaller towns, and a clutch of smallholdings, as well as the two main cattle-breeding centres, at Gratton Ridge and here at Calgarth.

Ten thousand people.

All the heat seemed to drain out of her body.

Nought point nought one.

Not even a whole person. There shouldn't have been enough of her left to do the maths.

A cramp stabbed through her stomach and up into the space beneath her ribs, doubling her over.

Breathe.

It was just an estimate. Maybe other people had done what she'd done, and locked themselves away the second they'd felt that first itch in their throat. But then it hadn't been hard for her to follow the emergency advice. There was no one depending on her, no one wanting her close. But if she'd still been with Daniel, would one of them have given in and crawled to the other, seeking warmth and comfort and the reassurance of another heart beating near theirs?

Daniel.

His name slammed into her, and she put her hands to her head, waiting for the reverberations of that thought to stop, so that she could start feeling something.

Nothing.

Daniel, she thought, more deliberately this time. The man with whom she'd spent the last thirteen years. The man she'd loved.

Still loved.

Maybe.

No.

That was a distraction she didn't need right now.

She stood up straight, moving slowly and carefully as though the air might shatter at an incautious movement, and reached for the towel hanging beside the sink. It was a thread-bare rag of a thing that looked as if it had been here since the first settlers, but towels were just one of the things she'd forgotten when she left Alegria. She'd arrived with only a handful of clothes and essentials, plus a few personal bits and pieces. Daniel had taken it as a good sign. *Your stuff is all where you left it*, he'd told her, in one of his mails. *Whenever you want it.*

Whenever you want me. That's what he'd really been saying. *I want you now.*

The thought caught her by surprise. She'd turned that question over and over in her mind since she'd been out here, in an endless inverted *he loves me, he loves me not*. She'd analysed every memory, replayed every argument, every tender moment, and she'd come up with a different answer every time.

Clearly she'd needed to wait until the world had ended before deciding that she did love him.

Loved him, wanted him. It was the same thing, wasn't it? A pull, a stretching of the tether that started with the other person and ended somewhere deep in your chest. She'd felt that tug when they'd talked on the long-distance airwave at the port. When was that? Three weeks ago? The conversation was stilted and artificial. Even though he'd shuttled out to the capital cluster's long-range station, the time delay was so marked that while she was speaking, the mouth of his crackled doppelgänger was still moving to the echo of his last remark, as though he was talking over her. He was going to Earth for a few weeks, he told her. Work. He just wanted her to know. In case . . .

That *in case* had been left hanging between them. That was when she'd felt that tug. It wasn't strong enough to make her say what she knew he hoped she'd say. But when he asked if they could talk again when he got back, she agreed. She'd even found a smile for him as they said goodbye, although it hadn't quite felt like it fitted, and she didn't know if he'd seen it before the connection was severed.

He'd been heading for Earth.

Four billion people on Earth. Four thousand survivors.

What were the chances of them both making it? She felt suddenly weak and couldn't work it out. Panic was starting to swirl up inside her chest.

Breathe.

She walked over to the cupboard. Underwear, a pair of jeans. She pulled them on. No T-shirts.

The washing line. She'd been hanging out laundry when the first spasms had sent her to her knees, and then, by slow increments, to the medicine drawer.

She stood still. Until she went outside, this could all just be a game of *what if?*

Nought point nought nought nought one.

'Shut up.' Her voice sounded thin and rusty, and she swore, another harsh scrape of sound, then opened the door.

The sun was high overhead, the sky its usual denim blue, fading to smoky marl at the horizon. Outside the croft a half-line of washing swayed in the breeze. At one end, a bed sheet trailed from a single peg, the line sagging under its weight. The laundry basket was on its side, her clothes streaked and crumpled in the dirt.

7

She realised she'd instinctively wrapped the towel around her before stepping outside, just as though one of the farm-hands might wander by with a casual wolf whistle.

Little things, she thought. It was too easy to forget, to fall back into past habits, paying too much attention to all the tiny, insignificant things.

She kept the towel clamped against her sides until she'd unpegged a grey T-shirt, and pulled it over her head. Her boots were abandoned by the door, as usual, and she sat to lace them up.

The birds had scattered over to the boundary fence, their quarrel muted by distance. The turbine turned quietly, and the cattle grumbled from the barn. She stood up, stretching her cramped limbs, forcing herself to look around. The main house was still and silent and she turned away, towards the open land beyond the station fences. A couple of faint scraps of cloud drifted over the hills, carrying a vague promise of rain.

Her thoughts were spiralling out, beyond the simple fact of the warm breeze and clear sun. This world had long growing seasons, regular rainfall, a simple infrastructure. It would be an easy enough place to survive, if surviving became all there was.

No.

The door of the main house was closed, but the curtains were open. Someone could be looking out right now. Or perhaps someone had heard her. Maybe they were stumbling to the window as she stood there.

But she didn't move.

There was a rumble from the barn. If the Calgarth herd had been milkers, they'd have been protesting their swollen neglect long and loud. But these were breeders, and their complaints were probably focused on being barn-bound and out of feed. If those basic needs were met, they wouldn't be troubled by the decimation of the human world.

She turned away from those empty windows, and walked down to the barn, swinging back the bar that kept the cattle from the yard. She found the herd outside, gathered in the shade of the back wall, near a trough of greenish water and a pile of fodder spilled from an upended bin. The scattered feed spoke of someone using their last strength to make sure the herd had enough to last until . . . for a while.

Her heart felt small and hard, as if her illness had turned it into something other than flesh. She hadn't spent much time with Jim Cranwell, who ran the farm, despite being his resident veterinarian, but he'd always been courteous. She'd had more to do with his grandchildren, who'd run in and out of the barn, clambering between stalls and treating the cattle like oversized pets. At first she'd wished they would leave her alone. She found their constant questions distracting, and she veered between patronising, oversimplified answers and curt, too-adult responses. But she'd got used to their presence, even playing the odd game with them, although she always tired of it before they did.

She'd have to go round the station and prop all the gates open. There was a stream near the boundary fence, so the cows would have water. She wasn't sure what to do about the bulls. If she left them roaming free, they'd fight, but if she kept them separate, there'd be no new calves. What happened when there was no prospect of anything beyond this generation? What happened when . . .

She gripped the edge of the door frame, her breath growing ragged. There'd be other people who'd beaten the odds. She had to find them. Until she did, these thoughts would keep piling up until she was crushed beneath them.

She stood for a moment, breathing slowly, trying to think

about nothing but the blue of the sky and the curve of the hills. Then she turned and walked, slowly and heavily, towards the silent house.

It's summer and a girl runs down a path towards a beach. The sun hangs low in a clear blue sky, like every memory of every summer evening there ever was.

Her stepmother comes to the gate and calls to her.

Jamie. Jamie. Take your sisters with you.

She hates the way her stepmother always says sisters, not half-sisters, as though she's trying to rewrite history, so that there was only ever the way things are now.

Jamie's the one who feels like a half. She's felt like that for years now. Ever since the night her mother drank one glass too many and let an old secret come spilling out, about the scar on Jamie's chest. She'd always thought it looked like a zip-fastener, running breastbone to navel, as though someone had opened her up and scooped something out.

It was a simple enough procedure. That's what the doctors had said. Just some cartilage to snip away.

Jamie often wondered what her mother saw when she looked at her daughter. Her living child, or her two-for-the-price-of-one babies, who'd been wheeled away to come back as one alone? Her mother kept telling the story, probing at the choice they'd made, like it was a rotten tooth. And every time she told it she cried and clutched at her remaining child.

You know I love you. Don't you? Don't you? You're all I've got left.

But all Jamie heard was that she'd taken too much. She'd come into the world with someone holding on to her, and that

11

almost-self had been sliced away, leaving her with more than her fair share.

Her stepmother calls to her again. But Jamie keeps running, down to where the wet sand fades into the shallows. The water is almost still, the weight of the coming night already damping down the waves. She pulls off her shoes, steps barefoot into the sea. It's cold, but she's done this many times before. She knows the first chill will soon fall away. She walks out beyond the shallows, her light summer clothes clinging to her. When she's deep enough, she tucks her knees underneath her and kicks out into the slow press of the tide.

When she grows tired, she leans back, sculling gently, counting stars. She'll stay here until the cold has soaked right into her bones, forcing her back to shore. Then she'll carry her shoes back up the beach and along the path to the house. Her stepmother will see her from the kitchen window, and she'll come out, holding a towel she's warmed on the Aga. And Jamie will sit at the kitchen table, listening as the older woman tries to find the right words, the ones that will break open the brittle shell of her stepdaughter's silence.

But Jamie is fastened up tight, her zip pulled safely over her heart, and she'll never let anything dangerous slip out again.

CHAPTER TWO

Jamie hesitated before pushing the front door open.

'Hello?'

Her voice cracked. She swallowed and tried again.

'Mr Cranwell?' That sounded childishly formal. 'Jim?'

The kitchen was tidier than usual. His daughter used to invite her in for a cup of tea sometimes.

'Cathy?'

Even the washing-up had been cleared away. An image flared in her head. Cathy, leaning heavily on the kitchen side, drying cups and stacking them slowly away, refusing to acknowledge the pointlessness of the task. One cupboard door was ajar, with a broken dish nearby. Maybe she'd crawled to her bed, like Jamie had. But Cathy's bed wouldn't have been empty. She would have climbed in and wrapped her arms around her children, breathing in their contagion, not knowing any other way of being.

Jamie walked down the hallway to a white-painted door. She stepped into a bright, airy room with doors opening onto the grass behind the house. Dust flecks drifted in the slanting sunlight.

Dust.

The sheets were grey with it, the covers tipped into a tangle on the floor.

There wasn't much. Not when you thought of the measure of a person.

Three people.

You'd have imagined there'd be more heft to a human life.

Jamie stood for a moment, watching the slow play of light and dust, then stepped backwards into the corridor and closed the door behind her.

Upstairs, she checked each door until she found a bare-boarded room, furnished with just a bed and a chest of drawers. There was a cross on the wall and a sprawl of abandoned clothes on the floor, topped with Jim Cranwell's belt, the one his grandchildren had bought him, with the buckle shaped like a running horse.

The covers were drawn up, almost as though the bed had been made, and the pillow was dusted with grey.

Back outside, Jamie leaned against the wall and closed her eyes. There was a pushiness to the sun's warmth.

Come on, come on. Things to do, things to know.

When she opened her eyes, her gaze fell on one of the crofts down beyond the barn. She stared at it for a moment, and then pushed herself upright and set off across the yard.

Her circuit of the station took longer than it should have done. The virus had diminished her. She checked the six crofts, as well as the dorm that housed the younger farmhands. Some were as tidy as the main house, while others bore signs of an occupant who'd done everything they could not to go quietly into the night. But there were no signs of life, and everywhere she went, she saw dust motes drifting in the uncaring sunlight.

When she was done she went back to her own croft. Her skin felt dry and scuffed, and she found herself rubbing at her palms, as though that dust was clinging to her skin.

Suddenly she was on her knees, folded over, forehead pressed to the floor as though she was praying. Which way did Muslims pray? Towards Mecca. How did they know which way that was, all these millions of miles away?

Her thoughts were twisting tighter and tighter until there was nowhere to go but to the place she'd been trying to avoid. She shouldn't be alive. Somehow the little world had got lucky. Was there any realistic chance that its luck had held more than once? And if not . . .

No.

There were other worlds. There'd be other survivors.

But the statistics were wrong here. What if they were wrong elsewhere? Her thoughts unwound again, spinning out beyond the walls of the croft, beyond the skies, out into the endlessness of space. An empty universe, with just one pinpoint of life, curled and numb on a dusty floor.

She fought for control. She knew there were survivors. The emergency messages had been clear.

Terminal in almost *all cases.*

Almost. A lot of life could fit into that one small word.

It all came down to the central worlds. Two thousand survivors. Enough for searches, for rescue missions.

But what if they thought two thousand was enough?

Her hope was strung on elastic, slackening, then snapping tight again.

If no one came, what then? How did it work, being alone, day in, day out?

You wouldn't speak. There'd be no one to talk to. You wouldn't touch anyone and no one would touch you. No one would stroke your hair, or tap you on the shoulder and say, *Hey, I thought that was you.* No sex. No one inside you but you, and yet you would somehow feel too full, too crowded, with no room to breathe.

Jamie curled tighter.

Stop.

Her heart was beating a tempo it couldn't sustain without shaking her apart. And she couldn't break apart because there was no one to put her back together again. If she broke, then her pieces would blow away on the wind, like the others. Dust to dust and . . .

Stopstopstopstopstop.

She'd survived. There'd be others. There would.

That thought was a handhold in the shifting swell of panic, tiny and fragile, but just enough for that tight knot inside her to unwind a little.

There'll be others.

She stayed bent over for a long moment, and only when she was sure her legs would support her did she climb slowly to her feet.

She stripped off her clothes, and walked over to the corner cubicle to pull the shower lever. The water was cold, but she closed her eyes and tipped her head back, letting it run over her face and neck, and down the line of the long, pale scar towards her stomach, which still had the faintest suggestion of a swell from her lost pregnancy.

Once she was done, she dressed and went back outside, over to the boundary fence. The horizon was blurred with a slight heat haze, but she could just make out the distant out-line of the turbines that served the port. They were still turning, ghost-pale against the bleached blue sky.

What if there were other people out there staring at their own empty skies? Each of them trapped in their own lonely skin on their own lonely world. Perhaps they'd take a leap of evolution and learn to send their thoughts across the void.

Hello. I'm here. I'm alone.

Jamie caught herself on the verge of making a sound that could have been a cough of laughter, or a sob, or any number of incoherent things in between.

I need space, she'd told Daniel, ignoring the sour clang of the cliché. She hadn't just been talking about their relationship. Wherever you went, there were always too many people trying to squeeze into that piece of the world. On Soltaire there'd been room to breathe, with no one pushing her to explain the exact shape and tone of each breath.

Be careful what you wish for.

Perhaps if she wished again, the turbines would falter, then start turning backwards, unwinding it all. Someone would say, *Oh no, that wasn't supposed to happen*, and they'd take it back.

But the great shadow-arms kept turning.

Back inside the croft Jamie moved around, touching things. Her ancient screen stayed a speckled, dull grey when she pressed the button. No electricity. The generator was down. When she picked up her comm-pager from the bedside table, the battery light was flashing, but there was still enough power to light the screen when she tapped it. One word appeared.

Message

Her hand jerked so hard that she almost lost her grip on the device. She tightened her fingers around it, and when she unpeeled them again, those blocky letters were still squatting there. When she tapped them with her fingertip, they gave way to a couple of lines of text.

Central Time 15.7.10 – 18.42

Duration 15 seconds

There followed a long jumble of incomprehensible data, marking the trail of comm satellites that had bounced the message across the void of space.

Her hands were shaking. The fifteenth of July. Less than two days ago. Soltaire was remote. The central worlds had gone silent several days before the virus took hold here.

She touched the screen lightly, as though that might use less power. The pager spat out a crackle of static, which gave

17

way to a high-pitched whine as the message ticker moved across the screen.

. . . eleven twelve thirteen . . .

Another burst of static, wrapped around something that might have been a human voice, like a faded ghost in the machine.

Then nothing.

She hit the replay button. Again, the seconds counted down, and again, the static flared, carrying with it that tantalising hint of a voice. Then the pager went dark.

'No. *Fuck.*'

She smacked the device with her palm, but the screen stayed blank. Panic scraped at the inside of her ribs. If she could just listen one more time, she might be able to figure it out. She might be able to . . .

Stop.

She drew a deep breath. There'd been nothing there. And it didn't matter. The simple existence of the message was the point. It had been sent two days ago, long after the disease had completed its rampage through all but the most outlying worlds. Someone else was alive. And in all the vastness of space, she could only think of one person who would be trying to contact her.

Daniel. He was alive.

The room lurched around her.

A memory surfaced. She'd taken him home with her once. It was three years ago, after her father died. She hadn't wanted to go back for the funeral, but Daniel had pushed and pushed until she gave in and booked them places on one of the fast clippers. It hadn't been as hard as she'd feared. The service was simple and understated, and she'd managed to hug her stepmother and half-sisters and make the right noises, without too much of their shared history gaping between them.

They'd only stayed in Northumberland for a couple of nights, but Daniel had been taken with the place, and they'd been easier together than they had in a long while. On the second evening they'd walked on the long, crescent-shaped beach at Belsley, watching the sun sink beyond the headland. He'd made a comment about it being a reasonable place to sit out a zombie apocalypse – an old joke of theirs – and she'd laughed and agreed.

It's a plan. He'd smiled at her. *If the world ends, we'll meet back here. Whoever arrives first can write their name on the sand so the other one knows they're here.*

Okay, she'd said, *but make sure it's above the tideline.* When he kissed her, she'd leaned into him, thinking that maybe they'd make it after all.

Jamie drew in another ragged breath. He'd been heading to Earth when they'd last spoken. That old promise had been made in jest, but he'd remember. He remembered everything. But she was stranded here, with light years of space between them and no way of crossing it. A sudden rush of vertigo tipped the floor beneath her feet, and she bent over, wrapping her arms across her body, waiting for the world to steady. There had to be a way. She could go to the port. There might be other survivors. There would be.

Other people. A ship. Someone might know how to fly it. Someone could learn. She could learn. They'd get off the planet, head to Earth, to Northumberland, to Daniel.

Her thoughts were tumbling over one another with a buoyancy she didn't want to examine too closely.

They'd get to Earth and Daniel would be waiting for her. She'd look at him and be sure for the first time. He'd be alive and she'd be alive and that would mean something. It *had* to mean something.

She looked around the croft, her pulse beating an urgent tattoo.

Hurry, hurry, hurry.

Her old rucksack was stuffed at the back of the cupboard. It was a tattered canvas thing that had once belonged to her grandfather. Jamie had taken it on school camping trips, along with his heavy, oilskin-backed sea blanket, which was folded in the bottom of the bag now. It had taken up a fair chunk of her baggage allowance when she left Earth, but somehow she couldn't bring herself to leave it behind. She grabbed the rucksack, shoving some clothes inside, before heading out of the croft.

Down in the field the cattle ambled behind her as she opened the three gates that would give them access to the stream and the best grazing. She hesitated over the gates to the bulls' enclosures, but eventually propped them open too.

The station's battered off-roader was missing from its place behind the barn, and her ID wasn't logged for any of the other vehicles. She knew there were various ways of circumventing the security systems, but she had no idea where to start with that sort of tinkering. Her gaze fell on the paddocks to the side of the house. She couldn't see the three scrubby cattle ponies, but when she whistled, Conrad lifted his greying head, and wandered over to nose at her pocket. The swaybacked roan had endured years of little feet drumming at his sides, and he had an air of world-weary patience. Jamie rubbed his neck, her breath snagging on the sudden lump in her throat.

The cattle, the birds, their presence hadn't made a dent in her sense of *alone*. But Conrad was different. She knew him – his name, his quirks and foibles – and seeing him here gave her a pang of emotion that fell somewhere between relief and despair.

Conrad made no objection to being tacked up – beyond a

token exhalation that meant she had to set her shoulder against his side and dig him with her elbow to get the girth tightened.

'Sort yourself out.'

He shoved her hard with his head, leaving green-tinged slobber down her side.

Jamie tightened her rucksack across her shoulders and pulled herself into the saddle.

'Come on, then,' she said, clicking her tongue to push him into a rolling plod.

The spaceport was a couple of hours away. Conrad settled into a steady enough pace once he realised he was in it for the duration. Jamie even broke a clunky canter out of him at one point, although she couldn't persuade him to maintain it. She still had that *hurry, hurry* beating inside her head, but she knew Conrad wouldn't *be* hurried. His hoof beats were hypnotic, and by the time Jamie realised she was counting them, she was already well into the hundreds.

Counting kept the other thoughts at bay. She'd been so sure when she'd set off, but the closer she got to the port, the more that *nought point nought nought nought one* shouldered its way in. How could she expect to find survivors with those desperate odds?

It was mid-afternoon when she arrived. Her mouth was dust-dry, and there was a dull throb at the back of her head. When she'd been here before the port had been one great clatter of noise from the shipyard and the trade depot, but today the stillness was unnerving. At least at Calgarth there'd been a backdrop of sound, as the non-human world went about its business. But there was no birdsong here, the silence broken only by the scrape of an open door swinging in the breeze.

She dismounted in the square and Conrad wandered over to the scrub of grass in front of the shop. He wouldn't need tethering. Give him a patch of unfamiliar green and he'd be happy for hours, like a gourmand sampling some new fare.

Jamie walked over to the open gate of the shipyard.

The concrete landing site was empty. No ships in port.

It didn't matter. It didn't. There could be ships up there, just waiting for a signal from any survivors.

There was a speaker system mounted outside the yard office. She remembered it shrilling on the day of her arrival, loud enough for most of the settlement to hear.

Inside the scruffy little office she found a microphone on the desk, and when she flicked the main switch a red light came on. The electricity was working then. She felt a lurch of relief. There'd been a nagging fear in the back of her mind that she'd get here to find the power down, and no way of contacting the outside world.

'Hello?' Her voice was thin and uncertain. 'If anyone's here, I'm at the shipyard.' She paused, then added, 'My name is Jamie,' as though that might sway some undecided listener. She repeated the message a couple of times, then replaced the microphone, before heading back outside and round the corner to the comms station.

When she'd come here after that last mail from Daniel, the portmaster himself had set up the call. She hadn't watched what he did, not sure she wanted to be here at all. The public booth still smelled the same now: sawdust mixed with a whiff of cleaning fluid. The chipboard walls had holes drilled for wires, and the stool was bolted to the floor. A couple of the fastenings were loose and the seat tipped under her weight as she sat down.

When she flicked the biggest switch, a few lights came on, and something began to click beneath the counter. She tried another switch, and the display flickered with a few darts of static. She turned the tuning dial slowly back and forth in the hope of catching something, but the screen stayed stubbornly dark.

She pressed the microphone button anyway.

'If anyone can hear this, I'm on Soltaire. At the port. My name is Jamie Allenby and I'm a veterinary scientist at Calgarth.'

She paused, conscious of her flat, monotone delivery. But was an impassioned plea for aid any more likely to be answered than a matter-of-fact message? Was it about deserving rescue? Earning it?

She took a deep breath before continuing. 'I don't know if there are any other survivors here. If there's anyone out there, this is Jamie Allenby at the port on Soltaire.'

It felt like there was more she should be saying, but she didn't even know if the message was transmitting. She left the console switched on, and sat there for a moment, as though there might be an instant reply.

Got your message, be there soon, pip pip, over and out.

She'd sat like this after speaking to Daniel. Well, he'd done most of the talking. But she'd listened, as hard as she could through the static and the lag, for the things that must be there, hidden in the cracks. The things that would mean there was a way back to him.

When she thought of Daniel as a whole, she couldn't make up her mind if she missed him. But if she broke him down into small, specific things, she felt a little nip of something. The conspiratorial smile he flicked at her when someone they didn't like said something particularly stupid. The sound of his home-coming routine – shoes carefully removed inside the door, then thrown, unceremoniously, into the hall cupboard.

The way he made toast for her – soft and buttery, and much tastier than when she did it herself.

Shaking the memories away, Jamie turned off the console, and walked out of the booth.

Back outside, she looked along the street towards the bar where she'd waited the day she'd arrived. Cranwell had been late, and she'd found a table in the corner, away from the serious business of drinking going on at the bar. She'd surprised herself by ordering a fruit juice. She'd been drinking more alcohol since she lost the baby. It dulled the sharp edges of the world, muffling the constant questions and platitudes. She knew the reason well enough, but she hadn't expected that need to fall away so sharply when she left Alegria.

Now she could feel that old craving tightening around her. The sharp taste of alcohol on her tongue. The slow-creeping haze, blurring sense and memory.

The bar was a scruffy-looking establishment, with peeling window frames and a couple of letters missing from the sign above the door. Inside it was tidy enough, but there was a layer of dust on the floorboards.

It would be so easy to go round behind the counter, pour a measure of whisky and throw it down her throat. But once she started she wouldn't stop, and there was no one here to pick her up off the floor, no one to get her into bed and hold on to her as the world pitched and spun.

She was suddenly bone-tired. Her whole body felt heavy, and she wanted to slide down onto the floor, close her eyes and never move again.

The whisky would help.

No.

With a wrench of will, she turned her back on the bar and headed back outside.

The port was sinking into night, the last dregs of sunlight draining away below the horizon, and the first pinpoints of starlight just breaking through. Soltaire's twin moons were facing off across the sky, one a bare sliver, the other swelling close to full. They were always out of time with one another, one waxing as the other waned. They kept to their own corners of the night sky, never meeting, never reaching a consensus.

The port's distinctive scent of oil and soldered steel was sinking into the background as the chalky smell of night won out. Funny how darkness smelled the same everywhere. She could have been anywhere in the universe, anywhere at all.

One of the guesthouses was unlocked, and she found an empty room, made up for someone who'd never arrived. It didn't feel as intrusive as sleeping in someone's own bed. There were no remnants of human life here.

No dust.

As soon as she lay down, she felt herself tipping towards sleep. The darkness that rose up to meet her was deep and viscous, and she just had time for a flash of fear and a sharp stab of a thought before the world slid away.

Alone.

CHAPTER THREE

Three days passed in a tangle of fear and loneliness, broken by the occasional lighthouse-beacon flash of hope.

Jamie tried to find a routine, to stop herself from getting lost in the endless hours. She ate her breakfast at one of the tables in the dining room, everything laid out just so. After washing up she'd head out to the square where Conrad was steadily working the grass down to stubble. She'd linger over the task of grooming him, and then she'd saddle up and ride out.

She drew mental trajectories around the port, mapping out the space around her, just as she mapped out the hours. At every settlement and smallholding, she'd stop to check for signs of life, but everywhere she went she saw the slow, empty drift of dust.

In the evening she walked through the streets of the port, feeling the tug of temptation every time she passed the bar. By the third night she no longer had the energy to resist.

Inside, she found a bottle of whisky and a glass, and made her way to a table next to one of the windows.

The whisky sounded a familiar note. It had been her drink of choice after the baby. It was an efficient drink: short and sharp and to the point. She and Daniel had already been fighting about her refusal to discuss the baby. Then they fought about her drinking and her refusal to discuss the baby. He'd laughed once, leaning on the kitchen counter, fingers spread as though he'd been stretched beyond any hope of snapping back. *Most people talk too much when they're drunk. You shut down even more.* He'd rubbed his hand across his eyes. *It was my baby too.*

She took a deep gulp of whisky, swirling the liquid around the glass before the second mouthful. The sun was setting, the window just starting to turn opaque. Her reflection looked back at her. She'd never carried much extra weight, but her slightness had always had a strength to it. Now she looked fragile. Her complexion didn't suit pallor. She was drawn and sallow, her face all shadows and hollows.

Nought point nought nought nought one.

At that moment she believed it. She felt like a fragment of a person.

Something shifted behind her reflection.

At first she thought she was mistaken, that it had just been the glass catching her movement, mocking it back to her. But as she leaned closer, her reflection fell away, and the street came into focus.

A man. A woman. Walking towards the bar.

The glass skittered across the table as Jamie's hand lurched. The man was pointing towards the window. The woman followed the line of his gesture, shielding her eyes with her hand.

A surge of adrenaline took Jamie to her feet, her chair crashing to the floor. Her heart was hurling itself against her ribs as the door creaked open and the man stepped into the bar. He was small-statured, in his late sixties or thereabouts, his white hair peppered with remnants of an earlier steel-grey. He wore a loose, collarless tunic over cotton trousers. The woman behind him was younger, early fifties perhaps, thin and gaunt with eyes a sharp enough blue to be striking, even from a few metres away. Her hands were tucked under her armpits, as though she had to hold herself together.

Jamie felt an incongruous surge of triumph, as though she'd beaten some unseen opponent in a complex game of chance.

The statistics were wrong.

The corners of the man's mouth lifted in a cautious smile. 'Hello.'

Jamie tried to reply, but something caught in her throat. She coughed and scrubbed at her face with the back of her hand.

'I'm sorry.' She tugged her sleeve up to wipe the tears from her other cheek. 'I thought . . .'

The man crossed the room and took her hand. There was something cool and reassuring about his grip. He didn't hold on too tight, or lean in too close. It was just a touch, just a simple *I'm here, we're here, we made it.*

She breathed in hard. 'I'm sorry. I'm okay.'

The woman walked over to join them, moving with a jerky, hesitant gait that made her look as though her knees weren't jointed properly.

'This is Rena,' the man said. 'I'm Lowry.'

'Jamie.'

'Jamie,' he repeated. 'Are you from here?' A brief smile twitched at his lips. 'The settlement, I mean. Not the bar.'

That smile scraped against her emotions, trailing a scratch behind it. How could he be standing there, all smiles and casual introductions, as though they'd met at some party? But there were two of them. They hadn't had to work their way through the full horror of being alone, maybe the last one alive.

'I was working,' she said. 'Out at Calgarth.'

'From the capital, originally?' Lowry tilted his head. 'That's not a local accent.'

'I lived on Alegria for a few years.' Jamie felt a squirm of discomfort at the idea that her life was marked out in the way she spoke. It wasn't even an accent. It was what was left when you stripped accent and dialect away, leaving neutral vowels and measured beats. It wasn't the way she'd spoken when she was young. One day she'd woken up and realised she sounded like everyone else around her. She'd felt a little stab of guilt, and it was the memory of that feeling that made her add now, 'But I was born on Earth.'

'Long way from Earth,' Lowry said.

'Yes.'

A pause. Jamie reached about for something to break the silence.

'What about you?' The usual courtesies felt brittle and irrelevant. There were more important things to say, surely. Who were they? What did they want from her?

What did she want from them?

But they seemed to be stuck in some social holding pattern, all polite introductions and mundane questions.

'We're from Longvale,' Lowry said. 'Out near the Lhun valley.'

'The monastery.' She'd heard the farmhands joking about what the holy men must get up to alone out there.

Lowry smiled. 'No monks. Just a few people in need of a bit of space from the world.'

'Are you . . .' She didn't know anything about Longvale beyond the jokes and speculation.

'I'm a preacher.' Lowry correctly interpreted her uncertainty. 'I travel a fair bit, but I come back every few months. I was on retreat when the virus hit. Like Rena here.'

'Was it just the two of you?'

Lowry shook his head. 'There were others.' He looked away, his gaze falling on the whisky. A faint smile twisted his lips. 'Is that for sharing?'

'It could be.' Jamie couldn't find a smile of her own for the idea of the three of them sitting together, drowning their sorrows. But she could have been drinking alone, drinking until she could drink no more.

She went to the bar for two more tumblers, while Lowry

and Rena sat down at the table. When she pushed the bottle towards him, Lowry poured a generous measure into each glass.

'There should be a toast.' There was a wry twist to his lips again. 'To the human race? Still here despite it all?'

Jamie looked down at her glass. She didn't want to be the human race. It sounded too big a responsibility. She hadn't even been able to keep one tiny not-quite-person alive inside her.

'To salvation.' Rena's voice was lower than Jamie had expected from someone of her sparse frame. She was rubbing at her glass with her thumb, a frown furrowed between her brows.

'To salvation then.' Lowry took a cautious sip, grimacing as the drink hit the back of his throat. 'An acquired taste, whisky. And I never seem to be around it long enough to do the necessary acquiring.'

'Don't clergymen abstain?' Jamie said.

Lowry grinned. 'Most do. Every religion seems to have something that's apparently the root of humanity's troubles, whether it's wine, women or song. If they were all right, there'd be nothing left we could touch without damnation.'

'What church do you belong to?' Jamie asked.

'No particular denomination. Longvale has something of an open door policy.'

There was something bitingly unreal about the situation. Drinking whisky and talking about faith in an empty bar on an empty planet.

'So what do you do?' Lowry asked.

'I'm a vet,' Jamie said. They were all clinging on to the present tense. 'I was working with the breeding stock at Calgarth.'

'I've heard of it.' Lowry hesitated before asking the inevitable question. 'Any others?'

When Jamie shook her head, he pressed his lips together, dipping his chin, as though offering a silent prayer.

Jamie had never been religious, but she'd spent a few of her formative years at a Catholic school. Her mother's faith came and went in broken bursts, but she'd cared enough to fight her ex-husband over Jamie's schooling. Or maybe it was just the fight she cared about. Lowry seemed very different from her school's dogmatic visiting priests. He had a calm and easy manner that was apparent, even at a first meeting as fraught and unreal as this one.

She glanced at Rena. There was a fidgety intensity about the older woman. Her hands shifted constantly on her glass, occasionally going up to tug at some stray strand of greying hair, or to the corner of her mouth so that she could chew on the edge of a blunted nail.

Rena looked up suddenly, catching her staring. Jamie stumbled into a clumsy question. 'What about you? What do you do?'

The other woman started to put her glass down, then seemed to change her mind, her fingers tightening around it. 'I was a research scientist. On Alegria. I was . . . I left.' She stopped abruptly, lifting her chin to give Jamie a look with a hint of challenge in it. 'Why are you here?' Her gaze flickered. 'I mean . . . all the way out here in the colonies.'

'A bit of space.' Jamie glanced at Lowry. 'Like you said.'

'Plenty of that out here.' Lowry hesitated. 'Have you lost anyone?'

The moment stretched out. 'Yes,' Jamie said, and then felt guilty because it wasn't true. Not in the way he'd meant. Her baby had been gone long before everyone else, but it didn't seem right to tell them that. There were too few of them to start diversifying their tragedies. And it didn't matter. He was still gone.

31

There was a stark intimacy to the scene: the empty bar, and the three of them huddled around the little table, with the darkness pressing against the window.

'What was your job on the capital?' Lowry changed the subject. 'Not many cows on Alegria.'

'Research.' She glanced at Rena, with the faint thought of drawing her into the conversation, but the other woman was looking at Jamie's left hand, where her travel ID circled her ring finger.

'That's an upper echelon mark,' she said. 'Why would you need to come out here for a job?'

Jamie dropped her hand to her lap. She hated the way people always looked for your mark when they first met you. Sometimes it was just a quick flick of a glance, buried in the middle of the conversation. Sometimes it was more blatant. It was an indelible marker of what your life meant to everyone else.

And more than that. It was a reminder of all those protests and lost causes from Jamie's youth on Earth. She'd done all the right things. She'd joined the campaigns against the resurrection of the old forced emigration programmes. She'd been in the marches, protested against the casual ousting of whole communities from the planet just because they'd suddenly been deemed undesirable in the greater scheme of things. When she'd left Earth it had been on one of the protest ships. *If they have to go, then we go too*, that had been their tagline. And then the measures had been forced through anyway. First the emigration programmes, then the mandatory ID marking, and somehow she'd found herself turning up to register, the same as everyone else.

She'd seen a couple of other old protesters at the ID office, and they'd avoided one another's eyes, concentrating on their forms. No one in authority ever admitted that the data on those forms was used to sift the population into groups, and there was no acknowledgement that the placement of the ID mark had any meaning. But everyone knew. After the procedure, the sting of the lasering process already fading, Jamie felt as though a piece of her had been scuffed away. It was official. She was part of the upper echelon, a member of the stratum of society that had forced people from their homes and burned their value into their skin.

Rena was rubbing the edge of her shirt between the fingers of her left hand, her own upper echelon mark visible. Lowry's was in the same place, a little worn, but functional enough.

'We were on retreat,' Rena said defensively, when she saw where Jamie was looking.

'And I was on a cattle station.' Jamie couldn't keep the sharp edge out of her voice, and Rena shifted in her seat, her frown deepening.

Jamie turned back to Lowry. 'How long were you at Longvale before the virus?'

'A couple of months,' he said. 'Rena only came in, what, a month ago?'

'Five weeks.'

'That long?' Lowry said. 'I suppose it was. You got in about a week after we spoke on the long-range.'

'You knew one another before?' Jamie said.

'We worked at the same hospital a few years ago.' Jamie noticed that Lowry glanced at Rena before answering. 'I was the visiting priest.'

'You're Catholic?'

'I was. I'm a little less strict these days.'

Rena made a sharp gesture. 'All beliefs come back to the one God. It's all the same in the end.'

'The end?' Jamie felt a kick of blurred and off-beat anger.

'We seem to be there. But I'm not seeing trumpets and the gates of heaven opening up.'

Rena glared at Jamie, and Lowry put his hand on her arm.

'There are different types of salvation,' he said diplomatically.

'No.' Rena shook him off. 'There's only one. In the voice of God, speaking through the space between the stars.'

The words had the resonance of a prayer, and Jamie almost expected Lowry to dip his head and say *amen*. How had they moved so swiftly from *what do you do* to *what do you believe*?

Rena looked down, a tear glistening on her cheek, and Jamie felt a pang of something that might have been guilt. Just three of them here, and she still couldn't find a gentle word for another broken soul.

She looked around the bar, feeling for a change of subject. 'Do you think it's like this everywhere?' Something was nagging at her. Something about the statistics. 'It's odd,' she went on slowly. 'Most pathogens want to survive.'

'Want?' Rena interrupted, her tone suddenly brusque. 'They don't want. They just are. You're a scientist. You know that.'

'Want,' Jamie said. 'Need. Everything pushes towards life. What's the point of a parasite that destroys its host?'

'That's what viruses do,' Rena said. 'They kill.'

'But most don't burn their host away to nothing.'

'Things happen.' Rena was fidgeting again, tugging at her cuff. 'Sometimes things go wrong.'

Silence settled over the table once more. It was Lowry who broke it, turning to Rena. 'Do you think we should check the signal?'

'I set an alert. If anyone answers, we'll hear it over the speakers.'

'An alert?' Jamie said.

'We set up a distress signal,' Lowry said. 'It goes off every

34

three minutes. If anyone comes within range, they should pick it up.'

'The system was turned off.'

Rena shook her head. 'Not in the booth. The main unit in the office. The public system hasn't got the power to reach further than the first relay.' She was brisker, more focused when she talked about practical things.

'Do you think there's anyone out there?' Jamie said.

'We listened on the airwaves for a while,' Lowry said. 'There were some traces. Nothing close, but it sounded like people trying to get through to someone.'

'People will come.' Rena pressed her palms together, like a child saying her prayers. 'Then it will begin.'

'What will?' Jamie said.

'The new world.' Rena looked surprised that Jamie had to ask. 'We'll start again. Build something better.' Certainty blazed briefly on her face, and then faded, leaving her looking lost and unsure. 'We'll start again,' she repeated. 'That's what God wants us to do.'

It sounded so simple. The world they'd known, over and done with. Time to start again, and get it right this time. There was an attraction to the idea, like a book of fairy tales, with every *The End* followed by a turn of the page and another *Once upon a time.*

But even if there were other survivors, there were vast swathes of empty space between them. What if the three of them had to find a way to start again right here?

It felt like all that space was contracting around her, the emptiness of it pressing close like a second skin.

'Hey.' Lowry touched her arm. 'It's all right.'

She shook her head, wrapping her arms tightly across her body. Her breath was growing shorter, more laboured.

'Jamie?' Lowry's voice sounded further away.

She couldn't feel her fingers. She couldn't feel anything. Perhaps she wasn't here at all. Perhaps she was still lying in those musty sheets out at Calgarth, wandering the tangled paths of her final, failing dreams.

'Jamie.' Lowry reached for her shoulder. Somehow she shoved herself back from the table, her chair scraping on the floor. It was vitally important that he didn't touch her, although she couldn't work out why. Her thoughts were splintering. Lowry's voice stretched out, vanishing into a rush of white noise, like water or static. Her last coherent thought was that he'd never been there at all, that the maths had been right all along.

Nought point nought nought nought one.

CHAPTER FOUR

When Jamie came back to herself, she was lying on the floor with Lowry sitting next to her, holding her hand. As she tried to push herself up, he put a soothing hand on her back.

'Steady.'

Rena appeared, looming above Jamie. Water slopped over her wrist as she shoved a glass towards Jamie's lips.

Jamie twisted her head away. There were too many people trying to occupy the same space. All this empty world, and here they were, crowded together on a metre-square bit of floor.

She sat up. Lowry shuffled back, but Rena was still hovering, and Jamie took the glass, forestalling another attempt. It had the flat taste of water sitting too long in the pipes, but it eased her dry mouth and she drained the glass in a few gulps.

'Thanks.'

'I'll get some more.' Rena seized the glass and scuttled off. When she returned, she handed it over with the first smile Jamie had seen from her; just an uncertain stretch of her lips that made her seem out of practice.

Jamie looked at Lowry. 'Sorry. I'm not sure what happened.'

'Nothing to apologise for. We're all going to have our moments, I'm sure.'

'So what now?' The stilted calm of their odd meeting was broken, and she felt cramped and restless. She climbed slowly to her feet.

'We've got the signal set up,' Lowry said. 'Not much else we can do. We'll have to set ourselves up somewhere while we wait.'

And if the skies stayed empty? How long would it be before they stopped calling it waiting, and found some other name for it?

'Let's say someone does come,' she said. 'What then? Where do you want to go? The capital?'

'Where else would we go?' Rena said.

'Earth,' Jamie said. 'I need to get to Earth.'

'Do you have people there?' Lowry asked.

'I'm from there.' Jamie looked away, not quite sure why she wasn't telling them about the blank message, about Daniel. Maybe it was because she could picture the precise shape of the look Lowry would give her, before gently dismantling her reasons for thinking Daniel might be alive.

'Whereabouts on Earth?' Lowry asked.

'England. The Northumbrian coast.'

He tilted his head, looking interested. 'I spent some time on Lindisfarne. Holy Island. Whichever name you prefer. I was thinking recently that I might go back there sometime.' He frowned, pinching at his forehead. 'Or maybe I dreamed it. When I was sick. It's been in my head for some reason. Where did you live?'

'Belsley. Just down the coast.'

'I know it,' Lowry said. 'Beautiful place.'

Jamie was assailed by an image so crystal clear that she might have been looking at a photo. A great, sweeping curve of pale sand, brushed by a blue-green sea.

Home, she thought, feeling her way around the shape of that word.

And then, a heartbeat later, *Daniel*.

'Why don't we go too?' Rena's face was suddenly alight. 'We could go back there.'

Back?

'Earth's a long way away,' Lowry said. 'And we've no idea what state things are in. Let's not get ahead of ourselves.'

'But it's a sign.' Rena stepped close, clutching his arm. 'Three of us here, connected by the same place.'

Her expression was fervent, but with an edge of something that looked almost like desperation.

You hadn't even thought of it till just a moment ago, Jamie thought, with a flash of irritation.

Lowry shook his head. 'I was only there for a while, and it was a long time ago.'

'It's a place of pilgrimage,' Rena pressed. 'We could start over.'

Lowry gave her a searching look. There was a wary tenderness about his expression.

'A new start,' Rena said again, her voice low, and with a hint of a tremor.

Lowry rubbed his face, then gave a faint smile. 'Well, we have to go somewhere, I suppose.'

Jamie found herself wanting to scream at them. Here they were, trapped on a deserted planet, playing at lives they couldn't have. That thought scraped at her like sandpaper, and some of that roughness found its way into her voice. 'What now?'

'How long have you been here?' Lowry asked.

'Three days.'

'No sign of anyone else?'

'No.'

'There could be others,' Rena said. 'There are other settlements.'

'I'd imagine any survivors would make their way to the port,' Lowry said. 'We're probably best off waiting here.'

There it was again. Waiting. *Of course there's someone out there. Of course someone will come.*

That's what waiting meant. You waited *for*. You waited *till*.

Jamie made herself speak in a level tone. 'It's getting late. I've been staying at the guesthouse on the square. Where are you going to sleep?'

Surely she should be urging them to take two of the other rooms there? Wouldn't that be the normal thing to do? But the guesthouse suddenly felt *hers* in a way it hadn't before.

'We left our things at a place on the edge of town,' Lowry said. 'We can go back there tonight and move closer tomorrow.'

There was another pause, as though none of them quite knew how to bring the encounter to a close. Once again, it was Lowry who broke the silence, his tone brisk. 'We'll come by the guesthouse in the morning, shall we?'

'Okay.' Jamie forced a smile. 'Well, goodnight.'

'Goodnight.' Lowry reached for her hand. 'I'm glad we found you.'

'Yes.' She should smile again, but when she lifted the corners of her mouth it felt more like a grimace. 'Yes.'

She cleared away the glasses, lingering over the task until Rena and Lowry had gone. She could feel the whisky as a sluggish flow in her veins. It had dulled the edges of her feelings, like it had after the baby. Tomorrow she'd feel like she should.

She wasn't alone. They had the signal. They had hope.

But there was a cold feeling in her lungs. She'd been so focused on finding other survivors that she'd given no thought to what came after.

Outside, the port was silent, as though there'd never been anyone else here at all. She was tired. *It will be different to-*

morrow, she thought, as she went inside the guesthouse and closed the door.

Another day passed, and another. Jamie still rode out for most of the daylight hours, ranging further each time. The first time after finding Rena and Lowry, she had been going for an hour or so when she was seized by an overwhelming urge to turn around, ride back to town and check they hadn't disappeared. She felt exposed, like a child who'd wandered too far from its parents. When she got back later, the memory of that feeling made her gentler towards them, and she answered Rena patiently when the older woman quizzed her about her search, the questions framed within semi-coherent ramblings about God and his purpose.

In the evenings they ate together, sitting out on the guesthouse's little terrace. Lowry was a reasonable cook and he took on most of the culinary duties.

'I'm too old to be riding out,' he said, waving away Jamie's offers of help. 'But I can at least have dinner ready when the search party returns.'

On the fourth night, Jamie arrived back to find that Lowry had gone to extra effort, setting the table with the guesthouse's best dishes, and livening up their usual simple fare with a few fancy bits from the shop.

'A celebration,' he said. 'No, that's not the right word for it. Just a recognition. That we're here together.'

When they sat down for dinner, the shadows were just beginning to stretch out. As Lowry picked up the serving spoon, a siren shrilled across the settlement.

Rena started to her feet, hands flying up to her mouth. Then she turned, stumbling over her fallen chair, and set off across the square in a lopsided run.

The sound of the siren punched into Jamie's chest, almost

knocking the breath out of her. There had been so little noise over the last few days. It felt as though she'd lost the ability to process it, like a lifelong vegetarian who can no longer digest meat. She should know what it meant, but right now it was just *noise noise noise*.

Lowry was saying something, but it took a moment for her mind to override the distorted blare of the siren.

'. . . the signal. The comms station.'

The signal.

The signal.

That word swelled within her, until she was sure her lungs were stretched too tight to contain the pressure.

Lowry was on his feet, already moving across the square, following Rena, and, after a frozen moment, Jamie set off after him.

There was a mocking edge to the siren as she made her way along the corridor of the comms station. Just as she reached the door at the far end, the noise snapped off, leaving her ears throbbing with after-echoes.

In the office, Rena was leaning over a complicated mess of wires and switches. The screen was awash with static, with a half-formed *something* shifting in the fuzz of black and white.

'This is Soltaire station, code 318. Are you receiving?'

There was a twist of sound, something that might have been a response, but it faded into the static.

Rena turned a dial beside the screen. 'Are you receiving me?'

Jamie found that she was counting inside her head, counting down the seconds to the moment when Rena would turn away and say, *It was nothing, just a false alarm.*

A thin, artificial voice echoed through the little office.

'Soltaire station, this is trade clipper *Phaeacian*.'

Jamie stood very still. If she moved or made a sound, it

would break the moment, and the voice would disappear. Rena was stabbing at buttons, her hands uncharacteristically swift and confident.

'Soltaire station hailing trade clipper *Phaeacian*. Hold that frequency.'

The static flared louder, then fell away, leaving the pregnant, edge-of-hearing hum of an open connection. In the same instant, the crackle-glaze of the screen gave way to an image. It was distorted, curving at the edges, and flickering sideways every few seconds, but Jamie could make out the face of a man.

Four, Jamie thought. Four of them alive. Another precious step away from *nought point nought nought nought one*.

Through the imprecise greyscale of the transmission, she could see the man's mouth moving, but there was no sound. When Rena turned another dial, the room was filled with the tail end of whatever it was that he'd been saying.

'. . . planetside.'

'Could you repeat that, please?' Rena said.

A second's delay, then the man nodded. 'I said, how many survivors planetside?'

'Just three. As far as we know.'

'Who are the other two?'

Lowry stepped up to Rena's side. 'Two of us from a religious house,' he said. 'Myself and Rena here. Then a female veterinarian from a cattle station.' He smiled. 'No one dangerous.'

The man didn't return the smile. 'Let me see your third.'

When Jamie moved round to place herself in view of the screen, the man glanced at her and then turned away, as though she were of no more interest than some piece of cargo he was being asked to transport.

'What do you need?' he said. 'Supplies? Messages carried?'

Jamie felt a catch of fear, as though Rena might say, *No, we're fine here. Continue on your way.*

'We want to get off-planet,' Rena said. 'We're going to Earth.'

This time the pause was fractionally longer than could be attributed to the transmission delay.

'I'm not going to Earth,' the man said. 'I'm headed to the capital worlds. See how the land lies.' He glanced away, and when he turned back to the screen his expression looked resigned, although that might have been a trick of the static. 'You able to check the fuel situation? I don't want to get stuck down there.'

'You can't send your shuttle down?' Lowry asked.

The man shook his head. 'It was planetside when this whole thing started. It never made it back. There's an orbiting fuel station not far from here, but I can't raise anyone.'

'I'll go check,' Lowry said. 'Tell me what I'm looking for.'

The man ran through a few technical instructions and made Lowry repeat them back, correcting him with a hint of irritation when he stumbled.

When the old preacher had left, Rena launched into a series of quick-fire questions about life beyond Soltaire. Had he come across other survivors? Other ships? Any official communications? Any idea of numbers?

The man gave brief responses, making no attempt to nurture the conversation. There were other survivors. He'd caught the tail end of messages on the long-range comms channels. He didn't know how many. Nothing official yet.

The door swung open as Lowry returned, short of breath, but with confirmation of full fuel dumps.

'Fine,' the man said. 'I'll land.'

'You'll take us to Earth?' Rena said.

'To the capital worlds,' the man said, with a trace of impatience.

Lowry put his hand on Rena's arm in a warning gesture. 'How long before you can set down?'

'I'll start the entry sequence as soon as I get offline.'

Lowry nodded. 'Safe landing. And our thanks.'

The man's image winked out, leaving the screen blank.

'Do you think he's really going to come for us?' Rena turned to Lowry, fingers twisting together. 'What if he just refuels and takes off again?'

'He'll come.' Lowry gave her shoulder a quick squeeze. 'Otherwise why would he have answered the signal?'

Rena's fractured thoughts had already moved on to something else. 'What about Earth?'

'The man's not a hail-and-ride service,' Lowry said. 'We'll take him up on what he's offering, and maybe talk again about Earth at some point. We'd better get to the shipyard.'

As they crossed the square, Conrad raised his head, regarding them placidly. When Jamie patted his neck, he shoved at her with his nose, looking for treats.

'Ever hopeful,' Lowry said. Then his smile faded. 'I think you might be out of luck with the horse. I can't imagine there's space for livestock.'

'I know that.' The reply came out more sharply than she'd intended. There was an image in her head: the old horse standing alone on that ragged patch of grass, watching as a ship disappeared into the sky.

Just at that moment the real ship broke into sight with a dull roar of engines and atmospheric resistance. It was one of the old-style clippers, heavy-bellied and ungainly, like something growing old ungracefully.

They hurried round the side of the shipyard to the concrete forecourt, tucking themselves back against the wall as the ship rotated into place, before setting down with surprising lightness and precision for its bulk. It was half the size of the passenger liners that served the central planets, but still a fair bit bigger than the little, multi-purpose clipper that had brought Jamie out to Soltaire.

The engine fans were still rumbling to a standstill when the main door cranked open, and a gangway slid out. A man stepped out from the dim interior. Even without the distortion of the comm screen, he wasn't easy to age. There was grey in his dark hair – just a fine speckling at his temples and in the brush of stubble on his jaw – but his face was unlined. Jamie had always thought that men aged differently from women, in clear markers – the first grey, a thinning, a stooping – whereas for women it was a slower, smoother crumpling. Maybe it was because men didn't fight it as hard as women. She'd seen it all around her on Alegria, that ongoing battle with time, fought with lotions, with dye, with personal trainers, and with subtle surgery that they wanted you to notice, but *not* notice.

The man gave no indication as to what he thought of the motley group of refugees. He was tall enough that the bulk of the ship didn't dwarf him, and although his stance was relaxed, Jamie could clearly see the hilt of a gun at his hip. From the way his hand was resting on it, he intended it to be visible. Jamie felt a swift clench of fear. What if it hadn't been caution driving his questions about the survivors? What if he was just making sure he had the upper hand?

'It's good to see you.' Lowry stepped forward. 'Thank you for coming for us.' He paused. 'I'm sorry, we don't know your name.'

'Callan Jacobs.'

He regarded them for a few seconds, and then took his hand from his gun. As he stepped down onto the ground, Jamie's fear gave way to an irrational flash of resentment. Just like that, he'd assessed the three of them and found them no threat.

The preacher moved forward, holding out his hand. 'Lowry,' he said. 'And these two are Rena and Jamie.'

Callan walked down the gangway and shook Lowry's hand briefly, before turning to look across the landing site. The fuel dumps were off to the side, their hoses abandoned in a haphazard tangle.

'It'll take about a half-hour to fuel,' he said. 'And I need to stock up on some basic supplies.'

'If you give us a list, we can sort that out,' Lowry said.

Callan walked over to the office and ducked inside, emerging a few seconds later with a scribbled list.

The old preacher scanned the page. 'Fine. We'll see you back here in—'

'Half an hour.' Callan set off towards the rear of the ship. 'Don't be late. I want to be off-planet before it gets dark.'

In the square, Conrad was lying flat out on the ground, doing his trademark impression of a corpse. The effect was spoiled by the soft nicker he gave as Jamie approached, although he didn't trouble himself to lift his head from the ground.

Jamie gave his belly a gentle prod with her toe. 'Come on. Time to go.'

He rolled an indignant eye at her, but heaved himself up onto his knees, and then scrambled to his feet. Jamie leaned against his warm flank.

She knew it was irrational, this sudden, intense attachment to the old horse. But leaning against Conrad, she felt like she knew where she was. This world had been decimated, but it was, in a way it had never been before, her world. When she left here, she'd be at the mercy of those pitiless survival statistics once again. She'd have to deal with other people's tragedies, not just her own.

She turned her head to press her face against Conrad's neck, breathing in the warm musk of him.

'Good horse.'

Conrad snorted, and then his head jerked up. Jamie turned to see Callan crossing the square, a burlap sack in his hand.

'He yours?' he said.

Jamie nodded.

'Best get on and turn him loose.' He walked up the steps to the shop. 'We haven't got much time.'

Jamie nodded again, less definitely.

Callan gave her a look of detached curiosity. 'What's wrong?'

'I . . .' Jamie stopped, collecting herself. 'It doesn't feel right. Just leaving him to fend for himself.'

'There'll be abandoned stock all over the place.'

'I know,' Jamie said. 'I opened the gates at Calgarth, but there'll be livestock fenced in elsewhere. What's going to happen to them?'

Callan raised his eyebrows. 'What do you think is going to happen? They'll either make it or they won't.'

'But we're the ones who put them there.'

Callan opened the door to the shop. 'You can't save everything. Lot of the clutter's been wiped away from these worlds of ours. I suspect we may find the view in some places a bit too clear for our liking. But no point going around beating ourselves up.' He gave her an appraising look. 'You're a vet. Surprised you'd be fussing so much about livestock. Survival of the fittest and all that.'

'Aren't you supposed to be refuelling?' Jamie turned away to loop the reins over Conrad's neck.

'Fuel line's set up and running,' Callan replied. 'There's a couple of things I forgot to put on the list, that's all.' He looked pointedly at the setting sun. 'Time's getting on.'

Jamie ignored him, picking up the reins and turning Conrad towards the edge of the square.

As the old horse ambled along behind her, Jamie found herself wanting to tell him what had happened to their world, to explain why she had to leave him. When they reached the outskirts of the town, she took off his bridle and turned him in the general direction of Calgarth. Maybe he'd make his way back there to find his stablemates.

'Off you go.'

He didn't move, and when he turned to look at her, she thought she could detect a hint of disapproval in his gaze.

She gave him a slap on the rump. 'Go on. Go home.'

Conrad took a couple of rolling steps, then stopped and dropped his head to graze. Somehow it would have been easier if he were the one to walk away. As it was, there was nothing to do but turn and head back to town, not looking behind her in response to the horse's questioning whicker.

Back in the square, Jamie retrieved her rucksack and went into the shop. As she lifted items down from the shelves it felt like stealing – although there was no one to take her money, and what use was money now anyway? Still, she limited herself to basics. Some spare toiletries, a travel mug and ready-mix white coffee, a box of fruit snack bars, a notebook and pen. As she gave a last glance around, a small box on the counter caught her eye. It was stacked with imported chocolate bars, wrapped in silver foil and coloured paper. She hadn't had real chocolate since she arrived here. There was a local substitute but it had a bitter, artificial taste. She hesitated, then picked up the whole box, and shoved it into the top of her rucksack, resisting the urge to give a furtive look over her shoulder as she headed back outside.

The night seemed to have made a sudden surge, damping

down the daylight and sinking the port into shadow. Callan had said that he wanted to be gone before the light faded.

Just at that moment, she heard a roar from the shipyard as the ship's great engines leaped to life.

They were leaving. Leaving her here alone.

She stumbled into a run, her rucksack thumping against her shoulders and her heart hammering.

No no no no no . . .

The engines surged again, a deep, angry-sounding rumble. Jamie's lungs were aching, a lingering legacy of her illness, and as she tried to force more speed from her legs, she tripped and almost went down. She recovered herself and ran on, expecting to see the ship's great bulk lifting into the sky, in the heavy, improbable lurch she'd never quite learned to take for granted, no matter how many times she saw it.

As she reached the gate her panic spiked, and then fell away, leaving her off balance and breathless.

The ship hadn't moved from the landing site.

Lowry and Rena were standing by the gangway, while Callan was at the side of the ship, detaching the fuel hose. He straightened up just as Jamie dropped out of her halting run.

'Done?' he said.

She took a shuddering breath in.

Callan gave her a scrutinising look. 'Everything okay?'

'I thought . . .' She stopped for another deep breath. 'Doesn't matter.'

'Okay.' Callan turned away. 'Let's get going.'

As they followed him up the gangway, Rena was sparking with some emotion Jamie couldn't quite read.

'What were the odds?' she said. 'Of the three of us finding one another, and the ship being so close?'

'I don't know.' Jamie tried not to let her irritation seep into her voice. 'I suppose it had to be somewhere.'

'It's God's voice.' Rena's smile was pitying, as though Jamie was too slow to understand some simple truth. 'We just have to listen.'

'You might find the engines a bit loud for that.' Callan glanced back over his shoulder.

Rena flushed. 'That's not . . .' She shook her head, as though trying to dislodge something. 'I mean, this starts with *us*. Something new, something different.'

Callan gave her a contemptuous look. 'I wouldn't bet on it. It won't just be us. There'll be others, and people will do what people always do. They'll get together, form committees, make rules and regulations, and before you know it we'll have exactly what we had before. Just smaller, and with more space to roll around in.'

'Why are you heading to the capital,' Lowry said, 'if that's the way you feel about it?'

'Like I said, I need to see how the land lies. When things are up and running, people will need transport, and there'll be trade. Now are you coming, or would you rather stay put and wait for God to talk to you?'

Lowry shot a warning look at Rena, but she was silent, her lips pressed into a thin line.

As she stepped on board, Jamie could feel the low vibrations of the ship's reserve power, rumbling away just below the edge of hearing. The hold was lit by striplights curving along the ship's metal ribs. Near the far end, shipping crates had been stacked to form a wall, and through a gap in their ranks, Jamie could see something that looked incongruously like a wood-framed sofa.

'Welcome on board,' Callan said, pulling down a handle to the side of the doors. There was an edge to his tone, as though he was expecting them to look around and say, *Is this it?* As the doors began to close, he walked over to the crates. 'You can put your stuff through here for now.' He gestured towards the gap. 'This isn't a luxury transporter – things are pretty basic. The galley and rec space is just at the back of the hold.'

As she walked across the hold, Jamie felt a tug of nausea. The floor felt as though it was shifting slightly, and there was an unpleasant pressure in her ears. She knew from experience that she'd adjust to the artificial gravity soon enough, but the first few minutes on board were always uncomfortable.

Behind the crates a steel kitchen unit had been fastened to the wall with brackets. It held a single hotplate, a microwave, a hot-water dispenser and a small dishwasher. A narrow cold box stood alongside, its wire disappearing underneath the unit, and its door held shut with a bungee cord.

Two ancient sofas stood nearby, their cushions age-shiny and sagging. The low table between them was so covered in drink rings that it was hard to make out the original shade of the wood. Jamie dumped her rucksack on the nearest sofa, and headed back out through the gap, making room for Lowry and Rena to stow their bags.

Callan was doing something over by the doors. As Jamie hesitated, he turned back towards her. 'How long till we can get up and running?'

She stared at him in surprise. 'What . . .'

'She hasn't cooled down much.' The response was unfamiliar and female, and it came from somewhere behind Jamie. She turned to see a woman standing on the steps at the side of the hold. She was well built, probably in her fifties or thereabouts, with cropped grey hair. 'We can be off-planet in less than ten minutes.'

Callan turned to Jamie, jerking his head towards a row of fold-down seats near the doors. 'You three strap yourselves in. It can be a bit bumpy, and I'd rather not deal with broken bones from people who haven't got their space legs yet.'

'How long do we need to stay strapped in?' Jamie said.

'Until I tell you otherwise.' As he set off up the stairs, the grey-haired woman was already disappearing through a doorway at the end of the landing.

As they strapped themselves into the jump seats, the ship shuddered, the engines beginning a hard bass crescendo. The noise wasn't muted by any passenger-friendly soundproofing. Here they were just cargo, and cargo didn't need to hear itself think. Rena was saying something, her mouth moving, her fingers pulling at the straps across her thin chest. When Lowry put his hand on her arm she fell still, although her face remained creased and anxious.

Lowry glanced at Jamie, eyebrows raised.

You okay?

She nodded. As the engines rose she was aware of an unexpected sense of elation. She was here, in her skin, feeling the sensations thrumming through her. She wasn't dust, mingling with the dirt of a frontier world. She couldn't tell the exact moment when they left the ground, but she felt a heaviness settling on her limbs, as though her body was fighting the rise of the ship, struggling to stay earthbound.

Beside her, Lowry had closed his eyes. Rena was twisting her hands together, lips moving as though in prayer. As the engine roar fell to a dull rumble, then eased further to a lower vibrato, her voice started to break through, disjointed and fractured.

'. . . the meek, the dispossessed . . . shall inherit . . . in the void, in the space between the stars . . . his voice . . .'

Jamie closed her own eyes. The heaviness was increasing, weighing her down. There was a muffled darkness just below the bottom edge of her thoughts. If she fell into it, it would be like floating in space, out there between the stars and beyond the world.

I'm tired, she thought, surprised she had room for something so ordinary.

Her thoughts were fragmenting as exhaustion flooded through her. Odd words and random images ricocheted off one another, broken and meaningless. The sea rose around her, and her mother's voice said *two* and *it didn't work*. Then the ocean tipped sideways and she slid through it, as a woman who'd once lived on the floor below talked about algebra. *Earth always sings*, she thought, and in that moment it made perfect sense. Daniel was watching her. He always brought a loaf back from the bakery when he went out for a morning run. It made him smell of fresh bread. Then he'd shower, and call her to join him, and sometimes she would, and his hands would be on her, and she'd smile, lean back and close her eyes.

There was a voice nearby, but Jamie didn't know if it was real.

'. . . the void . . . broken pieces . . .'

She made an effort to focus.

What were the odds of survival again?

No. They'd made it. They were alive.

And with that last flare of coherent thought, Jamie tipped over the edge into sleep.

It's summer and her baby is gone.

It was a slow unravelling of a loss. By the time they found the silence which should have been a heartbeat, he was long gone. How long, no one could say. No one was saying much at all. It was all hushed voices and unfinished sentences. Euphemisms, hands moving in helpless patterns, as though the necessary information could only be conveyed through some invisible cat's cradle.

Your loss.

The process.

Investigations.

No one came right out and said, Your baby's dead. He died inside you and you never even knew.

For a little while she thought that meant it wasn't true. There were no signs. He was still locked tight inside her body. Perhaps they'd got it wrong.

She held on to that thought, a faint grey line of comfort, stretching back to the time when he was a solid certainty inside her. She held on to it through all the silent scans and silent hours in between, right up to the moment when the nurse's masked face hung over hers, a professional smile crinkling her eyes.

And when she woke, scooped out and scraped clean, her stomach shrivelled to a slack, barely-there swell, she thought, There we go then.

Daniel wants to talk. He wants to hold her, to wrap himself about her in the dark. He wants to be so close that she wonders if he's trying to climb inside her, to occupy that vacated place below her heart. Sometimes she thinks that she might claw her way out of her skin, just so she'll be out of his arms.

She knows he's hurting, but his pain is different. It's cleaner than hers. She hadn't wanted a baby – it was he who had wanted it so much – and she sometimes wonders if that made it her fault. In the first weeks of pregnancy, she felt nothing but resentment. Every surge of nausea, every conspiratorial wink, everything she couldn't eat or couldn't drink or couldn't do, it all combined in a roiling mass of fear and loneliness.

Things changed when she felt the first shiftings of life inside her. There was no rush of love, no sudden understanding of what it all meant, but she became aware of a settled resignation. It was going to happen, whatever regrets she might be entertaining in the darkness after midnight while Daniel smiled in his sleep. As the baby grew, she found herself touching her stomach, very lightly, as though to avoid him knowing she was there. She started thinking of the two of them as on the same side. When people fussed over her with overdone smiles she'd send a sharp thought inwards to her baby, imagining him turning his head to listen. He was the only one who ever heard that inner voice of hers, and it made them co-conspirators against the world.

Now he's gone, and he's left a space inside her, all echoes and emptiness.

Daniel wants them to see a counsellor. She's still bleeding, and he wants her to sit there and find a way to put this hole in her racked and broken body into words. And once it's summed up and written down, that will be it for him. It will be done and they can move on.

There's a part of her that wants that for him, for both of them. But the greater part of her can only think of one word that would fit.

Over.

CHAPTER FIVE

There was a low thrum at the edge of her consciousness.

The generator at the main house playing up again.

No.

That wasn't right. She wasn't in her bed. She was upright, her neck cricked at an awkward angle, and there was something pulled tight across her chest.

She opened her eyes and looked out across the dim hollow of the hold.

The hold.

The ship.

The seats beside her were empty, but as she stared around the hold, she heard footsteps and Lowry ducked out from between the crates.

'You're back with us then.'

'How long was I asleep?' Jamie undid her harness.

'Less than an hour,' Lowry said. 'You didn't miss much. Callan's given us a brief tour, that's all. I'll show you your quarters.'

'Where's Rena?'

'Lying down. She's not a great flyer.'

Jamie glanced sideways at him. 'Have you known each other long?'

'Trying to work us out?' Lowry flicked her a swift smile.

Jamie started the automatic denial, feeling for some more socially acceptable motive for the question. Then she stopped. So few of them left. Why not just say what you meant?

'Yes.'

'That's all right. I know we must make a bit of an odd pair.' Lowry's smile stayed in place, but Jamie thought she could detect a slight wariness in it. 'Like I said, we were both based at the same hospital a few years back. I used to take services there. Rena was one of the regulars.'

'She's Catholic?'

'She was.'

Jamie had always thought that Catholic was something you were or you weren't, like being Jewish, but both Lowry and Rena had apparently left their old faith behind.

'So you stayed in touch?'

'On and off over the years. Then she contacted me when she wanted to come to Longvale, and that was that.'

Jamie thought that was very far from being that, but she didn't push the point. 'Fancy giving me the tour?' she said instead.

Lowry smiled. 'I don't think I'll be much of a guide. It all looked the same to me. But I'll do my best.'

Jamie followed him up the stairs and into a starkly functional corridor, with exposed pipes running along the ceiling, and bundles of wires that disappeared through jagged gaps in the walls. There was a dull, metallic smell, and the air tasted stale. At the far end there was a heavy door that clunked open when Lowry heaved a handle on the wall.

'We have to keep these shut.' He pulled another lever to close the door behind them. 'Callan was very clear about that.' He gave a slight grimace. 'His engineer was even clearer.'

'Engineer?'

'The tall woman. She's . . . formidable.'

After a short flight of stairs, they came to a hallway with doors along both sides.

'That one's yours, I think,' Lowry said, counting along the doors. 'Rena's at the far end. I'm next to her.'

When he turned the handle, the door clanked sideways into the wall cavity. The quarters beyond were cramped and utilitarian, with a drop-down bunk folded up against the wall. Below, there was a metal desk that looked as if it would also stow flat. A pair of slimline lockers flanked the door, and at the far end Jamie could see a low cupboard that probably hid a toilet and sink. The only other piece of furniture was a wooden chair tucked under the desk, its top edge splintered and cracked, as though the cabin's previous resident had repeatedly forgotten to move it out of the way before dropping the bunk down.

Jamie didn't want to think about that unknown occupant, but their presence was unavoidable. A coat hung from a wall hook, and there were a few bits and pieces on the desk and some pictures propped up on a small shelf.

'I'll leave you to get settled,' Lowry said. 'I was thinking of scraping some sort of dinner together if you feel like joining me? Unless you want to go straight to bed.'

Jamie could see blankets trapped between the bunk and the wall. The bed hadn't been stripped since it was last slept in. 'I'll come down.'

Once Lowry had gone, Jamie turned to the row of photos on the shelf. One showed a young man and woman holding hands on the steps of a small house. She was tiny and blonde, with cropped hair, and he was tall, a little gawky-looking, but with a sweet, tilted smile.

Had this been his cabin, or hers? Jamie felt a dragging reluctance to know the answer to that question, but she went over and opened one of the lockers. The clothes inside clearly belonged to a woman. She closed the door gently, and turned to her own belongings.

She sat down on the chair with her rucksack propped between her knees, and started to empty out its contents. She stacked the things from the shop on the desk, and then unpacked her clothes, her canvas shoes and the little bag with her toiletries, piling them on the floor beside her feet.

The bottom of the bag was taken up with things that she couldn't claim to need, but hadn't been able to leave behind. She took out an old wooden cigar box with an incongruously elaborate catch. Her grandfather – her mother's father – used to collect stamps in it, but now it held odd fragments of Jamie's life. A tiny Paddington Bear, hatless, fur rubbed away in places, letting the plastic show through. A little pewter horse. A patchwork roll holding a sewing kit that had belonged to her grandmother's grandmother. A silver christening spoon engraved with her name. A pack of miniature playing cards. Three plain gold wedding bands, distinguishable only by the fact that her mother's ring hadn't worn as thin as those of her grandmother and great-grandmother. At the bottom of the box there was a bundle of postcards, the top one showing the great sweep of the bay at Belsley.

She placed the box on the table, along with a multi-current charger, her e-reader, wrapped in an old jumper, and a couple of print books – old favourites bearing the stamp of the second-hand bookshop she used to visit when she was young.

The sea blanket was at the bottom of the bag, rolled tight around a glass jar with a crackle-glazed ceramic lid. The contents were packed too close to rattle as she turned it upright. It was full of sea glass, bright-hued fragments with their broken edges worn smooth by years of tumbling against the Northumberland shoreline. Most of the pieces were the greens and blues that you found at every Belsley low tide, but she could also see scarlets, ambers and a few of the multi-coloured fragments from the old Victorian glass factory down at Seaham.

Her grandfather had taken her there a few times, and they'd combed the tideline, intent on their task, speaking only to say, *here, look, look at this.* The old man made jewellery from the sea glass, setting it in fine silver wire for bracelets and necklaces. The Seaham glass was the most popular, but he always let Jamie keep the best of it.

In between the bits of glass she could glimpse fragments of pottery: curves of delft and slivers of rough-thrown terracotta. She used to have one jar for glass and one for pottery, but just before she left Earth she spent a whole evening sifting through, shedding all but the most striking pieces.

Her thumb briefly caressed the jar's smooth flanks, then she placed it on the desk and stood up. She piled her clothes on the chair, reluctant to oust the cabin's former occupant from her locker. She hesitated for a moment, then took the stack of postcards out of the cigar box. Turning to the shelf, she pushed the frames gently to the back, so that she could lean her postcards against them. She didn't turn the cards over, but she knew what she'd see if she did. Her stepmother's handwriting was sloped and untidy, and she never left room for everything she wanted to say, having to finish sideways along the edge, or crammed in below the address. There was never anything vital, just little moments in a life that had kept rolling on after Jamie had left. The cards had come at regular intervals when Jamie first left Earth, and while they'd become more infrequent in recent years, they'd still turn up every now and again. Perhaps there was one sitting on the sideboard in her old flat on Alegria.

We're all well. The weather's been unsettled but it's getting better now. The tourists are here, and there's a little girl next door who has a purple hat just like that one you used to wear. Hope you're well and happy. All love.

Jamie felt a chill of discomfort, as though she was an interloper in this little room. One of the cards had slipped down, revealing the picture behind. The blonde girl stared out into the cabin, her smile frozen.

It's not my fault, Jamie thought, almost aggressively, but she'd lost any desire to linger there.

Outside, she tried to retrace Lowry's directions, but found herself in an unfamiliar passage with a row of open entryways along the wall. She was about to turn back when she caught the faint echo of voices. She stepped through the first doorway and squeezed along a narrow service passage lit by emergency strips. It gave out onto a hallway with an open door at one end. The grey-haired engineer was standing in the doorway, her back to Jamie.

'I just don't see why it had to be us who picked them up,' she was saying to someone out of sight.

'We're heading to the capital anyway.' It was Callan's voice. 'It's not like we're going out of our way.'

'Shouldn't we be finding out what shape the central worlds are in before we start collecting waifs and strays?'

Jamie took a cautious step back, and then froze as the engineer turned her head slightly.

'We know there are other survivors,' Callan said.

'But we've no idea whether there's any sort of administration, or just a load of people running around like headless mice.'

'It's done.' Callan raised his voice. 'It's my ship, and I made the call. If you don't like it, you don't have to stay.'

'I didn't *say* I didn't like it.'

'You didn't have to,' Callan replied. 'Now, unless there's something else . . .'

The woman shrugged and turned away, her gaze immediately falling on Jamie.

Her expression tightened, and she walked over and fixed Jamie with a level stare. 'You shouldn't be up here. What are you doing?'

'I'm sorry. I got lost.' She stuck out her hand with a conciliatory smile. 'I'm Jamie, by the way.'

For a moment she thought the other woman was going to ignore her outstretched hand, but then the engineer reached out and gave it the briefest of shakes. Her nails were blunted and oil-stained.

'Gracie.'

'Are you two the only crew?'

'There were five of us,' Callan said. He was standing in the doorway, watching them. 'But the other three were planetside on Nassau when the quarantine kicked in. When we set down there was no sign of them. No sign of anyone.'

'No one at all?'

Callan shrugged. 'There were no signals and we weren't exactly in a position to perform a fingertip search. Our people were gone.'

'I'm sorry,' Jamie said. It felt trite and ham-fisted, like all the people who'd said they were sorry when they'd heard about the baby.

They stood in silence for a few seconds, until Gracie muttered something about the engines, pushing past Jamie to disappear into the service passage.

Jamie waited until she was out of earshot before turning back to Callan.

'She didn't want to pick us up.' She wasn't sure why it needed saying.

'No.'

Christ. Talking to him was like pulling teeth.

She tripped over that thought. Daniel had once said those exact words to her.

She looked away. 'I should go and find Lowry.'

'I came up from the galley a few minutes ago,' Callan said. 'He'd only just started dinner. You can give me a hand first.'

'With what?'

'I loaded a crate of medicines from the Soltaire depot,' he said. 'I need a rundown on what's in there. I know the basics, but we always made sure we had a crew member with some med skills.'

'I'm not a doctor,' she said.

'No.' He sounded impatient. 'But you're a vet and that makes you better qualified than me, so I'd appreciate you taking a look. Okay?'

She followed him to a small storage bay where he dragged a plastic crate out into the hall and tore open the wrapping with a lock-knife.

The top layer was standard stuff. Amphitsellin, tetraclin, levomycin.

'Broad-spectrum antibiotics,' she said. 'You know what they're for?'

'Pretty much anything.'

'Anything bacterial,' she corrected. 'Don't overuse them.'

She put them on the floor and reached down to the next layer. 'Tryptine. That's a prescription-strength painkiller.'

She ran through a few more basic supplies, putting a couple of packages to one side to double-check.

Callan leaned against the wall, watching her. 'I guess the medicines for people and animals aren't that different.'

'They're pretty different,' she said. 'But I did a couple of years in med school before I swapped to veterinary science.'

She wasn't sure why she'd told him that. It made her earlier remark about not being a doctor seem deliberately obstructive.

'Must be trickier with animals,' Callan said. 'They can't tell you what's wrong.'

Jamie didn't tell him he'd hit on her precise reason for making the switch. People could and did tell you, not only what was wrong, but why it was wrong, and what else was wrong, and how that made them feel. And they thought you should be able to make it all better. She'd tried to cultivate a detached, professional calm, but people always leaned too close, and held on too tight.

Callan nodded at the crate. 'Anything in there that would have done any good against what just hit us?'

Jamie sat back on her heels and looked at the little stack of medicines. The culmination of mankind's long battle against disease, and it might as well have been a load of herbs and holy water for all the good it did when it came to it. Perhaps it had never been more than one great multi-faceted placebo. They'd become used to thinking of themselves as invincible. Whatever happened, the human race would go on.

'No,' she said. 'Long incubation period, drug-resistant, and with the way it mutated we didn't stand a chance.' She glanced in the crate. 'That's everything.'

Once she'd repacked the medicines, Callan replaced the lid and pushed the crate back into the storage bay. As he stood up, he stretched a little, his hand going to his hip.

'Bad back?'

'Just an old injury.' He instantly straightened up, giving her the barest hint of a smile. 'Or maybe just old age.'

Jamie almost asked him how old he was, but the question felt too intimate. She'd guess late forties, but he could be a few years younger or older than that.

He leaned back against the wall, folding his arms and considering her. 'So what are you going to do? When we get to the central worlds, I mean.' He nodded towards her hand. 'That's an upper echelon mark. There'll be a place for you there, no doubt. Especially with medical skills.'

'They'll have better medics than me.'

'Not if they did their job,' he said. 'I'd be surprised if there's a practising doctor left alive on the central planets. They were right on the frontline, and frontlines aren't usually left standing when it's all over.' He tilted his head. 'So what do you think you'll do?'

Daniel's face rose in her mind. She'd have the chance to put things right.

'I want to get to Earth,' she said. 'Same as the others.'

'You a believer too?'

'A believer?'

'The other woman was on about it. God's will. A new world. A pilgrimage to some island.'

'No, I don't believe.' How did every conversation come back to this? 'I'm from Earth. That's all.'

'What were you doing all the way out here?'

'Working.'

'Long old way to go for a job.'

'I was on Alegria for a few years first,' she said.

'But you don't want to head back there?'

'No.' The exchange was circling closer to the thing she wasn't saying, and she was sure he'd catch the shape of it, outlined in her half-truths and vague answers. 'I just want to get back home.'

'Fair enough.' Callan closed the storage bay doors. 'You should go and eat.'

'Are you joining us?' she asked on impulse.

He shook his head. 'I've already eaten,' he said, and walked away towards the far door. Just as he reached it, he glanced back and gave her a brief smile. 'Thanks. For your help.'

CHAPTER SIX

When Jamie woke the next morning, the cabin was growing gradually lighter. The previous occupant must have set the lighting to simulate a natural dawn, although on board a ship like this, day and night were nothing more than a consensus.

She washed as best she could in the sink before pulling on a blue T-shirt and the long denim skirt she used to wear on warm evenings back on Calgarth. There was a tiny mirror above the cabinet, and she brushed her hair and fastened it back. There were still shadows beneath her eyes, but her reflection didn't look quite so drawn as the one she'd glimpsed in that bar window back on Soltaire.

There was no one else down in the hold. She was conscious of a feeling of being out of place, as if she were a guest in someone's home with no understanding of the unspoken rules.

She made herself a coffee, and stood at the counter to eat a bowl of cereal and rehydrated milk. She'd almost finished when footsteps clanged on the stairs. A few seconds later, Gracie stepped through the gap in the crates.

She gave Jamie a cool nod. 'Morning.' She paused, as though scratching around for how this sort of exchange should go. 'Sleep all right?'

'Fine, thanks.'

Gracie opened the fridge, apparently satisfied that she'd met her conversational obligations. As Jamie hurried down the last few mouthfuls, not inclined to linger in awkward silence, there was a sharp crackle of sound, and Callan's voice echoed through the hold, distorted by the comm.

'Engineer to bridge immediately, please.'

The message snapped off. Gracie didn't show any reaction to the peremptory summons, throwing a hasty cup of coffee together and heading back to the stairs. There was a brief collision of voices as she reached the top, and after a few seconds Lowry appeared.

'Good night's sleep?' he said.

She nodded. 'You?'

He smiled. 'Not too bad. The engines take a bit of getting used to. Have you travelled much?'

'Not that much. I went from Earth to Alegria when I was twenty-two, then Soltaire a few weeks ago. I did a couple of short trips when I was living on Alegria, but that's about it.'

'Not back to Earth at all?'

'Just once.'

'Do you still have family there? I mean, did you have . . .' Lowry rubbed his brow. 'Sorry. There's no right way to talk about it, is there?'

'It's okay,' Jamie said. 'My father died a few years ago, but my stepmother was still in Belsley. I'm not sure where my half-sisters were living. We didn't really keep in touch.'

'And your mother?'

'She died when I was fourteen.'

'That must have been hard.'

Jamie looked away. Twenty-four years ago and millions of miles away, and people still always wanted to know what had happened and how she'd felt about it. It was as though you weren't allowed to leave anything behind.

The clank of a door provided a welcome distraction, and she looked up to see Callan walking through the gap. He nodded at the pair of them, before shoving his tin mug under the hot water tap and tipping a large spoonful of instant coffee into it.

'Morning,' Lowry said. 'Everything all right?'

Callan nodded. 'We may be making another stop. We've picked up a signal.'

Jamie's heart gave a hopeful leap. More survivors. More proof that the statistics were wrong.

'From where?' Lowry asked.

'Mining colony on Pangaea.'

'I haven't heard of it,' Lowry said.

'It's in the Gemmel cluster,' Callan said. 'Fairly wealthy, if I remember rightly. Small-scale platinum mining. Gracie's trying to raise someone.'

'Do we know who it is?' Jamie asked.

'No,' Callan said. 'It's your basic distress beacon. Date-stamped a couple of days ago.'

'So we'll be landing,' Lowry said.

Callan gave a non-committal shrug. 'Let's see if Gracie gets any response. Then we'll make a decision.'

'What do you mean?' Jamie felt a sharp surge of adrenaline. 'We can't just leave someone down there.'

Callan tipped powdered milk into his coffee and swirled it around. 'Well, we can. If we can't raise anyone, I'm not inclined to land on spec. We won't know the fuel situation.'

The memories were shoving for space inside Jamie's head. Her cold stone floor, gritty and unyielding. Her arms wrapped tight around her body as she tried not to break into pieces, alone. And running through her mind, that relentless fugue – *nought point nought nought nought—*

'No.' She wrenched her thoughts back.

Callan's eyebrows went up. 'No?'

'I didn't mean . . .' She shook her head, trying to clear it. 'I just . . . whoever's down there, they may think they're the only one.'

Callan was still looking at her, and she felt a flash of resentment. He'd never had to face that possibility. None of them had.

'Like I said.' His tone was level. 'If Gracie can raise someone, then we'll see.'

'What if they can't get to the comm in time?' Jamie could hear her voice rising. 'What if they're injured?'

'That's a lot of *what ifs*.' Callan tapped his fingers on the scratched surface of the kitchen unit. 'How about I add one? What if there's no fuel?'

'You stocked up on Soltaire,' Lowry put in, his tone neutral. 'Do we have enough to take off again?'

'Yes,' Callan said. 'But it would mean another stop somewhere. That's an unnecessary complication.'

'Unnecessary?' Jamie gave a harsh laugh. 'Saving someone's life?'

'It's an established settlement,' Callan said. 'It's not like we'd be abandoning them on some backwater to chase their dinner with a home-made bow and arrow.'

'But they'd be *alone*.' Jamie could feel a tremor trying to break through her. If she started shaking, she might not stop. 'You don't know . . .' She broke off. The memory of those first hours was too close, too personal. But she had to make them understand. They couldn't just sail off into the void, never looking back. 'I was alone,' she managed. 'I thought I was alone.'

Callan sipped his coffee, studying her over the rim of the mug. 'You must have known you weren't. The infomercials said—'

'It doesn't matter.' There was a panicked edge to her voice. 'When you wake up and there's no one . . .' She drew a deep breath. 'If we just fly on, and leave whoever's down there, we might as well have murdered them.'

'There'll be survivors all over the place,' Callan said. 'We're not responsible for every one of them.'

'But we're responsible for this one.'

'How do you figure that?' Callan said. 'If we'd never picked up the signal, we'd never have known there was anyone there.'

'But we *do* know,' Jamie said. 'We can't stop knowing it just because it's not convenient for you.'

A quick flash of anger crossed Callan's face. 'Is that what you think? That I just can't be bothered?'

'Looks like it from where I'm standing,' she shot back.

'You're standing on my ship,' Callan said. 'And if I hadn't picked the three of you up, you'd still be standing on Soltaire.'

'And we're grateful,' Lowry said. 'But Jamie's right. We can't just leave someone behind.'

Callan drained his coffee and put the mug down. 'Let's see what Gracie picks up.'

As he walked away, Jamie stared after him, a whole plethora of furious responses running through her mind. She wanted to scream, or hit something. But she knew she wouldn't. She never had. She'd always kept everything shoved down inside her, growing harder and denser, hidden away, but never forgotten.

'Let it go.' Lowry stepped up to her side. 'Let's see what happens.'

Back upstairs, she'd just reached the door of her cabin when the comm crackled and Callan's voice came on.

'Commencing approach to Pangaea in five minutes. Strap in for landing.'

The tight knot inside Jamie's chest loosened. One of the other doors slid open and Rena appeared. Her hair was clumped at one side of her head, as though she'd been sleeping, but her eyes were suspiciously red.

'What is it?'

'Survivors,' Jamie said. 'There was a signal.'

'More survivors?' Rena's hand went to her forehead, as though she were about to cross herself, but she caught herself on the edge of the movement, and pressed her hands together in front of her chest instead. 'How many?'

'I don't know.'

Jamie turned and walked along the corridor. After a few seconds there was a patter of feet and Rena fell in beside her.

She gave Jamie a quick, tremulous smile. 'It's starting. People will come together.'

'We need to get strapped in,' Jamie said, before the other woman could get into her stride. 'Come on.'

Callan's skill in handling the ship had been apparent when the *Phaeacian* had set down on Soltaire, and this landing was no less deft. Jamie barely felt a jolt as they touched down.

Callan appeared just as they were undoing their harnesses. 'You three stay well back in the hold,' he said, walking towards the door.

'Who's out there?' Rena asked.

'No idea.'

Jamie stared at him. 'Didn't you speak to someone?'

'No. So stay back.'

'You expecting trouble?' Lowry said.

'I don't know what to expect. You never know how someone will react when they're frightened, and stupid is hot-wired right into some people.'

Sharp sunlight cut through the gap as the doors opened. Callan took a couple of steps outside, his hand resting on his gun, and then stopped. He stood still, looking at something out of Jamie's view, before turning and beckoning to them.

As Lowry and Rena hurried forwards, Jamie hung back, conscious of an echo of the same feeling she'd had on Soltaire. As long as they stayed safely sealed inside the walls of the ship, she didn't have to think about what was out there. She could choose to believe anything at all; that they were alone in the universe, or surrounded by living worlds, full of living, breathing people.

By the time she reached the entrance the others were walking down the gangway. The port was bigger than the one on Soltaire, and they'd set down on one of three platforms around a central loading area. The sky was a darker blue than on any other planet she'd seen, giving the place a pregnant, storm-heavy look despite the white-gold glare of the sun.

There were two people standing a few metres from the end of the gangway: a girl who looked to be in her early twenties, with a tall, thin lad of around eighteen or nineteen standing a few paces behind her, arms soldier-soldier straight by his sides.

The girl was small and fair-haired, dressed in a pale blue dress that looked like something a child might wear to a party. It floated down to just above her knees, and her arms and legs were bare. Her expression was wary, and as Callan reached the end of the gangway, she held up a warning hand, shooting a quick glance over her shoulder at the lad.

'Sorry.' Her voice seemed too light and flimsy for the heavy, industrial surroundings. 'Could you stop. Please.' The lad had risen up on his toes, shifting his weight backwards and forwards, his gaze resting somewhere above the heads of the new arrivals. 'He doesn't . . . I mean, he finds people difficult. It was hours before he'd talk to me. But we get along fine now, don't we, Finn?' She smiled over her shoulder. It looked forced, but the lad stopped his gentle rocking and nodded, a quick jerk of his head.

'What's your name?' Callan said.

'Mila.'

'You the only two here?'

Something flickered across the girl's face. 'I haven't seen anyone else.'

'That's not an answer.' Callan had picked up on the careful shape of her response. 'Any sign of anyone else?'

Unexpectedly it was Finn who replied. His voice was flat, his words delivered without intonation. 'There's the bad man.' He had dropped his gaze slightly, so that he was staring at the flanks of the ship.

'The bad man?' Callan said.

Mila tried to smile. 'It's nothing. Just a joke I made when I thought . . .' She broke off, reaching up to wrap a strand of hair around her fingers. 'I keep thinking there's someone here. Someone's moving things. Or maybe I did it. Or Finn. I'm never sure.'

There was a shrill note in her voice, and Finn went up on his toes again. Mila instantly turned to him, dropping into a soothing monotone. 'It's okay, Finn, it's okay.'

Callan glanced around the landing site, and then looked back at Mila, regarding her appraisingly. As Jamie moved further down the gangway, she could see what he was looking at. The girl had the mottled shadow of bruising along her jaw-line and a healing cut in front of her ear. There was also the faintest suggestion of a fading black eye hidden beneath her careful make-up.

'What happened to you?' Callan asked.

Mila flushed. 'Someone hurt me.'

'I can see that,' Callan replied. 'Is that someone your *bad man*?'

'No. It was before.'

Callan nodded, his expression still contemplative.

Mila's face creased in an anxious frown, and then her expression changed, and she lifted her hand to push her hair back from her face. It was a slow, deliberate gesture, and when she smiled at him, there was a hint of practised coquettishness about it.

'So,' she said. 'Here we are.'

The words sounded too old for her. They didn't fit with her child's dress and her thin frame.

Callan gave her a long, level look. 'Here we are. What now?'

Mila glanced away, her mask slipping a little, as though she didn't have the right script for this. When she looked back, she was herself again, young and uncertain. It was as though she'd shrugged on someone else's skin for a moment, but it hadn't fit.

She chewed at her thumbnail. 'Can we come with you?'

'If that's what you want. We're going to the capital.'

'Anywhere with people,' Mila said. 'I don't care where it is.'

She glanced over her shoulder as she spoke, and Callan followed the direction of her gaze. 'You really think there's someone else?'

Mila shook her head slowly.

'What?' Callan's voice was sharp with impatience. 'What are you not telling us?'

'There was a gunshot,' she said, after another long pause. 'A couple of nights ago.' Her brow creased. 'At least I think there was. Maybe I dreamed it. I don't know.'

'Did he hear it?' Callan jerked his head towards Finn.

'He sleeps really deeply.' Mila's tone was defensive. 'But I know what I heard.'

'I thought you said you weren't sure.'

'I . . .' Mila bit her lip. 'I didn't dream it. I just told myself that. I know what it was.'

'Shots.' There was a hint of scepticism in Callan's voice. 'From a bad man who's hiding and doesn't want to be seen. Maybe he decided to end it all, and that's what you heard.'

Mila's expression darkened. 'No. I think there was someone else. The bad man . . . he's still here. Sometimes I hear him at night, scratching around, as if he's trying to scare us.'

'He?' Callan said, as though it had just occurred to him.

'That's what it feels like.'

'And you haven't gone looking for him?' Callan said.

A hint of anger sparked in Mila's eyes, but Callan held his hand up. 'That was a question, not a criticism. I'd have thought you'd have wanted to find out if someone else was here, and what their intentions were.'

'I didn't think . . .' Mila looked down. 'I was scared. He felt . . . it felt wrong. Like I said. Bad.'

Callan regarded Mila for a few more seconds, then turned away. 'Well, if there is someone here, he's got half an hour to present himself. If he does show up . . . well, we'll see. The two of you go get your things. I need to check the fuel situation.' He turned to Jamie. 'Can you find the port depot and see if there are some medical packs we can load easily? It might be a good idea to have something worth trading.'

As he walked away, Jamie followed him.

'Are you sure we should be wandering about the place?' she said. 'You heard what she said.'

'I heard her say she might have dreamed it.'

'She sounded pretty scared.'

He stopped walking and looked at her. 'They've been alone here for days. Of course she's scared. She's probably jumping out of her skin at every bit of rubbish blowing in the street. If there really was a *bad man*, why wouldn't he have shown himself? They're not exactly much of a threat. And . . .'

He stopped abruptly.

'What?'

He shook his head. 'Just thinking there are some things that probably never change. A girl like her, alone. There'll always be someone out for what he can get.'

'She's not alone,' Jamie said.

'The boy's hardly likely to be much protection,' Callan said, setting off again.

Jamie fell into step beside him. 'You really think she was imagining things?'

'I do. I can't see any reason why someone would hide from them, but I can see a whole load of reasons why someone wouldn't.'

There was a dark logic to his words, and Jamie nodded. 'I'll go check the depot. Anything in particular you want me to look for?'

He gave her a faint smile. 'You're the vet.'

Jamie found the depot easily enough. It was a wide-fronted prefab building, with the main entrance on a service lane leading off the landing site. Inside, Jamie checked the signs on the end of each aisle until she found the medicines, her footsteps echoing between the shelves, as if someone was keeping pace with her in a parallel aisle.

She loaded a stack of portable med kits onto a trolley, and pushed it round to a roll-up shutter at the back of the warehouse. When she tugged at the bottom edge, it didn't move, and as she adjusted her grip, her knuckles scraped against the concrete floor. She yanked her hand back. There was a puckered graze across the back of her fingers, with a couple of tiny speckles of blood beading on the skin. She was about to turn and push the trolley the long way round when she felt an irrational flare of certainty.

There was someone else in the building.

It wasn't a sound exactly, but a particular kind of silence, like someone holding their breath.

'Hello?' Her voice sounded high and thin. 'Is someone there?'

Was that a footstep?

Her pulse was beginning to thud. Mila's nerves had infected her. There was no one here. But somehow she didn't want to make her way back through the empty, echoing warehouse. She turned back to the shutter, reaching down to scrabble at the lower edge again. As she turned, feeling for a better grip, she caught sight of a lever just to the side of the door. When she yanked it down, the shutter clanked and strained, then slid slowly up into the roof. Jamie grabbed the trolley and shoved it out onto the sunlit landing site.

By the time she reached the ship, her pulse had steadied, and she was uncomfortably relieved that no one else had witnessed that irrational moment of panic.

Mila was sitting on the edge of the gangway, next to Lowry. There was a clutch of small bags around her feet, clothes spilling out their tops, speaking of hasty and indiscriminate packing. Finn was pacing nearby, his steps careful and precise. A small backpack sat high up on his shoulders, with the chest strap pulled tight, like a child on a day trip from school. Rena was standing a little way apart, watching the pair of them through narrowed eyes.

'Are you sure you need all that?' Jamie nodded at the bags. Reds and golds, chiffons and satins. From one bag a blue sleeve hung limp, covered in sequins, some of which had pulled away, leaving trailing threads. 'The ship's pretty basic.'

'These are the only clothes I have.'

Jamie looked out across the rooftops. Callan had said that the settlement was wealthy, but the port didn't look like the sort of place where women would have much call to float around in sequinned chiffon. It was solid, industrial, and flanked by the scrubby slopes of a miserly hillside.

'You're a prostitute,' Rena said suddenly. It was a pronouncement, not a question, and her tone was blunt and accusatory.

Mila flinched, and reached out to touch the sequinned sleeve with her fingertip. After a moment, she lifted her head, another of those bright, artificial smiles pinned on her face.

'Why not? Money's good, and it's not as though work's easy to come by in a place like this.'

Rena stiffened.

'Rena . . .' Lowry began, but Jamie cut in, pre-empting anything the other woman might say.

'I don't think we need to worry too much about money.' She tried to keep her tone light, but the girl's smile faded.

'Is it like this everywhere?'

'I think so. But there might be more people on the capital.'

Mila dropped her head to her knees and began to cry. Finn stopped his pacing and turned to look at her, his face puckering in the first emotion Jamie had seen there. One hand clenched into a fist, the knuckles rubbing on the back of his other forearm, as though he was trying to scrub something off his skin.

Mila gave her face a hard swipe, knocking the tears away. She scrambled to her feet and moved towards Finn, stopping a short distance away, hand raised but not touching him.

'It's okay,' she said, in a low, sing-song voice, like a mother talking to a troubled child. 'It's okay, it's okay.' Jamie was assaulted by an image that was both brutal and oddly tender: Mila, in her chiffon and sequins, lying back on a bed, a male head on her breast, her hands soft on the stubby hair. *It's okay, it's okay.*

Finn was still rubbing at his skin, and he'd started to rock a little. Mila stood up on tiptoe, trying to catch his gaze.

'Look up,' she said. 'Look at the sky. Look how blue it is. And look at the ship. It's going to take us up there.'

Finn shook his head violently, but he lifted his gaze to the sky. Gradually his rocking slowed and stopped. The rubbing continued, but with less force to it, slowing until it was just an occasional pluck at his skin.

Mila said something else, her voice barely above a whisper. Finn tipped his head, listening, although he kept his face turned up towards the sky. After a moment he nodded, turned away and resumed his careful pacing.

Mila looked back at Jamie. 'He's okay.'

'How did you know what to do?' There had been something simple and instinctive about the way Mila had soothed the lad.

'I just figured it out. He likes the sky, and open places. He doesn't like being touched. And he doesn't like people getting angry or upset.'

'How did you survive?' Jamie said, and then hesitated, not sure how to clarify her meaning with any sort of delicacy. The disease had been spread and re-spread through human contact. And Mila was . . .

'I wasn't working at the time.' Mila lifted her hand to touch the bruise beneath her eye. 'I had a client who got angry when I wouldn't . . . well, it doesn't matter. They told me to keep out of the way until I healed. He was someone important, and they didn't want trouble. I stayed upstairs and someone brought my meals up. When I got sick no one came.' She looked down, fingers twining together. 'I thought I was going to die. I tried to get downstairs. I could hear people. Some shouting. Someone crying. But I couldn't walk. And anyway . . .' She gave

Jamie a swift look, as though assessing how much this stranger might understand. 'I thought if I was going to die, maybe dying alone would be okay. Being with someone isn't always better, is it?'

Jamie didn't reply. What would have happened if she'd still been with Daniel when the disease struck? They didn't touch as casually as other people they knew. There were some couples who brushed one another's arm when they spoke, or leaned against one another, as though they had to keep reminding themselves that they were one of two. Daniel had learned when to touch her, and when to let her have her space. So maybe they would have made it, the pair of them.

Callan and Gracie appeared round the side of the ship. The engineer was shaking her head, and Callan looked irritated. Another dispute over this fresh set of survivors, no doubt.

Callan came over, casting his eye over the stacked trolley. 'That the medicines?'

She nodded.

'Is there likely to be any lycidine in there?' Lowry said.

'Probably not in the multi-packs,' Jamie said. 'But there were some more specialist supplies. Do you need some?'

He nodded. 'I've got a rather irritating little heart condition that surfaces at times of stress. If you tell me where the medicines are, I'll go and look.'

'Quicker if I do it,' Jamie said. With the moment of their departure growing closer, she had an irrational urge to go back to the depot, to prove to herself that there'd never been anyone there.

That they wouldn't be leaving anyone behind.

As she stepped through the door, Jamie could feel the back of her neck prickling.

It was just the sudden chill of the place. That was all.

Her gaze fell on a doorway tucked into the alcove at the side of the shutter. She could see through it into a small office. A desk was tipped on its side in front of the door, as though to form a barrier of sorts. Jamie walked over to look inside, stopping dead on the threshold. The little room had been converted into something resembling a bunker. There were crates stacked around the walls, and a mattress was pushed into the corner, with a tangle of blankets on top.

And the body of a man lay face down on the floor.

CHAPTER SEVEN

Jamie suddenly seemed to be breathing ice, fear crackling inside her lungs.

The man looked to be about fifty, with thinning hair and a muscled frame. Now he was slack and grey-skinned, the only colour about him coming from the rusty stains on the concrete floor, where the blood had seeped from the ragged wounds in his head and side.

For a moment the implications of the scene failed to register. There was just the utter shock of that lifeless form. In all the days since she'd woken from the fever, Jamie had never once seen death. Just dust. Just emptiness. But this was death in its most solid, undeniable form. As she took a stuttering step backwards, her foot twisted and almost gave way. She grabbed at the door frame as a scatter of flies leaped up from the body with a buzz of noise that echoed the sudden ringing in her ears. She twisted round, her breath catching in her throat, utterly certain that she would find someone there, watching her from the shadows.

The depot was still and silent but for the buzzing of the flies, but there was a sense of menace so palpable that she could almost feel it pressing against her skin.

The bad man.

Mila's voice echoed in Jamie's thoughts as she broke into a run, ducking out of the doors and onto the concourse. Her legs were just fractionally heavier than they should have been, the planet's unfamiliar gravity registering for the first time. It was like one of those dreams where you try to run and your body only half responds. As she reached the ship, Callan and Gracie stepped out onto the gangway. The engineer suddenly stopped and pointed, not at Jamie, but at something behind her.

Jamie looked back over her shoulder, and saw smoke rising from somewhere beyond the surrounding buildings. Her feet clanged on the metal gangway as she stumbled towards Callan and Gracie.

'The depot—' she began, but Callan cut across her.

'Forget it. Let's go.'

'Tank's not full yet,' Gracie said.

'We've got enough to be going along with.' He looked across at the smoke. 'I'm not inclined to hang around.'

'It could be a signal,' Gracie said.

'You think?' Callan gave the engineer a blistering look. 'Let's get going. Maybe the girl wasn't so far off the mark with this *bad man* talk.'

'She was right.'

They both turned to stare at Jamie.

'The depot. There's a body. A man. Someone shot him.'

Gracie hesitated for a moment, and then scrambled down the side of the gangway and jogged over to detach the fuel hose.

As Callan turned to watch her, his eyes suddenly widened and he spun back towards the ship, shouting his engineer's name.

Fire. Licking up the corner of the shipyard, close to the great fuelling tanks, the reflected flames dancing in the muted rainbow surface of a slick of spilled oil.

As Jamie stood frozen, there was a misleadingly quiet *thump* of sound, and that shimmer disappeared in a leap of flame, almost as high as the tanks.

'Gracie.' Callan yelled it again, grabbing Jamie's shoulder and shoving her towards the doors.

The engineer yanked the fuel hose free, then slammed the panel closed and ran for the gangway. The doors were already closing as she reached them, and she pushed through the narrowing gap, knocking Jamie aside.

There was an acrid stench in the air, and Jamie's throat was already starting to itch. Then the doors closed and the sharp sting of smoke gave way to the familiar, slightly stale taste of the ship's air supply.

Callan ran for the stairs, ignoring the other passengers, save for a swift 'Get strapped in' thrown back over his shoulder.

'What's going on?' Rena stared after him, one hand going to her throat.

'Fire.' Jamie stepped forwards.

Mila's eyes widened. 'The bad man?'

'Yes. No.' Jamie was already tugging the row of seats down. 'It doesn't matter right now.'

They were leaving. There was someone out there and they were leaving them alone.

She strapped Mila in and reached for Finn, but he twisted out of her grasp.

'Finn, we need to go.'

Mila was saying something, but her voice was high-pitched and frightened and it wasn't soothing him this time. He flailed at Jamie, stiff-limbed and silent, backing away from the seats, until she swore at him through gritted teeth.

Lowry stepped in, talking to the lad in a calm, matter-of-fact tone. Finn grew still, his head tilted as though he was listening, although he did not look at the old man. Lowry kept up his soothing patter and somehow managed to steer Finn towards the seats. As the engines leaped into life the lad stiffened, but Lowry kept talking, describing the take-off process in his soothing tone until his voice was drowned out by the ship's dull crescendo. By that time the edge of Finn's panic had blunted and Lowry had been able to strap him into his seat, where he sat with his knees drawn up, as though the floor was dangerous, his fingers curling and uncurling where they rested on his shins.

Jamie leaned back and closed her eyes as the ship carried them back to the safety of space.

Once Callan's voice had come over the speaker, giving terse permission for them to undo their straps, Lowry turned to Jamie.

'What happened down there?'

'I don't know. There was a fire.' There'd been a panicked unreality about those moments when the flames were leaping into life. Jamie had a sudden image of fires springing up all over the settlement, licking closer and closer to the ship, as though someone would rather see the whole world burn than share it with others.

Despite it all – the fire, the body – she felt a stab of guilt. Yes, that unknown presence had done everything in its power to ensure they saw it as a threat, but whoever it was, did they deserve to be alone, perhaps for the rest of their days? Her head said *yes*, but she was conscious of a scratch of unease at how readily that answer came to her. Life was life. If she started making judgements about who was worth saving and who was not, then where did that end?

She shook the thought away and gave the other passengers a quick, dispassionate account of the events that had led to their precipitous departure. Callan arrived just as she finished.

'So there was someone there,' Mila said, shooting him an accusatory look.

'Seems so,' he said levelly.

'Well, that's a lesson learned, I suppose,' Lowry put in. 'Not everyone who survived is going to welcome us with open arms. I thought . . .' He sighed and rubbed at his face. 'Never mind. Did we get the fuel?'

'Not enough,' Callan said. 'We'll have to make another stop at some point.'

He was looking at Jamie as he spoke, and she felt a flicker of resentment. Was he blaming her?

'Come on,' Lowry said. 'Let's get our new arrivals settled in.'

They put Mila up in the quarters next to Jamie's and left her to unpack, while Lowry checked the cabins on the other side of the corridor. One had been commandeered for extra storage, but the second was empty, with a bed made up. Finn was tense, standing stock-still in the middle of the floor and shooting suspicious glances around the cabin. It was a few moments before Lowry could persuade him to unstrap his backpack and place it on the desk.

'Do you want to unpack your things?' the preacher said.

Finn gave a quick affirmative jerk of his head, coupled with another furtive recce of the cabin's far corners.

'Would you like us to help, or do you want to do it yourself?' Lowry asked.

'Myself.'

'Do you want us to leave you to it, or shall we stay?'

Finn considered this, frowning down at the floor. 'Stay.'

Lowry nodded and stepped back. Finn opened the rucksack and took out some neatly folded clothes.

'Here.' Jamie opened one of the lockers, so that he could place the clothes inside, tops on one shelf and trousers on another. Then he went back to his rucksack and took out a hessian drawstring bag, printed with the logo of a well-known dry foods supplier. A comb poked out of the top and the contents clinked as he placed it carefully on the desk. A brown-covered notebook followed, along with a clutch of coloured pencils, fastened together with two elastic bands. The final item was a cracked and faded cardboard box, with a picture of a beach on the cover, and *1000 pieces* blazoned along one edge.

'You like jigsaws?' Lowry asked.

'Yes.' Finn was holding the box in both hands, his gaze fixed on the printed seascape.

'Would you like to do it now?'

'Yes.'

'How about we go down to the galley? There's a table there.'

Finn hesitated, glancing first at Lowry and then at Jamie. After a moment he nodded. 'Yes.' He blinked, a small frown puckering his face, as though he was trying to remember something. 'Yes please.'

When they reached the galley, the table was in use. Rena and Gracie were sitting on either side of it, drinking coffee and not talking. Finn shifted from foot to foot, his hands tight on the jigsaw box, and Jamie saw Rena shoot him a quick unsmiling look before turning away.

Jamie looked around. There were a couple of pallets just to the side of the galley area, and some boards leaning against a nearby crate.

'Here.' She slid one of the boards on top of the pallets. 'We can use this.'

Finn placed the box on the makeshift table and slid into the gap alongside, tucking his knees underneath him.

Lowry looked down at the slatted floor with a grimace. 'If I get down there, I may never get back up again. I'll leave the two of you to it, if that's okay.'

Jamie wasn't sure she would be as easy with the lad as

Lowry, but the old preacher was looking tired and his hand kept going to the side of his chest.

'Are you all right?'

Lowry gave her a wry smile. 'Just old age.'

Jamie suddenly remembered his request back on Pangaea. 'The lycidine . . .'

'I still have a few tablets left,' Lowry said. 'I'll take one and lie down for a bit. You carry on.'

Finn had already tipped out the puzzle. He was carefully turning the pieces face up to show scattered fragments of golden sand and blue sky. Jamie sat down opposite him, noting the neat, precise way he handled the puzzle. Was he as focused as he appeared to be, or was his fear and confusion playing out in a loop, like her tangle of statistics? If he was in turmoil, he gave no outward sign.

'How do you like to do it?' Jamie kept her tone light and matter-of-fact, like Lowry's. 'Do you start with the edges?'

'Corners first.' Finn picked up four pieces in quick succession, laying them out at a precisely judged distance.

'You've done this before.' Jamie smiled at him, but his only response was a questioning look that made her feel stupid, talking about nothing at all when that kind of time-filling chatter was probably what he found most difficult. On Alegria, every social situation had been a seething mass of that sort of conversation. Even she'd sometimes found it hard to navigate. For Finn it was probably incomprehensible.

Finn was picking up straight-edged pieces of blue, some clear and featureless, others brushed with the faint suggestion of clouds. Jamie couldn't see anything to distinguish the pieces, but Finn laid them down without hesitation, leaving precise gaps. It wasn't a puzzle for him, she realised. It was a meditation, something he could do without having to figure out the whys and the wherefores.

The sofa scraped on the floor as Rena stood up, turning towards the galley. As she squeezed past, her skirt snagged the edge of the board, knocking a handful of pieces onto the floor. Jamie snatched at them, but only managed to save a couple before the others disappeared between the floor slats.

'Shit.' She slid her fingers into the gap. 'Sorry, Finn. I think we've lost them.'

Rena muttered something and tugged her skirt free, almost dislodging another piece. Jamie put her hand out to steady the board.

'Careful.'

A dull red flush rose along Rena's jaw. 'You were in the way. Can't he do this in his cabin?'

Finn was gripping the edge of the board, staring at the space where the pieces had been. At Rena's comment, he scrambled to his feet, grabbing at a crate for balance.

'Finn.' Jamie stood up, and put her arm out, not thinking. He shrunk away, and she immediately snatched her hand back. 'Sorry. Don't go. We might be able to find the pieces.'

Rena stalked away to the galley, where she slammed down her cup and busied herself with the hot water machine.

Jamie turned to Gracie who was sitting in silence, watching the commotion. 'Can we get under the floor?'

'Not without moving the crates and unscrewing the whole panel.'

Jamie looked back at Finn. 'I'm sorry,' she said again. 'Maybe we'll be able to get them back when the crates are unloaded.'

'That won't be any time soon,' Gracie said. 'They belonged to a family relocating out to one of the Mercian colonies. I don't suppose anyone's still waiting for them.'

Finn knelt back down and began shovelling pieces back into the box. There was a jaggedness to the movement, at odds with the deft way he'd been placing the pieces when the puzzle was whole. As Jamie watched the fragments of sea and sky disappear in a formless tumble into the box, an idea occurred to her.

'Wait there. I'm just going to get something.'

Up in her cabin she picked up the jar of sea glass, and hurried back to the hold. Gracie was gone, but Rena was back on the sofa, her hands clasped tightly together. When she saw Jamie, she rose out of her seat with an awkward, stiff-limbed movement.

'I'm sorry.' She made a vague gesture towards Finn. 'I didn't mean . . .' She stopped, her mouth working as though the words had suddenly become unpalatable. 'It was in the way,' she went on, more aggressively. 'I didn't mean to.'

'Okay.' Jamie knew she sounded short, but she didn't want to get drawn into a post-mortem, in which she'd have to navigate the uncharted waters of Rena's changing moods.

'It was in the way,' Rena said again. There was an odd, almost pleading note in her voice. 'It wasn't my fault.'

'It doesn't matter.' Jamie turned away. 'Just leave it.'

As Rena muttered something incomprehensible and stalked out of the galley, Jamie sat down opposite Finn, who'd finished packing the jigsaw away, and was sitting silently, knees tucked into his chest. When she opened the jar, he lifted his head, watching as she emptied out the fragments of glass and pottery. One piece, aqua blue and almost perfectly spherical, skittered across the board towards him, and he picked it up between finger and thumb.

'It's sea glass,' Jamie said. 'The pieces have been in the sea for years, so all the sharp bits have worn away.'

Finn replaced the blue marble and reached for a curve of deep red, running his thumb along the frosted surface.

'Pieces of what?' he asked.

'All sorts of things. You find it all along the coast where I grew up.' She ran her palms over the fragments, spreading them out so that the colours and textures were apparent. 'The clear pieces could be anything.' She picked up a green tear-drop. 'These are from old bottles. There was a glass factory just down the coast, and they used to throw their leftover glass into the sea.' She brushed through the pile until she found a smooth oval, shot through with lines of blue and amber. 'They call these pieces end-of-day glass. They came from the glass the factory workers used at the end of each day, with all the leftover colours mixed together.'

Finn reached into the centre of the pile, and picked up a piece of delft pottery, the faded sky-blue figures just visible against a crackle-grey background. He put it down in front of him and reached for another with a similar pattern, but stained with speckles of rusty pigment. He pushed the two pieces close, turning them round, trying to butt their corners together. Frustration creased his brow.

'They don't fit.'

Jamie put another piece down, dusty pink this time, with grey spider-thread lines across its smooth surface. 'They won't,' she said, adding a piece of terracotta tile, with a worn floral pattern carved along its edge. 'They're all from different things. And they've been worn away. Even if you had all the pieces, you'd never be able to put them back together.'

Finn reached for another piece of pink and grey. 'These are the same.'

'You do sometimes find pieces that look like they come from the same thing.' Jamie had always found that fascinating. All that great bulk of ocean and time, and some of the fragments had held together. She'd sometimes wondered, if you sat there long enough would you find the whole thing? And if you did, would there be a way to put it back together, so that it still held some vestige of what it had been before?

Her grandfather used to take her up to the pebble beach north of Belsley, usually on a Sunday morning when her grandmother was in church. You only ever found pottery fragments in any great number on that particular stretch of coast. Boulmer and Craster were for clear glass, and some light blues and greens. You got the cobalt blues at North Sunderland and Seaham, and the latter was the sole repository of the reds and purples and mixed hues. But Belsley was pottery, and she and her grandfather would walk up there when the tide was low.

They'd met a woman once, engrossed in the same activity. She wasn't local, too smartly dressed for the beach, with damp sand clinging to her suede toes. She had a whole handful of pieces of blue and white that looked as though they were from the same thing. A bowl most likely, from the way the pieces curved. She'd shown them, her face bright with discovery, and said that things like that were the reason she believed in God. Jamie's grandfather had smiled at the woman, and said it was why he didn't.

When they were alone, Jamie had scuffed the sand with her toes and asked him what he'd meant. He'd said that if God did exist, He'd give you all of it, or He'd give you nothing. He'd test your faith, or He'd verify it. He wouldn't leave it all so wide open that everything could be a pattern, or else nothing at all.

Finn ran his fingers through the fragments again, picking up a handful of tiny beads of glass. Jamie had always gone after the bigger pieces, the ones that caught your eye from a long way away, but her grandfather sifted through the fine shingle for the tiny scraps of almost-nothing, the ones that had been in the sea for so long that they were close to disappearing.

'What are they for?' Finn asked suddenly.

'What do you mean?'

'What do you do with them? If they don't go back together.'

'They're not for anything,' she said. 'My grandfather used to make jewellery, but I just liked to look at them. Sometimes I used to make pictures.' She moved a few pieces of red and blue around until she had two concentric circles, like a double-layered flower, and then she added a stalk and leaves of small green nuggets. 'Like that.'

'You're from Earth.' Finn brushed the glass petals with a careful fingertip.

'Yes.'

'The other lady said we're going to Earth. She said we were going to start again.'

'We want to go to Earth,' Jamie said. 'I'm not sure if we'll get there. And I'm not sure about the other bit.'

Finn nodded, and returned to his contemplation of the sea glass.

Jamie looked up at the echo of footsteps, and saw Callan approaching.

'Can I borrow you for a minute?' he said.

She glanced at Finn. 'Can we talk here?'

'No,' Callan said. 'I need you to do me an inventory of those new medicines. I want to know what we've got, and whether there's anything else we need.'

'Won't most places have stockpiled supplies?'

'The remote settlements may, but places closer in will have relied on regular deliveries.'

Jamie felt a brush of irritation and envy. What must it be like to see things as unemotionally as Callan did? They had no idea how many people had survived, or how any new society would function, but here he was, talking about stockpiles and inventories, as though they were on a run-of-the-mill trading trip, rather than making their way to the heart of a broken world, not sure whether or not they'd find it still beating.

'I don't want to leave Finn on his own,' she said, lowering her voice.

'He'll be fine. Not much he can get up to.'

'That's not what I meant.' Jamie glanced at Finn, who was studying a curve of green glass. 'He's . . . it must be hard for him.'

'He survived on his own until Mila found him,' Callan said. 'You don't have to treat him like a child.'

Once again Jamie felt a stirring of annoyance. What did he know about being vulnerable, and lost in a world you couldn't understand?

Callan leaned past her to address Finn directly. 'Boy.'

Finn didn't respond.

Callan raised his voice. 'Finn.'

Finn looked up.

'I need Jamie to help me with something,' Callan said. He spoke clearly and precisely, with a note in his voice Jamie hadn't heard there before. It sounded almost gentle. 'Will you wait here till she comes back?'

Finn tipped his head, considering this, and then nodded.

Callan turned back to Jamie, his tone brisk once again. 'See? He's fine.' Then he turned and walked out of the galley, leaving her with a faint, lingering resentment.

'You sure you'll be okay?' she asked Finn.

He looked up at her, his brow creasing. 'Yes. I told him.'

'Okay.' Jamie hesitated, but she couldn't think of any valid reason not to do as Callan had asked, and she wasn't sure why she was looking for one.

The task took longer than she expected, and by the time she returned to the hold, Finn was gone and there were signs of people having already eaten and dispersed. The sea glass had been placed back in the jar, and the makeshift table dismantled. She made herself a quick dinner, then returned to the sleeping quarters, where she knocked first on Finn's door, then on Mila's. There was no answer from either of them. She was about to go into her own cabin when she heard the scrape of another door, and turned to see Rena peering out. The other woman's eyes looked red and scuffed, and she was picking at the skin of her forearm.

'I looked for you earlier,' Rena said, her lips twisting into a tight rictus that was probably supposed to be a smile. 'I couldn't find you.'

'Callan asked me to catalogue the medical supplies.' Jamie reached for the door handle. Conversations with Rena were like some sinister obstacle course. One minute you'd be ambling along on solid footing; the next moment the ground had opened up and you were being sucked into a dark under-world, where fate and the gods waited to harangue you with their own version of why things were.

Rena took a couple of uncertain steps out into the corridor. 'I could have helped you.'

'It wasn't exactly a big job.'

'But I'd like to help.' Rena crossed her arms in front of her chest. 'You're helping, and I'm not doing anything.'

'You could try not upsetting Finn.' Jamie opened her cabin door. 'That might help.'

Rena looked down at the floor, her arms tightening around her thin frame.

'I'm sorry.' She sounded brittle. 'I didn't mean to make things difficult for you.' She moved her hands in a nervous gesture. 'People like you . . . you can talk to them and they understand what you mean. I don't . . .' She twisted her fingers together, and then continued in a rush. 'I always get it wrong. Say the wrong thing. People don't . . . I can't make them understand. I can't make them like me.'

'It's not about making things difficult for me.' Stiff with discomfort, Jamie decided it was safest to ignore the other woman's halting confession. 'It's about Finn. It must be hard enough for him without . . .' She caught herself before she could finish with the accusatory *you*. '. . . people making things worse.'

'It's not . . .' Rena stopped, nipping at her lip with her teeth. When she continued her tone was edged with something that sounded almost like defiance. 'I don't understand why he survived.'

'I don't know. I guess he must have been fairly isolated.'

Rena shook her head. 'That's not what I mean. So many dead. Those of us who survived . . . it must have been God's will. He has a plan for us, a place for all of us in his new world.'

Jamie stared at her for a moment, and then understanding dawned. 'You don't think Finn's good enough for this new world of yours. That's it, isn't it?'

Rena gave another shake of her head, a quick, spasm-like movement. 'You don't understand. It's not that simple.'

'Seems pretty simple to me.' Jamie's dislike was a sour taste on her tongue. 'Brave new world, but only by your invitation.' She deliberately let her lip curl. 'Or your God's.'

'I don't . . . you see? I never make people understand.'

'I understand perfectly.' Jamie turned away. 'I'll leave you to your plans for the perfect world.'

'Jamie.' Rena took a step towards her, her voice almost pleading. 'I'm sorry. I didn't—'

'It doesn't matter.' Jamie went into her cabin. 'Goodnight.'

As she closed the door behind her, she heard the other woman say something else, but she couldn't make out the words. She stood still for a moment, waiting to hear the sound of footsteps, but it was several long moments before they came. Her heartbeat was a dull, resentful thud, and she took a steadying breath. She was conscious of the faintest edge of guilt to the outbreath. There'd been something vulnerable about Rena in the first moments of that exchange. What would have happened if she'd been gentler with the other woman?

She walked away from the door, undressed and climbed into bed. It wasn't up to her to bring Rena into the fold. She just wanted to get where she was going and find Daniel. Then she'd know what all this was about. They could start again, just the two of them.

As her thoughts began to splinter into sleep, three words echoed through her mind in a mocking tone that sounded like Rena.

Brave new world.

It's summer, and the birds are singing at her mother's funeral.

She feels nothing. She's felt nothing since the two police-women came to her father's house and had that low-voiced conversation behind a closed door.

Or that's what she tells herself. The truth is that there is something hidden deep inside, but it's the wrong shape for grief, and she can't risk letting it out, because then everyone will see it and they'll know.

So she stands at the graveside and watches other people mourn. She's off to one side of the proceedings, with other people taking the central places. Her mother's sister has stepped into the role of chief mourner, although the two of them hadn't spoken in years. But somehow she finished up in the car behind the hearse, and somehow she was the one standing at the church door, draped in black and welcoming the mourners in. She shook Jamie's hand too, holding on for a moment too long, as though she had just remembered not to say, Thank you for coming, it means so much to us, *to the daughter of the deceased.*

Some of Jamie's classmates are there. It's the popular crowd, mostly. They're wearing black dresses and black eye make-up and their hair is loose and gleaming. They cry when the coffin's carried in. One of them has to be held up by her friends. Jamie doesn't remember if she ever met her mother.

After the service, her headmistress, a blunt-edged nun who's never spoken to her except to say walk *or* quiet *in the corridor, takes Jamie's face in her hands and asks,* Have you cried yet?

When Jamie shakes her head, her headmistress asks, Why not? *Jamie doesn't have an answer, and her stepmother steps in.*

Thank you for coming. It means so much.

The burial's not like in the films, where a serene-faced priest intones ashes to ashes, *as the mourners stand round a neat grave against a backdrop of blossom trees. The ground's uneven, with a pile of soil beside the open grave. There's another fresh mound to the side, so the mourners have to stand at the end like a disorganised bus queue, while the priest totters round the edge of the grave with a bucket of soil for them to throw. Jamie's near the back. Her stepmother tried to get to her, but the places at the front were already taken by then, and she'd have had to fight her way through the ranks of mourners. She stands behind a couple of her classmates and an elderly neighbour, and by the time she reaches the front, the bucket's almost empty. She scrabbles around for a moment, and manages to scrape together a pebbly handful of soil which she throws, overarm, into the grave. As it clatters onto the coffin, she wonders if it was too forceful, if her headmistress will find her and take her face in her hands and say,* Are you angry?

People are coming back to the house afterwards, but she doesn't think they'll notice if she isn't there. She can slip away down the path to the beach, and when she gets there she can run and run and run – until she's too far away for anyone to touch her, or ask her questions she couldn't answer even if she wanted.

CHAPTER EIGHT

It was still dark in her cabin when she was woken by a knock on the door. As she sat up, fumbling for the switch, the knock came again, sharp and peremptory.

'Okay.' She scrambled down the ladder and scratched around for something more suitable than the shorts and vest she'd slept in. She found a jumper and threw it over the top, before opening the door.

Callan stood outside, leaning on the door frame. As his gaze flicked over her, she was suddenly conscious of her bare legs beneath the baggy hem of the jumper. She resisted the urge to tug it down.

'I need you up on the bridge,' he said, with no preliminaries. 'We've made contact with a settlement on Gelta. A fair number of survivors apparently. They're willing to trade for fuel. I've offered medical supplies, but they want to know exactly what we're carrying. You did the inventory yesterday?'

'Yes.'

'Good.' He pushed himself off the door frame. 'Get up to the bridge as soon as you can. Better if you talk to their main man, rather than me relaying it.'

Jamie forced away the instinctive resentment. The request may not have been framed in the most graceful of terms, but it was a perfectly reasonable one.

When she made her way up to the bridge, she found Callan on the comm, talking to a middle-aged man. He gestured for her to take his place in front of the screen.

'This is Jamie, our medic.'

Jamie gave him a sharp look, but he just shrugged and handed her the stock-reader.

Vet, medic, whatever, she could almost hear him saying.

'Morning, doctor,' the man said. 'Name's Garrett. I seem to have wound up in charge of this settlement.' He gave her a quick smile. 'For my sins.'

'How many survivors are there?' she asked.

'Thirty-one.'

Jamie's heart gave a hard thud. Gelta wasn't a particularly densely populated world as far as she knew, so that survival rate wasn't *nought point nought nought nought one*. Not by any stretch of the imagination.

'How did so many people make it?' she asked.

'We're a mining settlement,' Garrett said. 'Mainly male labourers living in single workers' quarters. It was fairly easy to enforce a quarantine. Also, we had a delayed supply run, so we got hit a fair bit later than most places. If we'd got the news a day earlier, we wouldn't have let the ship land at all.'

'You've done better than most,' Callan put in.

'I'm sure. But thirty-one out of around fifteen thousand. It's taking a bit of time for us to feel lucky, if you'll forgive me for saying.'

'I understand you need medical supplies,' Jamie said.

He nodded. 'The last delivery was light of a few things. We were due a shipment of eripex. You got any on board?'

Jamie consulted the stock-reader. 'We've got two boxes. It has pretty limited uses, though. It's primarily a skin cancer treatment.'

'We've got a high carcinoma rate here,' Garrett said. 'Low ozone and strong sun. If we didn't have so many people working underground, we'd have far more cases. It's a good growing climate, mind, and we're fairly self-sufficient. Can't have everything, I suppose.' He looked down at a list. 'The rest is fairly standard stuff,' he said. 'Oxynril, diadrin, and we could probably do with some paxinell as well. If you're good for all that, then we can do business.'

Callan glanced at Jamie, his eyebrows raised. When she nodded, he turned back to the screen.

'You've definitely got enough fuel stocks? I don't want to land and find we're stuck.'

The man smiled. 'Trust me, captain. We don't want you stuck here either. We'll need other supplies in due course.'

'I should have mentioned we're at capacity in terms of passengers,' Callan said. 'I'm happy to carry messages, but if anyone's wanting off-planet . . .'

The man shook his head. 'We're not in any hurry to leave. The administration's never bothered much with us, beyond paying for what we dig up. We've got a decent enough set-up here. No point haring off hoping for a better deal somewhere else.'

Callan nodded. 'Okay. We'll be with you in less than an hour. We're running on standard time here, so early morning. What clock are you on?'

'Right now we're at central plus five,' the man said. 'A twenty-six-hour cycle, so plenty of daylight left. I'll see you at the landing site.'

The screen flicked off and Jamie got up, expecting Callan to take her place, but he was looking towards the doorway. Gracie was standing there, arms folded.

'Do you have something to say?' Callan asked his engineer.

Gracie unfolded her arms and shoved her hands into the pockets of her slacks. 'Is there any point me saying it?'

'Gets it out in the open.'

'Okay then,' Gracie said. 'I don't think we should land. I've run some calculations and we've just about enough fuel to get us to the capital – if we take it easy and don't make any more stops.'

'Or we could refuel here and not have to worry about eking out our tanks until we're running on fumes.'

'We've got enough,' Gracie repeated. 'We don't need to take the risk. You heard him. There are more than thirty stranded down there. You're assuming they're going to be happy to refuel us and wave us on our way, not knowing if they'll ever see another ship.'

'Thirty-one's a decent-sized community,' Callan said. 'And if they're mainly self-sufficient, they're in a far better situation than most survivors.'

'That's assuming he was telling the truth,' Gracie pointed out.

Callan sat down in the seat Jamie had vacated. 'Your comments are noted.'

Gracie didn't move. 'Why?' she said. 'Why are we suddenly hell-bent on being the conquering heroes?'

'What else are we going to do?' Callan said. 'Sit on the ship, twiddling our thumbs until we're about ready to kill each other just for something to do? Fly about until we fall out of the sky? Like it or not, we're part of whatever comes next, so we might as well get on with it.'

Gracie regarded him contemplatively. 'I thought you didn't want to help build a new world.'

'Well, it's going to be built, whether or not I choose to throw a few bricks in, and we'll have to figure out our place in it.'

'I thought that's why we were heading to the capital,' Gracie said.

Callan turned back to the helm. 'I don't think there'll be any big surprises waiting for us there. Okay, we don't know how many are alive. But there'll be stocks of food and medicine, same as everywhere. And the infrastructure's still working, for the most part. This isn't some nuclear wasteland. People and skills are the things that will be in short supply. As settlements are re-established they'll need us. They'll need our goodwill.'

'Or they could just take the ship. Cut out the middleman.'

'No one's taking anything of mine.'

Gracie shrugged and turned away. 'It's your ship.'

When she'd gone, Callan glanced at Jamie. 'You better go wake the others. Tell them to get strapped in.'

Jamie nodded slowly, but didn't move.

Callan gave her a sharp look. 'What?'

She fiddled with a piece of loose casing on the comms console. 'I just wonder if Gracie might be right.'

'Really? I seem to remember you being all for setting down and saving the day back on Pangaea.'

Jamie ignored the edge in his voice. 'That was different. That was someone asking for help, someone who might be alone. These people aren't alone.'

'So it's a numbers game, is it?' Callan hit a quick-fire sequence of buttons on the helm. 'How many people on a planet before they pass your *they'll just have to cope* test?'

Anger flickered up inside Jamie. For a moment she considered just walking away. But for some reason she needed to make him understand.

'It's not like that,' she said. 'It's—'

'We need to refuel,' Callan said. 'If we hadn't landed on Pangaea, we wouldn't. But we did. Partly due to your insistence. So we need to set down here.'

Jamie tried to keep her tone level. 'Gracie said we didn't.'

'How come Gracie's suddenly the font of all wisdom as far as you're concerned?'

'I just thought . . .'

Callan gave a faint smile. 'Well, thanks for the thought. Good job I've got so many people to do my thinking for me.

Now if you'll go and wake the rest of them, we'll get down, get fuelled and get on our way.'

The landing site was a wide concrete space, built for the vast cargo ships that served the industrial settlements. The port seemed to have been absorbed into the surrounding settlement, with narrow alleys and service roads leading off in all directions. To the west, the town had spread up onto the foothills, and beyond the edge of the built-up area a dirt road led off to where the mines crouched against the rising ground, ragged and bulky.

Garrett was waiting on the concourse, flanked by a couple of young lads. Jamie and the others waited at the entrance while Callan disembarked. After the two men had spoken for a few moments, Garrett nodded to his companions.

Callan walked back up the gangway. 'The lads will unload the goods. You've checked it?'

'It's all there.'

Callan turned to Gracie. 'You good to get on with the re-fuelling? He offered to find someone to help if we need it, but I'd rather not have anyone messing about with my ship.'

Gracie nodded. 'I'll get started.'

'Is there a shop?' Mila asked.

'I expect so,' Callan said. 'You need something?'

'A few bits and pieces.'

'You could see if there's any fresh food.' Lowry was looking out across the settlement. 'I'm going to take a walk. See how people are doing.'

'Planning on holding a prayer meeting?' Callan said.

Lowry smiled. 'If they want one. But I was just thinking they might be glad of a chance to talk to someone from off-planet. Being a preacher's sometimes like being a pressure valve. People see the collar and suddenly find they want to talk about things they've been keeping bottled up. Even the ones who don't believe in anything.'

'Fine,' Callan said. 'Don't be too long. I want to get on.'

'Is there any great hurry?' Lowry asked. 'We could always overnight here.'

'I want to get on,' Callan repeated, a little sharply. He shot a quick look at Garrett, waiting on the concourse. 'Besides, the man's courteous enough, but I got the impression he'd rather we just made the drop, refuelled and got going.' He turned to Mila. 'You get what you need and meet us back here. The preacher can take his walk while Gracie refuels.' He looked at Jamie and Rena. 'What about you?'

'I'll go with Mila,' Jamie said. She glanced at Rena, remembering that brief touch of guilt from last night. 'Do you want to join us?'

'I don't need anything.' Rena didn't look at her.

Jamie gave a mental shrug. She'd tried.

Finn was standing a little apart from the rest of the group, and Mila walked over to him. 'Do you want to come?' she asked. 'Or stay here?'

Finn looked out across the grey concrete of the concourse, and then shook his head.

'Fine.' Callan started back down the gangway. 'Those who are staying, keep out of the way. We'll be unloading soon.'

When Jamie asked Garrett for directions to the shop he was perfectly polite, but she could see what Callan meant. There was a definite coolness, and he didn't ask them any questions about their own experiences, or what they knew of the situation elsewhere.

'You'd think they'd want to talk to us,' Mila said, as they walked down the alleyway he'd pointed out. 'He doesn't seem interested in us at all.'

'Not everyone likes to talk.'

Mila peered along an empty side street. 'But where's every-one else?'

'Maybe they're working, trying to get the place up and running.'

'Maybe.' Mila kept looking around as they walked, as though she thought they might suddenly come across the other survivors, hiding round a corner with a banner saying *Surprise!*

They found the shop on the corner of the main street. It was a surprisingly well-maintained building, compared with the industrial dinginess of its surroundings. Its frontage was clean, and the goods were arranged in neat displays behind the glass. Through the window they could see basic supplies in wooden cubbies along the walls, and fresh food arranged in shallow crates on top of a pile of pallets.

The door had one of those old-fashioned bells that jingled as they entered, and a man appeared through a door at the back. He was thin-faced, with grey hair receding from his forehead. He stopped still for a moment when he saw the two women, and then he smiled, his whole bearing becoming more relaxed for some reason. 'You come in with the ship?'

'Just landed now,' Jamie said, but he must have known that. Funny how persistent it was, the need to fill empty spaces with words that added nothing of any substance.

'You staying long?'

'Just long enough to refuel and drop off some supplies.'

'The medicines,' the man said. 'Handy that you had those on board.'

Jamie nodded. 'We need a couple of things. Can we look around?'

'Feel free.' The man leaned on his elbows on the counter, watching them as they browsed.

'Any idea how many people have survived elsewhere?' he asked. 'Garrett seems to think we might be unusual here.'

'It was just three of us on Soltaire,' Jamie said, picking out a couple of items from the cubbies. 'And two on Pangaea.'

'What about the capital worlds?' the man asked. 'Any idea what's happened there?'

'Not yet.' She walked over to the counter. Mila joined her and put a few things down next to Jamie's haul, before pointing to the fresh food. 'What about some tomatoes? And maybe some carrots and onions?'

The man was checking through the little pile on the counter. 'I can do that for twenty.' He smiled. 'I'll give you a discount in exchange for that little update.'

'Twenty.' Jamie missed his meaning for a moment, and then she remembered. Money. It seemed about as relevant as the flimsy plastic counters in some child's game. 'You're still using money.'

'Money or trade. But mainly money. No reason to change things about. Guess we'll have to tweak the currency as time goes on. But we'll figure it out.'

Jamie was staring at him. He raised an eyebrow.

'Sorry,' she said. 'I'm just surprised.'

'Why?' the man asked. 'It's something that everyone understands. One of the basic rules of how we all live together. We keep those rules in place, things might just hold up until . . .' He broke off, looking uncertain for the first time.

'Until what?' Jamie said. 'Everything's changed. Even if we find a thousand people on Alegria, that's not enough to keep the world working like it did before.'

'Some things don't change.' His expression hardened a little. 'So how were you planning on paying?'

'We may have something on the ship,' Jamie said. 'What do you need?'

Mila suddenly spoke up. 'Or we might be able to come to some sort of arrangement.'

When Jamie turned to look at her, the younger girl had tilted her head to look at the shopkeeper, one eyebrow raised, her lips tilted in that same flirtatious smile that she'd tried on Callan.

The shopkeeper did a perceptible double-take, his eyes widening, and then he laughed.

'Oh, girl,' he said. 'I'm a bit past all that. Not that it's not a most enticing offer, but that's not really the sort of goods I deal in.'

Mila looked down, her face slightly flushed. Jamie couldn't work her out. Her first instinct was to offer her body when someone asked what she had that was of value, yet she wasn't so hardened to the idea of sex as a transaction that she could accept rejection with equanimity.

The shopkeeper was speaking again, ticking things off on his fingers. 'I could do with coffee powder. Milk and eggs, although I guess you won't have much fresh stuff.' He looked around his shop, considering. 'A few luxuries wouldn't go amiss.' He gave her a lopsided smile. 'A man cannot live on bread alone and all that.'

'Luxuries,' Jamie said slowly. 'I may have something. Just give me a minute.'

She left Mila in the shop and jogged back to the shipyard. There were a few more men standing around, and Callan was inside the entrance to the hold, speaking to Lowry who looked unsettled. As Jamie passed, Callan reached out and caught her arm.

'Where's Mila?'

'Still at the shop. I'm just getting something. Shopkeeper wants to trade for goods.'

Callan didn't let go of her arm. 'Be as quick as you can.'

'We're in a hurry, I get it.'

Callan tightened his grip. 'Just do it. Get what you need and get back here.'

He released her, and turned to speak to Gracie who had appeared from the back of the hold.

Jamie wasn't sure what was behind the sudden urgency, but her heart had caught the rhythm of his edginess. It was beating a little harder as she retrieved the box of chocolate and headed back down to the hold.

As she passed Callan, he put his arm out again, turning his body to block the view of anyone outside.

'Here. Take this.'

'This' was a small telescopic baton, like the ones carried by the capital's security officers.

'What? No. Why would—'

'Don't argue.' He pushed it into her hand. 'Just put it in your waistband, out of sight. Please.'

There was something in his expression that made Jamie's pulse pick up still more, and she followed his instructions without further comment. As she walked back across the ship-yard the baton felt bulky and obvious beneath her shirt. There were a couple of men standing near the alleyway, and one of them said something as she passed. She didn't catch what it was, and she didn't stop to ask. Even more than the baton, it was that *please* from Callan that had thrown her. He didn't ask people to do things. He told them what he expected, and that was that.

Back at the shop, Mila seemed to have got over her embarrassment, and was chatting to the shopkeeper. She had a dress in her arms, and when she saw Jamie she held it up against her. It was dark red and knee-length, made of some floaty, luxurious-looking fabric.

'Have you seen this?' she said. 'There's a whole crate of them.'

Jamie wanted to tell her to hurry up, but something stopped her from showing her unease in front of the shopkeeper. 'Can't imagine there being much call for dresses like that here,' she said, trying to keep her tone light.

The shopkeeper smiled. 'No. They must have got a shipment muddled up. When I opened the crate, that's what I found.'

Jamie placed her box on the counter and the shopkeeper leaned forward to look in.

'Yes, that should pretty much cover it.' He glanced at Mila. 'Take the dress too.'

'Are you sure?' Mila stroked the fabric.

'Yes, go ahead. Like you said, it's not like anyone here is going to be queuing up for it.' His smile turned a little sad. 'And besides, when you smiled at me before, it reminded me of the days when I might have taken you up on that offer of yours.'

When Mila brought the dress over to the counter, Jamie took it and started to stuff it into a canvas bag with the other bits and pieces. Mila reached over and pulled it back.

'Careful. It'll get creased.' She rolled it up and placed it gently on top of the groceries she'd already packed into a small rucksack.

'We need to go,' Jamie said.

The shopkeeper gave her a hard look. 'Anything wrong?'

'We're just heading off, that's all. I don't want to hold them up.'

The shopkeeper glanced out of the window to his right, as though something had caught his attention. 'Yes,' he said slowly. 'You should get going.'

'What is it?' Mila said, tightening the rucksack on her narrow shoulders.

'Some things are in short supply here, that's all.' The shopkeeper raised a hand to them. 'Get back to your ship, and safe journey.'

CHAPTER NINE

Outside the shop, Jamie broke into a jog.

Mila trotted along at her side, shooting anxious looks around. 'What is it? What's wrong?'

'I don't know.' There was a prickle of goosebumps across the back of Jamie's arms as they hurried along the alleyway. 'Callan—'

Two figures stepped out of a side entrance, almost blocking the way. Jamie couldn't be sure, but she thought they might have been the ones standing at the edge of the shipyard earlier. They were fairly young, probably early to mid-thirties. One was dark-haired with a scratch of stubble along his jaw, while the other had the light skin that goes with fair hair, and a tell-tale scatter of blotches on his forearm, where he'd had moles removed.

'Hey.' The dark-haired one was straight in Jamie's path.

She changed course slightly. If they just kept moving, the ship wasn't far. And perhaps this was no more than a couple of young men doing what young men do. A little harmless flirting, and they'd be on their way.

'Hey,' she said.

Mila had tucked in close behind Jamie.

The dark-haired man shifted, blocking Jamie's path again. The thumping in her chest became a series of hard hammer blows.

'Excuse me.' She kept her accompanying smile pleasant but distant.

'There's no rush, is there?' He gave her an answering cool smile.

'There is, actually.' Her voice was too high. Behind her, Mila pressed a little closer. 'Our captain's permanently in a hurry.' She swallowed and tried to muster up a more confident tone. 'He's probably on his way to chase us up right now.'

'Not very friendly of him. We were thinking you might like to stay a while. Get to know us.'

'Sorry.' Jamie tried to edge past. 'I don't think he's going to be keen.'

'And what about you?' The other man moved again, so that she had to stop or walk straight into him.

'What about us?'

He tilted his head to look past her at Mila. 'Are you in as much of a hurry as your captain?'

'I suppose so,' Jamie said. 'We're heading for Alegria. There should be more survivors there.'

'Garrett seems to think we're better off here,' the fair-haired man said. 'He keeps on about it. What a great set-up we've got. But we don't all agree with his way of thinking. Seems to us there's one thing in particular we don't have.' His gaze travelled slowly and deliberately down to Jamie's legs, and back up to her face.

Some things are in short supply here, that's all.

All the options flared in Jamie's mind, along with a sharp certainty that whichever she chose it would be the wrong one. Fight. Flight. Freeze. Keep talking. Behind her, Mila drew a ragged, frightened breath, tipping Jamie into a decision.

She shoved the bag at the blond man, and hurled herself forward, driving at him with her shoulder, trying to replicate the movement she'd often used on pushy cattle. As he stepped back heavily, she reached for Mila's hand. The girl stumbled, then righted herself, and for a moment Jamie thought they were in the clear. Then Mila's hand was jerked from hers, as the girl went down, dragging the dark-haired man with her. Mila screamed, kicking out at her attacker, who was swearing and grabbing at her legs. For a second or two Jamie's mind was a roiling mass of white noise and panic, and then an image flared: Callan's face, as he shoved the baton into her reluctant hand.

The other man was reaching towards her, but she twisted out of his grasp. Then the baton was somehow in her hand, and swinging out, almost in slow motion. It came down on the dark-haired man's skull with barely a sound, but he stopped scrabbling at Mila's legs, and folded in on himself, crumpling onto the ground.

Mila was sobbing and scrambling to her feet. As Jamie reached for the girl, a hand closed on her arm. She swiped wildly, and felt the baton connect. The man swore and let go, and then Mila was up and they were running for the end of the alley, with footsteps coming hard and fast behind them.

Jamie didn't stop when they got clear of the alleyway. She dragged Mila along with her, running for the ship. Callan was standing to the side of the bay doors, checking something. He straightened up as he saw them coming, and turned to say something over his shoulder. Gracie appeared alongside him.

They were almost there. The rattle of their footsteps changed to a metallic clang as concrete gave way to the steel of the gangway. Then her arm was nearly yanked out of its socket as Mila stumbled and went down again. Jamie pulled the girl back to her feet, and then froze.

Callan had his gun out, pointing it at something behind her. She turned slowly, and saw another gun, in the not-quite-steady hand of a lad who looked no older than Finn.

'Don't move.' The lad's voice was shaking as much as his hand.

'What's going on?' Garrett appeared at the edge of the concourse. 'Davey. Put that gun down and don't be stupid.'

'It's not stupid,' the lad said. 'It's got to be done. You were going to let them get on their ship and fly off. Leave us here like this.'

'Like what?' Garrett spread his hands out. 'We've got everything we need right here. What else are we going to do? Run off to whatever's left of the capital worlds and beg for handouts? We can build something good here.'

'What's the point?' The fair-haired man from the alleyway walked over to join the lad with the gun. 'We stay here, and we've got no future. Not unless you've got some way for men to breed with men.'

Garrett made an impatient gesture. 'You're talking a long way ahead. There'll be other survivors. We make this place work for us, and other people will want to come, make their home here.'

'How do you know?' the lad said. 'What if everyone gets to the capital and decides to stay right there? What if there are no more ships?'

'Jamie.' Callan had to say it twice before she could drag her gaze away from the gun. 'Get on board.'

'Don't move.' The lad lifted the gun a little higher.

'Jamie.' Callan raised his voice. 'Do as I say.'

Her whole body was cold, anticipating the bullet. It could go anywhere. With an effort that left her shaking, she reached for Mila's hand and took a slow step backwards up the gangway.

'No.' The lad pointed the gun straight at her. She froze again, her heart contracting hard and fast inside her chest.

'Boy.'

The gun swivelled towards Callan.

Jamie took a deep breath in, and stepped backwards again, as slowly and smoothly as possible.

'I'll make sure people know you're here,' Callan said. 'When we get to the capital. They'll need settlements like this.'

'And what if there's no one?' the lad said.

'Then you're on your own. Just like the rest of us.'

'You're not, though.' The blond man spoke up again. 'On your own, are you? You've got a nice little set-up. A ship, a crew.' He paused, his face darkening. 'Women.' He jerked his head towards Jamie and Mila. 'Which one of them are you fucking?'

Jamie felt a tightening in the mood of the crowd. She risked another couple of steps. She was only a few metres from the doors, but the lad had noticed. The gun twisted to point at her again.

'Stop.' There was a desperate, hopeless note in his voice.

'No.' The shopkeeper was standing at the entrance to the alleyway, a shotgun in his hands. 'You stop.'

He fired.

It was a warning shot, above the lad's head, but all hell broke loose.

The lad turned, firing wildly, and Jamie saw the shopkeeper go down, as she hauled Mila the last few metres to the doors. Gracie had already hit the lever, and the gangway was moving under Jamie's feet, the doors starting to close.

'Go. Get in.' Callan's gun was still up.

Then he lurched back, as another shot cracked out. His hand went to his side, and he staggered and almost went down. Mila was screaming. Jamie's head was one white-hot flare of noise and fear. Adrenaline was surging up inside her, so hard that she thought she'd choke on it. Somehow she shoved Mila inside, then turned, reaching for Callan. He was off balance, tipping forwards, away from the safety of the hold, and the retracting gangway was almost to his feet.

She grabbed at his shirt, bracing herself against the weight of his fall. Another gunshot, and something struck the side of the ship, just above the doors. She was losing her hold on herself. Her body wasn't responding to her muddled commands.

The drag on her arms eased. For a terrifying moment she thought she'd let go, but then she realised Gracie was beside her, holding on to Callan. They hauled at him, staggering backwards, and then they were through, sprawling painfully onto the ridged floor, as the door slammed shut behind them.

Mila was still screaming, shrill and panicked, the sound slicing through the ship's metal insides. There were too many people. Too many voices, too many pairs of hands.

'Give them room.' Lowry's voice raised above the rest, calm and authoritative.

Jamie leaned over Callan. His eyes were open and he was trying to shove himself up on one elbow, the other hand pressed against his side. Jamie could see blood on his fingers and she tried to push him back down. He shook her off and sat up, teeth gritted.

'Gracie.' The engineer nodded, and ran for the engine passage.

Callan dragged himself up to a half-crouch. She could see the blood clearly now, staining his shirt.

Jamie reached for him again. 'You need—'

'I need to get us in the air,' he said. 'Hull's solid enough, but if they think to open the fuel port, we're in trouble.' As he climbed to his feet, he breathed in hard, his hand tightening against his side.

'Here.' Lowry stepped forwards. 'Lean on me.'

Callan forced himself upright with a visible effort. 'I'm all right.'

The preacher didn't let go. 'Then you'll be even more all right with me helping, won't you?'

Mila was standing next to Finn, the back of her hand pressed against her mouth, as though that was the only way she could stop screaming. Finn was hunched over, his fingers shoved into his ears.

Speak no evil, hear no evil. Jamie had a sudden urge to laugh. If she covered her eyes, they'd have the full set. And she wouldn't have to see the deepening stain on Callan's shirt.

Up on the bridge Lowry helped Callan into the helm seat. As the engines began their steady crescendo, Callan jerked his head back towards the door. 'Go.'

'I'm staying,' Jamie said. 'What if you pass out?'

'You going to fly?' Callan pressed a rapid sequence of buttons.

'I'm staying,' she repeated.

'Fine.' Callan's teeth were gritted.

Lowry was hesitating, and Jamie turned to him. 'Go help Finn and Mila.'

When the preacher had gone Jamie reached for Callan's harness but he brushed her hand away. 'Leave it.'

She decided against arguing. She pulled the jump seat out of its slot, sat down and tightened the straps across her body.

As Callan hit a final button on the console, the ship juddered beneath them, and Jamie felt that now-familiar shift of air and gravity as they lifted off. She couldn't see out of the front view-panel from the jump seat, but she imagined the men scattering from the ship's vicious downdraft.

Callan took them up fast. He had to be burning fuel at a relentless rate, but the blood seeping from his side seemed more relentless still. The speed of their lift-off was the only sign he gave that he was in pain. His hands were entirely steady on the controls and when he spoke to Gracie on the comm, his voice was calm.

It was the first time she'd been at the front of the ship for take-off. She watched the clear blue of the sky fade into off-white, and then there was a moment when that white seemed to give way to something that was the opposite of colour, a not-quite nothing that made her look away for a moment. Then all of that fell away as they cleared the atmosphere. When you were down there looking up, it was light that you saw. But up here it was all black, with only the pinpricks of the stars to lift the darkness. It was as though the sun was an illusion, designed to keep you happy there, trapped against whatever little piece of the universe you'd decided to call home.

The ship banked, then levelled again. Up front, Jamie was more aware of its impossible bulk. It was difficult to picture something so unwieldy carrying them up here, its velocity as swift and brutal as a child's lost helium balloon. Jamie had a sudden image of that lad, the gun limp in his hand, watching their ascent.

What now?

Callan let out a slow breath, almost a groan, and slumped back in his seat. When Jamie scrambled across, he gave her the bare shadow of a smile.

'Think I might need a vet.'

'Don't worry.' She tried to keep her tone light as she lifted his shirt and saw the mess of torn flesh and blood. 'I'm pretty sure I've got some horse tranquillisers.'

There was no medical bay on a ship this size, and no room to treat him on the cramped bridge.

'My cabin,' he said. 'Just down the corridor.'

'I can't treat you in a bunk.'

'I've got a proper bed.' He gave another faint smile. 'Captain's prerogative.'

It took a couple of attempts to get him out of the seat, and she was just wondering whether to go and find help when Gracie appeared, and ducked under his other arm. Together they managed to get him along the corridor and into his quarters. His cabin was more spacious than the passenger berths, with a small bathroom off to one side. The bed wasn't much more than a generous single, but it would do.

Jamie eased his shirt up, and turned to Gracie.

'Do you know what a trauma kit looks like?'

Gracie shook her head.

Jamie swore, and stood up. 'Stay here. I'll go.'

She collided with Lowry in the corridor.

'Where's Callan?'

'His cabin. Back there.'

She took the steps three at a time, and skidded along the passage to the storage bay. The bright red trauma kit was still sealed and sterile, thank God, and she grabbed it and sprinted back to Callan's quarters.

Lowry was already there. He'd found some scissors and cut up the seam of the blood-stained shirt to give her access to the wound. Callan was lying on his side, teeth gritted, his face a sickly grey-white, no longer making any attempt to hide the fact that he was in pain.

Jamie's hands were trembling. Once again, the face of that lad flashed in her mind. He'd been as out of his depth as she was now, although she had treated a bullet wound before. Her first job had been at an animal hospital on Alegria. Most of her patients there were expensive thoroughbreds brought out from Earth by the über-rich elite who'd turned the new world into their playground. One day a young mare had been brought in, bleeding from the shoulder. She'd been hit by a stray round from a party out hunting imported pheasants. Jamie had managed to extract the bullet, but the owner had decided to have the mare put down, rather than spend the vast sums involved in complex tissue repair.

Jamie tried to steady her hands as she broke the seal on the trauma kit. She found the sterile wipes and a syringe of local anaesthetic, and laid them out on the edge of the bed next to a pair of surgical tweezers.

'I'm going to give you a shot for the pain.' She was surprised at how calm her voice sounded.

'Wasn't it a shot that got me into this trouble?' Callan said, looking up at her with a grimace.

'Don't make jokes.' She wiped her hands with antiseptic gel. 'If you laugh, it's going to hurt like fuck.'

'No laughing here.' He closed his eyes as Jamie slid the syringe into the ragged edges of the wound. 'Ow.'

'Give it a second to kick in,' she said, injecting him again at small intervals around the injured area.

He held his breath as she worked, but by the time she'd finished numbing the area she could feel a little of the tension draining out of the tight muscles just below where her hand was resting.

'That's better,' he said.

'This is still going to hurt.' She dropped the syringe back onto the bed and picked up the tweezers.

'Shouldn't you be telling me it won't hurt a bit?' He twisted his head round to look at her. 'I think you were right to switch to animals. Your bedside manner could use work.'

'Keep still.' Her hands were full, so she used her elbow to nudge his head back round.

'That how you treat the cattle?'

'No.' She ran a sterile wipe around the edges of the wound.

'Only people who won't stop talking so I can take bullets out of their sides.'

'It's still in there? I thought it might have just grazed through.'

'No, it's still in.' She used another wipe, laying the wound clear. The bullet glinted just below the surface layer. 'It's not deep, though. I may be able to get it out in one go.'

'How many goes does it usually take?'

'You're assuming I've done this before.' She was surprised to find that the exchange was helping her. She usually found it impossible to concentrate while people were talking, but her mind seemed to have split into two separate parts. One part was standing back, watching her work, exchanging idle remarks with the prone Callan. The other was just a tiny sliver of consciousness guiding her hands.

Callan shifted, as though he was about to speak, but she put her hand on his side again. 'Keep still,' she repeated. 'I'm going to try and get it out.'

She had to rest one knee on the edge of the bed to steady herself enough to go in. As she eased the tweezers into the wound, she felt him stiffen again, his breath shortening, but he held rock-still as she increased the pressure, feeling for the edge of the bullet.

There. She felt metal grate on metal, and then the tweezers slid free, scraping against the torn flesh. He jerked under her hand but made no sound.

'Sorry.' She tightened her grip on his side. 'It's at an awkward angle.'

'I don't need a running commentary.' He was curt, the black humour gone. 'Just get it out.'

'Here.' It grew brighter as Lowry stepped up to her side, holding a torch.

'That's perfect.' She reached into the wound again. 'Keep it steady.'

This time she could see the curve of the bullet. It was wedged against his ribcage. There were two ways of doing this. She could ease it out, a millimetre at a time, until it dislodged enough for her to fish it out, or she could go for it in one vicious yank. Callan had closed his eyes again. She could ask him, but she already knew what he'd say.

'Still as you can,' she said, more to mark the decision as made than from any real need to say it.

She went for the bullet. The tweezers grated against bone as they closed round the metal casing, and Callan twisted against her, one arm jerking out to grab the edge of the bed. But the bullet was safe in the tweezers, its silver flanks glistening with blood and a couple of strands of tissue. She let go of it and it clanged onto the floor and rolled a little way. It didn't look like anything much.

She turned back to Callan, reaching for the sterile gauze to stem a fresh spurt of blood.

'It's out,' she said, noting the sheen that had broken out on his face. 'I just need to stitch it now.'

Gracie spoke for the first time. 'I better go check the helm.' Her own face glistened with the faintest suggestion of a cold sweat, and she kept her eyes averted from the mess of blood and discarded wipes.

Lowry propped the torch up on a shelf beside the bed. 'If you don't need me, I'll let the others know everything's fine.'

'I'm not sure I'd go that far,' Callan said.

Lowry gave him a quick pat on the shoulder. 'I would,' he said, and headed out of the cabin.

Left alone, the two of them lapsed into a silence which

somehow made it harder to focus. For the first time, Jamie was conscious of the fact that she had her hand resting on him.

'You stitching?' Callan looked back over his shoulder.

Jamie repositioned herself, sitting side-on to him. She couldn't quite get the angle right, and she shifted along, bringing one leg up onto the edge of the bed, so that she could rest her elbow on her thigh to steady her hands.

'You carry on like that, people will talk,' Callan remarked.

Jamie slid the needle into the first scrap of torn flesh. 'Oh yes?' she said, not really thinking about what she was saying. 'What will they be talking about?'

There was a long pause, during which Jamie suddenly thought how flirtatious that must have sounded.

She felt him draw breath to speak again, and she tapped him with her free hand. 'Don't talk.' It didn't really matter if he did, but the conversation was becoming a distraction now. She couldn't concentrate on both things, and she had a sense that it was the talking that was likely to go awry, not the stitching.

The silence stretched out as she slowly pieced him back together. By the time she was done, her neck was aching and her leg was cramped.

'Finished,' she said as she fixed an all-in-one antiseptic dressing over the stitches. Dropping the needle down into the open lid of the trauma kit, she stretched both arms up, flexing her complaining muscles.

Callan shifted cautiously onto his back, lifting his head to inspect her handiwork.

'Good job,' he said. 'I assume I'm going to live.'

'I should think so.'

She was dead tired, she realised, fighting against the impulse to lie down on the bed, head to toe with her erstwhile patient.

'You okay?' Callan was studying her.

She rubbed at her neck, pressing her fingers into a sore spot. 'Just about breathing again after all the excitement.'

Callan nodded slowly, his eyes searching her face. 'How are you feeling?'

She found a smile for that. 'Shouldn't I be asking you that question? You're the one who got shot.'

He didn't smile back. 'I mean after what happened back there.'

'I know what you meant.'

Jamie was acutely aware of the way her leg was resting against his side, as though they'd just flopped down on the bed together. Close up she could see that his eyes were much darker than she'd realised, almost navy blue. Or maybe they were just clouded by pain. She got up, abruptly enough to make him push up on his elbows and look at her.

'You sure you're okay?'

'I'm fine.' She crouched down and began clearing up the mess on the floor. 'You should probably stay lying down. Once the local wears off, I can give you a shot of something a bit longer-acting.'

'You look like you could do with a lie-down yourself.'

She packed the waste into the empty trauma kit and closed the lid.

'Maybe I will.'

He was still looking at her, although his eyes were already taking on the glaze of tiredness she'd often seen after treating injured animals. 'Tell me something,' he said, lying back on his pillow. 'Why do you want to go to Earth?'

The question caught her off balance. 'How come you're suddenly asking me that?' she said, playing for time.

You're looking for Daniel, a little voice in the back of her head reminded her.

'I just wondered. Can't work you out.' He blinked, turning his head to hide a yawn.

She should walk away.

'It's home,' she said. 'It's where I grew up.'

'They're not necessarily the same thing,' he said, closing his eyes.

'Where's home for you then?'

He didn't answer straight away. Just as she thought he'd fallen asleep, he opened his eyes again. 'Home's what's left over when you've figured out all the places you don't want to be.' His lips lifted in a brief smile. 'Sounds stupid, doesn't it? But that's what we do. We say *not there* and *not there* and *not there*, until there's only one place left.' He stifled another yawn. 'It's like triangulating something. Work out why you don't want all those other places, then follow the lines and see where they cross.'

His hand wafted vaguely, as though drawing some diagram in the empty air. She should go. They'd both be awkward over this conversation when he woke.

She moved towards the door. 'Get some sleep.'

'Jamie.'

She turned.

'There's someone,' he said, fixing her with a suddenly clear gaze. 'Someone you're looking for. Isn't there?'

She hesitated for a long moment. 'Yes.'

'Thought so.' He gave her the faintest of smiles, and closed his eyes.

Jamie watched him for a moment, before letting herself out and closing the door behind her.

Back in her quarters, she climbed straight into bed. She was lead-limbed with tiredness.

She really should go and check on Mila. And Lowry. He'd mentioned a heart problem.

As she closed her eyes, her thoughts flicked back to when she'd been leaning against Callan. She had an absurd urge to climb back down, and go and find him and curl against his back. Just to be close to someone else who must be feeling a little of what she was feeling.

Daniel. His name fell into her thoughts, sending ripples of shock running through her.

He stared back at her, accusingly, from the shadows at the corners of her mind. *You never wanted to be close to me.*

She rolled over, wrapping herself in the blanket. She had wanted him. But when she let him in, he seemed to fill the space she gave him, and still want more of her, digging away at her closed-off corners, the ones clearly marked with a sign saying *No through road.*

She couldn't imagine Callan pushing like that.

Again, she felt needles of shock and guilt. Those moments in his cabin when she'd felt a tug of . . . *something*; it was classic. Two people thrown together, in the heat of an intense moment. It was easy to see things that weren't there. Tomorrow he'd be distant and polite once again.

She yawned and rubbed her cheek against the pillow, looking for a cool spot. The lights were still on, but that didn't matter.

Sleep made a swift surge for her, and she let go.

Daniel, she thought, as she fell.

But it was Callan who stared back at her, unsmiling and himself again.

CHAPTER TEN

There were voices outside her quarters.

Too soon. Jamie turned over, feeling for the edges of sleep again. But it was slipping away from her.

She found Mila and Lowry in the hold, drinking tea, while Finn was sitting beside another makeshift table, sorting the sea glass by size and colour. When Jamie stepped through the gap in the crates, he looked up with the faintest suggestion of a smile. It faded fast, his eyes flitting away, as though he wasn't quite sure whether he had it right.

'How are you feeling?' Lowry stood up. 'Coffee?'

'Please.' She stepped over to the pallet table and picked up a piece of blue glass.

'There.' Finn pointed at a stack of medium-sized blue. Jamie deposited her piece on top, setting off a little landslide which Finn halted with the side of his hand, never looking up from the pile of striped glass which seemed to be giving him some trouble.

'I looked in on Callan a few minutes ago,' Lowry said, handing her a steaming mug. 'I couldn't find him, but Gracie said she'd seen him checking something in the engine corridor.' He smiled. 'I don't think he's the staying-in-bed type.'

'I'll need to give him another shot soon.' Jamie didn't know what Callan's type was. She'd thought she did, but that exchange in his cabin had left her unsettled.

'Will he do any damage being up and about?'

'He'd probably heal quicker if he stayed put, but the stitches should hold.'

'Well, you can always stitch him back up again,' Lowry said. 'That might teach him to slow down a bit.'

Jamie made a non-committal noise and sipped her coffee. She didn't want to have to stitch him up again. There'd been an odd, painful intimacy to that scene in his cabin. It was something she'd felt in her early days as a trainee medic: that sense of you and your patient knotted tight together by your involvement in their pain. It was a brutal closeness, your hands, cool and untender, moving over places that weren't usually touched by someone who wasn't a lover. People sometimes reacted strangely. You never knew what they might say.

It was as though skin was a barrier, keeping the person inside and the world outside. When that barrier was broken, unexpected things leaked out. She'd had someone turn to her, just before going under anaesthetic, and tell her that they didn't love their husband, even as he waited outside, anxious and unknowing. One young woman had stared at the wall, stoic and silent, throughout her treatment. She only looked up at Jamie once, when they were almost done, to say that she'd been raped a few years ago, and never told anyone.

The feeling when she was treating Callan was just part of the same thing. It didn't mean anything. But still, she didn't want to sit that close to him again, close enough to hear the rhythm of his breathing, close enough that she wouldn't have to stretch out to touch him.

Mila stirred on the sofa, drawing her legs up.

'Are you okay?' Jamie said.

Mila looked up with a too-bright smile. 'I'm fine.' The smile faded a little. 'I'm fine.'

'Tell Jamie what you were thinking of doing later,' Lowry said.

Mila chewed on a fingernail. 'It sounds silly. But I thought . . .' She glanced at Lowry who gave her an encouraging nod.

'I thought we could have a proper dinner. I could make something, and we could all sit down together. Like a celebration.'

Jamie tried to imagine it: the seven of them sitting round the table, sipping wine and talking about the weather. The image was absurd enough to break a laugh from her. She instantly snapped it off, but Mila's smile fell away.

'I'm not laughing at you,' Jamie said quickly. 'Something . . . it doesn't matter. It's a great idea.'

As though she'd been waiting for Jamie's approval, Mila was off and planning. There wasn't room at the table, but they could move some crates, put a board on top. She'd cook something, and they could dress up. Well, the women could. She had some things that might fit Jamie. Maybe Rena too, if she wanted. Probably not Gracie. Unless Jamie thought . . .

Jamie didn't think.

Well, that didn't matter. Everyone could just wear what they wanted. It could still be a bit special. Didn't Jamie think so?

Jamie did think so.

After Lowry had been despatched to ask everyone to be down for dinner in an hour's time, Mila and Jamie dragged three of the smaller crates into place and laid a board on top.

Mila stood back, her face falling a little.

'It doesn't look much.'

'We could use a sheet to cover it,' Jamie suggested.

Mila brightened. 'That would work.' She looked around again. 'What do you think is in those crates?'

Jamie walked over and tried to lift one of the lids but it was fastened down. 'Gracie said it was a family relocating.'

Mila joined her and tried another crate. This lid was loose and she slid it off, revealing tight-packed shredded paper. 'I'll keep looking. There might be something we can use.'

*

Jamie found some spare bedding in one of the bays, and dug out a plain white sheet. On her way back to the hold, she was intercepted by Mila. The girl's face was flushed, and there was a secret little smile on her lips.

'I found something. You'll see. Don't come down till it's time. You can get ready while I cook. Here.' She opened the door to her quarters. 'I've got something you can wear.'

Mutton dressed as lamb. The snide saying floated through Jamie's head, although she'd never thought of herself as too old for anything before. Everyone was younger than they used to be. She was approaching forty, an age she remembered finding unimaginable when she was a child. But now, fifty, even sixty, didn't seem that old at all. The only time she'd really been aware of growing older was when Daniel dropped his little hints about her biological clock. He'd been frightened they were going to time out, that her reservations would outlast her fertility. Each birthday, he'd find some way to bring it up. Depending on how things were between them, sometimes she'd just smile and say, *Not yet*. Other times, it would trigger a row, and she'd finish up taking herself off to bed. He'd follow later, and they'd have sex, with Jamie feeling like they were doing it all wrong. If they were doing it right, surely there'd be a moment when they'd hold one another's gaze and know they both wanted it to be the time when they created that spark of new life.

Mila came back clutching an armful of pale grey fabric. Jamie relaxed a little. It wasn't frilled and flounced, and it didn't have sequins or lace. It was just a plain, floor-length dress with shoulder straps and a cross-over top. It looked like the sort of thing she might have worn for a summer barbecue or garden party, back before their lives grew more formal, and every social occasion started carrying its own agenda and dress code.

'This should fit.' She handed Jamie the dress. 'I thought you might like it.'

When Mila had disappeared downstairs with the folded sheet, Jamie collected her washbag and a towel, and took the dress with her as she set off for the showers. She'd found them on her second day on board, discovering that they were communal, the only privacy provided by shallow metal dividers. She'd chosen to wash in her cabin instead. But she was hot and sticky, with streaks of dirt on her knees, and Mila's dress smelled freshly washed. She wondered where the girl had worn it. Perhaps she'd changed into it after her last caller had gone, leaving her alone for the night.

Jamie felt a prickle of discomfort. It felt wrong to think of Mila that way; it was as though she was talking about her behind her back.

She closed the door behind her and stripped off, hanging the dress on a hook outside the stall. The water was warm, and she relaxed a little as the grime of the day rubbed away from her skin. She'd always felt safe in water. It kept things at a slight remove. The instant hot luxury of the capital planet apartment she'd shared with Daniel. The opulent, soft-water cradling of the building's rooftop pool, with the lazy river current that let you drift, switch off, gazing at nothing but the empty sky. Even the untrammelled chill of the North Sea, back on Earth. There was no cold like the cold of the sea after sundown. But there was a simplicity to it. If you didn't fight it, then it didn't fight you. You could just lean into the swell and watch the stars ease in, and there'd be no need to think of anything beyond that moment.

She gave her hair a quick wash, then turned the shower off. As she bent over to dry her legs, the door slid open, and she straightened up, clutching at her too-small towel.

Rena stared at her from the doorway, a dark red flush rising to cover her face and neck.

'Sorry.' Jamie scrubbed at herself with the towel.

Rena continued to stare, until Jamie felt her own face growing hot. Surely even Rena could work out the basic etiquette of running into a naked fellow traveller?

'What's that?' Rena was looking at the scar on Jamie's chest.

Jamie bent and gave her legs another rub, hiding that long crackle of bleached skin.

'I had a heart problem.' That was the answer she'd always given, even to Daniel.

When she stood up, reaching for Mila's dress, Rena had her head tilted, considering Jamie as though she was some scientific problem.

'That's not a heart surgery scar,' she said. 'It's old. It almost looks . . .'

There was something about the twist of Rena's mouth that raised a flicker of memory; an old, stale emotion, too faded for bitterness.

The way she'd felt when she'd found out what the scar meant.

'What does it look like?' Jamie's voice was harsh.

'It looks like something I saw. A study I worked on.' Another twist of her lips. 'Congenital . . . defects.'

That old emotion was licking into life now, changing colour, changing shape, until it was so close to anger that Jamie couldn't tell the difference. She'd never said it out loud before. It had always been a secret so close and physical that she couldn't imagine ever dropping it into casual conversation. It would have been like slicing herself open and spilling her guts onto the table at some polite dinner party.

But Rena was still looking at her, and that anger – it had to be anger – was hot against the inside of her ribs, and the truth was so old, it didn't matter. It couldn't hurt her, and her mother was long dead and past caring. Even through the heat, Jamie knew there was something off about her anger. It was blurred, out of focus, and she could feel all sorts of thoughts and emotions elbowing for space inside.

'I had a conjoined twin.' She held the other woman's gaze. 'They thought they could separate us, but something went wrong. She died. I didn't.'

Such a brief, fractured account of a brief, fractured life. But that was how she'd always thought of her lost twin. Not in detailed might-have-beens – the two of them growing up together, sharing a room, fighting over their place in the family – but slantwise, with a quick flick of a glance, then looking away again before she could see too much. A face that was her own, yet not her own. A fading pulse in a tiny chest, struggling to match Jamie's stronger, luckier heartbeat. And sometimes something older and vaguer. A faint haze of red, and the feel of someone's cheek against her own. She knew that wasn't a memory, just something her subconscious was trying to sell her as the truth. But she'd never quite shaken it away, even after nearly thirty years of knowing.

Rena flinched, a look of revulsion twisting her face.

'That's what we wanted to stop,' she said. 'Things that went wrong. We were figuring out the genetics, but we couldn't stop people making poor decisions, even if they knew what was in their genes.'

'They don't know what caused it.' Jamie pulled the dress over her head. The anger was fading, leaving a hollow feeling just behind the white line of the scar.

'There's always a reason. We hadn't figured it all out, but we would have done. Given time.'

'And then you could have stopped people like me being born.' Jamie felt a cold distaste. 'How do you square that with your God? Isn't it all God's will? The Lord giveth and the Lord taketh away?'

Anger flashed in Rena's eyes. 'God has many faces. He's a God of death, as well as life.' Her voice was growing louder, echoing in the metal-lined confines of the shower room. 'We're supposed to work with what we're given, refine what God has made.' She paused, and made a visible effort to steady herself. 'We were doing something good,' she went on, more quietly. 'The human race is broken. We could have fixed it.'

Jamie moved towards the door, but Rena blocked her way.

'There's something I'm missing. We've been given the signs, but I can't quite make out the pattern. It's like God became tired of waiting for us to get it right. Cut away the bad in one go.'

Jamie raised her eyebrows. 'He's saved you a job then. It's all perfect and meant to be. We'll all live happily ever after.'

'Perfect.' Rena's brow furrowed. 'We're not perfect. Look at us.' Her face hardened. 'A whore. A boy who barely knows what day it is. And . . .'

'And me.'

'That's not what I—'

'It is.' Jamie took a sideways step, aiming for the door again.

Rena slumped, seeming to curl in on herself. 'I'm not seeing it. There's something, a pattern. But I will. I'll find it. Then I'll know what's to be done.'

Jamie turned her body so she wouldn't touch the other woman as she moved past. 'You do that. Let me know how it works out for you.'

It's summer, and she's leaving.

He's begged and cried and told her the story of the two of them over and over until it's just words, and she can barely hear them any more.

He's gone out now, leaving her alone. She walks around the flat, staring at things, unable to work out whether she needs them. When her rucksack is full, she finds she can't remember what's in there. It doesn't matter. She just wants to be away, and done with this business of leaving him.

She's asked him not to come and see her off, but she knows he'll be there anyway. He thinks she'll change her mind, if he can just keep putting himself in her way. He thinks something will click back into place and she'll remember that she loves him and he loves her and that's the way it's supposed to be, forever and ever.

Her thoughts are fraying and unravelling. She can't focus on anything for more than a few seconds. Perhaps that's the only way she can leave him. In snatches and splinters. The door closing behind her. The port. The ship. A hand raised in a blur of goodbye. All the ways he's found to say don't leave me. *All the ways she's found to say nothing at all.*

CHAPTER ELEVEN

When she got back to her cabin Jamie found that her hands were trembling.

She'd lied about that old scar for years, and now she'd just tossed it out there, as currency in an argument she was never going to win.

She flexed her fingers, trying to dispel her discomfort. Mila would be expecting her downstairs.

When she checked her reflection, she was struck by how pale she still looked. It didn't matter, of course. Everyone on board had seen her at her grubby, exhausted worst, but on a sudden impulse she rummaged in her washbag and found a tube of tinted moisturiser, and a stubby kohl pencil. She rubbed the cream into her cheeks, and ran the pencil around her eyes. Then she fastened her hair up with a battered silver hairclip, pulling a few tendrils down to frame her face. It was a definite improvement. She wasn't going to be turning any heads at a society dinner, but it would do.

When she ventured downstairs, there was no sign of Rena. Lowry was setting the table with what looked like fine bone china, while Finn followed him around, straightening the cutlery. Mila was at the hob, stirring something in a battered cooking pot. The red dress the shopkeeper had given her had wide elbow-length sleeves which she kept pushing back. Her hair was loose, and she'd put on a silver necklace, and a couple of bangles that jingled with every movement.

Jamie suddenly wished that she'd left her face and hair

alone. As she hesitated at the gap between the crates, Lowry looked up and saw her.

'You look lovely,' he said.

She'd never known how to deal with compliments, but nothing Lowry said ever felt barbed or layered.

'Thank you.'

'We're almost ready,' Mila called over. 'The others should be down soon.'

'Is everyone coming?'

'Not Callan,' Lowry said. 'But the other two said they'd be down.' He grinned. 'I'm not sure Gracie intended to say yes. I think I just caught her on the hop and she couldn't think of an excuse.'

Jamie nodded towards the china. 'Where did that come from?'

'Mila found it in one of the crates.' Lowry's smile faded. Jamie knew what he was thinking. These had been someone's pride and joy once. 'I suppose it's better that they're used, rather than sitting in a crate forever.' He found another smile. 'There's more to see. Mila came across all sorts of things.'

Mila grinned at Jamie over her shoulder. 'Just a second.' She wiped her hands on a cloth and gestured to a space to the side of the eating area. 'Finn helped me move some of the crates.'

At the back of the cleared space there was a large packing case, with the front and top removed to reveal something so out of keeping with its surroundings that Jamie laughed out loud.

'A piano.' She walked over and brushed her fingers across the yellowing keys.

'A grand piano,' Lowry said. 'And a Bechstein at that. It's got to be a couple of hundred years old.'

'A piano,' Jamie said again. 'And that china. Someone was taking their whole life with them. You'd have thought they'd have wanted a new start if they were going to the trouble of moving all the way out here.'

'No one ever starts over,' Lowry said. 'Not really. They had their Bechstein. You have your sea glass.'

A voice spoke from behind them. 'What's going on?'

Jamie turned to see Rena staring at the piano. Their eyes met for a fraction of a second before the other woman jerked her head away.

'Mila found it,' Lowry said.

'Can you play?' Jamie asked him.

He laughed. 'I could probably manage that tune . . . what was it? Everyone learned it in school.' He pantomimed playing the piano with two fingers. '"Chopsticks".' He looked at Rena. 'You used to play, didn't you?'

She shook her head. 'I don't remember how.'

'Maybe you can give it a go later,' Lowry said.

'I don't remember.' Rena turned away, and walked over to sit down at the table.

Mila looked around. 'We're ready. Where's Gracie?'

Lowry took the seat next to Rena. 'We should probably start. She may have been held up.'

Or she might have thought better of the whole idea. Jamie walked over and took a seat at the opposite end of the table to Rena.

'We've got rice,' Mila said, tapping a battered spoon on the side of the cooking pot. 'And a tomato . . . thing. I just mixed the onions and carrots in with the tomatoes and some other bits.'

'I'm sure it will be lovely,' Lowry said. 'Pass your bowls over. I'll serve.'

Gracie arrived as Lowry was still dishing up. She made no apology for her lateness, and took the seat on the end. As soon as Lowry had served her food, she picked up her fork, not waiting for anyone else.

'Where's Callan?' she said, between mouthfuls.

Lowry shook his head. 'He wasn't too keen on the idea.'

Gracie gave him a cool smile. 'You mean he said he'd rather chew his own balls off than sit down to dinner with the rest of us.'

Rena gave Gracie a look of intense dislike, but Lowry laughed.

'He didn't put it quite like that.'

'How is he?' Jamie asked. 'I was going to find him, give him another shot, but I was . . .' Rena was a heavy, glowering presence at the other end of the table. 'I got distracted.'

'He seemed all right,' Lowry said. 'Moving a bit slowly, but that's about it.'

They lapsed back into silence. Mila looked strained and unhappy, shooting furtive glances around the table to check that people were eating. Her gaze fell on Rena, who was chewing slowly, her face creased in a frown.

'Don't you like it?' Mila said. 'I could make you something else.'

'It's fine.' Rena spoke without looking at Mila.

'I'd make the most of it,' Gracie said. 'We'll be on tinned and frozen for the rest of the trip. We've got enough fuel to get us to the capital, so we're not likely to stop again.'

'What if we come across more survivors?' Mila asked.

Gracie stopped, her fork halfway to her mouth. 'Really? Because our last stop worked out so well, didn't it?' She finished that mouthful and washed it down with a swig of beer. 'Besides, we've got no more space. Unless you fancy sharing a bunk.'

Rena laughed, a vicious bark that she immediately

142

smothered with the back of her hand. Mila flinched, looking down at her lap.

Jamie felt a surge of hatred. 'Well, I don't think anyone's going to be lining up to share with you,' she said to Rena. 'Not that you'd want us.' When Rena turned to glare at her, Jamie held her gaze. 'It's a pity the rest of us survived. I'm sure you'd have been much happier alone, with all us sinners turned to dust.' She found a hard little nub of laughter of her own. It didn't sound like her. None of this sounded like her. And the odd thing was that she didn't care. She and Rena would never be able to live alongside one another. Not if they were the only two people in the universe. 'That's the kind of thing they went in for in the Old Testament, isn't it? Maybe your God sent this plague to sort out the sheep from the goats. Only you got stuck with the goats.'

Rena stood up, her stool crashing onto the floor, and Mila flinched again. Finn was gripping the edge of the table with both hands.

'I don't have to sit here and listen to you mocking my beliefs.'

'No,' Jamie said. 'You don't.'

'Jamie.' Lowry reached across the table. 'I know today was—'

Jamie pulled her hand away. 'This isn't about what happened today.'

'Then what is it? Rena? What's—'

'The virus was nothing to do with God.' A muscle twitched just below Rena's eye.

'Really?' Jamie raised an eyebrow, deliberately provocative. 'I thought you said he'd got tired of waiting for us to get it right.'

'No, I don't . . .' Rena put her hands to her forehead.

'Maybe . . . I don't know, I don't know. But we're the ones He saved. He must have a plan for us all.'

Jamie felt a little of the heat go out of her anger, leaving a sharp metallic taste in her mouth. 'Then maybe you should get on board with that plan.' She picked up her fork again. 'Like it or not, we're what's left.'

Lowry righted Rena's stool. 'Sit down,' he said quietly. 'Please.'

Rena resisted for a moment, and then sank slowly into her seat.

Lowry looked around the table. 'This is new ground for all of us. But we have to make room for everyone. For everyone's beliefs. That's the only way this will work.'

'The space between the stars.' Rena was plucking at her skin again. 'The space between the stars.'

The sound of footsteps broke into the tension, and Callan appeared through the crates, moving slowly but straight and upright. He seemed about to walk past to the galley, but Mila stood up, seizing the distraction.

'There's some of this left. I can get another bowl.'

Callan looked around the silent table, his eyes meeting Jamie's for a brief second. 'Okay.'

Mila pattered off to the kitchen and came back with a bowl, while Lowry pulled another crate over to the table. Callan lowered himself carefully onto the makeshift seat.

'Thanks.' He picked up his fork.

'How are you feeling?' Lowry asked.

'Fine. The vet did a good job.' He turned to Gracie. 'Everything okay with the ship?'

'Yes, she's running fine. Enough fuel to get us to the capital in one push.'

'Right.' When he spoke again, he didn't look up. 'May need to make one more stop.'

'There's a signal?' Lowry said.

'No. Just a stop I need to make.'

'Where?' Gracie stared at him.

'Methuen.' Callan got up and went to the fridge for a beer, which he opened on the sharp edge of the counter.

'What's on Methuen?' Gracie asked.

'Just something I need to check.' He gave Mila a brief smile as he sat back down again. 'Good food. Maybe I should give you a job.'

Jamie expected Mila to return the smile, but instead she ducked her head again, her hands knotting together on her lap. Was it always the first thing she thought of when someone spoke to her? *Do they know what I do?*

'When will we be there?' Finn spoke for the first time since they'd sat down. He had separated his food into two sections, not touching one another, and he was carefully alternating mouthfuls of rice with mouthfuls of sauce.

'To the capital?' Callan said. 'About a day and a half.'

Finn shook his head. 'Earth. She said we were going to Earth.'

Callan loaded rice onto his fork. 'We don't know what we're going to find on the capital. No point worrying about what comes after.'

'But you could take us.' Rena leaned forward. 'You said you didn't know where you were going after the capital. Why not Earth?'

'Rena,' Lowry said warningly.

Rena kept her gaze fixed on Callan. 'You said it yourself. You want to see the lie of the land. There'll be survivors on Earth. There'll be people wanting to get from there to the capital, people needing supplies.'

Callan raised an eyebrow. 'Earth's a pretty big place. Can't think they're going to need anything shipped in from the settlements.'

'Well, there might be other people wanting to go there,' Rena persisted. 'It won't be overcrowded any more. Everyone could go back. Anyone who wanted to.'

Callan laughed. 'Oh well, that's one bonus of most of humanity being wiped out. Pity we didn't see it coming. If we'd known the population was going to be reduced anyway, we might not have bothered with all those forced emigration programmes. We might have left people where they wanted to be.'

Rena tipped her head, searching his face. There was something about her contemplative gaze that reminded Jamie that the other woman was a scientist. She'd caught a glimpse of something and was turning it over in her mind, trying to work out how it might be used.

'Is that where you wanted to be?' Rena asked. 'Did you have to leave?'

Jamie saw her eyes flick to Callan's hand, and she found herself doing the same. His ID mark circled his left forefinger, its sharp lines marred by a scar just below the knuckle. Funny how he hadn't had it redone, slightly lower down. A damaged mark generally meant all sorts of hold-ups and problems every time you had a brush with officialdom.

It took her a moment to register the meaning of the mark's positioning.

Forefinger.

Lower echelon.

She'd probably have assumed middle, if she'd given it any thought at all. Someone who'd rejected the steady respectability of that level of the social hierarchy and gone his own way. Perfectly well educated, but without the expensive polish of a stint at university. Once again, Jamie was conscious of a faint discomfort. She kept getting him wrong. Not that it mattered.

He was just the owner of the ship that happened to be taking them to Alegria. That was all.

'Lots of people had to leave,' Callan said.

'Then maybe this is what we're meant to be doing,' Rena replied, her eyes blazing with a sudden certainty. 'Going home. Getting everyone back home.'

'Everyone?' Jamie's dislike leaped up so readily that she couldn't avoid the thought that maybe it was a mask for something else. 'Do you really mean everyone, or just the godly?'

'You don't have to come.' Rena rounded on Jamie.

'Don't talk as though you're doing me some favour,' Jamie said. 'Graciously allowing me to tag along on your great pilgrimage. Northumberland's not even your home. It's just something you're using to convince yourself there's some pattern, that God's chosen you. No one's chosen any of us. We just survived, that's all.'

'And that's enough,' Lowry said. 'We survived, and now we have to work out a way to live in whatever this new world is going to be.'

'We have to shape that world,' Rena said.

'We do that by living in it,' Lowry said. 'Together.'

Jamie gave a sharp laugh. 'That's working out well so far.'

Lowry tapped the table with his palm, the first trace of irritation Jamie had seen from him. 'I don't mean we have to live pressed up against one another. There's going to be space enough for everyone.'

'There always was,' Callan said. 'The problem is that most people seem to want everyone else to believe what they believe, like that will make them more right.' He took another swig of his beer. 'Seems to me that a lot of our problems would disappear if people stopped believing in things, and just settled for knowing things.'

'It's the same thing,' Rena said.

'It's not,' Callan countered. 'When you know something, it's just how it is. Believing isn't as certain as that.' He gave a lop-sided smile. 'People who believe are always looking for proof, always trying to twist the world to make it fit, so they can say, *There you go, I was right all along.*'

'Believing means following through.' Rena's voice was growing high and agitated. 'Doing what you know is right.'

'And you know what's right, do you?' Jamie couldn't let it go.

'There was too much in the way before,' Rena said. 'I couldn't see clearly. But now . . .'

A line from an old song floated incongruously through Jamie's mind.

I can see clearly now the rain has gone.

'What can you see?' she said. 'What's God showing you?'

'The pieces of a puzzle,' Rena replied.

'Really?' Jamie raised her eyebrows. 'That's got to be a puzzle with a fair few broken pieces. And missing ones. You'd have thought God would give you better stuff to work with.'

'He doesn't show you everything.' Rena's hostility had given way to a sudden fervour. 'Just enough to figure it out yourself.'

'Why?' Jamie thought of her grandfather on the beach, talking to a woman with a handful of sea fragments and faith. 'If God did exist, why wouldn't he want you to be sure?'

'He tests us.'

Jamie laughed again, a tight, humourless sound. 'So how are we doing?'

Finn was gripping the edge of the table again. Callan glanced at him, then turned to Mila.

'Well, this is all very lovely, isn't it. Bet you're glad you came up with this idea.'

'I'm sorry.' Mila's voice was low. 'I just thought . . .'

'Hey,' Callan tapped his fork in front of her. 'This.' He gestured around the table. 'Not your fault. Some people could do with calming down a bit.' His gaze flicked to Jamie, who felt another surge of anger. It was duller this time, with the heat gone out of it. She could fan it as much as she wanted, but it was going to go out sooner or later, leaving her cold and guilty.

'Fuck you.' She shoved her stool back from the table and walked out, her feet over-loud on the metal floor.

Callan caught up with her outside her quarters.

'What was all that about?' He was looking at her with detached curiosity, as though she was some malfunctioning part of his ship.

Jamie shook her head. 'All that crap about God's will, and destiny, when she's the one who's built a career out of fiddling with nature.' It was a weak excuse for such a vicious exchange, but she wasn't going to tell him about the conversation in the shower room. 'I'm not sure even she knows what it is she believes. It seems to change every day to fit with whatever's going on.'

'Isn't that what people do? The world around us changes, and we have to change to keep up?'

Jamie shook her head again, and didn't answer.

'You could have let it go,' Callan said. 'It might all have calmed down if you'd just shut up.'

She felt a last shove of anger, ragged and limping. 'Don't tell me what to do.' She sounded ridiculous, like the stereotypical teenager she hadn't been. Her father and stepmother would probably have preferred her to scream and break things. Anything but that impenetrable silence; any conflict met with a sharp withdrawal.

'For fuck's sake.' He ran an impatient hand through his hair. 'Want to tell me I'm not the boss of you while we're at it? It's my ship. I'm not exactly enforcing martial law, but if I do tell you to do something, I expect you to do it. We're all cooped up in a glorified tin can, with an awful lot of space around us. Even more than there used to be. I've seen shipboard arguments go very badly wrong. I don't need someone going space-crazy and trying to eject us all into the void, because you and she can't sort out your differences. It doesn't matter who believes what.'

'It's not just about what she believes,' Jamie said. 'She looks at Mila like she's something the cat's dragged in, and she doesn't look at Finn at all, if she can possibly help it.'

'And what happened between the two of you?' Callan went straight to what she wasn't saying. 'I'd have thought you'd be just her cup of tea. Upper echelon, respectable.'

'It doesn't matter.'

Callan stood up straight, his hand going to his side. 'You're right. It doesn't. There's no room on a ship this size for all that clutter and baggage. It's exactly why I rotate my crew regularly. Clean things out before they can turn bad.'

'Isn't that hard?' That idea distracted Jamie from the main thrust of her anger. 'Living so closely with people, then just moving on?'

'Much easier than living with the consequences when it all goes wrong.'

Jamie leaned back against the door. Her anger had given way to curiosity. And something more. An unsettling sense that she needed to understand him, to make another connection, like that brief moment in his cabin when he'd seen more than she'd meant to show. But wasn't this exactly what he was talking about? They were just travelling together. When people started pushing too close, filling the spaces between them with their own beliefs and hurts and needs, that was when things went wrong.

'Why did you pick us up? Why bring more people on board when you don't seem to think that much of people in general?'

He gave her a faint smile. 'I don't mind people. As long as they keep all their peopleness to themselves, and don't try to make everyone else buy into it.'

'That seems to be the problem,' Jamie said.

His smile fell away. 'Well, it better stop being a problem.'

Her resentment flared again. 'Is that another order?'

Frustration flickered across Callan's face, and he looked away, as though feeling for what he wanted to say. But when he turned back to her, his expression was cool. 'Yes,' he said. 'We've only got a day and a half till we get to the capital. Shouldn't be too hard to keep the peace.'

'And then?' There was a hollow forming behind Jamie's ribs at the idea of what came next. Callan hadn't committed himself to the second leg of their journey, but she realised that she'd assumed he would agree to take them on. Perversely she found herself wanting to push for confirmation of her suspicions that Alegria would see him discharge his responsibility for them. 'I suppose you'll be glad to see the back of us and get off on your own again.'

Callan stared at her for a moment, then shrugged, a bare hitch of his shoulders. 'Probably for the best,' he said, and then turned and walked away.

Jamie watched him go, aware of the urge to call him back and say . . . what? He'd never wanted them on his ship. That much was clear. Whatever impulse had led to him bringing them on board, it was spent, and there was no reason for him to offer them any more of his time or thought. If she wanted to get to Earth, she'd have to find another way. There were other ships out there. Gracie had seen traces. Someone would be going to Earth, sooner or later. This was just a step on her journey.

Nothing more than that.

CHAPTER TWELVE

Jamie stayed late in her bunk the following morning, and when she finally ventured downstairs, she found the galley area deserted, and all signs of the dinner party cleared away.

She took her coffee back to her cabin, settled in with her e-reader and tried to forget where she was. She heard the occasional echo of footsteps, but no one knocked on her door.

She finished one book without much of its meaning sinking in, and started another, picked out at random from her unread list. She had to read the first page three times, and she still hadn't finished the chapter when the tannoy crackled, the static giving way to Callan's clipped tones.

'We will be setting down on Methuen in approximately fifteen minutes. Get ready for landing.'

Down in the hold she found the others already in their seats. Lowry nodded to her and Mila gave her a small smile, but Rena kept her gaze averted.

'Has he said why we're stopping?' she asked.

Lowry shook his head. 'He hasn't been down this morning.'

It was a rockier landing than usual, and the ship pitched slightly before setting down. Callan arrived in the hold before they'd finished undoing their harnesses.

'Sorry about that.' He barely gave them a glance as he headed over to the door release. 'Ground looked smoother than it was.'

'We're not on the landing platform?' Lowry said.

'A couple of miles out of port.'

Weak sunlight washed in as the doors creaked open. Callan didn't bother with the gangway, sitting down on the edge of the bay and dropping to the ground.

'I won't be long,' he said. 'There are shops in town if you need anything, but bear in mind we'll be on Alegria soon.'

Jamie walked over to the doors and looked out. The ship was resting on an expanse of grass beside a well-maintained road. A fairly sizeable town lay to the right. Callan was walking briskly in the opposite direction, towards the open gates of a large, institutional-looking building set in expansive grounds.

'Shouldn't we look around?' Lowry joined Jamie at the open doors.

'There were no beacons.' Gracie appeared behind them. 'I checked the comm on approach.'

'Still worth a look, surely,' Lowry said.

'Fine.' Gracie sat down and swung her legs over the edge. 'I might see if I can find the comms station anyway. I've tried a couple of times, and there's some static, but our set isn't strong enough to reach Alegria.'

'Anyone else?' Lowry looked at the other passengers.

Rena spoke first. 'I'll come with you.'

Jamie shook her head.

When the others were gone, Jamie sat down on the edge of the cargo bay. The sky was overcast, with the odd patch of sun breaking through. The grass had that slight bluish tinge that characterised all the worlds in the central part of the system. It had taken her a while to get used to it when she first came out from Earth. You didn't notice it so much up close, but when you looked out across the hills, the blue grew more acute, and more alien.

The town was the usual mix of modern builds and old-world nostalgia. The buildings on the outskirts were detached residential properties, with wooden porches and well-clipped lawns, just starting to grow out. Beyond them Jamie could see a few higher-rise structures, in the usual glass and clean steel lines. Funny how the tower block had become the symbol of overcrowding on Earth, with the emigration infomercials promising open vistas and spacious living; yet still they built upwards, even with all the space they had out here. Perhaps it was something instinctive, the need to go higher, see further.

Mila came and sat next to her, tucking her dress up around her knees.

'Sorry about last night,' Jamie said.

Mila shrugged. 'Maybe it wasn't such a good idea. I just thought . . . I don't know.' She paused, gathering her thoughts. 'I thought people might find they liked one another, if they gave it a chance.'

'Everyone's very different,' Jamie said cautiously. 'I don't think any of us would have been spending time together if this hadn't happened.'

Mila looked down, her fingers twining in her skirt.

Jamie felt an awkward flush rising in her cheeks. 'I mean . . . we just all had very different lives.'

'It's okay.' Mila gave her a small smile. 'It's true. You, Lowry, Rena, you're all upper echelon. You're from Earth. I was born in a brothel on an outer world colony. We would never have met.' Her smile faded. 'And if we had, you'd have thought I was trash, selling my body to anyone who wanted it.'

'That's not true.' But there was a prickle of unease at the back of her thoughts, telling her that Mila probably knew more about those invisible divides than she did.

'It is true.' Mila shook her skirt out, and looked out across the settlement. 'I could have stayed on Pangaea.'

'What?'

Mila met her gaze levelly. 'Why not? They didn't want anything I've not been selling since I was seventeen. I would have had a place there. What am I going to do on the capital? Or on Earth?'

'Anything you want,' Jamie said.

Mila shook her head. 'I think there's a place for all of us, somewhere we fit better than anywhere else, even if it's not what we want. We've got to belong somewhere, haven't we?'

'Not there,' Jamie said. She wanted to touch Mila, put an arm around her, but she didn't know how to shape herself against somebody else's need like that.

Not there. Callan had said something about that, just after she'd taken the bullet out. *Not there, and not there, and not there.* Our desires shaped by the negative space around them. She hadn't started wanting Daniel again until she realised he might be gone. She hadn't missed Northumberland until she became aware that it might be out of reach forever.

'Maybe not,' Mila said. 'But I don't know where.'

'Things will be clearer when we get to Alegria,' Jamie said. 'There'll be more people there, and then we'll know . . .' She hesitated. She'd had a vague but persistent idea that the capital worlds would be full of people who'd know what to do. But now it occurred to her that it could equally be full of other people who couldn't even get through dinner without falling out. Or maybe everyone would expect *them* to have the answers.

Mila tucked her legs underneath her and climbed to her feet. 'I'm going to go check on Finn.'

When Jamie was alone, she leaned back on her elbows and tilted her head up. The heavy bank of cloud was fraying into ragged tatters, with more blue showing through. But that blue felt like a lie, after so much time spent up above it, in the black of space. It was just something to hide beneath, to avoid seeing how wrenched and scattered among the stars they all really were.

A movement caught her eye. Callan was closing the gates of the building behind him. He didn't look around as he walked back to the ship, and when he drew closer Jamie could see that there was something tight and shuttered about his expression. She expected him to climb past her, straight into the ship, but instead he swung himself up to sit beside her.

'Everything okay?' she asked.

Stupid question.

'Fine.'

'Were you looking for someone?' She kept her gaze on the distant hills. It felt less personal if she didn't look at him.

His eyes were also fixed on the horizon. 'I just needed to be sure.'

Jamie shot a surreptitious glance towards the building. There was lettering above the gate, but she couldn't make it out. A hospital? Some sort of care centre? It had that look of something kept neat and safe and neutral by people with no stake in making it any more than that.

An elderly parent?

A sick child?

She dismissed that idea as soon as it formed, but there was a more intimate thought ready at hand. A wife. A lover. Sick or injured, and he'd had to carry on working. But there'd been no photos in his cabin, no incongruous little touches that might have indicated someone else's taste, tolerated in gifts, or tangled up in a pile of possessions left behind after a visit.

'Did the others say how long they'd be?' he asked.

'They only went to the shops. And Gracie was going to try the comm.'

They sat in silence for a few minutes until they saw the other three returning.

Callan stood up, stretching carefully. 'Better get ready to go. We may make Alegria late tonight if we push on.'

She nodded, expecting him to turn and walk away, but he didn't move.

'My brother,' he said.

'What?'

He nodded towards the gated building. 'That's who was in there.' A pause. 'In case you were wondering.'

Those last words were delivered with an odd inflexion. Jamie couldn't quite work out whether they were a jibe, or a warning, or whether he simply needed to say it to someone.

'I'm sorry,' she said, not quite sure at which of those inter-pretations she was aiming her apology.

He acknowledged it with a small smile as he turned and walked away. Just as he reached the stairs, he stopped and looked back.

'I'll take you to Earth,' he said. 'If you still want to go.'

When she twisted round to stare at him, too surprised to respond, he gave her a quick nod and then headed up the stairs.

Jamie stayed where she was until the others had reached the ship. Rena still looked sullen, and she kept her gaze averted from Jamie. Lowry swung a canvas bag up onto the bay floor and leaned against the ship.

'We got through to Alegria.'

Jamie's pulse picked up. 'And?'

'There are survivors,' Gracie said. 'A few hundred or there-abouts. The operator didn't have an exact number.'

'He said people are starting to drift in,' Lowry put in. 'A ship arrived yesterday, and they've had contact from another.'

'A few hundred?' She felt a sudden chill. 'Is that all?'

So many lost. Her survival estimate for Alegria had been in the thousands.

'The capital was too full.' There was more disapproval than

sadness in Rena's voice. 'People crushed up against each other.'

'I gave him all our names.' Gracie scrambled up into the ship, then reached a hand down to Lowry. The old man took it, gratefully, and with her help managed to heave himself up onto the bay floor.

'Thanks. I would have felt a bit daft having to ask for the gangway to be put out just for me.' He grimaced as he climbed to his feet. 'Old age. It's supposed to be dignified.'

'Who was on the comm?' Jamie asked.

'No idea.' Gracie walked over to the door lever. 'We need to get ready for take-off.'

The day passed slowly. Jamie read, wandered down to the galley and back again, read some more, tried to sleep. Later, she sat with Finn, watching him sort through the sea glass, laying the fragments out in ever more complex patterns. Spirals and loops and things that looked like manifestations of mathematical formulae. When she asked him what they were, he shrugged. 'They're in my head.'

She ate dinner with Mila and Finn and Lowry. Gracie joined them for a little while, but she ate fast and said little. Rena was lying down in her cabin. A headache, Lowry said. He seemed distant, barely reacting to the news that Callan had agreed to take them on to Earth. Perhaps it was just the proximity to the capital, to the moment when they'd know what their world had become.

After dinner, Gracie disappeared, but the rest of them lingered. There was no point going to bed, and Jamie doubted she'd be able to sleep anyway. She played poker with Mila and Lowry, but couldn't keep track of her hands. Eventually she put the cards down, shaking her head at Mila when she tried to deal her in again.

'I'm not concentrating.'

'Not long now,' Lowry said. 'How are you feeling?'

'Fine.'

Lowry held her gaze. 'You sure? You lived here, after all. There might be people you know who've survived. Is there anyone you're hoping to see?'

'No one here.' Then she realised how that sounded. 'I mean, there are people I knew. I'd be glad to see them, of course.'

'But no one in particular?'

'Not here.'

'On Earth then?'

She hesitated. She'd kept Daniel from them for reasons she couldn't articulate. Perhaps it was just that she only had that blank message to go on, and she didn't want to see the sympathy in other people's eyes when she told them how she was sure it meant he was alive. But somehow it felt more matted and complex than that. Callan's closed face flitted through her thoughts. He'd kept a secret too. But then he'd told her, unasked and matter-of-fact, that he'd had a brother, and that brother was gone now.

'There is someone. I mean, there was . . . I don't know. We said we'd meet on Earth if the world ever ended.' She found a smile for the memory, but it was brief and quick-fading. 'I know it's stupid.'

'It's not stupid,' Lowry said. 'Hope is never stupid. It lets us work things through, and figure out all the *what ifs*.'

'Isn't it worse?' Mila put in. 'Hoping for something and not getting it?'

'I don't think it is,' Lowry said. 'Hope isn't the same as having. There's room in it for all the ways things could be.'

But this didn't feel like hope. It was nothing but a thin thread of almost-longing stretching out before her, and a tangled mess of regret trailing behind. The urge to honesty had passed, and she felt as raw as if she'd scraped away a layer of skin.

Just then the galley speaker buzzed, and Callan's voice came on. 'We're here. Everyone strap in.'

Jamie felt a lurch of something like vertigo. They'd got here too quickly. She hadn't had time to think about what they might find.

All the what ifs, Lowry had said.

She wanted to find Callan and ask him not to stop, just to keep flying. She needed more time out here, between the unknowing stars.

She wasn't ready.

It was a slow, steady landing, the engines straining to hold the ship in whatever entry pattern Callan was following. After an interminable period of shifting and turning, there was a final surge of engine noise, signalling the last effort, and then they juddered and sank onto the ground.

Everyone seemed slow to undo their harnesses. Callan and Gracie were already down by the time they'd gathered in a loose knot by the bay doors.

'Where are we?' Lowry asked, as Callan pulled the door lever.

'The dock at the administration headquarters.'

'Why not the main port?' Jamie asked.

'This is where they told us to come in. Presumably no one wanted to trek all the way out to the port at this time of night.'

As the doors slid open, the bay was lit up by the hard glare of the floodlights on the side of the administration headquarters. All steel and glass and carved marble panels, sweeping up some fifteen floors, the administration building was the beating heart of humankind. As she looked up, the floodlights flared in her eyes and she blinked away a blur of tears. There were voices outside the doors. Callan was walking forwards, with Gracie at his side, Lowry falling in behind them. Mila was hanging back with Finn, while Rena hovered off to one side, her face tight and drawn. As Jamie moved to follow Callan and the others, her toe snagged on the edge of one of the cargo rails and she stumbled and almost fell. Lowry caught her arm, steadying her.

'Okay?'

'Fine.' It sounded snappish, and she tried for a smile to soften the effect. It felt like a grimace, stretched across her face. She was all over the place. It was late, and the lights were—

'Jamie?'

Her head jerked up. The voice was familiar, but she couldn't place it. She took another numb-footed step forward, blinking in the glare.

'Jamie.' Footsteps clattered on the gangway, and a figure loomed in front of her, backlit into a monochrome blur. It moved closer, resolving itself into a familiar shape.

Marc.

The name dropped into her memory where it hung, detached and meaningless, a label for a stick figure she'd drawn one day and cast aside.

He took another step, growing more solid.

Marc. Tall, dark-skinned, with a light brush of stubble that used to snag against her face when they kissed. They'd worked together a few years ago, and then he'd moved over to an administration job, finishing up in Daniel's division. Their brief fling had been over long before she met Daniel. It had been one of those fleeting attractions that falls away swiftly and cleanly, leaving no ill feeling behind.

'My God, Jamie.'

As he pulled her into a hard hug, her arms hung limp by her

sides. He'd held her before but she couldn't remember how it had felt. Maybe it hadn't been real at all. Or maybe it had happened to someone else. He let her go, taking a step back to look at her.

'When I saw your name on the list just now, I couldn't believe it. We never . . .' He stopped and rubbed his face. 'Sorry. It's just . . . it's good to see you.'

Jamie nodded. All the words she thought of saying were the wrong shape in her mouth.

Marc glanced down the gangway. 'Daniel should be here any minute,' he said.

Except he hadn't.

Of course he hadn't said it. It was her racked imagination sliding Daniel's name into the space between his words. She tried to focus, but Marc was still talking.

'I sent someone with a message as soon as I saw the list. Then I had this awful thought, what if it's someone else? The same name but not you.'

'Daniel?' Her voice sounded muffled, and she tried again. This time his name caught in her throat, and she had to stop and cover her mouth with her hand.

'He's on his way now.'

'From Earth?' She was talking as though it was real.

Jamie suddenly realised that she'd never truly believed that he was alive. It had only ever been a distraction; something to stop her having to look at what was left of her world, her life.

Marc laughed. 'Earth? No. He's here, at the headquarters.'

It wasn't real. He must be talking about something else, but she'd blocked it out somehow, replacing it with another version of this world in which Daniel was alive, and here.

'He was going to Earth.'

'He only got as far as Earth station when the landing embargo kicked in. He was turned back.'

Her mind was working too hard to fill in all those details, desperately searching for a reason why he might have beaten the statistics. You had to get the details right, or you couldn't relax into the fantasy. Something would trip you up.

'No.' There. She was back on script. That's what she'd be saying if he was telling her that Daniel was dead.

Nought point nought nought nought one.

She took a step back, colliding with someone behind her.

'Jamie . . .' It was Lowry, but she couldn't focus on what he was saying, because there were footsteps on the gangway again, and a figure coming closer.

'Jamie?'

Nought point nought nought nought one.

'Jamie.' As the figure rushed forwards her arms came up and she turned, so that they collided, awkward and side-on, her elbow digging against his ribs, her jaw pressing against his shoulder.

Daniel. She wasn't sure if she'd said it out loud or not, but it didn't mean anything. It had no connection with the arms around her and the body pressed against hers.

His hands were on her face, tipping her head up to look at him. She could feel his breath on her cheeks and see the flecks of blue in his grey eyes.

Too close. She put her hands against his chest. He dropped one hand and folded his fingers over hers, misunderstanding her gesture. She was numb, cold in his arms.

'Jamie.'

She looked up. There were tears glinting on his lashes as he leaned closer, his lips feeling for hers. She turned her head, so that the kiss fell on her cheek.

She was out of step, out of sync.

He folded her close again, her face pressed against his chest. He was saying something, but it was muffled. She shifted, turning in his arms so that she could look past him. Callan was watching them, his expression unreadable, and when their eyes met, he looked away.

Callan's reaction snapped everything into focus. If someone else could see them, then this was real. He was real. He was here.

She stepped back out of his embrace. 'How are you here? I was going to Earth.'

'I didn't make it.' He took her hand, turning it over to stroke her palm. 'And I knew if there was any hope of finding you, it would be back here.'

'No.' She wasn't making him understand. 'I thought you'd go to Earth. To Northumberland. We said we would. If . . . don't you remember?'

He stared at her, blank incomprehension in his eyes, and then he laughed.

'Oh God, that old joke.'

'I was looking for you.' Jamie thought it needed saying again.

'Well, you found me,' he said, and smiled. 'By accident, it seems.'

She was about to argue, to remind him that they'd agreed, but there were conversations overlapping all around her, and she couldn't focus. Callan was talking to a man with an e-pad. Gracie was checking something over by the doors. Lowry and Rena were standing with another couple of people. Lowry was smiling, but Rena was turned half away, her arms wrapped tightly across her body. The man with the e-pad nodded at Callan, then walked over to Jamie and Daniel.

The man glanced at his pad. 'Jamie Allenby?'

'Yes.'

'And you've come in from . . .'

'Soltaire.' Daniel answered for her.

'Oh, yes. One of the smaller settlements. Three of you from there, is that right?'

'Yes.'

'Any chance that anyone else survived?'

'We didn't find anyone, but we only checked the area around the port.'

The man frowned, and seemed about to ask another question, but Marc stepped up beside them, giving Daniel a quick slap on the back that set Jamie's teeth on edge. There was something congratulatory about it.

'Look, it's late,' he said. 'Let's debrief in the morning.' He turned to Jamie. 'We're putting new arrivals up in the conference wing for now. We've still got a few rooms free.'

When Daniel's arm tightened around Jamie, Marc smiled. 'Guess you won't be needing one. Why don't you two turn in for the night? I'll get everyone else settled.'

Jamie hesitated, watching Marc walk away towards Callan and Gracie, but when Daniel squeezed her arm and said, 'Come on,' his voice low and tender, she couldn't think of a good reason to linger.

She followed him out of the ship and down the gangway.

CHAPTER THIRTEEN

Daniel had a suite on the top floor, with a bedroom, small sitting area and spacious bathroom.

'Perk of an administration job,' he said, when he saw her looking around. 'We figured we'd probably be needed here for a fair while, so we might as well be comfortable.'

We?

They stood for a moment, not speaking.

'Why don't you take a bath?' he said eventually. 'I assume things on the ship were pretty basic. You were lucky that Callan guy was in the area, mind, or you'd still be stuck on Soltaire.'

Jamie looked away. 'There must be plenty of people in that situation.'

'I know. We're going to send out search parties, but we're short of ships and people to fly them. And we need to keep an eye on fuel supplies. It's going to take careful planning.'

'Couldn't you send a ship out to transmit messages,' Jamie said. 'Let people know it's not just them? I nearly . . .' She stopped. She couldn't talk about that.

Daniel shook his head. 'We don't want to waste fuel. Better to wait till we're ready to start picking people up.'

Jamie didn't have the energy to argue. She'd speak to someone tomorrow.

'It's late,' Daniel said gently. 'Have a bath and then we'll go to bed.'

It was cold in here, the air-conditioning turned down low.

That was why there were goosebumps suddenly brushing her arms. She went into the bathroom, and closed the door, making sure the lock clicked as quietly as possible. Then she filled the sharp-edged marble bath with scalding hot water, before trickling the cold in, until it was just cool enough for her to lower herself in, millimetres at a time.

She usually took long, lingering baths, but tonight she couldn't settle, climbing out after just a few moments, when steam was still rising from the surface. She dried herself on one of the soft towels, then hesitated over her clothes. She couldn't very well put her filthy shirt and trousers back on, but her other things were still on the ship.

She shoved her hair back. This was Daniel. He'd seen her naked a million times before. But not for a long time. After the baby, it had taken a while for her body to return to its pre-pregnancy shape, as though it was reluctant to let her forget. She'd fallen into the habit of covering up, sleeping in a T-shirt. It hadn't been shame at her changed body. There was something solid and visceral about her half of their shared loss. It was written in the fine silvery lines on her stomach, and soaked into the blood that seeped from her, steady and pitiless, for those first weeks.

The bathroom floor was cold beneath her bare feet. She had to go out there.

She eventually slipped her shirt on, half-buttoned. Then she opened the door.

Daniel was lying on the bed, reading something. As she came out of the bathroom, he sat up, dropping the pad to one side. She didn't know how to move or what expression she should be wearing. She looked around the room, putting off the moment. There were a few things from their flat on the sideboard. The digital frame with the pictures of his family. The abstract sculpture she'd bought him a few years back.

Some of his books. She ran her hand along the titles. *The Bone Clocks*. That was hers. And the pewter bowl overflowing with odds and ends, that was hers too.

'I brought some of your things.' He stepped up behind her. 'Just in case. Everything else is still at the apartment.' His lips brushed the sensitive spot where her neck met her shoulder. 'I never gave up on you.'

His hand was sliding up under her shirt, stroking her ribs, just brushing the underside of her breast.

She should turn and kiss him. Once she'd kissed him, she'd remember how this worked.

When she edged round to meet his gaze, he smiled and lifted his hand to brush back her hair. As his mouth came down on hers, she felt a flutter of panic. She couldn't remember how they used to kiss.

He took a step, easing her back towards the sideboard, his hands on her hips. She gave way, letting him lift her up onto the cold polished wood, one knee caught up between their bodies. He shifted, using his hip to gently push that leg to the side, so he could move in closer. His hands were tugging at her shirt, and she lifted her arms, letting him undress her.

When he dropped his head to kiss her breast, she brushed her hands over the soft burr of his hair. That touch carried memories, familiarity, and it brought a rush of relief. She knew the way from here. She even felt a faint flicker of arousal. But was it enough?

There'd been a time when every corner of their apartment had been home to some aspect of their desire. The sofa, the table, the sun-soaked carpet in front of the window, where any passing hovercraft could have seen them.

Now the wood was cold beneath her bare skin, and she wanted to be in bed. She didn't know him well enough for this. Not any more. It was as though they'd only just met, and people who'd only just met hid their awkwardness beneath the forgiving covers. They didn't have sex on sideboards, unable to contain themselves for a moment longer.

She dropped her hands to his chest, pushing him away. When he looked at her, hurt flaring behind his eyes, she found a smile she hoped would fit, and said, 'Let's go to bed.'

They made their separate ways across the floor, and she slid in beneath the sheets, turning to watch him undress. The lines of his body didn't look quite right, as if she were trying to draw him from memory and getting it wrong. He climbed in next to her, pulling the covers right up to their necks, making a joke of it. She smiled back, blinking away the tears that were pricking behind her eyes. He knelt up, the sheet falling to his waist, and swung one leg over hers, before dropping down onto one elbow so that he could kiss her breast once again. His weight was awkward, and she shifted, pushing up with her knee. He didn't understand, pressing down on her, one hand catching her wrists and pinning them above her head while the other moved down between her legs, fingers splayed against her thigh.

His eyes were dark as he kissed her again, a long, tender kiss that she tried to mirror. If she kept mimicking his passion, her own would surely follow, breathing those faint embers into a proper flame. The kiss went on, until she found herself wanting to push on to the next, inevitable, stage. She leaned back against the bed, lifting her hips. He felt the movement and breathed in hard, bearing down, feeling his way into her.

There was that moment of resistance as they shifted and edged against one another, and then he was inside her, and she was arching her back, trying to remember how it felt to want this. Something was swelling hard behind her ribs, and there wasn't room to breathe. She let out a gasp. He heard it, and drew a sharp breath of his own.

It was too fast. Too full. The wrong place, the wrong moment, and suddenly she needed him out of her, off her, because this wasn't what she'd thought it would be, and it was too soon, too fast, too much. This was Daniel. This was her. But it wasn't right.

Stop.

He was still moving. Why hadn't he stopped?

She'd only said it inside her head.

Stop.

Still silent, not projecting beyond the confines of her skull.

'Stop.'

There was a fractional falter in his rhythm, but he hadn't heard her, or perhaps he'd heard her wrong.

'Daniel, stop.'

This time his head came up, confusion writing itself across his face.

'Daniel, I can't.'

She could see the hurt on his face, stark and livid. His weight was still pinning her down.

'Jamie . . .'

'Get off.' Her throat was so tight that she could barely force the words out. 'Get off me.'

She tried to pull her hands out of his grip, and for just a fraction of an instant he held on. That brief second stretched out as though time had warped around that single sharp beat; his hands still holding on to her. In that still moment, she felt a tiny click, like a small bone breaking.

Oh God, I don't love you.

She wrenched her hands away, shoving him hard in the chest. As he pulled back, she twisted out from under him.

'Jamie?' There was concern in his voice, but a hint of anger too. 'What the hell?'

She sat on the edge of the bed, tipped forwards, holding herself tightly. 'I can't.'

'Can't what?' Anger had the upper hand now. 'Can't look at me? Can't touch me?' He gave a humourless laugh. 'Why am I even surprised? Same old Jamie. End of the world, and it's still all about you. What *you* want, and don't want.'

She stood and walked over to pick her shirt off the floor. The bed creaked as Daniel got up. He followed her and put his arms around her.

'Look,' he said. 'It's late. Let's not say anything we don't mean. Come back to bed. Just to sleep.'

'I can't.' She tried to extricate herself as gently as possible. Her heart was a dead weight. She didn't love him any more. She was sure of that. But she had loved him. Maybe it was fatigue, or grief, but she couldn't separate out the loving from the not loving. 'I'm so sorry. I thought I could. I thought if we both made it, then . . .'

'It would mean something,' he finished. 'It does. It has to.'

She shook her head. 'It just means we both survived. And that's not enough. Just not dying. There are all those other people out there who didn't die. How does it mean we're meant to be with each other, rather than with any one of them?'

His expression changed. 'There's someone else.'

'No.' She said it too quickly, but that didn't mean it wasn't true. 'I was just . . . I don't know what I'm saying. I'm sorry.' He was still holding on to her. 'Daniel, let me go.'

'I can't. You've got to give this a go. Let's just try.'

'Let go.' She had to get his arms off her.

'Jamie . . .'

'No.' She wrenched herself out of his grip, stumbling against the sideboard. Daniel tried to catch her, but as she twisted away from him, off balance, her forehead cracked against the edge of a shelf.

'Christ, Jamie.' Daniel made no attempt to touch her again. 'Jesus Christ.'

She lifted her hand to her face. It hurt, and when she looked down there was blood on her fingers.

He was here, and she was bleeding again.

'Here.' Daniel went into the bathroom and came back with a pad of wet tissue which he held out to her at arm's length. She pressed it to her head while he pulled his clothes back on. 'I'll sleep somewhere else.'

She shook her head. 'This is your room. I'll go.'

'Where? You haven't been allocated a room. Everyone assumed . . .' He looked away.

'I'll sleep on the ship,' she said. 'My things are there anyway.'

She went into the bathroom to get dressed. When she looked in the mirror, there was a tiny cut on the edge of her brow, wrapped in swelling and discolouration. She brushed her hair across it before leaving the bathroom. Daniel was sitting on the edge of the bed. He didn't look up, and she almost left without speaking. But there was something inside her that felt like it was being tugged and torn, like someone taking off a plaster too slowly. She stopped, halfway out of the door.

'Can we talk in the morning?' she said.

He rubbed his face, still not looking at her. 'Okay.'

She nodded, although she knew he couldn't see it, and closed the door behind her.

CHAPTER FOURTEEN

When the door closed, Jamie stood still for a moment, trying to get her bearings. There was a lift at the end of the corridor that would take her down to the exit nearest to the landing-bay. She hesitated, and then set off in the opposite direction. She followed the twists and turns of the corridor until she arrived at the lift at the far corner, pressed the button and waited. After a few seconds the doors slid open with a perky ding, followed by a female voice announcing 'executive corridor'. That smooth artificial voice sent a shiver of discomfort through her. Most people were dead and dust, yet the world they'd made was still ticking over, waiting for them to figure out how to live in it.

She watched the struts and girders slide past as the glass lift sank smoothly down the side of the building. Who had thought it would be a good idea to let everyone see the mechanics of their descent? Most people just wanted things to work. They didn't want to know how or why.

Another ding, and that level, unaccented tone announced her arrival on the third floor. Jamie crossed the foyer to the double doors that led to the executive bar, a wide, opulent room, with floor-to-ceiling windows. The bar was made of thellum, the mahogany-like wood that was the cornerstone of Alegria's wealth. Polished slabs from the vast trunks had been shipped back to the boardrooms and power corridors of Earth, the new colony growing steadily richer and more powerful, until it found itself furnishing its own administration offices.

The main lights were off, the only illumination coming from the dimmed strips over the bar. Outside the city was in darkness, but through the low-glare glass Jamie could see the blaze of stars in the sky. You didn't notice them when the city was lit up.

As she walked over to the bar, she expected the familiar craving to kick in, but there was only a dull ache where that sharp need had always bitten. She scanned the rows of bottles: wines, spirits, beer from a dozen different planets, a locked cold-crate of bottles of the much-celebrated Keplan champagne, each one capped with a digital security top. What would happen if she were to smash her way into the crate, break a bottle at the neck and pour its contents down her throat? Would someone come running to wrestle it off her? Or were things only valuable when there were enough people around who couldn't afford them?

She opened one of the wine fridges and took out a bottle of the expensive Kapteyn wine. As she reached up for a glass, a voice spoke from behind her.

'I've got whisky, if that's your tipple.'

The glass slipped through her fingers, exploding in a shower of splinters on the countertop.

'Fuck's sake,' she muttered. Callan was sitting in the semi-darkness, over in the far corner. She shook shards of glass off her sleeve, and sucked at a fleck of blood on the back of her hand. 'What are you doing?'

'Drinking.'

'I can see that. Why didn't you say something when I came in.'

'Thought it might be a flying visit. Picking up some celebratory champagne.' He took a sip of his drink. 'I can't imagine they've got room service up and running yet.'

'What are you doing here?' She tipped a generous measure

of the Kapteyn into another glass. 'I thought everyone would be asleep.'

'Guy in charge wanted to speak to me about a couple of things.'

She walked over. He was sitting in a high-backed armchair, feet up on a padded stool. Jamie sat down on the small sofa at right angles to his seat, so that they wouldn't have to face off across the table, like one of them was interviewing the other.

He lifted his drink. 'Cheers.'

She took a swig of her wine. 'Guy in charge? Who's that?'

'Name of Buckley,' Callan said. 'You know him?'

'Slightly,' she said. 'He was under-secretary to one of the cabinets, I think.'

'That figures. He knows his stuff, but not much charisma. Kind of guy who spends his time running things so other people can look like they're running things.'

Jamie almost smiled at that. 'Plenty of people like that in the administration. What did he want to talk to you about?'

'The ship.' Callan swirled his whisky. 'My plans.'

'And what are they?' She found she was mirroring his movement, her wine sliding round the curve of her own glass. She tightened her grip on the stem. 'Did you tell him you're going to Earth?'

Her own words caught at her, and it took her a second to realise what it was that had caused that snag.

She'd said *you*, not *we*. She felt a flicker of resentment, irrationally aimed at Callan, as though he was the one who'd jumped to conclusions.

She and Daniel, whatever they'd been together, it was over. But there were other decisions still to be made. If the old world could be rebuilt, it would happen here. Maybe there'd be a place for her.

'We didn't get that far.' Callan looked out across the dark

city. 'He just wanted to know if I'm willing to help with the search and rescue plan they're working out.' He gave her a quick glance. 'So, Daniel. That's who you were looking for. Odds have got to be astronomical. You both surviving.'

She stared at her drink. 'I suppose so.'

'What happened?'

She looked up to see Callan staring at her.

'What?'

He reached over and touched her brow. Her skin prickled beneath his fingers.

She leaned back, trying to make the movement casual. 'Bumped my head.'

'On what?'

'Just a shelf.'

His expression was entirely neutral, but she found herself wanting to bolster the explanation.

'I was tired, not paying attention.'

He nodded. 'Must have been a shock for both of you.'

'Yes.'

'So why are you sat down here, drinking alone?'

'I'm not drinking alone.'

'Planning on it, though.'

She took another slug of wine. 'Like you said, it was a shock.'

He nodded slowly. 'How come you were out on Soltaire on your own? If you're with him.'

'Work.'

'Wouldn't have thought you'd have needed to trek all the way out there to find work.'

There was a barely perceptible blurring at the edge of his voice. If the bottle had been full when he started, he was at least three shots down.

'Why are you so interested in my life story?' She nodded towards the bottle. 'Are you drunk?'

'Maybe. But it's a reasonable question.'

'I needed a bit of space.' She wasn't sure which question she was answering: the one about Soltaire, or the unanswered one about her presence here in the bar.

'So you're going to stay?'

She almost said yes. *Yes, of course.* While she'd been letting him fill the gaps in the conversation with assumptions, she'd almost forgotten the truth. She didn't love Daniel.

'I don't know. I . . .' Maybe it was the wine kicking in, but she suddenly thought it might be a relief to say it. 'I'm not sure it's going to work. Him and me.'

He considered this, his expression still neutral. 'Situation like this, it's got to be hard to deal with.'

She shook her head. 'That's not . . . things weren't right. Before.'

'So why were you trying to find him?'

'I don't know.' That was all she seemed to have said since they'd arrived here.

She got up and poured herself another glass. When she came back, Callan nodded at her forehead.

'He do that?'

A jolt of shock ran through her. 'No. Of course not. He . . .' She stopped. 'We were fighting. I pushed him, and lost my balance.'

'Seems to me if two people have the energy to fight, it means there are still feelings there.'

'Of course there are feelings. We were together for thirteen years.'

'Long time. What went wrong?'

Jamie didn't answer straight away. All her instinctive responses began with *he*.

He pushed me.

He didn't give me space.

He changed.

What would Daniel say, if it was him sitting here?

She never let me in.

She wouldn't try.

The wine had made her too honest to blame him completely, but she didn't see why she should shoulder the whole weight. That left only the thing that should have been something of each of them.

'There was a baby.' She fixed her gaze on the distant stars. 'Or there should have been. His heart stopped. Somewhere around thirty weeks, no one was sure exactly.'

'I'm sorry.'

'Why?' Her voice was too loud in the empty bar.

'What?'

'Why are you sorry?' Her chest was too full. Things were trying to force their way out between her ribs. 'You barely know me.'

His gaze narrowed. 'Because, despite what you seem to think, I'm not a complete arsehole. Someone tells me they lost a baby, that it broke their relationship, what else am I going to say? Congratulations? Well done?'

'I don't have to listen to this.'

'No,' Callan said. 'You don't.'

That's what she'd said to Rena that night at dinner. She breathed out slowly and took another sip of her drink.

'Sorry.'

'You could give things another go,' Callan said. 'You could try for another baby.'

'No,' she said, so quickly that she tripped over the ends of his words. She took another deep breath, steadying herself, and on the outbreath she let go of the other half of that tight-wound secret. 'I never wanted a baby. He was the one who wanted children. Then I lost it and . . .' She ran out of coherent words.

Callan waited for her to continue, but she shook her head and took a deep slug of her drink.

'So it's over?'

'I think so.' She gave a hard little laugh. 'Funny. All the stories say that love is forever. And the songs. All you need is love, and all that.'

'There are other songs.' He didn't smile. 'Too much love will kill you. Sometimes love ain't enough. What about those?'

'See?' She laughed again. 'If even the songwriters can't reach a consensus, what hope do the rest of us have?'

He shook his head. 'The problem with stories and songs – no, scratch that, the problem with *words* – is that they make us squeeze all the messy bits of life into something small and snappy. All the things you feel. The times you hate one another. The times you want to tear open your skin and let the other person climb inside. All that, and only one word for it.' His smile was edged with something she couldn't quite read. 'It's like there's only one way of doing things. You get it right or you get it wrong. But no two people are the same. If you're trying to follow some blueprint for what loving someone ought to be, it's probably doomed from the start.'

'Maybe people can never fit together,' she said. 'Not properly.'

'Or maybe we've made our expectations too big, and our definition too small. One word for being with someone. There's got to be room in that word for everything we drag along with us, and for most people I don't think there is.'

'Baggage,' Jamie said. 'You mean all our baggage.'

He grimaced. 'You could call it that. I just think it's . . . us. The things that shape us.' He tilted his head, meeting her eyes.

'But no. I don't think two people are ever a perfect fit. Too many bits have been snapped off along the way. And people always think they can fix you, if you just let them in on the secret of what it was that broke you in the first place.'

'So what happened to you?' she said, the wine sharpening her recklessness.

'What do you mean?'

'If we're all broken, what broke you?'

'There you go,' he said. 'You're asking that question like there's a one-word answer.'

'Okay,' she said. 'Tell me one thing.' It was definitely the wine. She could feel her inhibitions just starting to blur.

He looked at her for a moment, his face blank and closed. Then he sighed and rubbed at the back of his neck. Jamie suddenly wondered what he would do if she stepped behind him and pressed her fingers into his shoulders, kneading the tension away.

'You really want to know?' he said.

'Yes.' Maybe it would distract her from that unsettling image.

He drained the last of his whisky, but kept hold of the glass, twisting it in his hands. 'I had a brother. He was disabled, severely autistic, with some other problems. When he was eighteen and I was sixteen, we came out from Earth with my parents. It was during the first of the forced emigrations. The worst thing was that my parents wanted to go. We lived in one of the most crowded parts of St Louis, Missouri. They thought it might be better. A new start.' He laughed, a dark, hollow sound.

Jamie felt a hard jolt of understanding. The early colonies had an ugly history. Whole settlements had been lost.

'I was in the homeland protests,' she said.

He gave her a sardonic look, his gaze flicking towards her ring finger.

'I left because of it,' she said, stung. 'I came out here on the *Phoenix*, one of the protest ships.'

'And landed on the capital, where you finished up living with a member of the administration and working for the ministry of whatever it was you did. You really stuck it to them, didn't you?'

'At least we tried. And the programme did eventually stop.'

'It would have stopped anyway,' Callan said. 'They'd got rid of enough undesirables by then.'

'At least we tried,' she repeated, with a little more heat. 'What else could we have done?'

'Nothing. I'm not blaming you. It's just . . .' He made a vague gesture. 'I don't know. Sorry. Not your fault.'

'No, I'm sorry.' She felt clumsy and stupid. She'd done what people always did and tried to make a connection to someone else's story. 'It felt like doing something at the time.'

'Doesn't matter now, I suppose.'

'I guess not.' Most of the people who came out on those colony ships were dead, along with those who'd enforced the programme, and those who'd protested against it. 'So what happened?'

He didn't answer for a long moment. Jamie wondered if he'd changed his mind about sharing the story.

'The ship wasn't well stocked,' he said eventually. 'There was rationing, fights over who should be prioritised. This was one of the first colony ships, remember. Trip took a month when it would be less than two weeks these days. Anyway, things went wrong pretty fast. Maybe we'd have worked it out, but then there was an outbreak of cholera.'

'Christ. You were on the *El Doradao*.' The *Plague Ship* was how it had become known.

He nodded. 'You know the story. Not enough vaccine. People died.'

Everyone knew the story. The fledgling settlement had disintegrated into chaos, and the administration had been forced to send a salvage team in to deal with the outbreak and restore order. They'd saved maybe half the settlers, but it had taken years before Thetis was anything approaching a fully functioning colony. It was spun, of course, as these things always were. Greedy settlers, unable to self-govern. But the truth had seeped around the edges of the administration whitewash, staining the early days of off-world settlement.

'The overseers had to manage the distribution of the vaccine while waiting for back-up supplies. They decided to prioritise adults. They decided it was better to let the children take their chances, rather than finishing up with a whole lot of orphaned kids needing care. All of those over eighteen should have been vaccinated.' He refilled his glass, and took a good-sized mouthful before continuing. 'Except they wouldn't give my brother his dose.' His tone was level. 'My parents gave us their doses. They told me to look after him if the worst happened.' He smiled, a cold twitch of his lips. 'The worst happened. It generally does.'

'And you looked after him.'

'I looked after him.' Another sip of whisky. 'For a while.'

'Must have been difficult. You were very young.'

'It was. But not in the way you probably think. He wasn't like Finn. He could barely speak. He had a breakdown if anyone looked at him for too long. Violent outbursts. I never even knew if he understood who I was. I never knew if he felt anything for me, or if I was just another part of a world he couldn't cope with.'

'What happened?'

Callan sat back in his chair, stretching his legs, as though the story was some ache that could be eased. 'We managed. I found work, did all right at it. I'd had better schooling than most people around me. My mother was a teaching assistant before we left Earth.' He smiled, a proper smile, although one that was edged with sadness. 'She had no problem knocking an education into me.' The smile faded. 'Then I was offered something much better. Good pay, good prospects. But it was shipboard, and I couldn't take Ed with me.' It was the first time he'd said his brother's name. 'They'd set up a facility by then. A residential home.'

'On Methuen.'

He nodded. 'It was a good place. It wasn't like I was leaving him to be locked up in some old-world asylum. But . . . the bottom line was that I left him.'

'It would have been the best thing for him,' Jamie said. 'Even if you could have taken him, it wouldn't have been good for him, being dragged all over the place.'

'That's what I told myself.' Callan's gaze flitted to the starlit sky again. 'But I wasn't doing it for him. I was doing it for me. I wanted my own ship, my own space.' He shook his head. 'I went to see him sometimes, but he didn't seem to remember who I was. So I stopped going so much. I still called in when I was near, but for the most part I left him to the staff.'

'It wasn't your fault.' Jamie reached out to touch his arm, but she lost her nerve at the last moment, leaving her hand hovering awkwardly between them. She pulled it back and wrapped it around her glass again.

'It was. I made that choice.'

'But it wasn't your fault you were left looking after him.'

'No,' he said. 'But just because it was someone else's fault as well, that doesn't get me off the hook.' He lifted his glass again. 'Anyway, it's over and done with now. I just have to live with it.'

Live with it. That's what everyone had wanted her to do after her mother died. Live with it. Deal with it. Talk about it. Work it through. Just like when she lost the baby. At least with the baby she'd been an adult, in charge of her own choices, including the choice to run. But that other time, she was only fourteen, and there was nowhere to run to, except into silence.

Callan was looking at her. 'What is it?'

For a moment she thought she might tell him. But she couldn't think how she might start that old story, and the impulse passed. 'Nothing. Just thinking about what comes next. Now, I mean.'

'And what does come next?'

There was an odd clarity about the moment, as though the wine had sharpened her thought processes, instead of blurring them. While she and Callan had been grappling their way through that fraught, tangled conversation, her subconscious had been working away, making the decision. 'There's nothing here for me,' she said. 'I'll come to Earth with the rest of you. New start.' She gave a faint smile. 'I sound like Rena.'

He was looking out of the window again, his face half in shadow. Her smile faded.

'Sorry,' she said. 'You came here for a quiet drink, not to talk about the past.'

He put his glass down on the table and stood up.

'It doesn't matter.' He still didn't look at her. 'It's late. I'm going to get some sleep.'

After Callan had gone, Jamie sat looking out at the stars, the too-honest conversation replaying in her mind. She wasn't sure what they'd been trying to say, or if the whole thing had been just one of those meandering, drink-fuelled rambles, that only ever makes sense at the time.

She shoved the cushions up to one end of the sofa and lay down. As soon as she closed her eyes she could feel the wine pushing at the edges of her senses, as though it had been waiting for its moment. She turned over, curling into the crease of the sofa, and let go.

CHAPTER FIFTEEN

When Jamie woke, the sun was glaring in through the windows, dragging back the fug of sleep. There was a dull ache in her head, and when she lifted her fingers to her forehead, they brushed the edges of the swollen cut, setting off a sharper throb of pain. She could smell the stale musk of last night's wine on her skin, and her mouth was sticky, her stomach roiling with a sullen hunger that she knew would turn to nausea if she tried to eat.

She got up and walked over to the window, squinting against the glare. In the daylight the city looked no different from how she remembered. There was no haze of death hanging over the rooftops, no fires burning in the streets. Was it like this everywhere? Just a neat, closing-up-shop type ending of mankind's hold on its world?

Another image rose in her mind. Wide, empty skies above a wide, empty shore. The sun was high, glinting off the faint shimmer of waves breaking along the tideline.

Home. She let that idea hang in her mind for a moment, until she felt a little tug of . . . something. It wasn't certainty, and it wasn't longing, but it was there. *Home,* she thought again. She'd go back to where she'd started from. Maybe then she'd know what she was supposed to do. She'd told Callan she'd come with them to Earth, but he hadn't looked as though he believed her. She couldn't blame him. The conversation had been full of all the things she didn't know, or wasn't sure about.

She'd find him, tell him again. There would be no *I don't know*. Just her decision, clean and simple.

Down at the landing site, the ship's bay doors were open. Lowry and Rena were standing to the side of the gangway with a small group of men, while Mila and Finn hovered nearby. Rena's voice was raised, and Mila looked as though she'd been crying. When Jamie looked up the gangway, she could see Gracie standing just inside the hold, arms folded.

As she walked towards the ship, one of the men glanced up. He said something to the man next to him, and then headed over to intercept her.

'Excuse me, ma'am. Can I ask what you're doing?'

'Is there a problem?'

The man was tall and broad-shouldered, with a speckling of silver in his hair. He was dressed in the grey uniform of senior capital security, with a comms clip on his collar, and a bulge at his hip. There were other security uniforms in the group, and when Jamie looked around, she could see another couple of officers over by the main entrance to the dockyard. All of them were visibly armed, and all had the cool, neutral expressions of men trained to take in every detail of a situation without letting slip any hint of what they thought of it.

It occurred to Jamie that she'd seen several uniformed officers last night, both on arrival, and as she'd followed Daniel through the main building. How had so many of the security service survived? Surely they would have been frontline when the virus took hold? She had no time to ponder this anomaly, as Rena detached herself from the group and scuttled over, her disjointed gait even more pronounced than usual.

'They're saying we can't leave.'

'I think there's been some misunderstanding.' Lowry joined them. 'I was just trying to find out who I need to speak to, in order to clear this up.'

'No misunderstanding,' the man said. 'I've been trying to explain to Mr Lowry and Ms Casella that no one is allowed to leave the capital without the express consent of the temporary administration committee. Emergency protocol.'

'But this was just a stop-over,' Jamie said. 'We're heading to Earth.'

'No one's going anywhere. Not until things settle down.'

'You're grounding the ship?' Jamie said. 'Why?'

The man shook his head. 'I believe the ship and its crew have been cleared for search and rescue.'

'I want to talk to someone else,' Rena said. 'Who's in charge here?'

'I am,' the man said. 'Down here at least.'

'Not you,' Rena said scathingly. 'Someone in authority.'

'Can I help?' The man walking towards them looked faintly familiar, but Jamie couldn't quite place him.

'Carl Doxton,' he said. 'I'm assistant to Evren Buckley, who's in temporary charge of the administration.'

'Why can't we leave?' Rena demanded.

'Ah.' The man's gaze flickered towards the ship. 'Well, at this point I understand that's not an option. The *Phaeacian* will be taking part in our search and rescue operation. I believe they'll be heading out within the next twenty-four hours.'

'We're going to Earth,' Rena said flatly. 'Callan agreed.'

'Plans change,' Doxton said, with a polite smile. 'And besides, we need to gather everyone here. If we're going to rebuild, we need to find out where we stand. Survival rates. Skills. I'm sure individual preferences can be considered in due course. But right now we're in a state of emergency. I'm sure you understand.'

'I'm not sure we do,' Lowry said. 'We can't hope to rebuild what we had. We need to find a new way. There'll be people who don't want to come here, places where there are enough survivors for viable settlements.'

'It's not just about numbers,' Doxton said, as though explaining something to a recalcitrant child. 'It's about skills, balance, finding formulas that work.' He smiled again. 'But no need to worry about all that now. Take a bit of time to rest and recuperate. Once things are more settled, if you still decide you want to move on, the situation can be reviewed.'

'Is it true?' Rena took a couple of steps towards the gangway, shouting up to Gracie. 'Is he leaving us here?'

Gracie glanced over her shoulder, as though looking for someone. She looked tense and unhappy, but made no attempt to answer Rena's question.

'Could we speak to Callan?' Lowry said. 'There may be some crossed wires here.'

Doxton put his arm across Rena's shoulders in an attempt to steer her away. 'No crossed wires. I promise you.'

Rena shook him off furiously. 'You can't do this. We're going to Earth, and you can't stop us.'

Jamie turned and walked away towards the main building. Inside she found a young woman at a desk in the main foyer, dealing with queries from a trail of dazed-looking people. As she walked straight to the front of the queue, a discontented mutter rose behind her.

'Where's Daniel Orton?' Jamie said.

The woman blinked, then gave Jamie a tight smile. 'If you could just—'

'I need to find Daniel. Now. Where is he?'

The woman was looking around nervously. 'I can't give out personal information on administration employees.'

Something inside Jamie snapped. She placed both palms on the desk, leaning forward. 'I lived with him for thirteen years,' she said. 'I miscarried his baby and spent last night in his bed.

If anyone's in a position to dish out personal information on Daniel Orton, it's me.' Her voice echoed around the foyer, and she made an effort to lower her voice. 'I'm not asking for his inside leg measurements. I just can't find him.'

'It's all right.' She turned to see Doxton walking towards them. 'I'll take Ms Allenby up to the boardroom.'

'Wait a minute.' It was a man in the middle of the queue who'd spoken up. He was small and dark-haired, and his face was creased with anger. 'We've been here for hours, and she just waltzes up to the front and gets dealt with.'

Doxton nodded to a security officer loitering by some glass doors in the far corner, and then gestured to Jamie to follow him.

'I'm speaking to you.' The man's voice was growing louder, and it was underpinned by another low rumble from the gathered people. People were pressing closer together, and somehow, imperceptibly, the queue had become a crowd. 'We keep being told to wait. I've got . . .' He broke off, and Jamie saw his hand down by his side, fingers open, as though he was reaching for someone's hand.

The hand curled into a fist. Something ugly entered the man's voice. 'No one cares about people like us. Only about people like her.' As the guard reached him, the man took a step forward. 'It's always the same.' He was shouting now. The main doors opened and more security offers entered. 'Why are we still doing what they say? Why—'

His voice snapped off abruptly, and he pitched forwards, his arms wrapping across his body. It took Jamie a second to realise that the guard had his baton in his hand.

'Miss Allenby.' Doxton had hold of her arm. 'Please. The guards will handle this.'

The other officers were pushing forwards, the sound of the crowd changing from angry to fearful.

'Please,' Doxton said again. 'I think it would be better if you left.'

Jamie couldn't move. There was a bloodless chill in her hands and feet. She felt strung out, like a wire, stretched between the struggling crowd, and the insistent, oh-so-logical voice of the man at her side, slightly chiding and full of the promise of quiet, *normal* corridors beyond those doors.

The crowd was being pushed back. The dark-haired man was still on his knees, dazed from the blow, but his hands were half raised in a gesture of surrender.

Or maybe it was despair.

'It's over,' Doxton said. 'Come with me. Please.'

Jamie let him lead her through the glass doors. He didn't speak, either to excuse or condemn what she had just seen, and she couldn't find the words to challenge him. Her thoughts kept making little sorties towards justification.

Things were on a knife-edge.

This whole thing was unprecedented.

They couldn't risk violence.

But all those reasons seemed to be spoken in someone else's voice.

Doxton's voice?

Daniel's?

No. Daniel wouldn't be part of something like this. Maybe there was nothing to be a part *of*. A one-off incident. There'd probably be a demotion for the guard. An apology, certainly.

Her hands were cold, and her throat felt tight.

They went up in the lift in silence, alighting on the fifth floor, and making their way along a wood-panelled corridor to another set of double doors. Doxton pushed one open and gestured for her to precede him into the room.

The large corner office was dominated by a thellum table, from which all the chairs had been pulled back, to give unrestricted access to the charts and computer screens laid out on the polished surface. Daniel was leaning over one of the e-pads, pointing something out to another man. He looked up as Jamie entered, his expression growing guarded.

'Ms Allenby was looking for you,' Doxton said. 'I brought her up.'

'Thank you.' Daniel's tone was cool. 'What's wrong?'

Jamie glanced at the room's other occupants. 'Can we speak somewhere else?'

Daniel hesitated and then nodded, before leading her out into the corridor.

'What is it?'

The face of the dark-haired man flickered through her mind, but she pushed it away and went straight to her reason for seeking him out.

'Why are we being told we can't leave?'

He raised an eyebrow. 'Where were you planning on going?'

'Earth. That's where we were always heading.'

He studied her. 'I thought you were looking for me.'

'I was, but . . .' She tripped over that tangle of intent. 'I thought you were on Earth.'

'Well, I'm not. I'm here. And if you're telling me you don't want to stay here, then I guess that makes your feelings pretty clear.'

'It's not . . .' The words weren't falling into place. 'I can't stay.'

He looked away. 'Well, no one's being cleared to leave right now. We're assuming most people will want to come to a place where there are other survivors, and a functioning infrastructure.'

'There'll be other survivors on Earth. What's the problem with us going there?'

'Well, there being no one to take you would be one big problem.' He tapped his fingers against the wood panelling.

'Callan agreed to take us.'

'Things change.' Daniel wasn't quite looking her in the eye.

Jamie stared at him. 'What's going on?'

'Nothing. Just a bunch of people trying to do their best for everyone.'

The man on his knees.

'For everyone?'

Resentment blazed in his eyes. 'Yes,' he said. 'For everyone. You think you could do a better job?'

'Maybe,' she said. 'Maybe I'd start by letting people make their own choices.' She looked straight at him. 'And maybe I wouldn't beat the shit out of people for objecting.'

'What do you mean?'

She described the scene in the atrium in a few brief sentences, and he ran his hand through his hair.

'That doesn't sound great.'

'Not great?' Her anger had been trapped somewhere down inside her, muffled by shock. Now she felt it shake loose. 'Is that all you can say?'

He rounded on her. 'What do you want me to say? No, it's not ideal. None of this is ideal. Do you have any idea how close we came to not making it? The human race, I mean. Just another percentage point in the mortality rate and we'd have been finished.'

Another nought in the nought point nought nought nought one.

A thought snagged at her.

'How did so many security and administration personnel make it?'

'There was a drug,' he said. 'Not a cure. And too late to help the settlements. But it boosted the immune system. Gave people a fighting chance. We used it on vital personnel first, obviously.'

'Obviously.'

Anger flared in his eyes once again. 'Maybe you should be running things. But you don't tend to stick around when things get difficult, do you?'

'Looks like I'm being forced to stick around,' Jamie shot back.

'We have to make sure the human race survives.'

'That doesn't mean you have to go around beating people up for opening their mouths at the wrong moment.'

'That's exactly what it means.' He almost shouted it, and she took a step back from him, a whip-crack of shock snapping through her.

He made a visible effort to collect himself, and when he spoke again his voice was quiet, dampened down with something that sounded more like regret than anger.

'We're too fragile. There've been other incidents. The whole thing is close to breaking right open.'

'People are *scared*,' she said.

'And that's why they're dangerous,' Daniel said. 'Frightened people aren't thinking straight.'

'Dangerous? They're broken. That man back there, I think . . .' She broke off, her voice snagging in her throat at the memory of his hand reaching for something she couldn't see. 'I think he'd lost a child.'

'So did we.'

There was pain in his voice, and she took a hard breath in. 'That's different. We never had it in the first place.'

'We could have had it,' Daniel said. 'If you'd stayed.'

'This isn't about us.'

'It could be.' He took a step towards her.

'Stop.' She held her hands up, fending him off. 'I'm talking about what's going on here. It can't be like this. People have to be able to make their own choices.'

He shook his head, looking frustrated. 'We can't risk it. If everyone splinters off into small groups, we're done for.' He stepped in close, his expression softening. 'We can rebuild. But we need everybody to contribute. We need people like you, with your medical knowledge. We need to train the next generation of doctors and engineers. And we don't have long to do it. Once skills are lost, that's it. Not everything can be learned from an e-book or computer.'

'And what about the others?' Jamie said.

'The others?'

'Mila,' she said. 'Finn. You could probably find something for Rena to do. But what about Lowry? Do you really need a preacher? A prostitute?'

'We need everyone,' he said. 'Farmers and labourers, as much as doctors and teachers.'

'And what if people don't want to be farmers and labourers? It's all very well for people like Doxton and the others. They're doing pretty much what they did before. But you can't just allocate people roles in some new society, and expect them to fall into line. What if it's not what they want?'

There was an odd look on his face, a mix of guilt and defiance, and it took her a moment to realise what it meant.

'You don't care about them,' she said slowly. 'Do you? You don't care what the little people want. Not as long as everyone does what they're told, and you're on the side that does the telling.'

He shook his head, but there was a heaviness to the gesture that made it look more like a concession than a denial. 'It's not like that.'

'It is like that. It's going to be like forced emigration all over again.' Callan's face flickered in her mind. 'Instead of making people leave, you're going to force them to stay and work.'

'Everyone's going to have to work.' Frustration coloured his tone. 'All of us. Do you see me sitting on my backside, pondering where I might like to go on a bit of a jaunt? No. I'm here, trying to help rebuild our world.'

'What is it you even do here? You worked in statistics. How does that equip you to help run things?'

'Someone's got to do it,' he snapped back at her. 'And realistically it's going to be—'

'The upper echelon,' she put in. 'That's it, isn't it?'

He rounded on her. 'How else do you think it's going to work? The people who finish up in charge are generally the ones best placed to be there. The ones who understand how things work, who can make difficult decisions. Not the ones who start fights in queues and try to raid the food stores. You don't get it, do you? Just what a big gulf there is between the people at the top, and everyone else, particularly out in the colonies. We used to have the luxury of pretending none of that was true, that everyone was just the same. But now everything's been stripped away, all but the bare bones. We can't keep on pretending.'

'My God.' She stared at him. 'What happened to you?'

'I spent some time in the real world,' he said. 'You know, the one you did your level best to avoid.' He put a hand to his forehead. 'Look. No one's saying this is a perfect plan, or that it will be a perfect world, but it never was. We all muddle through as best we can. And, to be fair . . .' He forced a small smile. 'The human race hasn't done too badly.'

'The human race has come close to being wiped out.'

'But we weren't.' Daniel reached for her hand. 'We've survived. We have to find a way to go on. We have to make it mean something.'

She pulled her hand away. 'More than being alive?'

'What's wrong with that? People have always tried to make their lives mean something. They've always been thinking about the future, the next generations.'

'The next . . .' She broke off. *That man. His empty hand.* 'How many children?'

He didn't answer straight away.

'How many?' she asked again. 'How many children survived?'

He looked away. 'None. As far as we know. Parents don't leave their sick children to fend for themselves. No children, and no parents of young children, except a few men working away from their families.'

'So when you talk about rebuilding, you're not just talking about the infrastructure, are you? You're talking about the human race.'

He nodded. 'There's got to be a next generation. Otherwise what's the point?'

She could feel the hollow space beneath the curve of her stomach, as clearly as if that loss was new. 'Us.' Her voice caught in her throat again. 'We're the point. We're not just a stepping stone for the future of the species. People have to be able to choose what kind of life to lead.'

'People have never had that sort of freedom,' Daniel said. 'There's never been a time when we could just please ourselves.'

'But things could be different.' She was losing track of what the conversation was about. 'People could make real choices. We could build something better.'

'We will. But it's not going to be as easy as you think.'

There was an odd tension in his voice.

'What?' She searched his face, but he wasn't meeting her eyes. 'What are you not telling me?'

He put both hands to his face, rubbing at his eyes. He looked bone-tired and she felt a pang of reluctant tenderness.

'The virus,' he said. 'It had an odd life cycle. It attacked the reproductive organs first. We've had several survivors complaining of stomach pains, and some women with bleeding. We don't have the personnel to do proper testing, but the preliminary indications are that at least a proportion of the survivors are infertile.'

'A proportion?' Jamie said. 'How many are we talking about?'

'It's possible that all survivors have sustained damage to their reproductive systems.'

He sounded as though he was making a public announcement, the impact of it muffled by a packing of medical terms and administrative jargon. She half expected him to urge her not to panic, and to stay in her home awaiting further information.

'So what are you saying? That this is it for the human race? It ends with us?'

'We're not giving up. It might not be everyone, and it might be reversible. But it's not going to be a case of people skipping off into the sunset with instructions to go forth and multiply. Nature might need a bit of help.' He held her gaze. 'And we need help. From medics and research scientists. We need you. Your area was fertility.'

'In animals,' she said. 'Not people.'

'The principles are the same. And there's only a handful of other people with relevant expertise. You could make a huge difference here.' He hesitated before adding, 'And so could women like your shipmate, Mila.'

'Mila?' She stared at him, unable to process what he was saying. 'What's Mila got to do with this?'

'She's young.' Daniel didn't bother trying to soften the blunt edges of his words. 'If there's any chance of reversing the effects of the virus, younger women are our best hope. And it's not as though . . .' He stopped and looked away.

'Not as though what?' Jamie said. 'Not as though she's got a choice?'

He gave a slight shrug, still not looking at her.

Understanding dawned. 'Not as though it matters. That's what you mean, isn't it?'

He gave a sharp shake of his head and finally met her gaze. 'You know I don't think like that. I just meant that she hasn't exactly had things easy so far. Why wouldn't she want a chance for something better? A chance to be part of something better?'

'So what are we talking about here?' Jamie said. 'Some sort of breeding programme? People forced to reproduce for the greater good? In between working in the fields, obviously.' She gave a cough of laughter. 'Christ, it's only been days. People are in shock, grieving, and you're up here planning some sort of state-sanctioned prostitution. What sort of society would we be, if it began with something like that? With sexual slavery? We'd be poisoned right from the start. We've got to be better than we were, or what's the point of any of this? What's the point of us surviving?'

His expression hardened again. 'We're just trying to come up with a plan that doesn't involve the human race dying out on our watch.'

'But why is it your watch? Why should people commit their lives to building something where other people get to sit on top and tell them what to do? If what you say is right, this may be the end. Maybe people should get to live out the last days of our race in whatever way they choose.'

'It's not the end,' he said. 'It can't be. And if some people can't grasp the need for us to work together, then that just drives home how *vital* it is for those who can see the bigger picture to take charge.'

'People won't do it,' she said. 'How will you make them?'

'Trust me.' His voice was quiet again. 'We can make them.'

Last night his hands had been all over her body. The thought made her feel sick. Every other time he'd touched her over the years, it all felt like collusion now, as if she'd always been a part of what was coming.

'I'm not staying,' she said. 'Find someone else.'

'You are.' His tone was harder than any he'd ever directed towards her. 'No one's leaving.'

'I won't. Not here, and not with you. I'm going to talk to Buckley.'

'Fine.' He turned back towards the boardroom. 'Good luck with that.'

Jamie waited until she was round the corner before leaning against the wall and pressing the heels of her hands against her eyes. Thirteen years. She'd spent thirteen years of her life with him, and this is where they'd been heading all the time.

She took a deep breath, straightened up and headed off in search of Buckley.

CHAPTER SIXTEEN

The day wound tighter and tighter around Jamie. Buckley wasn't available. His deputy was sorry, but sure Jamie understood how busy things were. Maybe if she came back later? The resettlement committee were sympathetic but it was out of their hands. The head of security was not at all sympathetic, and he most certainly did not want her to come back later.

Around lunchtime, she went in search of Lowry, but could only find Mila and Finn, sitting together in the far corner of the communal dining hall. As she walked towards them, a couple of young security officers stopped beside their table. One of them said something to Mila, running his hand down her arm in a quick, suggestive touch. The girl flushed and looked down.

'Is there a problem?' Jamie said, stepping up beside them.

The security officer's gaze flickered to her ID mark, his expression reforming into polite neutrality.

'No problem, ma'am. Excuse us.'

'What was that about?' Jamie asked Mila, as the men walked away.

'Nothing.' Mila's expression was closed, and Jamie let it go.

No, Mila hadn't seen the others since they'd been turned back from the ship. They hadn't even been allowed to unload their things. Could Jamie maybe speak to someone?

'You may not need to unload anything,' Jamie said. 'If I can just speak to Buckley, we may be able to sort something out.'

Mila shot her a dubious look. Jamie couldn't blame her.

'Just my bags,' the girl said. 'That's all I need.'

'When are we going to Earth?' Finn looked up at Jamie.

'He keeps asking that,' Mila said. 'I don't know what to tell him.'

'I'll sort it out,' Jamie said again.

She found Lowry out on one of the terraces with his arm around a weeping Rena. As Jamie approached, he gently disentangled himself, but Rena clung on, leaning into him, her spare frame racked by gasping sobs.

'What's happening?' Lowry asked.

'I'm trying to speak to the guy in charge, but he's pretty elusive, and no one else seems particularly inclined to help.'

'What about Daniel?'

'He can't help.'

'I can't stay here.' Rena twisted round to fix Jamie with a pleading gaze. 'They have to let us go.'

Lowry put his hand on her back. 'We'll get this sorted.'

'We might,' Jamie said. 'Or we might be stuck here until the administration figures out there are too few of us left to get away with treating people like something they can catalogue and stockpile.'

'Why are they so set on keeping everyone here?' Lowry asked. 'Surely it won't make any difference if the odd few want to go off and do their own thing.'

'Depends on who those few are,' Jamie said. 'Medics and those of childbearing age seem to be fairly high on their wish list.'

'They want to repopulate the world.' Lowry sounded resigned. 'That figures.'

'Not just that.' Jamie hesitated. 'There's something else. The virus . . . they think . . .' She broke off, staring at Rena.

The other woman's face was grey-white, her eyes dark and hollow. The old cliché echoed in Jamie's mind.

You look like you've seen a ghost.

'What about the virus?' Lowry said, dragging her attention away from Rena.

'They think it attacked people's fertility,' she said. 'They don't know whether anyone will be able to have children.'

'We have to leave.' Rena's arms were wrapped defensively across her body.

'I'm trying,' Jamie said. 'But like I said, they—'

'I can't stay.' Rena's voice was rising. 'I can't be here.'

I can't stay here had been the one strand of clarity in Jamie's mind, running from last night's encounter with Daniel to that final decision to carry on to Earth. Maybe Callan was right. Maybe people did live their lives in the negative.

I can't be here.

I don't love you.

This isn't what I want.

'Rena . . .' Lowry began, but the older woman twisted round and backed away.

'I can't,' she said again, and then her voice spiralled up into a near scream, although neither Lowry nor Jamie had tried to argue. 'I can't.'

She turned and stumbled away towards the steps at the end of the terrace.

'What's wrong with her?' Jamie asked.

'Long story.'

'I seem to have time.' She leaned against the low wall.

Lowry came and stood beside her, looking out across the city. 'It's a sensitive topic,' he said carefully. 'Fertility, I mean.'

'What do you mean?'

'Rena's infertile,' he said bluntly. 'Or as good as. She's got a genetic condition. She can conceive, but the defective egg will always be rejected by her body. That's why she went into that line of research. To try and find a way of overriding the damaged gene. It was the worst thing she could have done, of course. Her personal obsession got tangled up with all the demands they put on her. And I think they knew that. And used it.'

'They?' Every fraught encounter with the other woman was taking on new shades and hues, all coming together in a kaleidoscope of shifting motivations.

'Her employers,' Lowry said. 'The administration.'

'You think they manipulated her? Why?'

He was silent for a moment. 'You didn't know her then,' he said eventually. 'What you see now, it's just the bare shreds of the woman I knew. She was bright, super bright, with that kind of cleverness that sparks off in all sorts of directions, too fast for you to have any hope of keeping up. But she never made you feel stupid because you weren't as clever. She was kind, too.' He chewed on his lip. 'No, that's not the right word for it. She was desperately eager to do the right thing, and when someone was in trouble, she always wanted to help. But she was nervous of getting it wrong, so sometimes she'd stop just short of doing or saying what she should. Some people found her difficult. They didn't realise how hard she was trying, and when she attempted to explain herself, or put things right, they'd get irritated with her. I think her colleagues "got" her a bit more than most people. Anyway, from what I could tell, she was one of their prize assets. She came up with ideas, directions no one else had thought of. Some of her work jumped them forwards years in their research. They had to keep her, at all costs.'

'But why would they need to manipulate her?' Jamie said. 'If she was on board with what they were doing.'

Lowry shook his head. 'Even back then she had doubts, fits

of anxiety.' He gave a heavy smile. 'It was her faith, of course. What she was doing couldn't have been more at odds with the teachings of the Church. She had a couple of major crises over the years, disappearing for several days, saying she was going to quit. But they always managed to talk her back. I don't know exactly what they said, but I have my suspicions. She'd always be . . . different for a while afterwards. Uplifted. Like she'd seen something that really mattered.'

'What exactly *were* they doing?' Jamie asked. 'It all sounds . . . I don't know. A lot more cloak-and-dagger than any research department I had dealings with.'

Lowry shot a quick look over his shoulder. 'It still feels wrong saying it. Even after everything that's happened. Like someone's going to pop up from behind a pillar and "off" me. Not that the administration have ever worked that way.' His smile twisted. 'We left all that behind us, after all. That was the idea anyway. That we'd outgrown oppression. We'd escaped our overcrowded world and found somewhere with enough space for everyone.' He picked at a piece of grit, lodged in a crack in the stone wall. 'Except it turned out that all the fighting over immigration and borders was never about too many people. It was about too many of the wrong sort of people.' He placed the grit fragment down on top of the wall, and flicked it over the edge. 'Rena's department were working on ways to restrict the fertility of certain socio-ethnic groups. They'd identified some combinations of genetic markers – they called them keyhole genes – that were restricted to certain socio-economic communities. The kind of communities who had lived in the same city ghetto for several generations. Communities that had sprung up around old refugee camps. Ethnic groups with a tradition of close-kin marriages.'

'Christ.' Jamie stared at him in shock. 'It sounds like something the Nazis would have come up with. Why would they want to do that?'

They'd both lowered their voices, and she found herself throwing a nervous glance over her own shoulder.

'Exactly the same reason as the Nazis. Because they thought they could make the world into what they wanted it to be. They thought they could make the human race into what they wanted it to be. They'd already started working on it before we managed to get ourselves off Earth. They justified it as a way to control the worldwide birth rate. Then when population size stopped being an immediate issue, they figured it might be time for a fresh start, to make sure the new, space-age human race was smarter and healthier than before. The forced emigration programmes were all part of the same idea. Ship the undesirables off to a couple of colonies, and leave the home world for those who could afford to stay. Maybe a few decent people got caught up in the exodus, but greater good and all that.'

'How do you know all this?' Jamie asked. She couldn't quite take in the truly monstrous scale of what he was telling her, and she clutched at the thread of the smaller, more personal story running at the heart of it.

'I was Rena's confessor,' Lowry said, and then, 'I know, I know,' at Jamie's sharp look. 'But it's been twenty years, and that particular faith was ground out of both of us long ago.'

'But you kept it a secret until now?'

'Like I said, the confessional meant something to me back then.' He shifted his weight, one hand going to his lower back. 'No, it wasn't just that. I've been telling myself that for twenty years, but I've always known it wasn't the whole truth. The political situation was so delicate back then. I believed wholeheartedly – and I still do – that the colonisation of other worlds was the only chance our species had. I thought . . . or rather I convinced myself, that to make what I knew public would be to risk the stability of what we were trying to build.' He gave her another of those weighted smiles. 'The greater good. It's got to be the most commonly used justification for moral cowardice in the history of the human race. Anyway, there you have it. Rena was part of something she could never quite square with her conscience or her faith. And it ripped her apart.'

'And for nothing,' Jamie said. 'They never managed it. Thank Christ.'

Lowry looked out across the city. 'No.'

'I guess that explains why she's so horrified at the idea of being involved with some new fertility programme.' Even as she said it, she had a sense that the connection she'd made was too flimsy. That look on Rena's face . . .

But then Lowry had said it himself: Rena was just the shredded fragments of what she'd once been. There was no reason to think that her logic was sound, or her fears proportional.

'Do they know?' she asked. 'Buckley and the others? Do they know she was involved?'

Lowry nodded. 'Someone came to speak to her this morning. Lots of skirting round the subject with talk of skill sets and specialist knowledge, rather than coming right out and saying what he meant. But yes, they know.' He shook his head and looked away for a long moment. 'You think there's any chance of them letting us leave?' he said eventually.

'I don't know.' Jamie pulled her thoughts away from Rena. 'I'll keep trying.'

Back upstairs, she made another visit to Buckley's office, and this time she found him in situ. He listened, politely enough, and then explained, in distant, dispassionate logic, why his way was the only way. Jamie was close to losing her temper again, but she could see that it wouldn't dent Buckley's calm. She looked out of the window, searching for the right words.

The sky was clear, with the occasional vague wisp of cloud. It looked wrong, somehow, and it took her a moment to realise she'd never seen the Alegrian sky when it wasn't shot through with vapour trails.

That's how the Northumbrian sky would look right now, unmarked and endless. They'd come in on the coast road, the dunes rising up to guide them in, and then, when they crested those scrubby slopes, they'd see two expanses of blue: the thin, grey-blue of the sky meeting the deeper teal of the sea. She could picture them: Lowry, hand pressed to his chest; Rena, shading her eyes with one thin, shaking hand; Finn, shooting quick sideways glances at the sea, as though it might suddenly break its bounds and rush him; Mila, skirt tucked up above her knees as she paddled, with no one watching her and thinking *those* thoughts.

There was an ache inside Jamie's chest as she turned back to Buckley. 'Look,' she said. 'I'll do you a deal. You need medics. I'll stay, help you get things set up. Then we'll see about later.' She folded her arms. 'But you let the others go on to Earth.'

He sat back in his chair, and regarded her, his gaze level. 'I'm sorry,' he said. 'I'm not in a position to make any such concessions for your friends. The situation will, of course, remain subject to review.'

'But—'

'Miss Allenby, I've explained the position. And even if I were minded to make an exception, there are no ships available at this time.'

'The *Phaeacian* is available.'

'The captain of the *Phaeacian* has agreed to undertake search and rescue work as an administration contractor.'

'Contractor?' She almost laughed. Even with all that had happened, people were still clinging to the language of a world that no longer existed. 'You're paying him?'

'In fuel,' Buckley said, just beginning to show the first fault lines of impatience. 'We will ensure his ship is kept fuelled and supplied for as long as he continues to transport survivors from the outer worlds.'

'In . . .' She stopped, all hope falling away. She'd tried to do a deal with someone who was actually practised in that kind of horse trading. He'd found the one thing that would bring Callan to heel. Access to the fuel he needed to keep his ship in the air once the small planetary stores were exhausted. 'Transport survivors? You mean, bring you a workforce, slaves to keep the wheels turning, so you don't have to.'

Buckley stood up. He was taller than Jamie remembered, and as his shadow fell over her she found herself wanting to take a step back.

'We're done here, Miss Allenby.'

Down in the foyer, Jamie joined the much reduced queue for the information desk, and asked for a room. The young woman raised her eyebrows as she checked through her list.

'You're down as sharing with Daniel Orton.'

'No.' Jamie met her look for look. 'That's not correct.'

The woman hesitated, then gave a slight shrug. 'Room 521. Fifth floor. Shared sitting room.'

It took Jamie another hour to extract permission to retrieve her belongings from the *Phaeacian*, by which time she couldn't face queuing again to ask where the other passengers were roomed. She'd get her things and find out how long the ship was going to be there. Then she could let the others know the position.

The hold doors were open, but there was no sign of Callan or Gracie. Jamie packed quickly, shoving her belongings into her old rucksack with little care for the state of her already crumpled clothes.

On her way back down, she caught a faint clatter from a service passage. She hesitated for a moment, then dropped her rucksack and squeezed through, emerging by the bridge. Callan was lying on his back, head and shoulders wedged into a hatchway, shining a small torch up into the guts of the ship.

At the sound of her footsteps, he twisted his head to peer out.

'I came to get my things,' she said. 'Doesn't look like we're leaving any time soon.'

'No.' He looked back up at whatever he was doing. 'Guess not.'

'You guess?' Jamie's emotions were on a rollercoaster today. No sooner had she free-wheeled down into something like resignation, she'd find her anger gathering speed again, ready for the ascent. 'You're the one who took this deal of theirs.'

Callan took hold of the edge of the hatchway and eased himself out, then climbed to his feet.

'It wasn't exactly a choice,' he said. 'They've made their position clear. They weren't going to let you head off to Earth, even if I refused to help them out.'

'Did you even try? They might have agreed, if you held out. They aren't exactly overrun with ships. They need you.'

'They need the ship,' Callan said. 'What if they'd just decided to take it?'

'They need people to fly them too.'

'There'll be other people who can fly. I couldn't risk it.'

'So you sacrificed our freedom for yours.'

'Don't be so melodramatic,' Callan said. 'You weren't going anywhere. I could either finish up in the same position, or I could knuckle down and take what was on offer.'

'With the added bonus of unlimited fuel.'

'Can't rescue people without fuel.'

'And that's what's uppermost in your mind,' Jamie flung at him. 'Saving the day. Being a hero.'

'No.' Callan wiped his oil-stained hands on a rag. 'But fortunately what I want and what they want run hand in hand.'

'And what about the rest of us? What about what we want?'

He raised an eyebrow. 'You've figured out what you want, have you?'

She made an impatient gesture. 'You know what I mean.'

'I'm not sure *you* know what you mean,' he said, tossing the rag back down again. 'And I think you probably want to have a good hard look at what you're being offered. You could have a nice, safe life here, in your nice, safe upper-echelon world.'

'That's not what I want.'

'We don't always get what we want,' he said. 'Sometimes you just have to get over it and do the best you can with what you have.'

'You didn't,' she said.

'What?'

'You didn't get over it,' she said. 'You left your brother behind because you wanted your freedom. And you've never got over it. But you're doing it again. To us.'

'You're not my responsibility.' Callan's voice stayed level, but there was a muscle tightening in his cheek. 'Anyway, this is the capital world. Plenty of food and space and luxury for everyone.'

'Not everyone,' she said. 'That's not the plan. Those people you're bringing in for them, well, they'd better be upper echelon.'

'What's that supposed to mean?'

'Figure it out for yourself.' She started to turn away.

He caught her arm. 'Tell me.'

'What do you think I mean? Everyone's going to need to know their place in the new order, that's all, and their lords and masters are going to make sure they knuckle down. Lots of little cogs in the administration's big, shiny machine. Just like it's always been, only without even the illusion of choice this time. No chance of opting out of the breeding programme. But that doesn't matter, does it? As long as you have your freedom.'

'It won't be like that.' There was a hint of doubt just showing through a narrow crack in his composure. 'There isn't enough of the old administration left to enforce that sort of set-up.'

'How much time have you spent off the ship?' Jamie said. 'Have you seen how they're dealing with anyone who isn't happy with their plans?'

'Things will shake down. Governments are always heavy-handed when there's a crisis.' He shot her a swift look. 'And if they're so all-powerful, why are you blaming me for falling into line like the rest of you?'

'In a crisis?' Jamie ignored his last dig. 'And any other time they fancy doing something unpopular. You, of all people, should know that.'

Anger flickered across Callan's face. He turned away to crouch down by the hatchway again. 'I'm busy. If you just came to harangue me, then you can get off my ship. Or did you have any other business here?'

She shook her head, not trusting herself to speak.

'Okay.' Callan lay back down and pulled himself in through the hatch. 'See you around then.'

'I doubt that,' Jamie said, as she walked away.

CHAPTER SEVENTEEN

Jamie spent the rest of the evening in her room, listening to people coming and going outside her door. Once she heard someone crying. Around ten, Daniel knocked on the door and called her name. When she didn't respond, he went away without trying a second time.

After he'd gone Jamie climbed into bed and turned off the light. She had no sense that the morning would bring any relief, but at least she could hope for a few hours of forgetfulness. She tried to steady her thoughts, but they kept lurching from one dead end to another. Sheer exhaustion eventually tipped the balance, and she stumbled into unsettled sleep.

It could have been minutes or hours later when she was jerked awake. She lay still, eyes open, searching the grey-dark of the unfamiliar room, trying to work out what had broken her sleep.

It came again. A cautious knock, followed by a low, muffled voice, like someone pressed close to the door. 'Jamie.'

Not Daniel. But the voice was too distorted to make any identification beyond that.

Callan.

No. She dismissed that thought immediately.

She pulled her shirt over her head, and went over to the door, opening it a crack and peering out.

Lowry was fully dressed, a rucksack slung across his shoulders.

'What—'

He jerked a finger to his lips.

'We're going.' His voice was low and tense. 'If you want to come with us, get your stuff and head down to the ship.'

'The ship? He said—'

'Change of plan. Or change of heart. Doesn't matter. Are you coming?'

She hesitated. She'd been so sure just a few hours ago, but now . . .

'No time for that.' Lowry had seen straight into the roiling mess of her indecision. 'Come, or don't come.'

She breathed in hard. 'Okay.'

Lowry gave her a quick smile. 'Good. Go down the back way. Not through the foyer.'

'Isn't anyone watching the ship?'

'They were.' Lowry's expression was grim.

As he padded off, she ducked back inside her room. She dressed, but shoved her boots into her bag, before heading out into the corridor, her bare feet silent on the cold floor.

At the bottom of the emergency stairwell, she paused, looking out across the exposed concrete landing site. The bay doors of the *Phaeacian* were open, but the gangway wasn't down, and there were no lights showing. She couldn't see anyone moving, inside the ship or out on the forecourt. She let herself out, and jogged across to the ship, splinters of grit digging into her feet. She kept waiting for a warning cry, but she reached the ship without incident, and scrambled up into the cargo bay with her bag.

'Jamie.'

A small group of figures blurred into focus as her eyes adjusted to the semi-darkness. Lowry was standing off to the side with Mila and Finn. Finn had his little rucksack, while Mila had shed all but one bag which she was clutching with both hands.

'Where's Rena?' Jamie kept her voice low.

'Should be on her way.' Lowry edged over to the door and peered out. 'She said she had to pick something up.'

Jamie felt her pulse quickening. They didn't have time. Mila moved over to join them at the doors. Her face was set.

'What is it?' Jamie said.

'I don't know.' Mila pulled her bag tighter against her chest. 'I don't know about this.'

'What do you mean?'

The girl shook her head, tears starting in her eyes. 'I have to get off. I don't know why I came.'

'What are you talking about?' Lowry reached out to take Mila's hand. 'We're going to Earth. All of us.'

'What would I do on Earth? Rena keeps talking about a new world, but the people here want the old one back.'

'Was it kind to you?' Lowry asked. 'The old world?'

Mila looked away. 'No one's kind. Not to people like me.' She looked at Jamie. 'You were. Or you tried to be. But you know what you want. I don't, and there won't be a place for me where you're going. I don't want to be left on my own when I don't fit in.'

'Mila.' Lowry gave her a little shake. 'We'd never leave you alone. Come with us.'

'But you're going to that island, to the religious place. I couldn't go there with you.'

'Why not?'

She gave a convulsive shake of her head. 'It wouldn't work. I wouldn't fit.'

'What about me?' Jamie said. 'I'm not going to Lindisfarne. I'm just going . . .' She stopped. She'd almost said *home*. 'To the place I'm from. You could come with me. You and Finn.'

'And what about . . .' It was Mila's turn to break off.

'What about what?'

'It doesn't matter.' Mila looked away. 'I'd be in the way.'

'Mila,' Lowry tried again, but the girl took a step back.

'No,' she said. 'I want to stay here. I don't want to go with you.'

'You can't,' Jamie said. 'You don't know what they're planning.'

'I'm not stupid,' Mila said. 'I can figure it out. And what's to say it will be so bad? We're coming at this from different places, you and me. You look at this and think it's not going to be as good as what you had. But for me, maybe it'll be better. There might be a place for me. I might be able to do something good.'

'What's going on?' Jamie turned to see Callan moving through the gloom of the hold.

'Mila's not sure about coming,' Lowry said.

'Well, she better make her mind up quick.' Callan was walking towards the doors. 'We have to go.'

Lowry put his hand out to stop him. 'Rena's not here yet.'

'Where the fuck is she?'

'She needed to pick something up. She said it was important.'

'It better be. Because whatever it is, she may be staying here with it.' Callan's lips tightened. 'One minute, then whoever's on board will be coming, and everyone else will just have to take their chances.'

Lowry turned to Mila, but she was backing away.

'Take care of Finn,' she said, and then she scrambled down onto the concourse and set off towards the tower entrance.

Lowry caught Jamie's arm, holding her back from following. 'Don't.'

'Thirty seconds.' Callan's hand was on the lever.

Lowry shuffled to the edge of the hold. 'She must . . .' His head jerked up. 'There she is.'

An ungainly figure lurched into view, coming from some-where to the side of the landing site.

'Where's she been?' Jamie watched Rena hurrying towards the ship, a small bag clutched in her arms.

Lowry had no chance to answer, as a shout went up from somewhere out of Jamie's line of sight.

Callan swore and hit the lever, starting the slow, inevitable slide of the doors.

'Gracie.' He shouted it into the tannoy, then ran for the stairs.

Security guards were running in from all directions, guns in their hands. There was an explosion of shouting, of threats, but Rena kept stumbling towards the ship. Then a voice rose above the tangle of noise.

'Stop. Stop or I will shoot.'

Rena's gaze was fixed on the ship and its closing doors. The guard lifted his gun and trained it on her.

He wouldn't. They wouldn't.

But then Jamie saw the cold glint in his eye, and the way his hands shifted on the gun, and she knew what was going to happen, right there in front of her.

Rena had reached the ship, and Lowry was leaning down to grab her arm, as she scrabbled to pull herself up.

Another voice cut across the clamour.

'No.'

Mila was rushing forwards, her hands up, as though she could stop what was happening. A gunshot echoed around the shipyard, and the girl cried out and fell to her knees. All the noise seemed to be coming from far away. Jamie's lips had shaped themselves around Mila's name, but she couldn't hear her own voice. Lowry dragged Rena through the closing gap, turning sideways to squeeze inside. Just as the doors closed, Jamie saw Mila lift her head to look at the ship. One hand was pressed to her side, blood welling between her fingers. Then she was gone, and the engines were starting their swift-rising roar.

A howl went up, and Finn stumbled forwards, clawing at the doors. When Jamie tried to push him back towards the seats, he fought against her hold, writhing in her grasp with single-minded desperation. With Lowry's help she managed to wrestle him across the hold, but it was beyond their strength to force him into a seat. As he threw himself onto the floor, Jamie sank down with him, hanging on as tight as she could, and suddenly he wasn't fighting her any more. He was letting her hold on to him.

It was another hard acceleration, and Jamie had to brace herself against the wall, digging her heels into one of the grooves in the floor, to hold the two of them steady against the wrenching forces of the ship's ascent. Finn was still, with just the occasional spasm running through him.

Gradually the engines eased back, and Jamie felt the odd shift of gravity that told her they'd levelled off. She suddenly wished she was up front with Callan, or Gracie, or whoever had taken them up. Callan, she thought. She didn't know what made her sure of that, but there was something about the way the ship had moved, a certain exultant leap that made her think of his hands on the controls.

As the hold lights came on, Finn stayed curled tightly in her arms. She looked up at Lowry.

'What happened?' She wasn't sure quite what she was asking. Her head was a tangle of noise and motion; running, shouting, gunshots. And Mila . . .

'I don't know.' Lowry had chosen one of the more straight-forward versions of her question. 'Callan found me and said he'd take us to Earth, if we still wanted to go. I rather assumed you'd had something to do with his change of heart.'

'It's a sign.' Rena shook the harness off. Her face was lit up. 'We're *right*. We're going the right way. We just have to put our faith in God.'

Jamie felt a surge of something close to hatred. She disentangled herself from Finn and climbed to her feet. 'Pity we can't put our faith in you. We almost didn't make it. And Mila . . .'

As she broke off, unable to find the right words to frame what had just happened, Lowry put his hand on her shoulder.

'She'll be okay,' he said. 'They wouldn't have been shooting to kill.'

'But he wasn't aiming at her.' Jamie rounded on Rena. 'He was aiming at you. Mila saved you.'

Rena's expression was serene. 'God saved me.'

'God's not the one lying bleeding on the ground back there.' Jamie's anger was a hot blaze in her veins.

'That's not my fault,' Rena said. 'I just needed some things from my old lab.'

'What things?' Lowry said, turning to stare at her.

Rena's gaze flickered. 'Some medical stuff. I thought we might need it.'

'So Mila got shot for the sake of something you *might* need.'

Finn had his hands pressed to his ears, and Lowry stepped over to his side. He said Finn's name a couple of times, and the lad eventually dropped his hands and looked up at him.

'Why don't you go and put your things back in your cabin,' the old man said.

'Mila.'

'She'll be fine.' Lowry sounded certain. 'They'll be helping her right now.'

Finn nodded, but he was plucking at his sleeve.

'Go on,' Lowry said gently. 'Go put your things away. You know the way?'

'Yes.'

Jamie waited until he was out of earshot before turning to Lowry.

'They shot her,' she said. 'Just like that.'

Lowry touched her arm. 'She'll be okay.'

'And then what?' Jamie said. 'We should never have left her.'

'She made her choice,' Lowry said. 'Just like we did.'

Jamie's thoughts were too tangled and overwrought for her to argue the point.

'And what about Callan?' she went on. 'He's changed his mind once already. What if he changes it back again?'

'I said I'd take you to Earth.' It was Callan's voice, and Jamie looked up to see him leaning on the gallery rail, looking down at them.

'How do we know you won't get fed up with us again, and dump us on the next place we pass?'

He gave a slight smile. 'Last time I checked there were no habitable worlds between here and Earth.'

'You were going to leave us,' she said.

'But I didn't, did I?' His voice was quiet, but there was something beneath it that Jamie couldn't quite interpret. She opened her mouth to push the point, but he brought his hand up, cutting her off. 'We could argue this all night. You're here, aren't you? I'm not going to make you all sorts of promises, but I'll do what I can to get you to Earth.'

'Won't they come after us?' Lowry asked.

'There were no other ships at the landing site,' Callan said. 'By the time they get out to the port and get one ready, we'll be well on our way. Now if you'll excuse me, it's late. I need to get some sleep.'

'He's right,' Lowry said, as Callan walked away. 'We should all get to bed.' He looked at Jamie closely. 'Are you all right?'

She didn't answer. There was an odd, constricted feeling in her chest.

'Want to talk about it?'

She shook her head. 'Maybe some other time.'

Back in her old cabin, Jamie sat in front of the little desk, fiddling with a twist of wire. She felt muffled, dull-edged, as though the events of the last twenty-four hours had blunted her emotions.

Daniel.

His name brought a brush of ... *something*, but she couldn't quite interpret the feeling.

Her mouth was dry, but the tap in her cabin always produced a lukewarm drizzle that tasted of metal. She stood up, her chair scraping on the metal floor, and went out of her cabin, and down to the hold, where she fished a bottle of water out of the cold box, and took a gulp.

On her way back, she somehow found herself walking along the passage that led to Callan's quarters. She hesitated outside his door, and then knocked, a quick rattle of sound, over-loud in the empty corridor.

'Who is it?'

What was she doing? If she moved quickly, she could be out of sight before he got to the door, and he'd never even know she'd been here.

The door opened and Callan looked out, his eyebrows going up when he saw her.

'Problem?' he said. 'Or are you just here for round two of the accusations and recriminations?'

'Why did you change your mind?'

He looked at her for a long moment. 'Does it matter?'

'Yes.' Her mouth was suddenly dry again. 'It matters.'

He stepped back from the door, his expression unreadable. 'You'd better come in.'

She felt a rush of light-headedness as she followed him into the cabin. There was something unreal about the situation.

The door clicked shut behind her. For a moment they stared at one another, not speaking, and then he looked away, rubbing one hand along his jaw. There was a wariness in his eyes. 'Look,' he began. 'I don't—'

She stepped forwards and took hold of his face, pushing his hand away, spreading her fingers out so that she could tug his head down towards hers.

'Jamie . . .' He resisted briefly, and then his breath was warm on her face, and he was too near for her to do anything but close her eyes and open her lips. For a moment, breath was all there was, and then she felt the faintest brush of his mouth on hers. A stab of wanting went through her, strong enough to knock her off balance. She couldn't remember ever feeling like this before. Or was that how memory worked? The old passions fading, and edging away, self-effacing and trying to pretend they'd never been there at all? *Oh no, not us. You don't need to worry about us.* With Daniel, she'd . . .

No. She wrenched her thoughts away.

She must have made some inadvertent movement, because he pulled back a little. She opened her eyes to see him looking at her. That wariness was still there, playing about the edges of his expression, but there were other things there too.

'Jamie, I . . .'

She shook her head, a sharp gesture. 'I don't want to talk.'

She wanted him to touch her.

No, not him. And not her. That was how sex was, when it worked like it should. It wasn't you. There was just the feel of it, of his hands on your body, and your hands on his, and that great, swelling force inside your chest, driving everything else out, until you stopped being so *you*, and became something else entirely.

He moved away slightly. 'What do you want then?'

She didn't answer him. Just one step forward and their bodies were pressed close again. She rose up on tiptoe and brushed her lips down the line of his jaw.

'Stop.' He said it quietly.

She slid a hand in under the edge of his shirt, her thumb brushing over his ribs. There was a soft line of hair running down his breastbone. She could feel the slight curl of it against her fingertips. She brought her other hand up and eased the bottom button of his shirt through the hole, before moving up to the next one. She felt him take a hard breath in. The next button caught, and she had to use both hands to slide it free.

As though that snag had brought him back to himself, he made a sudden swift movement, catching both of her wrists in his hands.

'We're not doing this.' His eyes were dark, and there was a faint flush across his neck. 'You don't want to do this.'

'Does it look like I don't want to do this?'

'Okay.' He tightened his grip. 'I don't want to do this.'

When she looked up at him, he turned away, but not before she'd seen what was stirring behind his eyes.

She gave a low laugh that didn't sound like her. 'Yes, you do.'

He stood still as she curled her body against his again, reaching up to draw his face back down to hers. His lips parted, and then he was kissing her again, one hand coming up to twine in her hair, the other pressing against the small of her back, pulling her harder against him.

She felt the briefest flicker of uncertainty, but it was swept away in a surge of heat as their bodies pressed together. She wanted him. The thought carried a faint brush of surprise with it, telling her that this had started as something else.

He suddenly stepped back, pulling away from her, the back of one hand going to his mouth, as though he might wipe the taste of her away.

'Are you done?' he said, his voice low.

'Done?' Her lips felt raw.

He turned and walked over to lean on the desk, not looking at her. 'This isn't about you wanting me. This is about you not wanting him.' He gripped the edge of the desk a little tighter. 'Or maybe it's about you still wanting him. I don't know. But I'm not going to be your whipping boy. You're angry. I'm not quite sure I get what it is you're angry about, or who you're angry with. But it doesn't matter. We're not doing this.'

'You wanted to.' The room seemed to have dropped several degrees.

He laughed, a low, coarse sound, turning to face her again. 'I'm a man.' He didn't quite meet her eyes. 'What else do you expect, coming in all guns blazing like that?' His expression hardened. 'But I'm not going to fuck you while you think of him.'

'I'm not thinking of him.' She took a couple of steps towards him, and saw him stiffen. She stopped, a tremor running through her body. His expression changed, the anger giving way to something that might almost have been a reluctant tenderness. Following the pull of that look, she took another step, and another.

His hands came up, warding her off.

'You don't want to do this,' he said again.

'I do.' But she could feel a faint chill brushing the inside of her ribs, just where that jagged desire had risen a moment earlier.

'Why?' He sounded tired. 'So that we can hate one another in the morning? Or is that the point?'

'What do you mean?'

'That's how you work,' he said. 'Isn't it? Ticking off everything you don't want. Everyone you don't want, until there's nothing left.'

'No.' There was a hollow ring to her denial.

'Really? I found you on a barely populated planet at the arse end of known space. You'd apparently gone there to get away from someone who does a pretty good impression of being in love with you.' He gave her a heavy smile. 'There's a fine line, you know. Between having space and having nothing.'

That raised a muted flare of feeling. 'You would know.'

He looked at her, unflinching. 'Yes, I would.'

The admission damped down the heat of her anger, leaving just a dull emptiness. 'So what about you?'

'What about me?'

'Where are you going? What do you want?'

He walked towards the door. 'You should go,' he said. 'It's late and we're both talking nonsense.'

There was nothing to do but nod, and follow him.

Just as she was about to step out, he said her name. When she turned to look at him, he leaned forward, letting his mouth find hers, slow and tender and heavy with regret. Her lips parted in something that was closer to a sigh than a kiss.

When they pulled apart, he gave her a crooked smile, and brushed her cheek with the side of his hand.

'Goodnight,' he said.

'Goodnight.' She stepped out through the door and walked away.

CHAPTER EIGHTEEN

Jamie woke the next morning with an ache in her chest, a dull-edged pain that made her want to go back and find him and say, *I didn't mean it like that. It had nothing to do with Daniel.*

Instead, she dressed and went down to the galley, where she found Lowry making breakfast for Rena and Finn. The lad looked up as she entered.

'You okay?' she said.

He nodded.

'Bit of a scramble last night,' Lowry said, putting a bowl down in front of Finn. 'Let it cool down.' He wiped his hands on a tattered towel. 'Still, we're on our way now.'

'Do you think they'll come after us?'

'It doesn't matter,' Rena said. 'We've got God on our side. The old world's gone. They shouldn't be trying to bring it back. We need to strip away all the things we did wrong. Make something new, something better.'

The old world. A new world. Jamie was tired of hearing those words. Why couldn't it be something in between the two? Her grandfather used to pick up little coloured pieces of plastic on the beach. Nurdles, they were called. He kept them in a jar in the window of his little workshop in the village, like tiny, primary-coloured pick-and-mix. People would often ask about them, their mouths making puckered Os of disgust when they found out they were fragments of industrial waste. *All that mess in that beautiful ocean.* When her grandfather pointed them to the glass and the pottery, they'd say, *But that's different.*

It seemed like there'd been a cut-off point, somewhere in human history. Anything discarded before that arbitrary date was *archaeology*, *salvage*, sometimes *vintage*. Anything after that was *pollution* and *rubbish* and *we should be ashamed*. To her grandfather, it was all part of what we'd made the ocean mean to us, and he gathered it up and turned it into what the ocean meant to him. So tiny ships made of plastic pellets sat alongside bracelets of smooth pottery shards, and necklaces of sea glass wrapped in strands of silver filigree.

You can't pick and choose with history, he once said. *If you want the glass and the china, you have to take the other things too. And you can't wipe it away without unravelling the whole story of us and the sea.*

Somewhere above them Jamie heard the ring of footsteps on metal. She looked up and saw Callan and Gracie making their way towards the stairs. It was too late to make her excuses and slip away, so she went over to busy herself at the galley counter, not turning around for the brief flurry of greetings.

'We need to jettison some weight,' Callan said after the courtesies were over. 'They only gave us enough fuel for a short run to the other capital planets. We should make Earth orbital station, but it's going to be tight. The lighter we are, the further the fuel will stretch.'

'And what happens when we reach the station?' Lowry asked.

'If it's unmanned, then we refuel there,' Callan said. 'They gave me the access codes, so I could refuel on my runs.'

'What if they change them?' Jamie said.

'Then we have a problem,' Callan replied. 'But I don't think they can. Not remotely.'

'And then we're going to Earth?' Rena demanded.

'Depends,' Callan said. 'If there are any shuttles there, you can use one to get planetside. If not, and the fuel situation works out, then yes, I'll take you down.'

As Jamie poured herself a coffee, trying to look as though she was concentrating her entire attention on that simple task, Callan walked over and reached past her for a mug.

'Any more of that?' He put his hand on her shoulder, making her jump slightly, sloshing her coffee over the counter.

He pulled his hand away, leaving her skin cooling as the warmth of his touch faded. She thought there had been something in it. An apology perhaps, or a question.

Are we okay?

She cleared her throat. 'Yes.' It came out too loud. She tried again. 'Yes, I'll make you one.'

'So what if it's manned?' Lowry asked. 'Earth station, I mean.'

'Let's worry about that when we get there.'

'We're going to make it.' Rena's voice quivered with certainty. 'God is leading us home.'

'Great,' Callan said. 'But if you don't mind, I'll still take all precautions. I want most of these crates jettisoned. The airlock's over by the main doors. If you get them stacked inside, I'll open the outer doors.'

'Don't you want to check what's in them?' Lowry asked.

Callan shook his head. 'Just get rid of them.'

'I'll deal with that,' Gracie said. 'You need to go over the coordinates I set. I wasn't sure which route you wanted to take.'

'Okay.' Callan took the coffee that Jamie held out to him, wrapping his hand around it carefully, his fingers not touching hers. 'Thanks.'

*

Despite Callan's directive and Gracie's impatience, Jamie lifted any loose lid she found. She wasn't sure why it seemed so important to note the passing of the detritus of unknown lives. Maybe it was that the ending of those lives would have no other marker. So she opened the lids and peered inside at clothes, books, random pieces of clutter. An old-fashioned cast-iron casserole dish. An artist's workbox and sketchbook, filled with images of the sunset on some unknown world. A stack of diaries with the same girl's name on each cover.

When they'd dragged all the smaller containers across the floor to the airlock, Lowry walked over to the piano and ran his fingers across the keys. 'Anyone fancy getting a last tune out of this?'

When Gracie stepped forward, Jamie thought the engineer was going to brush aside his sentiment, and begin moving the stately old instrument to its final silence. Instead, she pulled out the stool and sat down. There was a moment of pregnant still, then her shoulders went back and she spread her hands across the keys. She sat bolt upright as she played, but the music that poured from beneath her fingers was an aching, swooping thing.

Jamie didn't know the piece, but there were odd little phrases – ripples of falling notes and contrapuntal shivers up the keyboard – that made the hairs on the back of her neck stand up, with the sense that this was something she'd once known, or almost known, and had somehow lost.

They all stood in silence as the piano sang, the flowing melody rising into the dark curve of the hold, merging with its own echoes. It grew louder, more insistent, with a throbbing ache in the bass line, set against the almost unbearable tenderness of the treble.

When Gracie suddenly stopped playing, pulling her hands back from the keys as though they'd burned her, Jamie felt the loss as a physical shock. The tableau held for a moment. The woman at the piano, straight-backed and silent. The rest of them, frozen between shock and longing. Rena was crying silently, and for a fraction of a heartbeat, Jamie thought of going to her, putting her arms around the older woman's gaunt frame and telling her that it would be all right.

A small sound from above pulled her attention from Rena. Callan was standing on the gangway, watching the scene below. As Jamie's gaze fell on him, he turned his head and looked down at her, unsmiling. They stared at one another for a moment, and then he turned and walked away.

'Come on.' Gracie closed the lid, keeping her back to the rest of them. 'Let's get this jettisoned.'

As Rena muttered something and stumbled away towards the stairs, Jamie remembered that odd impulse to tenderness, but the moment had gone and she could no longer recall how it had felt.

Two days passed. Jamie saw very little of Callan, and when they did encounter one another, their exchanges were brief and awkward. A couple of times Jamie found herself wanting to put out a hand to stop him walking away, and say, *Are we okay?* But she was frightened he'd look at her and say, *No*.

She spent a lot of time with Finn, sorting through the jar of sea glass as he created his elaborate patterns in shades of green and blue and amber. For the most part, he seemed to have come to terms with the random nature of the fragments, but every now and again he'd find two pieces that looked as though they might go together, and he'd spend a little while turning them against one another, trying to find the place where their sharp edges would slot into place.

He didn't seem unduly troubled when these efforts failed. Jamie was the one who was unsettled by them, as though she really thought there was a pattern there. Sometimes she'd think she could see it, and she'd find herself mimicking his actions, her fingers scuffing on the cracks and snags of the broken pieces. She preferred the older pieces, with their smooth curves and sand-glazed opacity. There was no temptation to try and force them together. Whatever edges and fault lines they'd ever had, they were gone now.

They didn't talk much. Sometimes Finn would make a fleeting comment on some fragment or other.

Blue.

Like a tear.

Tiny.

There was no value judgement in these passing remarks. He wasn't comparing one piece to another, and finding it wanting. She found herself replying in kind.

Like an eye.

Clear.

Whenever she spoke, Finn smiled; just a sidelong twitch of his lips, accompanied by a swift glance at her face. There was something soothing and undemanding about these exchanges. There was no subtext, no nuances to be teased out and worried over. It was simple, uncluttered, and Jamie sometimes found herself looking at Finn with something that might almost have been a cautious, faltering love twisting in her heart.

By contrast, Rena's moods were growing more intense and less coherent. She prowled the corridors of the ship at all hours. Sometimes Jamie would wake in the night and hear the sound of those familiar halting footsteps in the passage. Once they stopped outside her quarters for a moment, and Jamie thought she heard the faint brush of a touch on the metal door, like someone thinking of knocking, but snatching their hand away at the last moment.

She tried to be kind to the other woman, but her attempts felt stilted and clumsy. They always seemed to be talking at odds, their remarks glancing off one another and sliding away at an angle. Maybe that fleeting instant of empathy had been all there could ever be between them. Perhaps it had slipped out of the airlock to float out there beside the piano, turning endlessly in the silence between the stars.

Lowry was quieter than usual. He'd taken to spending time up on the bridge with Callan, although when Jamie passed by, they never seemed to be talking. When she asked him about it, he said he just wanted to see ahead of them. He looked tired, his face drawn. That old heart problem, he told her, brushing away her concern. It just slowed him down some-times. He'd be fine. When he got to the sea, he'd rest and recover. He'd be fine.

On the third day, Jamie was eating lunch with Finn and Lowry when Callan came to find them. The galley was exposed now, without its wall of crates, and the sofas looked small and out of place in the great vault of the hold.

'I've picked up a message,' Callan said. 'From Alegria. They must have bounced it off a couple of the satellites.'

'A message for us?' Lowry said.

'For Earth station. Telling them we're on our way, and that we don't have permission to land on the planet.'

'But there might not be anyone there,' Jamie said.

'The message sounded fairly sure. They must have had contact. I haven't picked anything else up, but I've only been monitoring sporadically.'

'So what do we do?'

'Not much we can do. We don't have enough fuel to turn back, and the nearest planet is Alegria anyway. We may be able to convince them that we're going back. Let them refuel us, and then land on Earth.'

'You think that will work?' Lowry asked doubtfully.

'I don't know,' Callan said. 'They're not going to want to keep us there, and they can't turn us back without refuelling us, or they lose the ship.'

Lowry nodded slowly. 'So how long before we reach them?'

'About twenty hours,' Callan said. 'Mid-morning tomorrow. I'll let you know when I've made contact.'

He nodded to them, bringing the discussion to a close, before walking away.

Jamie gave it a few moments before heading back to her quarters, but just as she reached her door, she heard her name, and turned to see Callan walking towards her.

'I didn't want to say anything in front of the others,' he said, stopping a couple of metres away. 'But there was another message. Sent direct to us.' He hesitated. 'Well, to you.'

'To . . .' She stopped. She knew what he was going to say.

'It's from Daniel.' He didn't look at her as he delivered that information. 'I didn't listen to it. Just enough to work out what it was.'

For a moment she considered just thanking him politely, then going into her quarters and closing the door. But whatever there had been between Daniel and her, there was still a single thread of it running from her heart to his. It was fraying, stretched thin by the events on Alegria, but it was still there, and it would tangle and knot itself inside her if she didn't find a way to break it once and for all.

'Can I listen to it?'

There was a second's hesitation from Callan before he answered, and it occurred to her that he might have been expecting a different response.

'I'll set it up.'

She followed him up to the bridge and stood by as he flicked a few switches, before stepping aside to let her sit down in front of the screen.

'Just hit the red button to start it. If you need me, I'll be in my quarters. If you need anything, I mean.'

'Thank you,' she said.

Just as he was about to duck out of the door, he glanced back at her. 'That blue button on the top right.'

'This one?'

'That's right. If you ever needed to return a call to a stored location, that's the button you'd press. While the message was playing. If there's a working relay off the satellites, it will connect automatically. Just in case you ever need it.'

After he'd gone, Jamie sat there for a few moments, before leaning forward and pressing the red button. The greyed-out screen flickered and gave way to Daniel's face, sudden and close up, haloed in static.

'Jamie.'

She almost responded, forgetting it was a recording, but the message rolled on.

'I hope you're hearing this. I wasn't sure whether to send it. The way we left things . . .' He glanced away, composing himself. 'I suppose that's the thing. We didn't leave things, didn't finish things, I mean. I thought we'd have time, or I'd never have walked away from you like that.' His gaze moved around, as though he was searching for her beyond the screen. 'Jamie . . . look, it's not too late to turn back. Everything you need is here. It wouldn't have to be how you think. You can be part of it, help us rebuild the world and make it better. You could . . .' He stopped and rubbed at his face. 'I'm not saying this right. That's not why I'm asking you to come back. I love you. I'll always love you. We can make it work. I know we can.' He broke off, glancing away from the screen again, as though someone had distracted him. When he turned back, he was brisk, businesslike. 'Contact me if you get this.' Another pause, and then he lowered his voice and said, 'I love you.' The message winked out.

Jamie stared at the blank screen. She shouldn't have listened to it. There was no going back from what had happened between them. So why was her mind suddenly working overtime, trying to unravel that certainty and replace it with a handful of *ifs* and *maybes*?

No.

He'd said his piece. She could delete the message and walk away.

She reached out, slowly, and pressed the blue switch. The screen broke into flickering bands of grey as the comm searched the airwaves. There were a few shadows moving behind the static, like ghosts floating out there between the stars, waiting for something to catch them and pull them in. But nothing else.

She reached for the switch again, only to snatch her hand back as the distortions on the screen took shape and form, and became Daniel.

The image was blurred, constantly jumping and shifting, its lips moving just out of sync with bursts of incomprehensible static.

'Jamie?' Another crackle swallowed his next words.

'Yes. Can you hear me?'

His image moved forwards, fiddling with something, and some of the static fell away.

'Can you hear me?' he echoed back to her.

'Yes, I can hear you.'

A pause, and then they both spoke at once. Or that's how it seemed, although he must have started first for them to clash across all the distance between them.

Another pause, then he said, 'You go.'

'I got your message.'

'Yes, sorry.'

'What?'

'No, sorry, someone came in. We're alone now.'

'I'm not coming back.'

The image wasn't clear enough for her to see his expression change, but he leaned back, briefly lifting his hands to his face.

'What went wrong?'

'I think it was just life,' she said. 'We stopped fitting together.'

'But you did love me? Once?'

'Yes.'

'Tell me,' he said, leaning forward again, the urgency and need in his tone evident even through the lag and distortion of the airwaves.

For a moment she thought he hadn't heard her say she'd loved him, but then she realised he was begging her for something more. She fought the sudden urge to flick that switch, and lose the conversation under the illusion of a broken connection.

Thirteen years.

The words were sharp and painful in her mouth as she began to speak. She told him how it had felt when he'd first smiled at her, how she'd felt when he first touched her. She told him about the toast, about the shoes and the hall cupboard. She told him that she'd wondered if the baby would have that same little crease above the bridge of the nose. She told him about the way he made her laugh by changing the lyrics of songs so they were about her cooking disasters or her attempt at painting the living room. She told him what she'd wanted for them, what she'd believed about them, and when she finally ran out of words, he was crying.

'There's a difference,' he said, when he could speak again. 'Isn't there? Between love and being in love.'

That's what you heard? she thought. *That's all you heard from what I just said?*

He was speaking again, but the screen was beginning to splinter and fragment.

'What did you say?' If they finished this properly and said goodbye, it would be an absolution of sorts. She said his name a couple of times but he was just a blur now, the static scratching and scraping over the airwaves, finally giving way to the grey crackle of a lost connection.

She sat there for a moment, then reached for the switch. Just as she took hold of it, the crackle suddenly fell away, yielding a last snatch of clarity. His voice, distorted but audible.

'. . . end of all things . . . meant to be.'

Then he was gone.

Jamie lifted a shaking hand to brush her hair back from her face.

We'll meet here, he'd said. *If the world ever ends.*

How had something so throwaway become the thing they returned to when everything else was breaking and falling apart?

There was a sound behind her, and she turned, her shoulders already tightening defensively against the look that she'd see in Callan's eyes. Instead, Rena was standing in the doorway, an odd, exultant expression on her face.

When Jamie got up and walked over to the door, Rena grabbed her arm.

'You heard that.' A blaze of emotion crackled over her face. '*Meant to be.* You heard.'

'Get off me.' Jamie shook herself free.

'You heard.'

Jamie wasn't sure the other woman was even talking to her any more. Rena was staring out at the distant stars, and as Jamie walked away she could hear what sounded like a muttered prayer, a thin rise and fall of sound that barely sounded like Rena at all.

It's summer, just like it's supposed to be whenever you're in love.

And she is. In love. She's sure of it.

It doesn't feel like the books or the movies. She's not lying awake at night thinking of him. When she sees him she doesn't run and throw herself into his arms, and he doesn't swing her round and round in the middle of a crowd while they both laugh and throw their heads back.

But that's not what love is. Not really.

He's nice. Not that smothering sort of nice. There's an irreverence to him, an edge. He believes in the things she believes in, and he laughs at the things she laughs at. They never run out of things to talk about. They don't do that thing where every conversation spirals smaller and smaller and tighter and tighter, always working its way down to the same thing.

Are we getting this right?

They talk about things that happen on other worlds. New books. New research. Out-there scientific theories someone in her department is trying to prove. They talk about further out, and far in the future. They talk about things that are bigger than them, wider than them.

And she thinks that maybe this is how it's supposed to be. Close, but not too close. Room to breathe, room to be.

It's not perfect. There are moments when it's still too much, when she gets that old, familiar feeling, as if the world's pressing too hard against her skin. Times when he looks at her and all she thinks is that she wants to be somewhere else. Times when they're *making love and she knows his eyes are open, but she keeps hers closed.*

Once, just once, he tried to get her to talk to him while he was moving inside her.

Tell me how you want me to touch you. Tell me what you're thinking.

It hurled her back into her skin. Suddenly she was aware of his weight upon her, the press of him inside her, all the places his body was touching hers. It was too real, as though they were acting out some clinical instruction manual.

Insert part A into aperture B.

Make sure part C is tight to part D.

Her breath caught in her chest and she found herself shoving and clawing her way out from under him.

I can't, *was all she'd said, shaking her head when he reached for her, his face creased in concern. When he tried to push the point she got out of bed, dressed and went home, leaving him alone. They didn't talk about it the following day, and the next time they had sex they moved together in silence once again, both of them with their eyes tightly closed.*

CHAPTER NINETEEN

It was almost noon when the call came. Jamie was in the galley, just making the third coffee of the day, when Callan's voice crackled over the tannoy.

'Everyone to the bridge, please.'

When they got up there, they found Callan and Gracie engaged in an argument which they broke off as soon as they saw the passengers. Gracie shoved her hands in her pockets and walked over to stare out at the stars.

'We've had contact from Earth station,' Callan said. 'There are survivors – four of them – and they've spoken to Alegria. They've been told to automate the station and come back with us.'

'They can't make us go back.' Rena's hands clenched into fists. 'We won't let them on board. We'll—'

'Rena.' Lowry touched her arm. 'Calm down. We'll figure something out.'

'There's nothing we can do,' Gracie said. 'They won't refuel us unless we let them code-lock the helm.'

'You're an engineer.' Rena took a step towards her. 'Can't you override it?'

'No,' Gracie said. 'That's pretty much the point of a lock. And I can't imagine the four of them will just stand around watching me try.'

'Can we land?' Lowry said. 'Find somewhere to refuel on Earth?'

Callan shook his head. 'There's no central fuel port on

Earth. Only the small shuttle points. Large ship refuelling is always done via the station.'

'We wouldn't make it anyway,' Gracie said. 'We're running on fumes.'

Callan leaned over to look at a dial. 'We might. We could use a load of smaller dumps to get the tank full, but we'd have to find one with stocks, and set down close enough for the first top-up.'

'It's too risky,' Gracie said. 'We'll be grounded if we misjudge it, even supposing we land safely.'

The comm alert shrilled, and Callan flicked the respond switch.

The man on the screen looked to be in his late fifties, with a cool, appraising stare.

'We're waiting for you to transfer control of your helm,' he said. 'The link's open. What's the delay?'

'Just getting a little closer,' Callan said.

'You're well within range,' the man replied. 'Get on with it. We've been stuck here long enough, and we all know you're not going anywhere without fuel. Out.'

As the screen winked out Rena lurched forward, lunging for the helm. 'We can't go back. If you won't put us down, I will.'

Jamie grabbed at her arm, but Rena flailed in her grip, catching her across the nose with her elbow. Sharp pain flared between Jamie's eyes, and she felt the warm spurt of blood. She put her hands up to stop the flow, vaguely aware that Lowry had hold of Rena, who was shrieking something about destiny and the voice of God. Callan pushed forward to join Lowry, and together they managed to force Rena back from the helm. Finn was crouched almost double, his hands pressed hard against his ears. Gracie was shouting something but Jamie couldn't make out the words. Rena's screams were a high-pitched throb as she writhed and fought in the grip of the two men.

Callan turned, still holding on to Rena, and looked at Gracie, then at Finn, and finally at Jamie. They stared at one another for a moment, and then he let go of Rena and walked across to the helm.

'What are you doing?' Gracie moved forwards.

'Landing.' He sat down at the controls. 'Go strap yourselves in.'

'We won't make it.' Gracie gripped the edge of the console. 'You'll kill us all.'

'I can do this,' he said. 'Get strapped in.'

'Callan . . .'

He turned on her. 'This is my ship. And I'm landing it. Now you can stand there and distract me, or you can do what I said.'

Gracie swore, and strode off the bridge.

'Go,' Callan said to the rest of them, turning back to the controls. 'And make sure you're strapped in tight.'

Jamie's thoughts were spiralling as she fastened the straps on her harness. One image kept recurring: the set, tight-lipped look on Callan's face as he'd made that unfathomable decision.

Beside her Rena was praying, eyes screwed up tight. Lowry had his eyes closed too, but if he was talking to God he was doing it in silence. Finn was on Jamie's other side, folded as far forward as the straps would allow, hands crushed together on his lap. Jamie hesitated, and then reached over to him. He resisted briefly, but then allowed her to uncurl his fingers and wrap her palm into his.

The engines were beginning their slow-growing roar, a great heft of sound rising up to swallow Rena's mutterings, and the relentless thudding of Jamie's heart. Was it her imagination, or were those engines more muted than usual? Was Callan holding back, saving fuel for the final descent? For the first time, Jamie wondered if they would die in this attempt. Would it be quick? Would they black out, before they were crushed in the great burning bulk of the dying ship?

Breathe.

Her chest stayed tight and restricted.

'Breathe.' She said it out loud, trying to give it more force.

The engines peaked, then seemed to fade a little, and the ship rocked. Jamie found herself tipping forward like Finn. Her fingers were numb, but she knew she still had hold of his hand.

Another hard lurch. And then the engines faltered.

For a terrible fraction of a heartbeat, there was silence, and then the ship revved again, harder than before. A picture flared in Jamie's mind: Callan, his knuckles white on the helm, teeth set, throwing all his hopes into a last desperate burn.

Finn's hand jerked in hers. She tightened her grip, tried to say, *It's okay*, but she couldn't find the right shape for those words.

The ship was screaming now, racked by forces it couldn't withstand for long, straining every connection to keep its improbable bulk airborne. Jamie imagined the helm bucking against Callan's control, twisting in panic like a horse that's seen the needle coming.

Another brief, dragging crescendo, then all that bedlam of sound fell away, leaving an echoing void in which Jamie could hear Rena's short, harsh breaths, and her own heart beating too fast, too hard.

The ship tipped, listing to one side, as if it had been caught by a wave. Then they were falling, her stomach forced up against her ribs, bile leaping into her throat.

She should be frightened, but all she could feel was regret.

They'd been so very close. And the way Callan had looked at her before he made the call, was it her fault? Could she have said, *No, let's go back*, and they'd be alive?

Someone was screaming, but she couldn't remember any names, or any faces. It was getting harder to breathe, and to think through the syrupy fog in her mind. But her thoughts were all she had left.

She felt around for something to focus on, something beyond the moment.

Daniel? She'd left him, and couldn't remember his face.

The baby? He didn't feel real, not real enough to hold on to.

The sea? But it was cold, and so very far away.

Stop it.

She was losing it. She was losing these last moments.

Callan. He was still up there, at the helm, holding his ship in his arms. Did he believe in anything beyond himself? Lowry did. And Rena.

For a moment Jamie strained inside herself, trying to feel the shape belief would make if it was in there, but her thoughts kept coming back to Callan.

There was a rending of metal, a last shriek of protest from the ship, and she was flung hard against her straps. It felt like she'd been sliced into pieces. They weren't falling any more. They were spinning, side over side, up becoming down becoming up again. Her mind was trying to keep up but it was a losing battle, and the nausea, the nausea. She didn't want to die vomiting. Her head struck something hard, sending a silver flare up the back of her skull. Any minute now the ship would crumple around her, like a sweet wrapper thrown into a bin.

Another crunch sent her into the straps again, hard enough that she thought she might break in two. Then the ship tipped forwards and lay still.

*

It was dark and silent for a long time.

Jamie teetered backwards and forwards on the edge of consciousness. One moment she was wondering where she was and how she'd come to be there. The next second she knew, with utter certainty, that she was here, in the carcass of a fallen ship, and that she had to get out.

The darkness was heavy with an incomprehensible array of sharp-throated smells. Engine oil and hot metal, and the low drag of burning machinery.

Burning?

That thought hurled her back to full awareness. She clawed at her harness. She couldn't undo the catch, and she realised she was using only one hand. The other was still holding on to Finn. She could feel his palm hot and damp against her own. That small awareness was a touchstone, and suddenly she could feel the hard ache in her ribs, and the throb in her skull.

She lifted her free arm and reached over to where Rena should be. Her hand collided with a warm body, and someone said something, but she couldn't make out the words through the buzzing in her ears.

The smell of hot metal and oil was overpowering.

She tried to extract her hand from Finn's, but he clung on, gripping so hard that she thought she could feel her bones grinding together.

'Finn.' The words sounded thick and clumsy. 'I need to get us out. You need to let go.'

There was no response, but he didn't seem to be holding on quite so tightly. She extracted her hand, and fumbled at her straps until the catch snapped open. When she stood up, the movement sent sharper shards of pain through the dull, constant ache of her body.

She took a few cautious steps forward, then stopped at the sudden clang of metal. When she tilted her head, she could just make out the sound of footsteps through the ringing in her ears. They were somewhere above her, slow and cautious, but not as faltering as her own.

'Anyone there?' It was Callan's voice.

Through the surge of relief, she had an irrational urge to ask him what he'd believed in, as the ship came down.

'Hello?' His voice came again, louder.

'Here.' Her ears were clearing. 'I'm here. The doors . . .'

'Stand still.' His footsteps were on the stairs now. 'I know the ship. You don't. Stay there.'

That *stay there* was shockingly close after the black emptiness of the hold. And it wasn't just his voice. She could feel him through the darkness, just inches away, another warm body in the void.

'Callan . . .'

He was moving further away again now, and she felt a leap of fear. She needed him close, so she'd know he was real, that this wasn't just the last oxygen-starved ravings of her dying mind.

'Callan?'

No reply.

'*Callan?*'

A low thud, then the scrape of metal. For a long moment the gears ground against one another, and then the doors cranked open, air hissing through the narrow gap, light breaking in through a haze of dust.

Callan was crouched by the door release. As Jamie looked at him, he pushed himself slowly to his feet, leaning on the side of the ship.

'Think I might have pulled some stitches,' he said.

She nodded, not sure what would come out if she tried to speak. Behind her Lowry was leaning over Finn, undoing his straps. Rena's harness was unfastened, but she was still in her seat, tipped forwards, clutching at her knees.

'Everyone okay?' Callan said.

Jamie looked around the hold. 'Gracie . . .'

'I'm fine.' The engineer was making her way down the steps, one hand pressed to her side. When she saw Jamie looking she took the hand away. 'How's the ship?'

'We'll find out when we get out there.'

'What happened?' Gracie asked. 'Fuel?'

Callan nodded. 'We were too high for the chutes, so I had to try and glide it in.'

'You can't glide a T-class,' Gracie said. 'You *know* that. God knows how we're still alive.'

'Well, we are.' Callan stepped up to the gap and sat down on the edge, before dropping out of sight.

Gracie muttered something, and followed him.

Jamie walked over to the doors, waiting to feel elation, or relief, or anything at all.

Home, she thought, trying to know it was true. *Home*.

As she stepped through the gap, she had to screw her eyes up against the glare. There was a perfect blue sky overhead, with a high sun beating down. Hills rose up in the distance, grey-green and craggy, with a narrow road winding up and out of sight. Scrubby grass and gorse stretched out all around them, and where the ground rose towards the foothills, fir trees marched up the slopes in artificially straight rows.

It could be anywhere. Callan had only had moments to plot their course. But there was a smell, or a taste, or something that was neither, but still tangible.

Home. The thought had a bit more weight to it this time.

The sun was warm on her skin, but there was a familiar brittleness to the heat. It didn't go down deep. If you rubbed a northern summer between your fingers, the warmth would crumble away like flaky pastry, revealing the chill underneath.

She dropped down onto the grass, landing slightly off balance. The ship was listing to the side, and one set of landing gear had been torn off. The impact had gouged up great clods of earth, and steam was drifting out from underneath the hull.

Callan was moving along the side of the ship, one hand trailing along her metal flank, while Gracie stood back, arms folded, inspecting the *Phaeacian* through narrowed eyes.

Lowry appeared at the doors. He was moving slowly, and he winced as his feet jarred onto the ground. Rena followed him, scrambling gracelessly over the edge and landing in a hurried sprawl. When she got to her feet, she was breathing hard.

'We made it,' she said. 'Thank God. Thank you, God.'

Jamie looked at Lowry.

'You okay?'

There was a grey tinge to his pallor, but he managed a half-smile. 'Not too bad as long as I don't take a deep breath.'

'Where does it hurt?'

'Just my ribs. I may have cracked something. I'll be fine. We're lucky if this is the worst of it.'

There was a sound from the ship and Finn shuffled through the gap in the doors.

'Here.' Jamie reached up to guide him down, but he shook his head, sat down and pushed off, landing in a crouch on the grass.

'Are you okay?' she asked.

Finn nodded. 'Earth?'

'Earth,' Jamie agreed.

The lad's lips twitched in a brief smile as he walked away to examine a patch of bright yellow trefoil flowers.

'Have we done the right thing?' Lowry was looking at

Callan, who had both hands pressed against the hull of his stricken ship.

Jamie felt a sudden drag of guilt.

'We all made the choice.' It came out much sharper than she intended.

'Do we know where we've landed?' Rena said. 'We need to go. To Lindisfarne.'

'No hurry,' Lowry said. 'We're alive. That's the most important thing right now.' He turned to Jamie. 'Any idea where we are?'

'I'm not sure.' She looked around again. 'It feels . . . I don't know, it looks like England. The north.'

'It better be.' Callan walked over to join them. 'I set course for the Wearside landing site. When our fuel ran out, I changed course to try and glide down onto open land northwest of there.'

'How much further north?' Jamie asked.

Callan shrugged. 'Fifty miles,' he said. 'Maybe a bit more. The system's down.'

'Fifty miles,' Lowry said. 'If that's right, then we're close.' He looked up at Callan. 'How's the ship?'

Callan's expression closed down. 'Probably repairable. But not going anywhere – unless someone's left a full fuel wherry somewhere handy, with the access codes stuck on a post-it note.'

'It doesn't matter,' Rena said. 'We have to go on, not back.'

'Rena . . .' Lowry began, but Callan just turned and walked away, one hand pressed against his injured side.

Jamie followed, catching him up just as he reached the doors.

I'm sorry, was what she meant to say. But instead she looked up at him, meeting his gaze squarely for the first time since that night in his quarters. 'Why did you do it?'

He shrugged. 'Maybe I just don't like being told what to do.'

'That . . .' She stopped and tried again, feeling her way around the edges of what it was she wanted to know. 'You didn't want to come. Why—'

He cut across her. 'You're *here*, aren't you? Don't tell me you've changed your mind now. If it was ever made up in the first place.'

'What do you mean?'

'Doesn't matter,' he said. 'Look, I'm not exactly sure I've done the right thing, so the last thing I need is someone going on at me about my reasons.' He hauled himself up onto the hold floor, breathing in sharply.

'I need to look at those stitches,' Jamie said.

'It's fine.' He disappeared into the cargo hold, leaving her staring after him.

It took about an hour for Callan and Gracie to get the backup power on. When the emergency lights were working, Jamie and the others went up to their quarters for their things. There were no obvious signs of damage inside the ship, but the lights kept flickering, and Jamie expected to be plunged into that complete darkness again at any moment. She packed as quickly as she could.

Back outside, Callan and Gracie were studying a hand-held map unit.

'Do you know where we are?' Jamie asked.

'Here.' Callan handed her the unit. 'Might mean more to you than us.'

'The GPS is working?'

'Why wouldn't it be?' Gracie said. 'The satellites are still transmitting.'

'It just feels odd,' Jamie said. 'Like those pictures you used to see of abandoned places. Chernobyl, or that place in Siberia after the chemical strike. Houses with plates still on the table, that sort of thing. How long do you think it will all keep running?'

Gracie shrugged. 'Depends. The wind turbines should keep pumping out voltage indefinitely. There's not much that can go wrong with them. Hydropower stations are a bit more labour-intensive. The solar panels should be all right for a while.'

'So we'll have power?' Jamie said. 'When we get to the coast, I mean.'

'Should do,' Gracie said. 'Some of the mechanics will probably outlive us all.' She gave a slight smile. 'I suppose that's an immortality of sorts, for the people who built them.'

'There's no such thing.' Rena had come up behind them. 'Only God can grant immortality. And we don't need the old world any more. It should all be stripped away. All the markers of what we did.'

Gracie ignored her, turning back to tap her finger on the map-reader. 'We're here. Do you know it?'

The map was zoomed right out, and Jamie had to squint to read the tiny place names.

Alwinton. Harbottle. Newton-on-the-Moor.

She looked up at the hills, trying to superimpose them onto the landscape of her memory. They couldn't be far from the main road between Rothbury and Alnwick.

'I think we're about twenty-five miles away. Thereabouts.'

'How are we going to get there?' Gracie asked. 'Even if we could find a vehicle, we won't have their access codes.'

'We walk, then,' Callan said.

'Walk?' Gracie looked horrified. 'But we'll have stuff to carry.'

'So we carry it,' Callan said. 'We won't need to take much.'

'You're talking like we're going with them,' the engineer said.

'I never signed up for this pilgrimage, or whatever you want to call it.'

'Where else are we going to go?' Callan said. 'Let's just get there, and then we can think about what comes next. Unless you want to stay put and hope the administration turn up to rescue you, of course.' He turned to Jamie. 'So which way from here?'

She pointed towards a line of trees. 'I don't think we're more than a couple of hundred metres from the main road.'

Callan nodded. 'Might as well get going, then.'

'What about the ship?' It felt wrong to just walk away, as though his sacrifice didn't matter at all.

'It's not going anywhere,' Callan said, turning to walk in the direction Jamie had indicated.

The road was an anonymous stretch of pitted tarmac, flanked by high hedgerows, but it sparked a random flash of memory – which could have been here or anywhere. Sitting in the back of the car with her two half-sisters, her stepmother in the front, talking too fast, telling them what they were going to do when they got where they were going, how much they'd all enjoy it.

'Which way now?' Callan said.

'We need to head towards Alnwick,' Jamie said. 'That way.'

Callan set off at a brisk pace, despite the heavy pack on his shoulders. Rena hurried along at his heels, almost stumbling in her haste, while Gracie followed at a more moderate pace that Jamie suspected might have more to do with reluctance than with the weight of her own rucksack.

Lowry brought up the rear with Finn, who was walking cautiously, as though the tarmac might be hot.

'Are you all right?' Jamie asked Lowry.

The old man gave her a wry smile. 'I'll get there. Maybe a fair few hours after the rest of you, mind.'

Jamie looked up at the sound of a low whicker, and saw a horse leaning over a nearby gate. It was a cobby chestnut, with a sprinkling of grey around the muzzle. Finn stopped dead, staring at it.

'No horses on Pangaea?' Lowry said.

Finn shook his head, keeping his eyes on the cob.

Jamie walked over and looked into the field, rubbing the horse's muzzle. There was a shelter near the far fence.

'Just a minute.' Jamie opened the gate.

Inside the shelter she found a purple halter and lead-rope, and a fleece rug with red and yellow stripes that had blurred into one another from too much washing. It took them a few minutes to load the heavier packs onto the horse's back, fastening them together in pairs of makeshift panniers. Jamie folded the rug into a pad, to stop the load from rubbing. Gracie insisted on keeping her rucksack, and Finn could not be persuaded to give up his small bag, but the others gladly offloaded their burdens.

The horse seemed untroubled by the weight, walking briskly alongside Jamie, the lead rope hanging slack between them. Finn walked on the far side. Every now and again, his hand would move towards the horse, but he always snatched it back at the last moment.

'You can touch him.' Jamie placed her own hand on the horse's warm neck. 'Like this.'

Finn stretched out and brushed his fingers along the horse's mane, pulling back sharply before reaching out again, to rest his palm against the horse's shoulder. They walked on like that, the two of them, connected by the swaying warmth of the old horse plodding along between them.

CHAPTER TWENTY

It was mid-afternoon when they reached the outskirts of Alnwick. It had taken them a while to find a rhythm that would suit all the members of the party. But they'd eventually fallen into a pattern of walking for an hour, then resting for twenty minutes or so, while the horse grazed on a loose rein.

'I'm wondering how much further we can go today,' Callan said, dropping back from his point position, a couple of hundred yards in front. He glanced at Lowry as he spoke. The older man had raised no complaint about the pace, but he looked pale and hadn't been talking much.

'We're about halfway,' Jamie said. 'If we can manage another hour or so, there's somewhere I know.'

Somewhere nice. It would have sounded foolish to say it. Like they were on a day trip to the countryside, looking for an upmarket teashop.

'Okay,' Callan said.

Gracie joined them. She had a reader of some sort, and was examining the screen. 'Something's transmitting around here.'

'A distress signal?' Callan asked.

Gracie shook her head. 'No, nothing like that. A wireless code. Like someone's uploading data on a local network.'

'Could it be automated?' Jamie asked. 'If everything's still running, then presumably the net will keep . . .' She hesitated, realising she wasn't entirely sure what the internet actually did. It was just one of those things that was always there. Like air, like weather. '. . . working,' she finished lamely.

Gracie gave her a faintly contemptuous look. 'It will only keep running if it was automated in the first place. The net's a lot more labour-intensive than people think it is.' She paused. 'Was.' When she carried on, her tone was more neutral, as though that little slip had made her less dismissive of someone else's ignorance. 'Besides, you can tell the difference between the background hum of the net, and someone actively making a change. There's someone working on a server, and they're nearby.'

'Any idea where?' Callan asked.

'I might be able to trace it.' Gracie glanced around the group. 'Assuming we want to take the time, that is.'

'Of course we do,' Lowry said. 'If we're going to be settling here, we should try and find other people.'

'Why?' Rena said.

When they all turned to look at her, she stared back, her mouth a stubborn line. There were fresh scratches on her arms.

'What do you mean, Rena?' Lowry's voice was gentle, as though talking to a child.

'Why do we need more people? That's what they were doing on Alegria. Trying to make everyone do what they want. *Be* what they want. We're beyond that now. Beyond all of that. We need to get there, and then we'll see.'

'See what?' Jamie asked.

Rena shot her an almost pitying look. 'Everything.'

Gracie had walked a few paces away. 'I think it's coming from this direction,' she said, as though Rena hadn't spoken.

'Come on.' Lowry took Rena's arm. 'We've got to live in this world. It's not just about getting here.'

'You don't understand.' Rena looked at Lowry, an odd, almost tender, expression coming over her face. 'You're always thinking about tomorrow, and you don't need to keep doing that. Not now.' She gave a flimsy smile. 'Tomorrow and tomorrow and tomorrow, and the world getting fuller by the minute. But not any more.'

Lowry returned the smile, although his was strained and quick-fading. 'You're right. We should try and think more about the moment. Now we have the time to slow down.' He grimaced, his hand going to his chest. 'In fact, we may have to slow down. A little bit, at least.'

Rena shook her head again. The movement went on for longer than it should have done, giving her the appearance of an emphatic child. 'That's not it.' Her tone was fretful. 'It's not—'

'Shh.' Lowry put his hand on her arm. 'Rena, we'll get where we're going, and it will be okay. We'll work it out. You don't have to make us understand.'

Callan and Gracie had already set off.

'We should go,' Jamie said.

Rena hesitated, but finally gave in to Lowry's gentle pressure on her arm, and fell into step beside him.

Gracie led them through the narrow streets, stopping every now and again to tilt her screen. When they reached the main road out of town, she stopped and looked up a cobbled slope towards a long building with a frosted-glass roof. 'It's coming from here.'

'That's the old railway station,' Jamie said. 'It's a bookshop now. They reopened the line during the first fuel crisis, but built a new station on the other side of the tracks. Maybe there's some sort of server there.'

Gracie shook her head. 'It's closer than that. I'm going to take a look inside.'

They made their way round to the entrance. When Callan tried the door, it slid open a few inches before jamming.

'There's something against the door,' he said. 'Looks like a bookcase has tipped over.' He gave the door another shove, but it didn't move. Jamie tethered the horse to a ring in the wall, and went over to join Callan, kneeling down and squeezing her arm through the gap until she could feel the edge of the book-case. When she pushed at it, it shifted sideways very slightly. She wriggled round so that she was almost lying on the ground and forced her arm a little further inside. When she pushed again, the obstruction slid a little further, allowing the door to open a few more inches, and then a few more, until Jamie could squeeze through and haul the bookcase out of the way.

'It looks like it was dragged there on purpose,' she said. 'There's nowhere round here it could have come from.'

Callan walked through the entrance hall, with its clutter of bookshelves and armchairs, into the high-roofed space that formed the main part of the shop. Jamie followed more slowly, running her fingers along the spines of the tight-packed books. She'd loved this place once. Often, when people were pressing too close and the village seemed too small and too familiar, she'd climb on one of the slow, sporadic buses and come here to lose herself in the maze of shelves.

'How would you ever find anything?' Gracie looked around disapprovingly. 'Is there any order to it?'

'Anyone there?' Callan raised his voice.

There was no reply. Jamie walked over to a room just off the main shop floor, where the children's books used to be. She stepped through the archway, and then stopped.

The central shelves had been moved closer to the wall, forming a little nook around a pile of camping mattresses, topped with a pillow and a mess of blankets. The bookcases had been dragged away from the wall to the right, and placed in front of the windows, sinking the room into a muted haze. Someone had begun the painstaking process of covering the bare wall with coloured illustrations, each one enclosed in its own decorative pane, like a cartoon strip, but much more elaborate than any Jamie had seen before. She moved closer, studying the first few panels. There was a depiction of the Alnwick town square, crowded with more people. The sky overhead was a clear blue, marred by a single cloud, heavy and low and picked out in ominous shades of purple and grey. In the next panel the square was empty, but for a shadowy figure in the entrance to one of the side streets. The same blurred figure featured in several other images. Walking down a street, the air heavy with a haze of dust. Standing in the doorway to the bookshop. Crouched between the stacks in the main part of the shop.

Callan came up behind her. 'What is it?'

'Someone's here,' Jamie said.

He glanced around the little room, and nodded. 'Be careful,' he said, walking back through the archway.

A memory stirred in Jamie's mind. That warehouse on Pangaea, not quite silent and not quite still.

She pushed that thought away, and followed Callan into the main room where a single central aisle ran the whole length of the space, stacks slanting away to both sides. Gracie was already moving down the walkway, skirting round the little clusters of low-slung chairs. As Callan followed her, Jamie moved to the side, taking the walkway that ran along below the high-arched windows at the front. You could play an endless game of cat-and-mouse in here, turning round one end of an aisle just as someone slipped away at the other.

As though that thought had taken real form, something flickered in the corner of her eye, and she twisted round.

There was nothing there. Just a trick of light and shadow, no doubt.

She moved on.

A sound. She spun round, this time fast enough to catch a flurry of movement at the end of the stack.

'Who's there?'

'Jamie?' Callan's footsteps came closer.

Jamie didn't answer. Moving as quietly as she could, she edged past the end of the shelves to look along the next aisle. Nothing. The next row was the last, and she inched forward to where she could see into the wider space at the end.

She found herself staring into the frightened eyes of a plump, crop-haired girl of about twenty, dressed in a rainbow-coloured skirt and loose kaftan top.

'It's okay.' Jamie lifted her hand as the girl took a step backwards, swivelling her head back and forwards as though trying to work out which escape route gave her the best chance. 'It's okay.' She risked a smile. 'We're not dangerous, I promise.'

'Who . . .' Callan appeared, and the girl started and scuttled across the space to press her back against the shelves that lined the end of the shop.

Jamie made a sharp gesture at Callan, and he fell still. Gracie appeared beside him.

'What's your name?' Jamie asked.

The girl's voice was barely more than a whisper. 'Elsie.'

'I'm Jamie. This is Callan, and Gracie. There are three others.' She smiled again. 'Somewhere in here. It's like a maze, isn't it? I used to come here years ago. I lived not far from here.' She'd fallen into the soothing tones she used on frightened horses, where what you said mattered less than how you said it. 'Do you live near here?'

There was a long pause, during which Elsie's gaze continued to dart between them.

'Here,' she said eventually. 'I live here.'

'In Alnwick?'

She gave a half-shake of her head. 'In the shop.'

'Is it yours?' Gracie asked. 'This place, I mean.'

Elsie gave another of those quick, nervous jerks of her head.

'I used to work here. I came here after . . .' She looked down at her toes, clad in heavy purple boots. 'After.'

'Is there anyone else?' Callan asked.

'I haven't seen anyone,' Elsie said. 'Not round here anyway.'

'But there are others?'

'I've talked to some people.'

'On the comm?' Callan asked.

'Online,' Gracie put in. 'That's right, isn't it?'

Elsie nodded.

'The signal,' Callan said. 'That was you?'

Another nod. 'There's an admin server hub across the tracks,' she said. 'I hacked it ages ago. When I was first working here.' She smiled for the first time, a sweet, curved lift of her lips. 'I used it to play games when we were quiet.'

'What are you doing with it now?' Gracie asked.

'Trying to keep some things running.' Her smile fell away, leaving a worried little crease between her eyebrows. 'There's a linked server network that supports a big chunk of the net. If it's not managed, the whole thing will start breaking down.'

'Does that matter?' Callan asked bluntly.

'Yes, of course it does.' Elsie looked at him as though he'd just asked her what colour the sky was. 'If it goes down, we may not be able to get it running again.'

Callan gave her an equally uncomprehending look. 'You do know how few people are left, don't you?'

'I do know,' Elsie said, a little defensively. 'But the network, it's not just computers.' She screwed up her face, clearly searching for a way to make him understand. 'You won't get it, if you're not . . . if you're not into that sort of thing. We built a whole world online.'

'There's a whole world out there,' Callan said, nodding towards the window.

'I don't like it out there.' Elsie hunched her shoulders. 'Not really. I don't go out. I mean, I didn't. My dad used to drive me to work and pick me up. It's too big outside. Too busy.'

'Not any more,' Jamie said gently. 'Not busy.'

Elsie shrugged. 'Still big. And the network, it's important. To lots of people like me. And some of them are still alive out there.'

'You won't be able to keep it running forever,' Gracie said. Her tone was softer than usual. 'Not on your own. Sooner or later things will start to decay.'

'I'm not on my own,' Elsie said. 'There are others. All over the place. A girl in Japan. A couple of guys in the States. Some-one in Delhi. I don't know whether they're a man or a woman. They won't say. I've had about twenty contacts, although one or two haven't been online again. We're working out how to keep it running long-term.'

'I don't get it,' Callan said.

'You don't have to get it,' Gracie said. 'I don't get why you crash-landed your ship on a planet you didn't want to come to in the first place. Not everyone wants the same thing. Not everyone wants to live in the same world.'

'It's not a world.' Rena was standing at the end of the row of shelves. 'Computers. The network. It's just data and numbers.' Her face twisted. 'It's not real. None of it. We're all looking in, when we should be looking out.'

'It is real,' Elsie insisted, her cheeks and neck flushing the mottled pink of sunburn. It made her look raw and vulnerable. 'People built it. Just like they built this station, or the castle down the road. Why are those things real, just because they're made of stone, not numbers?'

'Stones and numbers.' There was a fault line running through Rena's voice, Jamie suddenly realised. A crack that could gape open at any time, and swallow her whole. 'Nothing we make is real. Only the void. Only the empty places, where God can speak to us. Only the space between the stars.'

'Rena.' Lowry appeared at her side. 'Come with me. Come outside.'

'Outside.' Rena repeated the word like an incantation. 'That's where we need to be. Not trapped in here.' An offbeat smile. 'I knew you'd understand, Marcus. You just needed to remember.'

'Rena.' Lowry's voice was low, shot through with something Jamie hadn't heard there before. A sort of broken tenderness.

'Do you remember?' Rena was growing agitated again. 'I thought you'd forgotten.'

'I remember,' Lowry said. 'Come outside.'

Rena gnawed on the edge of her thumb for a moment, and then she gave Lowry another of those unsettling smiles, and allowed him to lead her away.

'What's wrong with her?' Elsie asked, once their footsteps had faded.

'Bad case of religion,' Callan replied.

'I think it's more than that,' Jamie said.

'Doesn't matter,' he said. 'Once we get where we're going she can sit on that holy rock she keeps going on about, and pray to her heart's content to the stars. Or to the sea or the funny-shaped stone she found in her shoe. No doubt she'll find something new to believe in soon enough.'

'Where are you going?' Elsie asked.

'Lindisfarne,' Jamie said. 'Well, Rena and Lowry are. I'm going to Belsley.'

Elsie stared at her. 'Why?' Then she blinked, and looked embarrassed. 'Sorry, I mean, it's beautiful there. I've seen pictures. But why there? With everything that's happened.'

Jamie glanced around the stacks. 'Why here?'

'I don't know. It's just where I wanted to be. I didn't have anywhere else to go.'

'That's pretty much it,' Jamie said. 'It's beautiful, and I lived there once, and I don't know where else to go.'

The place that's left when you've figured out all the places you don't want to be.

She glanced up at Callan, and found him looking back at her. For a moment, they stared at one another, and then Callan looked away, turning to Elsie again.

'We're carrying on for another hour or so today,' he said. 'Jamie knows somewhere we can spend the night. If you get your things together, we can head straight off.'

Elsie blinked. 'Head off?'

Callan raised an eyebrow. 'Well, you can't stay here.'

'Why not?'

He made an impatient gesture. 'Because you'll be alone.'

'I won't be alone.' She spoke slowly, a hint of strained patience in her tone. 'I've got all those other people online.'

'But they're not real,' Callan said, and then made another irritable gesture. 'Okay, you know what I mean. They're not here.'

'I don't need them to be here,' Elsie said. 'I like being on my own. When I woke up and everyone was gone, I panicked at first, but then people started coming online and asking if anyone else was out there, and then it was okay.' She smiled slightly. 'It's not that I don't like people. It's just that I like them better when they're a long way away, and I can switch them off if I need to.'

'But you can't—'

'Why not?' Gracie spoke, cutting him off. 'If everyone was up for doing what other people think they should, this lot would still be stuck on Alegria – and you and I'd be off doing shuttle runs between the colonies?'

'That's different.'

'It's not,' Gracie replied. 'People don't have to be what other people think they should be.'

'Fine.' Callan lifted his hands, palms up. 'Stay. But what if you change your mind?'

'I won't,' Elsie said.

'Give me the server details,' Gracie said. 'When we get where we're going, we can link up. Keep in touch.'

'I'd like that.' Elsie gave the engineer a quick smile.

'Fine,' Callan said again, turning to walk back towards the shop entrance.

'Where's your server link?' Gracie asked, and then headed off in the direction Elsie indicated.

Jamie stayed.

'Are you sure?'

Elsie nodded. 'I couldn't come with you.'

'You could try,' Jamie said.

'I don't want to try,' Elsie said. 'This is okay, what I've got here. I don't need lots of people around. No one ever seemed to get that. They thought I was weird. They kept trying to make me join in. Now I can be on my own, and there'll be no one to make me feel bad about it.'

'What will you do?' Jamie asked.

'Run the network.' Elsie smiled. 'Be in charge. Make it whatever I want it to be. And I've got all these books, and I've been writing, drawing. It's stupid, I know, but I've been making a comic, telling the story of what's happened.' She gave Jamie a quick, shy glance. 'Maybe you'll all be in it.'

'You can't do all that forever.'

Elsie shrugged again. 'What else should I be doing?'

'What about food?' Jamie asked. 'We'll all have to start thinking about the future.'

'I'll figure it out.'

Still Jamie lingered, unsatisfied. 'But what about . . . other things?' she said. 'You're human. Won't you need—'

'Sex?' Elsie broke in with an unexpected flash of a grin. 'That's what you mean, isn't it?'

Jamie nodded, a little embarrassed.

Elsie sobered. 'I tried it once. I didn't like it. Maybe that was just because I didn't really like him. It was just another of those things I thought I should do, because everyone else did it. But there's no everyone else any more, is there? And this is okay. Really.'

Jamie nodded slowly. This was something she ought to understand. All those times when she'd wished people would take a step back from her. But for Elsie, a step back wasn't enough. Jamie had always felt like the world was a jigsaw puzzle, and she was the broken piece. But maybe everyone felt like that. Maybe they were all pieces of different puzzles, trying to force their curves and edges together to make a picture that just wasn't there.

'Okay,' she said. 'But you know where we'll be if you need us.'

Elsie nodded. 'And you can stop by. If you're ever near.'

'You won't mind?' Jamie said.

'Every now and again,' Elsie replied. 'Every now and again is okay.'

CHAPTER TWENTY-ONE

Elsie didn't come out to see them off. They left her in the little room at the front of the shop, where she'd gone to show Finn her mural. He'd studied it for a few moments, and then he'd opened his bag and taken out his pencils, glancing at Elsie for permission. When she nodded he leaned in close, elbows pressed against the wall, brow creased in concentration. After a minute or two he stood up straight and returned his pencils to his bag before walking away, not looking back. When Jamie went into the room she found that he'd drawn Mila in the town square, the girl's face sketched out in clear and confident lines, a wistful smile playing about her lips.

As they walked away from the shop, Callan kept glancing behind him, as though he expected Elsie to run after them. *Stop, I've made a mistake.*

'She'll be fine.' There was a trace of impatience in Gracie's voice.

Callan shrugged, and picked up pace, joining Jamie at the front of the group. Finn was now leading the horse, and was taking the responsibility seriously, judging from the little furrow of concentration between his eyebrows.

Jamie glanced sideways at Callan who had his hand resting on his side again.

'You okay?'

He nodded. 'Might need a check over when we get where we're going. Where are we going, by the way?'

'Place called Walton Hall. I used to go there as a child. It had a tearoom, and you could walk in the gardens. There was a room with all these strange things. A fish that looked like a porcupine, and a scale model of the Taj Mahal. I used to imagine getting locked in there at night, and having to sleep in one of the four-poster beds.' He was studying her face, and she looked away. 'Daft, I know.'

'Not daft. Doesn't everyone do that? Imagine things they can't have?'

'It looks like I can have it,' she said, trying to make a joke of it. 'For one night, at least.'

'There you go. End of the world's not all bad. At least there are four-poster beds.'

She was seized by a sudden image. Callan sliding off his shirt and slipping in beside her, behind the closed drapes of one of those ridiculous canopied beds.

She turned away, looking out across the fields, in case he saw the thought sketched across her face.

It took them nearly two hours to reach Walton. Lowry had been walking more slowly since leaving Alnwick, and Rena seemed to be flagging too. She had a glazed look on her face and didn't respond when Lowry spoke to her.

They crossed a humpback bridge over a little river, heading for the four stone dragon heads that glared out across the road, marking the edge of the Walton estate. The square-fronted hall, with its ranks of floor-to-ceiling windows, sat at the end of the main drive, the woods forming a ragged mass behind it, dark and formless in the glare of the sinking sun.

'There's a lawn at the side,' Jamie said. 'We can let the horse graze there.'

'What's his name?' Finn said suddenly.

'Who?'

Finn jerked his hand towards the horse. 'Him.'

Jamie smiled at him. 'Why don't you choose one?'

Finn frowned. 'What are horses' names?'

'Anything you like.'

The frown deepened.

Jamie was about to tell him it wasn't something to worry over, but at that moment the hall's heavy wooden doors swung open and an elderly man stepped out. There was something wrong about him, and Jamie squinted for a moment before she realised that he was dressed like something out of an old period film. A high-collared coat with long tails, and breeches tucked into boots.

As Callan moved forwards the man held up a polished cane with a silver top.

'Can I trouble you to stay where you are and identify yourselves, please?' He enunciated each word with an unnatural precision.

'Callan Jacobs. My ship crash-landed half a day's walk from here,' Callan said. 'These others are my engineer, and survivors from two of the colonies. They've been trying to reach Earth.'

'It would appear they've succeeded,' the man said, lifting a monocle to his eye and peering at each of them in turn. 'We did see your ship pass over, but we weren't aware you had experienced such an unfortunate ending to your journey. Can I ask your intended destination?'

'Lindisfarne.' Jamie stepped forward.

'And you are?'

'Jamie.'

The man studied her for a moment, before walking down the steps, hand outstretched.

'Delighted to make your acquaintance.' He turned to look at the rest of the group. 'I'm Bernard Hendry.'

'Are you alone here?' Callan asked.

'Oh, good gracious, no,' the man said, smiling. 'There's a good little group of us.'

'How many?' Jamie said.

'How many? Hmm, let me see. There's myself, Miss Cavanagh, Mr Carter.' The man made a show of counting on his fingers. 'Mrs Denby, Mrs Lawrence, Mr Greenwood. Oh, I think we're a round dozen in number.'

'That many?' Callan said.

What had happened to those survival statistics? Maybe people were stronger, or more stubborn, than anyone had thought.

'We took all possible precautions.' The man glanced away, and when he looked back, his smile was in place once more. 'Please. Come in. You'll be needing to rest. Beds for the night, perhaps?'

'Will there be room?' Jamie asked.

The man nodded. 'We have a number of rooms free on the top floor. You will come in?' He smiled at Finn. 'Probably not the horse, but there's plenty of grazing.'

Callan didn't move. 'What are you doing here?'

The man tilted his head. 'I don't understand.'

Callan gestured towards the hall. 'Seems an odd place for so many survivors to gather.'

'Ah.' The man turned his monocle backwards and forwards between his fingers. 'A fortunate coincidence. We were here for an overnight event when the virus took hold. A historical re-enactment.'

'Did everyone make it?' Jamie couldn't quite process that idea. Funny how swiftly your mindset adjusted to a new state of things. It had become inconceivable that the natural state of the human race was more than ones and twos.

'Not all, no.' The man gestured towards the door. 'Please. Come in.'

Jamie went with Finn to let the horse loose on the green. Neat cottages ran along two sides, fronted by a wide gravel path. At the far end, the cottages curved round to meet a stable block, a coach house and an archway, topped by a clock tower. It was all so achingly familiar that Jamie felt a rush of vertigo, as though she might fall back into another time, when she'd run along those paths with her young half-sisters trailing behind her, crying, *Jamie, wait for us.*

'Emily,' Finn said, pulling her back into the present moment.

'What?'

'The horse,' Finn said.

'That's a girl's name.'

Finn gave her a narrow-eyed look.

'Okay.' She held a hand up. 'Emily it is.'

When Emily was settled, they walked back to the house and followed the sound of voices through to the central hall. It was a double-height space that had always reminded Jamie of the cloisters at a cathedral, with stone pillars marching around the edges and a gallery above. Painted panels hung between the pillars, and a frieze ran round the narrow stretch of wall between the lower and upper floors. Battle scenes. Banquet scenes. Hunting scenes. Remnants of an older world, now even more remote.

The others were there, surrounded by a small crowd of elderly men and women. Like Mr Hendry they were all dressed in old-fashioned clothing. Long dresses and shawls for the women, their creased faces powdered and painted in a long-lost version of beauty. For the men, it was morning suits or smoking jackets, accessorised with cravats and pocket watches.

'Jamie.' Mr Hendry spotted them. 'Do come and meet the others.'

He drew Jamie into a small group of his companions. Finn

trailed behind, hanging back from the group. Mr Hendry gave him a quick look, then turned away, making no attempt to include him.

'Mrs Denby, Mr Graham, Miss Ingram, this is Jamie.' He turned to her. 'I should really introduce you more formally, but I don't know your other name.'

'Allenby.' There was something about this whole set-up that was making her feel snappish and out of sorts. She didn't want to stand there discussing the fine points of an archaic etiquette, when she was yet to figure out the rules of the now.

'Miss Allenby,' Mr Hendry said, bowing from the waist.

'Bernard tells me you're travelling to Lindisfarne,' said the woman who'd been introduced as Mrs Denby. 'Do you have family there?'

Jamie must have misheard the question. She'd said, *Did you have family there.* Of course she had. It was an opening for them to share their losses. There'd be a new social code for this new world. You wouldn't talk about the weather, or what you did for a living. You'd talk about who you'd lost.

Then she looked at Mrs Denby's face, cool and polite, her eyebrows pencilled into perfect arcs that gave her a permanently questioning look. She hadn't misheard.

'I don't know.' Jamie's voice was too loud, and Mrs Denby's lips pursed in the faintest suggestion of disapproval. All around them, people were talking in low, measured tones, a civilised hum punctuated only by the occasional flutter of brittle laughter. 'I don't expect so. Given that everyone's dead.'

'Not everyone.' The man who'd been introduced as Mr Graham smiled, his lips drawing back from his teeth. 'Not by a long shot.'

'Near enough.'

What was the point of this charade?

'Well,' Mr Hendry put in soothingly. 'We're all here together now.' His face suddenly lit up, and he turned on the spot, clapping his hands until the room fell quiet. Callan was standing over on the other side of the room, arms folded, face closed. Gracie was standing a little way apart, making no attempt to join in the conversation. She couldn't see Lowry and Rena. 'Friends. Guests. This is a special occasion. I propose a night of celebration. Dinner in the great hall, and then a dance.'

There was a twittering chorus of agreement, and a couple of women clapped their own hands in an incongruous girlish gesture. One very elderly man drummed his hand on a sideboard in what appeared to be enthusiasm.

Hendry turned back to Jamie. 'I'll find rooms for your party.' He glanced around. 'Will everyone require their own room, or are any of you . . . er . . .'

Jamie cut across his exaggerated delicacy. 'We'll all need our own rooms.'

'Very well,' he said. 'I'll show you up.' He looked around at everyone again. 'What time shall we say for dinner?'

'I'll ask Lawson.' Mrs Denby walked slowly and stiffly across to pull on a worn velvet cord. A bell rang with a peremptory clang, and after a moment or two a woman appeared from between two of the far pillars. She was dressed in the traditional black and white garb of an old-fashioned housekeeper.

'Ah, Lawson,' Mrs Denby said. 'As you see, we have guests. We are intending to hold a formal dinner in celebration. What time could we all sit down to eat?'

'Around eight thirty.' The woman's face was expressionless.

'Perfect,' Mrs Denby said. 'Thank you, Lawson.'

The woman's footsteps echoed as she disappeared again.

'There.' Mrs Denby pressed her palms together, a satisfied smile on her face. She turned to Jamie. 'Lawson takes such good care of us. It's so fortunate that she turned up when she did. With her own vehicle as well. Without her, we would have run out of provisions days ago. And she makes such lovely food.'

'You have a servant?' Gracie appeared at Jamie's side. 'How does that work? Do you pay her?'

'Pay?' Mrs Denby wrinkled her nose. 'She doesn't expect payment. This is a mutually beneficial arrangement.'

'Let me show you to your rooms.' Mr Hendry stepped forward. 'I'm sure you'll want to bathe before dinner.'

Gracie hesitated, and then she shrugged and stood back to allow Mr Hendry to walk past her towards the stairs.

Jamie was assigned what must have been a young girl's bedroom, all pink flounces and bundles of lace. It wasn't one she remembered seeing before. When she turned the handle on a door in the far wall, it opened onto a tiny bathroom, with an old-fashioned toilet and a claw-footed bath. The tap clanked and sputtered when she turned the stiff metal wheel, but it eventually yielded a sporadic flow of hot water.

When the bath was full, she stripped off and climbed in, rubbing at her aching calves. There'd been no reason for them to push on so fast, but they all seemed to be feeling the same relentless need to get to where they were going.

Jamie closed her eyes and tucked her knees up, letting her body lift off the curved bottom of the bath. If she kept her hands moving beneath her, she could just about float. She could be anywhere. She could be in the ocean, or in that rooftop pool back on Alegria. It could be any place, any time. She opened her eyes. There was a time when she'd imagined herself here. Now that she was, her mind seemed set on conjuring up ways to let her pretend she was somewhere else.

She stood up, wreathed in steam, and climbed out of the bath. There were no towels, so she walked through to the bedroom naked and dripping. She dried herself on a spare blanket, then climbed up onto the high bed and slid in beneath the eiderdown.

When she woke, the light was fading. She looked at the clock on the wall. Eight o'clock. They'd said dinner at eight thirty. She climbed out of bed, wrapping herself in the discarded blanket, and rummaged through her rucksack, looking for clean clothes.

A knock at the door.

'Who is it?'

'Mrs Lawson. I have clean clothes for you.'

'Come in.'

The door opened a crack, and Mrs Lawson peered around it, looking away when she saw Jamie's state of undress. 'Shall I leave the clothes outside?'

'No, it's okay.' Jamie walked over and pulled the door open.

Mrs Lawson stepped reluctantly into the room. 'I'll put this over here.'

Jamie turned to watch as she laid a moss-green dress on the bed. 'What's going on here?'

Mrs Lawson carefully smoothed out the fabric, not answering the question.

'Why are you working for these people?' Jamie pressed.

'Why not?' The other woman straightened up. 'They need help.'

'But what do you get out of it? All those old people, acting like something from a period drama, and you running around after them. They can't pay you. They don't have anything you need.'

'They do.' When the woman looked up, Jamie saw a flash of something raw and haunted in her eyes. 'Do you know what

275

it's like to think you're completely alone? To think the whole world is dead but you?'

Jamie felt a flicker of angry resentment. She did know how that felt. And she'd been light years from anywhere she could call home. 'Yes. It was three days before I found anyone else.'

The woman gave a low mutter of laughter. 'Three?' She wrapped her arms across her body. 'I was alone for a week. I couldn't get the comm to work. I drove to Alnwick, and to Rothbury, then down to Newcastle. I couldn't find anyone. I was going mad. I climbed the monument in the city, meaning to jump. But it was all concrete and grey and I didn't want to lie there for the rats and the birds. I wished I was dust like everyone else.' She drew a deep, heaving breath. 'I thought, *If I'm going to kill myself, I want to do it somewhere nicer than this.* I broke a shop window and picked up as many pills as I could. Then I drove to Walton. I used to work here, back when the kids were at school. I used to dress like this . . .' She ran a hand over her uniform. '. . . and show visitors around. I thought I'd go down to the gardens, take the pills, and the leaves would bury me. But when I got here, I found Mr Hendry and the others. I fell down on the steps and cried.'

She looked down, rubbing at one sleeve as though she could brush the memories away.

'And then what happened?'

'It was pretty straightforward. They had a . . . vacancy.' There was a little twist at the corner of her smile. 'That's how they put it. It was all quite formal and businesslike, really.'

'But it's like being a slave,' Jamie said.

'It's not like that at all. I made a choice. Be alone, or be here like this. It's not like I could have just lived here, like I was one of them.'

'Why not?' Even as Jamie asked the question, she suddenly knew what the answer would be. She glanced at the woman's left hand. Sure enough, her ID mark was wrapped around her forefinger. Lower echelon.

The woman caught the glance and gave Jamie a faint, ironic smile.

'That's ridiculous.' Jamie felt a flush of anger, as much at Mrs Lawson's calm acceptance as at the old people's exploitation of her loneliness. 'None of that matters any more.'

'But you still looked at my hand.'

'I . . .' Jamie tripped over her own tangled thoughts and emotions. 'It's not right. This whole thing, the dressing up, the way they talk. It's insane.'

'It's just how they like things,' Mrs Lawson said. 'They used to do those historical events. Re-enactments. Mrs Denby said it was because they preferred an older time to how things are now. She said manners were better, and people showed respect.'

'But everything's changed,' Jamie said. 'There is no *how things are now*. There's only us, and what we do.'

'It doesn't matter.' Mrs Lawson gave the green dress another quick smooth with her palm. 'I've always worked. It makes me feel like things are normal. Like what I do still means something.'

'You don't have to stay,' Jamie said. 'You could come with us.'

'And do what?'

'I don't know. I just . . . we just need to get there. Then we'll figure it out.' God, she sounded like Rena. Like there was an answer there, waiting for them, written in the sand maybe, or washed up in a bottle. 'It's somewhere,' she went on, a little defensively. 'It's something. It's not just sitting around, wondering what the point of it all is.'

Mrs Lawson picked up her armful of clothes. 'And so is this.'

'Come with us,' Jamie said.

'I can't leave them.' Mrs Lawson shook her head. 'They wouldn't last a fortnight.' She walked over and fumbled at the door handle. Jamie followed and opened it for her. 'And besides, they're nice enough, most of them. I know it seems odd, but it works. And it's my choice.'

'But—'

The woman cut her off with a sharp gesture. 'My choice.' Her tone was harder this time. 'I don't even know you, and you're telling me to come away with you. I'm needed here, and that's something I never thought I'd say again. And you want me to just walk away, throw it all in for a promise of . . . what? How do I know what you're offering would be better than this?'

Jamie couldn't find an immediate answer, and Mrs Lawson gave her a quick nod, as though she'd expected none, and walked out of the room.

Jamie stood still in the middle of the floor. It felt as though there'd been some trailing end she'd missed, something that would have let her tug at Mrs Lawson's argument and unravel the whole thing.

She rubbed her face. There was something she was missing. All these people, all with different ideas about what the world should be. They couldn't all be right.

She picked up the dress and walked over to the mirror to hold it up against her. It was ankle-length, and simply cut, with an empire-line bodice and gold trim around the neckline and hem. She stared at herself in the mirror. Could she really go downstairs and pretend this was all right and normal?

My choice.

Jamie shook her head against the echo of Mrs Lawson's words, as though she could carry on the argument, even without the other woman here. What if some choices were wrong, or dangerous? What if you could clearly see a better one?

She turned away from the mirror. She was tired. The day

had been long and eventful. The crash. The walk. Elsie. The old people. No point tying herself in knots, trying to figure it all out. She'd dress for dinner and play along with the charade. Tomorrow she'd speak to Mrs Lawson again. Maybe get Lowry to help her. Together they'd persuade her to come with them.

The dress fitted like it had been made for her. Before her illness it would probably have been too tight, but now it clung to her like a second skin, moulding itself to the contours of her breasts, and skimming the curve of her stomach. She wound her hair up on top of her head and walked over to look at the accessories Mrs Lawson had left on the bed: a green and gold stole, and a pair of elbow gloves in faded gold satin. She hesitated, but the whole situation was so bizarre that it seemed perfectly reasonable to roll the gloves up her arms, and drape the stole across her shoulders.

She looked at the clock again. Eight fifteen. Where were the others? Where was Finn? She went out into the corridor and rapped gently with her knuckles on the next door along.

Silence.

She was about to tap again when the door jerked open, and Gracie looked out. She was wrapped in a towel, her hair damp and clinging to her skull. It made her look smaller, and softer round the edges.

'What?'

'Sorry,' Jamie said. 'I was looking for Finn.'

'That one.' Gracie pointed to the door at the end.

'Are you coming down?' Jamie asked.

Gracie paused in the act of closing the door. 'Yes. I'm hungry.'

'Are you . . .' Jamie hesitated, not wanting to expose herself to Gracie's scorn. '. . . dressing for dinner?'

'Well, I'm not coming down naked, if that's what you mean.'

279

The engineer gave the faintest suggestion of a smile. 'I'm dressing, but probably not as they hoped.'

Then she closed the door.

Jamie walked along the corridor and knocked on the door Gracie had indicated. There was a long pause, and when Finn finally answered, it sounded as though he was standing right on the other side of the door.

'Yes.'

'It's Jamie.'

There was the sound of a key turning in a lock, and then the door creaked open. Finn had clearly done his best with the unfamiliar clothes, but the wing collar had defeated him. It hung open, the cravat looped into a lopsided knot over the top. He'd managed the row of fiddly shirt buttons, but one of the long tails was bunched up at his waist.

'Here.' When Jamie reached for his cravat, Finn flinched, but then held still.

'I couldn't do it.'

'I'm not sure I'm going to do any better,' Jamie said, holding the loose silk ends. 'Shall we leave it off?'

'The lady said I had to wear it.'

'You don't have to do anything. Not if you don't want to.' She looked around. She remembered this room. It had a single canopied bed, and there were toys scattered about the place. At the far end, there was a narrow ladder leading up to a little gallery lined with dolls' houses. On the floor, ranks of lead soldiers faced off, as though about to join battle. The formation was broken in one corner, with a clutch of red-coated figures scattered face down, balancing awkwardly on their protruding muskets and swords.

'I'm sorry.' Finn had followed the line of her gaze.

'Don't be silly,' Jamie said. 'They're just toys.'

Finn continued to stare at the prone figures, rubbing one finger and thumb together in a compulsive, repetitive gesture.

Jamie looked at him. 'Do you want to stay here?'

He gave her a quick glance, a hopeful light flickering in his eyes.

'I could get some dinner sent up,' she went on. 'If you don't want to come down.'

'Yes please,' was all he said, but just as she turned away, he reached out a hesitant hand and tapped her arm with his fingertips.

She turned back, thinking he wanted something, but he was already kneeling back down by the fallen soldiers. It took her a moment to realise that it had been an attempt at affection or thanks. She watched as he reached to pick up one of the little infantrymen, setting it back on its feet with infinite care.

'Okay?' she said.

He nodded. 'Okay.'

CHAPTER TWENTY-TWO

When she left Finn, Jamie walked round the gallery to the stairs. A single flight of steps led down to the middle floor, and then the stairs split, meeting at a landing halfway down, before merging, grandly, into their final curving descent.

As she walked down the right-hand flight, Callan was just reaching the landing from the other side. He paused, one hand on the bannister, and looked up at her. Jamie was surprised to see him dressed in a morning suit, complete with wing collar and a wine-red cravat, just like the one that had defeated Finn.

'I didn't have you down as the dressing-up kind,' she said, as she reached the landing.

He raised an eyebrow. 'What kind did you have me down as?'

She busied herself straightening her hem.

'I just mean . . . this whole thing is so odd, I thought maybe I was the only one daft enough to go along with it.'

Callan shrugged. 'It's one night, and then we'll be off again.'

'But it's not just one night. Not for them. This is how they live.'

'It doesn't matter,' he said. 'It's just another way of editing things to something they like better. And for us it's just one night.'

And what did that one night mean for him? What part of his life was he editing, standing there in his dress suit, in a place he'd never wanted to come?

'What about Mrs Lawson?' Jamie said.

Callan gave another shrug. 'I offered her a chance to come with us. She said you'd tried as well. I guess she's made a choice. Just like that girl back in Alnwick. Just like Mila.'

'I know,' Jamie said. 'It just feels *wrong.*'

'I know.' Callan echoed her words, with a small smile. 'But like I said, just one night.'

He lifted his hand from the bannister, stretching it out towards her, palm up. For a moment she didn't understand, and then he gave her another of those lopsided little smiles, and tipped his head towards the next flight of steps. Her heart gave a hard thump, and then she stretched out her own hand and placed it in his. For a second it just rested there, and then he closed his fingers around hers, dipping his head in an ironic little bow.

Just one night. They could let go, pretend none of it had ever happened.

'They're probably waiting for us,' he said. 'Shall we go down?'

She let him escort her down the stairs, and round the gallery to some open double doors, through which she could hear a low hum of conversation and the descant clink of glasses.

They stepped through the door into a dark-panelled room, in which ranks of flickering candles vied with the low rays of the sinking sun. A heavy mahogany banqueting table was laid with what must have been the best china: cream with an oriental pattern around the edge. Four steaming tureens sat at equally spaced intervals, and each place setting had the full ceremonial array of forks and spoons and more knives than anyone could possibly use.

'Ms Allenby, Mr Jacobs.' Mr Hendry hurried over to greet them, bowing over Jamie's free hand. 'So glad you could join us. Will your companions be down soon?'

'Finn won't be coming,' Jamie said. 'I was going to ask if he could have a tray in his room.'

'Of course.' Mr Hendry bowed again. It was beginning to get on Jamie's nerves. 'I'll ask Lawson to see to it.'

'I can take it up,' Jamie objected, but Mr Hendry wafted his hand.

'Lawson will be happy to oblige. And the others? Mr Lowry, Ms Casella, and the other lady, I didn't catch her full name.'

'I'd stick with Gracie.' Callan gave a faint smile. 'She's not one for standing on unnecessary ceremony.'

'Of course,' Mr Hendry said. 'Whatever you think is best. We want all of you to be comfortable.'

'If you want them to be comfortable, then you'll stop talking in the doorway and get them a drink.' One of the older women came over, leaning on a walking stick, topped with what looked like ivory, yellowed by age and the rub of many hands. She had a slight stoop but she moved briskly enough, despite the stick, and the gaze she turned on Mr Hendry was sharp and disapproving.

'Of course,' he said. 'Red or white?'

'Red, please,' Jamie said, thinking that this could have been one of those interminable parties on Alegria. Everyone talking about nothing, and drinking to take the edge off it all.

'Red's fine for me,' Callan said.

Mr Hendry walked over to a heavy wooden sideboard, where a row of dusty wine bottles stood in a row.

The woman turned to Jamie and Callan with a malicious grin.

'Might as well keep him busy,' she said. 'He's terribly tedious when he gets into his stride. I sometimes think he really believes all this . . .' She wafted her hand vaguely. '. . . whatever you want to call it.'

Jamie felt a little sag of relief, as though the woman's words had created a crack in the facade of this strange situation.

'You don't like it?'

The woman shrugged, adjusting her weight on the walking stick. 'I wouldn't go that far,' she said. 'Cora Barton, by the way. I don't think we've been introduced. All these manners and affectations getting in the way. No, I wouldn't go as far as saying I don't like it. It passes the time. If we didn't have something to take our minds off it, we'd just be sitting around waiting to die.' She lowered her voice. 'Don't let them hear me say that, mind you. It's pretty much blasphemy. Most of them are still twenty-one inside their heads.' She nodded towards one of the other women, fluttering a fan in front of her painted smile, her head tilted coyly to listen to something one of the men was saying. 'See what I mean? Still, it's harmless.'

'Harmless?' Callan said. 'Would Mrs Lawson agree?'

'Ah.' The other woman tipped her head to the side. 'You think we've got her imprisoned here, scrubbing the floors while we ugly stepsisters swan around in silk and flounces.'

'Pretty much.' Callan leaned back against the wall, his gaze flickering around the room.

Cora shook her head. 'It's not like that. It's all part of the game. It's been ramped up for your benefit, of course. Most nights, the majority of us eat in the kitchen. Mrs Lawson too. We compare our varicose veins, and Mrs Zechiel over there puts her feet up on a chair, and Mrs Sutton makes tea and it's all very ordinary. One or two of them . . .' She jerked her head towards Mrs Denby. 'They insist on eating in here, every breakfast, lunch and dinner, but then they've always had a stick up their backsides.'

'But you only let her stay if she waited on you,' Jamie said. 'How is that a game?'

'Is that what she told you?' Cora asked. 'Well, I suppose you could interpret it like that.'

'What if she'd said no?' Jamie pressed.

'She didn't.' There was a certain wariness in the other woman's eyes, and Jamie suddenly wanted to take a step back from her. This place, all this play-acting, how could you ever know what was the truth and what was just part of the show? The room was stuffy and close. Too many bodies. Too many layers of stiff, starched clothing. Why didn't they open one of the French windows?

Mr Hendry returned with two large glasses of wine in his hands.

'A good vintage, this,' he said. 'We're fortunate to have a well-stocked cellar.'

As Jamie took a sip of her wine he watched her, eyes bright with expectation.

'Good?'

She nodded, and then turned at the sound of footsteps as Lowry and Rena entered the room. Lowry was wearing a plain grey suit, the trouser cuffs turned up to accommodate his small frame. Rena was dressed in a dark red crepe dress, long-sleeved and fitted, with black lace at the collar and hem. It suited her, giving her shape where there was none, and lifting her pallor a little. For the first time Jamie wondered what the other woman had looked like a few years ago, before she'd been worn down to just skin and nerves. There was something about the tilt of her head, the play of light and shade across her features, that made Jamie think she might have been almost beautiful.

Rena and Lowry were followed into the room by Gracie. Mr Hendry did an almost comedic double-take, eyes widening in clear disapproval. Gracie was wearing a man's grey morning suit over a cream silk shirt and cravat. Her short hair was smoothed down, and the suit hung perfectly from her tall, broad-shouldered frame. There was a stiff, uncompromising beauty to her, although Jamie suspected she wouldn't have thanked anyone for such a compliment.

Callan gave his engineer a quick, conspiratorial smile just as a chime sounded nearby. Jamie turned to see one of the men holding a small silver hand bell.

'Ladies, gentlemen. Will you please take your seats. A quick headcount has revealed equal numbers of men and women this evening, so please do adhere to the traditional seating arrangement of gentleman-lady, and perhaps our guests could spread themselves out, so that we have a good conversational mix.'

As people started tugging high-backed wooden chairs out of the tight ranks, Jamie hesitated. Two round-faced old men were beaming at her, gesturing to the seat between them. She'd have to squeeze in, all clashing chairs and clumsy apologies, and then they'd sit wedged together, unable to move or turn without pressing against their neighbour. Was it too late to make an excuse? She could say she felt unwell. She could go up and sit with Finn. But somehow she was still walking towards the table, as though social convention was as strong as gravity.

Don't make a fuss. Don't offend.

Fit in, however many of your edges you have to rub away to get there.

A hand cupped her elbow, steering her towards the end of the table.

'Here.' Callan let go of her arm to pull out two chairs.

Mr Hendry fluttered over. 'I don't think . . . Would you not prefer to sit—'

'These are fine.' Callan gave him a bland smile. 'We're comfortable here.'

Mr Hendry hesitated, then inclined his head. 'Very well.' He marched away to the middle of the table, where he took a place next to Rena. Lowry was at the far end, with Gracie a couple of seats along from him. She was beside a man who was quite possibly entirely deaf, judging from his vague smile, and the way he kept nodding in response to nothing at all. On her other side, there was a tall, elegant-looking man, one of the younger members of the group – although that still put him at least in his seventies. He was leaning in to speak to her, and Jamie thought she could detect a hint of admiration in his face.

The tureens were uncovered, and plates handed along. Jamie was relieved to see that Mrs Lawson wasn't expected to serve them. While she was waiting for her own portion of what seemed to be a vegetable stew of some sort, Jamie turned to Callan, searching for something to say.

He was already looking at her, and when their eyes met, he tilted his head in a mocking impression of Mr Hendry's repeated bows.

'So, do you come here often?'

She glanced along the table at the close-pressed mass of wool and silk and papery skin.

'It's my first time,' she said. 'How about you?'

'Oh, all the time. But I think standards are slipping a little. I don't think I'll come again.'

'Any better offers?' Jamie said.

'I'm holding out for one. But we'll see.'

Mr Hendry clinked his knife against his glass. 'Grace,' he said.

'Here.' Gracie raised her glass.

Callan gave a quick laugh, and a couple of the women tittered. Mr Hendry ignored the interruption, turning to Lowry. 'Would our visiting clergyman be so good as to lead us in prayer?' He folded his hands and dropped his head in an ostentatious gesture.

'Of course.' Lowry cleared his throat. 'Beyond the stars, beyond the sun, beyond the ending of the worlds there is life and hope and love. We give thanks for those blessings. In the name of all gods. Amen.'

There was a muttered chorus of *Amens* and then the woman next to Lowry turned to him.

'What church did you say you were from?'

'None,' Lowry said with a smile. 'Freelance, you might say.'

'How unusual.' The woman picked up her fork and poked at her food. 'This smells wonderful. Lawson really is amazing, isn't she?'

All around the table, people were making the usual empty social noises. The food. The state of everyone's health. Would it rain tomorrow? Might they take tea in the garden?

There was an invisible barrier separating the wood-panelled room from the world outside, and it seemed to be stretching thinner and tighter.

Any minute, Jamie thought, *any minute now and it will snap*.

Callan spoke up, his voice loud enough to carry to the far end of the table. 'So, what are your plans?' The conversation fell away as all heads turned towards him. Only the old man next to Gracie kept smiling and nodding.

'I'm afraid I don't follow,' Mr Hendry said.

'What next?' Callan said. 'You can't be planning on staying here.'

A woman laughed, a nervous scatter of sound. 'Why ever not?'

Callan rested his elbows on the table, oblivious to the little chorus of disapproving sniffs. 'Do you know how few people are left? It's not a question of just waiting till someone comes to rescue you. You need to be thinking in terms of years, not just living day to day. What will you do when your food stocks are exhausted? What if you need medical help?'

Silence. No one was looking at him any more.

'Lovely wine,' a woman said eventually, tilting her glass to examine the blood-red liquid. 'What year?'

The conversation rose again, a swift, relieved surge.

Callan stared around the table for a moment, then shrugged and picked up his cutlery.

When the meal was finished, Mr Hendry herded everyone into the hall, where a modern music dock sat, incongruously, on top of a harpsichord.

'Unfortunately none of us play,' he said.

Jamie glanced at Gracie, but the engineer was leaning against a pillar, arms folded.

When a formal, baroque melody started up, several of the old people paired up, and commenced circling the hall in a slow, arthritic minuet. There was a sort of dignity to the scene, despite the ludicrous costumes and the garish make-up. With a pang of pain, Jamie thought of Mila, and how the girl would have loved this. She would have been among the dancers, smiling, flirting gently, never thinking of anything but how wonderful the moment was.

'Top-up?' Callan appeared at her elbow with the remains of a bottle of red. 'I'm told it's a good vintage.'

'What does that even mean?' Jamie lifted her glass so that he could fill it up. 'Did the winemakers tread them for longer? Use better corks?'

'Don't know.' Callan discarded the empty bottle on a nearby sideboard, with supreme disregard for its antique veneer. 'It's one of those things where you should just nod and pretend to agree.' He took a slug of wine. 'Like that Beltran caviar that everyone raves about. I met a trader who'd transported some and swiped a tin. He said it tasted like old men's feet.' He shook his head. 'Never asked him how he knew. You get all sorts on the outer trading runs.'

When Jamie laughed, Callan gave her a sidelong look.

'I don't dance,' he said. 'Fancy getting out of here?'

'Where to?'

'You know this place,' he said. 'You said it was beautiful. Show me.'

It was easy enough to slip away. All eyes were on the dancers. As they walked down the drive, the sun was setting, and the air was that odd blend of fading heat and burgeoning chill; not cold enough for an extra layer, but cool enough to make you shiver every now and again.

The path to the woods was across the road. Jamie glanced both ways, and caught him looking at her.

'Habit,' she said defensively.

'How long ago did you leave Earth?' he said.

'Fifteen years.'

As they wound their way through the sparse woodland, they were trailed by a clamour of late birdsong, their passing marked by shrills and whistles, and stubborn loops of two- or three-note melodies.

At the far end of the little lake, a flight of shallow stone steps led down to an ornate iron gate. They emerged onto a statue-lined walkway running the length of the sunken gardens. Below them, a flight of stone stairs curved down onto a paved terrace, with another few steps leading down to a tangle of little paths and hidden bowers that formed the garden itself.

The bright scent of lavender merged with the deeper musk of damp moss. The noisier birds had stayed behind in the woods, and the only song inside the garden came from a lone thrush, perched on top of a green-stained lead satyr.

Callan moved over to lean on the low wall that had always made Jamie's stepmother nervous.

Careful. Be careful.

Jamie joined him, resting her elbows on the rough stone.

'It's not what you expect, is it?' she said. 'I don't know why they tucked the gardens away down here.'

'Maybe they wanted a place to come to when they needed to get away,' Callan said. 'From all the bowing and scraping up at the hall.'

The sun was a bare sliver of red now, just clinging to the craggy outline of the distant hills. In the garden the shadows deepened, darkness welling up and spilling over the wall into the fields beyond. The first stars were pricking into life, each one starting as an uncertain blur in the dark blue, only growing clear when you didn't look straight at them. Strange how the stars didn't change after you'd been out there. Wherever in the universe you stood, it was impossible to think of them as anything but pinpricks in a sky belonging to your world alone. You were always the centre of the universe, with the spheres and the stars and other people's stories turning around you.

'What are you thinking?' Callan was watching her.

'The universe,' she said, wafting a hand at the darkening sky. 'Our place in it all. Little things like that.'

'Ah. Those sorts of thoughts. Reached any conclusions?'

'Nothing that makes much sense.'

He looked up. 'All those years spent trying to get off this planet. Then close on a century digging ourselves in, setting up shop on every rock that looked like it could hold us. And here we are, unravelling it all, making our way back to a random little corner of the world in which it all started.'

'We had to go somewhere,' Jamie said. 'All those end-of-the-world movies. They were always about surviving. People looting and fighting. No one ever made a film where the main character had enough food, and no one to run away from, where they looked around and said, *Right, what now?*'

'So, what now?' he said with a faint smile.

'I don't know.' She tried for an answering smile. 'I'll tell you when I get there.'

He stepped in front of her, standing close enough that she thought she could feel the warmth of his body.

'Why not tell me now?'

There was such a thin sliver of space between them. If he just shifted his weight a little, they'd be touching.

'Jamie.' He said it quietly, and somehow she managed to lift her gaze. He was looking down at her, his face shaded by the almost-dark. He lifted a hand and placed it on her shoulder, sliding it round so that it was resting on the nape of her neck, his thumb moving in barely perceptible circles on her bare skin.

Her hands were down by her sides, feeling heavy and clumsy. She thought of touching him, but she couldn't work out how. He shifted closer, his body just brushing against hers, his other arm coming up to rest across her back.

'What . . .' She stopped. She knew what this was. It was beating in the air around them, writing itself into her skin. But she didn't know what it would be, if she leaned back and tipped her face up to his. One night, and then they'd both pretend it hadn't happened? A few days together, trying to make it into something more, breathless with the sense of time running out?

His hands were moving gently across her back, and she wanted to lean into his touch, pressing his palms harder against her skin, so that she'd be able to feel every contour and callus. But they'd been here before, and she remembered the look in his eyes as he told her they'd only hate one another in the morning.

That was before he'd trapped himself here. What had changed? Had he looked at her and thought, *This will do*?

The wall behind her prevented her from stepping back, so she slid her hands in between them, placing them against his chest.

He drew back a little. 'What is it?'

She shook her head, her palms still flat against his body, just enough pressure behind them to be clear that she was pushing him away, not holding on to him.

He stood still for a moment, and then breathed out hard and took a slow step back. The shock of not touching him sparked in her fingertips.

'Okay,' he said.

The air between them felt colder than it had been, as though night had finally rubbed away the last vestiges of the day's warmth.

He glanced towards the gate. 'I suppose we should head back.'

She nodded slowly. 'Okay.'

The woods were almost silent as they made their way back to the hall. The evening birds had all settled down for the night. She wanted to say something, but she couldn't find any words that wouldn't sound trite or foolish. She wanted to tell him that she needed to finish this journey, and then she could think about what came next. She needed time to unravel everything that had happened. And then . . . but she couldn't say that. It would sound like she was asking him to wait for her to make up her mind, and that wasn't it at all.

When they reached the house, he held the door for her, and she thanked him politely. The dance was still going on, but they skirted the edge of the hallway, round to the bottom of the stairs, where he said goodnight, and went upstairs without looking back.

After he'd gone, she wandered on along the corridor, too restless to think of following him upstairs. Where was that room with all the strange things? She tried a couple of doors. A parlour. A study. Then a locked door. If she remembered rightly, all the rooms on this side of the house were connected. The next door was unlocked, and she opened it and stepped into the library. She'd loved this room, with its ranks of perfectly matched spines, stretching from floor to ceiling.

The far door had no keyhole, but when she turned the handle, it didn't budge. When she looked up she saw that it was bolted at the top. There was a set of library steps nearby, and she pulled them over, picking up the hem of her dress so she could climb up and drag the bolt back.

The room beyond was much darker than the library. She felt along the wall and found an old-fashioned brass switch. The lights stuttered into life, their dull glow revealing a sitting room hung with faded tapestries of birds, pressed behind glass panels. Groups of low-backed chairs formed little furniture archipelagos, and the heavy wooden shutters were chained shut.

The room was full of dust. It lay in greying piles on the worn carpet. It was heaped up by the main door. The air was thick with it. She pressed her hand across her mouth.

Footsteps sounded behind her, and an odd, off-beat *tap tap tap*.

'Close the door,' a voice said. Jamie dragged her gaze away from the room of dust, and turned to see Cora Barton leaning heavily on her stick as she made her way across the room. 'There's nothing to be done here.'

When Jamie didn't move, the old woman muttered something, reaching past her to pull the door shut.

'How many?' Jamie stared at the closed door.

'Sixteen.'

'Why did they all die in there?'

'What else could we have done?' the other woman's voice was sharp.

'You locked them in there?'

Cora was small and stooped, but Jamie had a desperate urge to turn and run and keep running until there was no chance of hearing the *tap tap* of that stick coming along behind her.

'We were here when the quarantine began,' the old woman said. 'It was all terribly civilised to start with. All of us – the staff, the guests – agreed to isolate ourselves as best we could. Sleeping in different parts of the house, and in the cottages. Eating at different times. Then the reports began coming in. About what was happening on the central worlds. How the virus worked. How few people survived. The staff broke the quarantine and went home, and we were left here. We knew what we had to do. Stay right away from each other. Even the couples. But some people panicked. They didn't want to die alone. They wanted to be held.'

'So you just locked them in?' Jamie was shaking as she walked over to grip the back of a chair.

'If we hadn't, we'd all have died,' Cora said. 'We couldn't save them. And they wouldn't save themselves.' She shook her head. 'Dying for the sake of a touch.'

'There are worse things to die for,' Jamie said, and immediately wondered if she believed it.

'How did you survive then?' the other woman said, narrowing her eyes. 'None of us are in any position to judge. We're all here because we didn't go to the people dying all around us.'

'Was your husband in there?'

Cora turned away. 'It doesn't matter. It's done. We're here. They're not. And it's not as though we're going to be called to account for what we did and didn't do in the last days of the world.'

'The last days?' Jamie said.

'What else would you call it?'

'Life,' Jamie replied. 'Not an end. Not a new beginning. Just another bit in the middle, and who knows what comes next?'

'Nothing,' Cora said. 'There's nothing left to come. This is the end, and all we can do is live it as best we can.'

Jamie laughed, a harsh burst of sound that caught in her throat. 'This is the best you can do?'

'What are you doing?' Cora said. 'What makes your way of ending better than ours?'

Jamie couldn't be in this room any longer. Not with the old woman huddled there like some emissary of death.

'No,' she said, not sure what it was that she was answering, and then she turned and walked out of the room, stumbling a little on the hem of her ridiculous dress. She didn't look back, but she could feel the other woman watching her until she was out of sight.

CHAPTER TWENTY-THREE

Jamie didn't expect to sleep well, with the dust of that room swirling in her mind. But when she closed her eyes, she didn't open them again until the sun was up.

Once she was dressed she headed downstairs, waiting until the kitchen was empty before slipping in to throw together a hasty breakfast. She found Finn around the side of the house, sitting on a bench with a mug and a plate of buttery toast.

'Not eating with the others?' she said, sitting down beside him.

'They talk funny.'

'They're pretending,' Jamie said. 'Pretending that it's a long time ago.'

He gave a quick shake of his head. 'Not that.'

'What do you mean then?'

He frowned down at his hands. 'What they say, it doesn't fit.'

'Fit?'

'With their faces. They don't look like what they're saying.'

For a moment Jamie was back in that dust-soaked room. She took a hard gulp of her coffee. 'It doesn't matter,' she said. 'We'll be gone soon.'

'What will they do?'

'I suppose they'll live here.'

'Until they die?'

'I guess so.'

Finn was silent for a moment. 'There are no babies,' he said eventually. 'Are there?'

'What do you mean?'

'You have to have babies. They're what comes next. After people are dead, their children have more children and that's how it all works. But Rena said there would never be any more babies at all.'

'We don't know that.' There was a little ache in her stomach.

'But if there are no babies, what will happen?'

'I don't know,' Jamie said. 'We just have to live our own lives and not worry about what happens after us.'

'Until we die?'

She nodded.

'And one day there'll be no one left?'

'I don't think that will happen,' Jamie said. 'Nature's cleverer than we are.'

'I'm the youngest.' Finn was staring out across the hills.

'The youngest?'

'You're older than me. And Callan, and Lowry, and Rena. And the people here. You'll all die first. I'll be last.'

'We don't know what will happen.' Her throat felt tight. 'They haven't tested properly. It was just what they thought might happen. We won't know until . . .' She broke off.

'Until you try,' Finn said.

'That won't . . .' The conversation was twisting and tangling, drawing in all sorts of ideas she didn't want in her head right now. 'I won't be having a baby.' She forced a smile, trying to make a joke of it. 'I'm getting a bit long in the tooth for that.' As Finn glanced at her mouth, she waved a hand. 'No, I just mean I'm older than most people are when they start having babies. And I don't have . . .' She ground to a halt again.

'A husband,' Finn said. 'You need a husband to have a baby. Yours is still on Alegria.'

299

'He wasn't my husband.'

'Will you go back?'

'No.'

He was still considering this when the crunch of gravel signalled someone approaching.

Callan stepped into view, hesitated, and then walked towards them.

'We're about ready to head off.'

'I'll need to get my things,' Jamie said.

'I've packed my bag,' Finn volunteered.

'Very efficient.' Callan gave him a quick smile, but Finn was looking out across the fields again.

Jamie tipped the dregs of her coffee onto the grass. 'I'll just be a minute.'

'No hurry.' Callan sat down next to Finn, stretching out his legs. 'I think the old folk would be happy if we stayed longer, but I said we wanted to get on. Unless you want to spend the morning here?'

'No.' Jamie's voice was sharp.

Callan raised an eyebrow. 'Okay. See you round the front.'

Jamie rinsed her mug, then went upstairs to pack. She'd loved this place once, but now she wanted nothing more than to be away. She needed to finish this journey before she lost hold of everything she'd ever been. Little pieces of her were splintering away with every step she took. Old loves, old dreams. When they were all gone, what would be left?

The old people had gathered on the steps to see them off. Someone had repacked their bags on Emily's back, and Finn was holding on to the lead-rope. Callan and Lowry were shaking hands with some of the men, while Mr Hendry looked on, palms pressed together under his chin in an affected, contemplative pose. When he saw Jamie, he dipped his head, his steepled fingers tipping towards her.

'It's been such a pleasure,' he said, to a fluttering chorus of agreement from a few of the women. 'When you are settled, you simply must come back and see us.'

Jamie nodded, but didn't answer. Mrs Barton was standing a little to the side, and when their eyes met, she inclined her head, her expression cool and watchful.

'Let's go.' Jamie started to walk down the path.

As they reached the road, Lowry fell into step beside her.

'What is it?'

She shook her head. 'Doesn't matter.'

'Well, it obviously does. You couldn't wait to be away from there. It was all a little odd, I'll grant you, but harmless enough.'

'Harmless?' She gave a hard laugh. 'You ask them what they did to survive?'

'No. And I'm not sure any of us would like to be asked that question.'

'I've got nothing to hide,' Jamie said sharply.

'So what were you doing on Soltaire?' Lowry asked. 'That young man of yours, did he want you to go?'

'We didn't know what was coming. It's not like I left him so that I could survive.'

'No,' Lowry conceded. 'But you probably survived because you left him.'

'So did he.'

'That's true,' Lowry said. 'But first you broke his heart.'

'Are you saying I should have stayed with him, just because he wanted me to?'

'Not at all. I'm just making the point that none of us goes through life without blame sticking to us for something.'

Jamie shook her head, impatient with the conversation. 'It doesn't matter. We're going. They're the ones who have to stay and live with it.'

'We all have to live with what we've done and seen,' Lowry said. 'That's all we can do.'

'I'm going to walk on ahead.' Jamie picked up pace. 'See where we are.'

'I thought you knew the way,' Lowry remarked mildly.

They made better time than Jamie had anticipated. It was early afternoon when she suddenly realised she was walking through countryside that was as familiar as breathing. They followed the road through its illogical twists and turns, passing a few groups of sheep grazing contentedly on the verges. At one of the bigger farms, a couple of rangy collies came bounding out, sniffing and wagging. The sun was beating down and the tarmac ahead seemed scattered with deep puddles, the sky reflected in a shifting, shimmering mirage that Jamie knew would fade and disappear as soon as they got close.

Jamie found herself mentally ticking off the markers along the way.

The bridge over the dried-up stream.

The dirt track, where she'd parked up with her first boy-friend. An inexperienced fumble that had ended in her kneeing him in the groin, before getting out of the car and stomping off towards home. He'd driven past her, fast and close, screamed, *Bitch*, and left her to walk the two miles back to Belsley.

The stone lions at the old manor house.

The row of vast and silent turbines ranged along the horizon, their great arms turning slowly.

'Look at them.' Jamie hadn't realised that Rena was so close behind her until the other woman spoke, her voice curling with distaste. 'Ugly great things. That's all we did. Spoil what God made for us.'

'I never minded them,' Jamie said. She'd always thought they fitted with the vastness of the northern landscape.

'We don't need them,' Rena said. 'The old world gobbled up power and spat out filth. There was never enough to keep everything running.'

'They weren't just for electricity.' Jamie didn't know why she was engaging. 'The newer ones had pods to disperse seeds or treatments for crop diseases. They used them for artificial pollination when the bee populations were low.'

'They should be pulled down,' Rena said, her voice rising. 'Like all the things we did wrong.'

'Okay.' Jamie was tired of the conversation. She picked up her pace a little, moving on ahead. 'I'll leave that with you.'

As they approached the turning for Belsley, Finn suddenly stopped walking, his head going up, as though he'd caught some scent on the wind.

Jamie suddenly realised what it was. There was a low, resonant rush, almost on the edge of hearing. If you'd ever heard it, you'd be in no doubt as to what it was – and if you'd never heard it, you'd have no idea what it meant.

She walked over and held out her hand to him. He was still clutching Emily's lead-rope.

'Come on.'

He hesitated, then reached out slowly to place his free hand in hers.

Jamie tugged Finn into a shuffling run, the horse breaking into a reluctant trot to keep pace. As they jogged along the narrow lane, Jamie could smell the sharp tang of sand, and salt and dune grass.

At the little car park where Jamie and her sisters used to buy ice creams, Finn dropped to a walk. Sand had drifted across the tarmac and he lifted his feet up high, placing them carefully, his eyes narrowing suspiciously as the footing shifted beneath his weight.

'It's okay.' Jamie wanted to laugh, and then cry. It was more than okay. They were *here*. All those millions of miles, all that dust and loss and *nought point nought nought nought one*, and they were finally here.

At the edge of the dunes, Emily dug his hooves in, refusing to follow. Jamie tied the lead-rope to the gate across the trailer slipway. Then she took Finn's hand again, and pulled him up the dunes, slipping and sliding. They scrambled up one false summit, and another, and then they were over the top, with the great, golden curve of the beach sweeping off towards the headland. The old lime kilns squatted at the entrance to the little harbour, with a cluster of guesthouses pressed up against the crumbling stone walls.

And there was the sea.

It was a deeper green than she remembered it, with the sun a shifting glaze of silver across the waves. She could feel herself rising on her toes ready to run down the dunes, across the beach, feeling the ground growing damp and hard beneath her feet, until she was running through water, not on sand. There were wide shallows just offshore, and she'd wade and wade until that moment when there was nothing beneath her feet but the ocean, and it could be a few inches, or it could be full fathom five, and it would make no difference.

Finn said something, but his voice was muffled by the thudding of blood in her ears. It might have been, *That's it.*

That's it.

One of those moments when the world contracts around you, fitting like a second layer of skin. And you're just the right shape for this piece of world, and if you spoke, you'd say the right thing, and if you heard music, it would be the most perfect song, and if someone touched you, it would be true love.

It will pass. The more cynical part of herself was muttering at the back of her mind.

I don't care. I'm here now.

Overhead the scythe-winged gulls wheeled and shrilled at one another.

People. People. Leftover sandwiches. Fish bones. Chip papers stiff with salt and vinegar. People. People. People.

There were voices behind her. The scuff and scrabble of people climbing the dunes, and then Lowry was panting beside her. Rena was talking, her voice high and fast, but she was just static in the background. The sea filled Jamie. She was buzzing, manic, but she didn't care.

The sea.

CHAPTER TWENTY-FOUR

Callan came up beside her and stood looking out across the beach.

'Beautiful place.' The words should have been inadequate, but there was an odd note in Callan's voice. When she turned to look at him, he gave her a tilted smile, sadder and less guarded than any she'd seen on his face before.

'Never seen the sea before,' he said. 'My mother was from the west coast, and she always wanted to go back. But it was always *next year, next year,* and when next year came, there'd be something we needed more than a trip to the beach.' He glanced at Finn who had started down the dunes towards the beach, cat-stepping and cautious. 'Maybe it was just as well. Ed wouldn't have cared about this. It would have been too hot, or too windy, or too bright. It would never have stopped until we were home again.'

'It wasn't his fault,' Jamie said, looking at Finn.

'No,' Callan said. 'Doesn't mean I don't regret some of the things we didn't have.'

Regret. That word sounded an off-key note inside her. The elation was fading, and she could feel old memories stirring, as though she was starting to resonate at the same frequency as the space around her.

Finn was crossing the sand, still lifting his feet up high, like it might bite him.

'I'd better go with him.' Jamie set off down the dunes, the sand slipping and sinking around her. She caught up with Finn just as the damp sand was giving way to the first thin sheen of water.

'Careful.' She pointed down. There was a dark line of damp just above the rubber soles of his boots.

Finn lifted his foot and examined the wet sole.

'You could take them off,' Jamie suggested.

He gave her a suspicious look. Clearly this went against his understanding of how the world worked.

'It's okay. It's what people do . . .' She caught herself. 'What people did on the beach.'

Finn contemplated this, and then nodded and started to sit down. Jamie laughed, and caught at his arm. He didn't flinch, she noticed. 'Not here. Come back onto the dry sand.'

As they moved back up the beach, the others walked down to join them. Only Rena hung back, shading her eyes to peer along the coast.

'What are you doing?' Lowry asked.

'Paddling,' Jamie said with a grin.

She helped Finn unlace his boots and roll his trousers up to his knees. He plucked briefly at the uneven twist of one of the hems, trying to straighten it, and then stood up, curling his toes into the sand.

'You ready?' Jamie said.

He nodded, and took her outstretched hand. When she started to run towards the sea, he ran beside her, his eyes fixed on the waves.

They were in up to their knees, and there were dark splatters on their trousers, but Finn didn't seem to have noticed. He was looking out towards the horizon.

'Further in?' he said.

Jamie laughed and shook her head. 'Not today. We're not exactly dressed for it. But sometime. You'll have to learn to swim first.'

A splashing behind them heralded the arrival of Lowry. He had his own trousers rolled up, and his hands pushed into his pockets.

'We made it,' he said.

'Yes.' She glanced up the coast to where the uneven silhouette of Lindisfarne was just visible. 'Well, almost.'

Lowry followed the line of her gaze. 'We need to wait for low tide. Unless we can find a boat.'

'Can you sail?'

He gave her a quick grin. 'How hard can it be?'

She raised an eyebrow. 'Maybe you'd better start with a rowing boat.'

He laughed. 'Or maybe I'd better wait for the causeway.'

They stood for a moment, watching Finn wading about in the shallows, occasionally bending down to examine something beneath the surface.

'What about you?' Lowry said. 'Are you coming to Lindisfarne?'

Jamie looked across the waves. Whenever she'd thought of getting here it had been this she'd pictured. The sea, the sand, the great sweep of the sky beyond it all. Nothing else. But if she walked just a little way along the shore, she'd see the white-painted fence and gate of her old house, just behind the kilns. The gate used to creak, and her stepmother would come to the door if she heard it. If you'd been up to something you didn't want her to know about, you were better off coming up the path from the headland, and sneaking under the kitchen window.

'Can you watch Finn?' she said. 'I just want to see something.'

Lowry nodded. 'Of course.'

She waded back to the shore and headed towards the kilns and the slope that led up to the lane. The gritty surface of the road nipped at her bare feet as she passed the holiday cottages, their windows off-season empty. Past the guesthouse, past the old Dixon place, and round the curve of the lane to where her old house stood.

The windows weren't as sparkling clean as her stepmother had kept them, and the upstairs curtains were closed, but otherwise it looked just the same. The familiarity jarred somehow, as though she'd been expecting some Sleeping Beauty's castle of gnarled thorns and crumbling stonework. The only signs of neglect were a little posse of stinging nettles swaggering at the front of the flower bed, and the wilted rose petals on the path.

The front door was closed, but not locked. Jamie turned the handle and used the very tips of her fingers to push it open. The hallway was tidy, with rows of boots lined up neatly, and coats hanging from the driftwood hooks.

She stepped inside. The flagstone floor was gritty underfoot, as though someone had trodden sand in, and hadn't been sent to clean it up with a dustpan and brush. The door at the far end of the hallway was open.

The living room was bright and high-ceilinged, with white-framed windows looking out to the sea beyond the headland. Books crammed the alcoves on either side of the fireplace, and the mantelpiece was covered in framed family photos. Jamie walked over and ran her fingers across the glass covering her own face. Her eyes were screwed up against the sun, her lips twitched into a reluctant smile. Her half-sisters were beside her, their faces open and untroubled.

There was no dust here, no sign that anyone had spent their last days in this room. Her stepmother's desk was still in the corner, tidy and clear, with pens crammed into a pot decorated with pieces of sea glass.

She'd made that, hadn't she? She went over and picked it

up. A couple of pieces had come loose, showing the cheap white china underneath. She remembered gluing the glass onto the surface, but she couldn't remember what had been behind the gesture. All her memories of her stepmother were from a distance, with no sense that there had ever been a connection between the two of them. And yet the pen pot was still here on the desk, holding the old-fashioned fountain pen that her stepmother had always insisted on using, preferring pen and paper to whatever technology came along.

Her psychology books were lined up on the shelf above the desk, and a couple of cardboard folders sat next to them. Her case files. Had she still been working when the virus struck? She'd have been, what, sixty-two?

Jamie ran her hand down the spines, with their names and case references. She remembered some of her stepmother's clients coming to see her in her office at the back of the house: younger ones in school uniforms, shepherded in by parents who smiled too much and talked too fast, and monosyllabic teenagers, slouching in with headphones wedged in.

Those children would be adults now, perhaps with children of their own. Had they managed to leave their troubles behind? Or had they passed down to another generation, like something in the blood?

Then Jamie remembered. They were gone. The children, and their children. Whatever their troubles, they'd blown away as dust on the wind.

About halfway down the pile there was an unnamed folder, marked only with a set of dates from the year that Jamie had turned fifteen.

She picked up the folder and opened it, conscious of a prickling unease, as though someone might come in and find her leafing through confidential information. The papers inside looked as though they'd been torn from a notebook. They were covered in her stepmother's slanted handwriting. There were no bullet points, no medical abbreviations, just a solid block of text, like a stream of consciousness.

. . . *sleeping fine, school work good, no obvious troubled behaviour other than complete lack of engagement in any discussion of personal matters, complete silence, some regular distraction techniques . . . selective mutism?* No. *Don't overcomplicate.*

It sounded like they just wanted to be left alone, whoever they were.

. . . *no obvious progress, no overt signs of grieving, hasn't cried, or has hidden it well . . .*

Jamie turned the page and found a more coherent passage. The pen strokes were thicker and pressed harder into the paper, as though her usually measured stepmother had been agitated when she wrote it.

I'm getting this wrong. When it matters the most, I can't get through. I know the theory, but it's not working. Maybe we're making it worse. There's something I'm not getting and it feels like I'm running out of time.

There was something sharp lodged at the base of Jamie's throat.

When it matters the most.

Below that passage there was a list, with some of the entries scratched out with what looked like another vicious pen stroke.

Dinner at Bamburgh.

Trip to the spa.

A memory took shape. She'd been about fifteen, and her stepmother had suggested that they did something, just the two of them. She'd come up with a little clutch of ideas for what they could do. *We could go to a spa. Just you and me. I'll book.* Jamie had fiddled with her bracelet and smiled the vague, distant smile she'd perfected for moments like that. And then she'd made another arrangement with someone from school, and pretended she'd forgotten her stepmother had ever made plans.

Something twisted painfully behind her ribs.

I'm getting this wrong.

But what if there hadn't been a right?

'Were you right?' A voice spoke from behind her, echoing her thoughts, and she turned to see Lowry standing in the door.

'What?'

He took a couple of steps into the room. 'I said are you all right?'

'Oh.' She put her hand up to push her hair back from her face. 'Yes. Sorry. Where's Finn?'

'With Callan.' He walked over and put his hand on her arm. 'I don't think you are. All right.' He searched her face. 'Are you?'

She shook her head slowly. 'No.'

'What happened?'

She glanced down at the page again, and then put both hands up and rubbed at her face. 'God, it was years ago. I should be over it by now.'

'I don't think it works like that,' Lowry said gently. 'When things happen, they'll always have happened, no matter how many years go by. There isn't a switch that turns it all off.'

She tried to smile, but it slid away, half-formed. 'Really? A switch would be good.'

'What happened?' Lowry asked again.

She turned and walked over to the window.

Oh God, the view. That was always the first thing guests said. But when she lived here, she'd stopped noticing it. It was just part of the background to their lives.

'My mother died when I was fourteen,' she said.

'I'm sorry.' Lowry didn't say, *You already told me that*.

'No.' Jamie could hear the impatience shading her voice. 'That's not it.' Her breath was condensing on the window, turning a little patch almost opaque. Maybe she could write her story in the steam, so that it would stay there, invisible, until she came back and breathed on it again. 'I mean, that's not all. My parents divorced when I was nearly five. And then he married again, and my mother went to pieces.'

'Must have been hard for you,' Lowry said. 'Did you still see your father?'

Jamie nodded. 'This was his house. I used to come and stay most weekends.' She took a deep breath. 'And then I'd go home and my mother would have been drinking the whole time I was away – and she'd tell me how sad she'd been while I wasn't there, and how she couldn't stand the thought of my stepmother looking after me, and that I didn't understand how hard it was for her.'

'Those were some big emotions for a young child to unravel.'

'I didn't even try,' Jamie said. 'I hated it when she was like that, so I wouldn't talk to her. It felt safer. Because when I did tell her anything about my father and stepmother, she'd cry, or get angry. But she hated it when I wouldn't talk to her too. I couldn't win.'

'No,' Lowry said. 'There aren't usually any winners in situations like that. Certainly not the children.'

'But I should have tried harder,' Jamie said. 'When I was older, anyway. I could have tried to talk to her. But I think . . .' She stopped. The admission that was taking shape wasn't something she'd realised she knew.

'It was something you could control,' Lowry finished.

Jamie didn't answer for a long moment. All those times she'd battened down the hatches against her mother, her stepmother, Daniel, she'd always felt under siege. Like her silence was something that had been forced upon her, not something she'd chosen. Had there really been a stubborn little nub of satisfaction, right down at the bottom of it all? She turned over a couple of memories, examining them. Daniel, after the baby, begging her to talk to him. Her stepmother, coming up with idea after idea for things they could do together.

'Yes,' she said. 'I think that was it.'

'Understandable enough,' the old man said. 'And the situation wasn't of your making.'

'No.' Jamie's throat was dry. They were approaching the heart of it, and she wasn't sure she was ready to slice open those old stitches and expose the damage she'd done. She had to force the words out. 'But there's something else.'

Lowry waited.

Jamie rubbed her face again, her breath shuddering in her chest. 'I'd been here for part of the summer, and my father asked me if I wanted to stay longer. My mother had been really hard to live with. My father must have realised.' She glanced at the folder on the desk. 'Actually, it was probably my stepmother who picked up on it.'

'Were you close to her?' Lowry asked.

'No. But I think I probably should have been.' She brushed her hand over the page of handwritten notes. 'Anyway, my father asked me if I wanted to spend more time here. I said yes, and he talked to my mother about it. They had a blazing row. I heard the whole thing, and when she put me on the spot, asking me if I really wanted to leave her on her own, I said yes. I think I'd just had enough, so I gave her a straight answer for once. She went mad, screaming at me, telling me I was breaking her heart, saying I hated her, that I'd probably be happy if she was dead.'

She looked down at her hands. This was it. The hard little lump she'd always been able to feel at the heart of her life. She had to say it. She'd come this far, and the story felt like it had a sort of momentum.

She looked up again, meeting Lowry's compassionate gaze. 'I said I wished she was dead. I said I did hate her.'

'You didn't mean it, though.'

She gave a half-smile, bitter as old blood. 'I think I did. In that moment, I really did.'

'What happened?' Lowry asked, but he must have figured it out by now. She'd given him enough to piece it together. Maybe he thought she needed to say it.

'She slapped my face. Knocked me right across the room. Then she cried and tried to hold me and said she was sorry. I wouldn't let her touch me.' She gave another bitter smile. 'Not much change there, to be honest. But I wouldn't talk to her or look at her. I rang my dad to come and get me, and I moved in there for the rest of the summer. I didn't tell them what had happened, just that we'd had an argument. When school began, I refused to go home. All hell broke loose. She kept ringing and ringing and I wouldn't speak to her. She got a solicitor, who must have told her there was no way of forcing a fourteen-year-old to live with her if they didn't want to.'

'You must have been very angry with her,' Lowry said.

'That's the thing,' Jamie said. 'I don't remember feeling that angry. I just felt heavy and stuck. It was like a sort of inertia. Like this was the situation, and it was just easier if it didn't change, and I didn't have to deal with any of it.'

'There are different sorts of anger,' Lowry said. 'Not all of it's about screaming and shouting and hating.'

'Maybe,' Jamie said. 'Anyway, there were a couple of days when she didn't call, and then two police officers came to the door here and she was dead.'

'Did she kill herself?'

Jamie gave a small, tight smile. 'No. Not quite. She fell down the stairs drunk and broke her neck. Doctor said there was so much alcohol in her system she probably hadn't been sober for days. So there you go. I said I wished she would die, and she obliged me.' Lowry was silent, and she gave him a mocking, cynical look. 'Isn't this the bit where you tell me it wasn't my fault?'

'I can't tell you that. Maybe it would have happened anyway. Maybe it wouldn't. All I can say is that nothing that happens is down to just one person, or just one action. It was part of life. Yours, and hers, and your father's.'

'Part of life's rich pattern,' she said. 'Is that honestly what you're telling me? That it meant something?'

'That's not what I'm saying at all. If there is a pattern, it's way beyond our understanding. Maybe we're just not clear-sighted enough. Too much getting in the way.'

'If none of it means anything, then what's the *point*?' Jamie was suddenly bone-tired, as though she'd run a marathon in the time it had taken to tell him that short, sad story.

'Life is its own point,' Lowry said. 'It's just a series of moments, some of them memorable, some of them not. There's no redemption but what we're prepared to grant to ourselves. No point when we're finished becoming what we're going to be. There's just this breath, and the next one, and the next one. Each one of those breaths, each of those moments helps to shape us. And then there's other people. Sometimes we figure out a way of rubbing along together. Sometimes we break someone else, or they break us.'

'Then maybe it's better to keep your distance. If you don't get too close, then you can't hurt one another.'

'Really?' Lowry gave her a keen look. 'Tell me this then. How long did you stay with Daniel?'

'And look how that worked out.'

Lowry raised an eyebrow. 'You're telling me you were with him all that time, and didn't have a single happy moment?'

Jamie gave an irritable shake of her head. 'Of course not. We used to be happy. But it didn't turn out well in the long run.'

'The long run's not what it's about,' Lowry said. 'Not from where I'm standing anyway. It's the now that you feel. Everything else is just what you imagine, or what you remember, and that's only second-hand living.'

'So what do we do now?'

'I can't tell you that,' Lowry said with a faint smile. 'I can only tell you what I'm going to do. I'm going to Lindisfarne, I'm going to grow vegetables. Raise chickens. Think about things I haven't taken time to think about for a long time.' His smile faded. 'Help Rena, if I can. What about you?'

'I don't know. Shouldn't I feel differently about it all now I've come back here and told you what happened? Isn't that how it's supposed to work?'

Lowry smiled. 'Do you need me to answer that?'

Jamie found an answering smile. 'Just another moment, right? I don't even know why I told you all that.'

'It's the preacher effect,' Lowry said with a quick grin. 'It makes people come over all confessional.' He grew serious. 'I think it's because they're not really talking to you. They're talking to whatever god they believe in. And that means they're really talking to themselves.'

Jamie raised an eyebrow. 'Shouldn't you be telling them that God is listening when they talk?'

'The thing about being a preacher is that everyone fills in the gaps in what you say. They decide for themselves what you believe in. And most people assume that's a single, all-powerful god, sitting up there on a cloud and watching us all run about making mistakes.'

'It's kind of part of the job description, isn't it?'

Lowry shook his head. 'Religion's about what you do, not what you believe. God's the smallest part of it. If God was up there watching us, and we were all living good and generous lives and looking out for one another, then He . . .' He gave another small smile. 'Or She, for that matter, could just shut up shop. They'd have no purpose any more.'

'You don't believe?'

'I do believe,' Lowry said. 'But if you mean in the traditional sense, then no, that's not where my faith lies. Not any more. Maybe it never did. I believe that people make their own gods, out of whatever they have to hand.'

Jamie looked out at the shifting face of the ocean.

'What about me?' she said. 'If I were in the market for a god, what would you suggest I use?'

Lowry smiled. 'This place,' he said. 'The sea, the sky, the people who came here with you. You build your gods out of the same materials you use to build your life.'

'All this way, and you're telling me I still have work to do?' she said, trying to make a joke of it.

'Always,' he said, and walked away, pausing at the door. 'We'll be on the beach, when you're done here.'

CHAPTER TWENTY-FIVE

When Lowry had gone, Jamie moved about the room, picking things up and putting them back down again, pieces of the conversation replaying in her mind. There was a dog barking somewhere. Not far away. Some family pet, wandering and confused. A pause, and then it started up again, closer this time, a flurry of noise that carried an impression of a frantically waggling rear end and a thumping tail. And was that a voice, almost lost under the barking? Lowry was no doubt being subjected to the over-exuberant attentions of a lonely dog.

She looked down at the page again.

I'm getting this wrong.

A footstep echoed in the hallway, and she turned, expecting to see Lowry. Instead a small tan and white dog came waddling in, lopsided and arthritic, tail thumping from side to side.

And then her stepmother stepped into the room and said, 'I knew it would be you.' She was leaning on a walking stick, and her hair was lighter and thinner than it should have been. She should have been steel-grey, ash-grey, not this pale, wispy shade of age. 'Of all my girls, I knew you'd be the one who came home.'

'Home?' Jamie said irrelevantly, her voice sounding small and far away. She shook her head. 'I don't . . . I mean, I thought . . .'

Then she was shaking; great shuddering tremors that started somewhere deep inside her. She put her hands to her face, hiding her eyes for a moment. When she took them away, she'd be alone. This wasn't real.

When she lowered her hands her stepmother was still standing there.

Those scribbled words took on life, echoing through Jamie's thoughts as though her stepmother had spoken them out loud.

I'm getting this wrong.

No. She'd never said it, but she should have done. Years ago, she should have turned to this woman and said, *It's not you. This is just the way it is.*

The space between them felt wrong. The thought of taking the first step was like falling, but someone had to cross the room.

She took a step, and then another, and another, and then she had her arms around her stepmother, and the other woman was holding on to her.

Thank you . . . knew you'd . . . sorry . . . love you . . . love you . . . love you . . .

They fit together better than Jamie remembered, the older woman curled against Jamie's more sturdy frame. There were still places where bones knocked against one another, or where a curve and a hollow didn't quite slot together. But it was close enough.

They held on to one another for a long, long moment, the older woman gradually becoming more real and solid in Jamie's arms, like a developing picture, slowly warming into focus. She could feel her stepmother's heart beating hard inside her too-slight frame. She could feel how close her bones were to the surface, how thinly her skin was stretched over those bones. She could feel things that shouldn't be there: hard swellings running to either side of her stepmother's spine.

She pulled back slightly.

'What . . .' she began, but her stepmother eased herself away.

'Can't have everything,' she said, with a faint smile. 'Surviving one thing doesn't mean that something else won't come calling.'

'Is it . . .'

'Yes, it's cancer.' Her stepmother was brisk. 'I was in remission, but it came back a few weeks ago. I found a lump in my neck, and a few days later they were all over.' She gave another little smile. 'Like it didn't want me to be in any doubt about its intentions this time.'

'No.' Jamie couldn't work out what was happening. The moment was the wrong shape, and she couldn't get hold of it. All the space between them, all the odds they'd beaten, and her stepmother was telling her it might be just a fleeting instant before the statistics won out after all. 'We can go to Newcastle. The hospital. I can find the right drugs, work out—'

'Jamie.' Her stepmother put her hand on Jamie's arm.

'It went into remission once. We can beat it. We can.'

'Jamie.'

No. She tried to say it again, but there was a hard lump in her own throat, as if her stepmother's cancer was contagious.

Her stepmother's arms came around her again, gentle and patient, and for once it didn't feel wrong to let someone hold her as she cried.

After a few moments she lifted her head and wiped her arm across her face.

'Sorry,' she said, with another deep, shuddering breath. 'It's just . . . I came all this way, and I never thought you'd be here.' She rubbed her face again. 'How did you survive?'

'I was in isolation,' her stepmother said. 'And I suppose I was so full of system-boosting drugs that even the virus didn't stand a chance.' She gave Jamie a sad, tender look. 'You were alone, weren't you? You left him.'

'How did you know?'

'I spoke to him on the comm,' her stepmother said. 'I'd written to you on Alegria. Daft and old-fashioned, I know. But I was telling you I was going to die, and it didn't feel like something I should say in a mail. Daniel opened it, and called me. He told me you'd gone. That was just before the virus hit Alegria. When we had the first outbreaks here on Earth, I tried to send you a comm message, to say goodbye, but it cut off.'

'That was from you?'

Her stepmother nodded. 'It got through?'

'Just a blank message. I thought it was Daniel.'

'Maybe he survived too,' her stepmother said. 'If—'

'He did.' Jamie looked away. 'He's on Alegria.'

Her stepmother nodded, and didn't ask any more. 'I need to sit down,' she said.

Jamie helped her to an armchair. The dog trotted over and lay down on her stepmother's feet as the older woman looked up at Jamie.

'I thought it would be you who made it back, if any of you did,' she said. 'The other two . . .' Her voice broke slightly. 'They weren't good at being on their own. My fault, I think. But I thought perhaps you'd be strong enough.'

'I wasn't alone because I was strong. Pretty much the opposite.'

'You were strong,' her stepmother said. 'What you had to deal with—'

'I didn't deal with it,' Jamie cut across her. 'Not by a long shot.'

Her stepmother looked down at her hands, rubbing her thumb across one knuckle. The skin there was so fine that it looked translucent, the bone almost glinting through. 'We just made things worse, didn't we?'

'No.' Jamie tripped over the tail end of her stepmother's question. It suddenly felt like they needed to say all these things as fast as they could. *In case there's not another time.* 'You did everything you could. It's just that . . .' She stopped, gathering her thoughts, feeling for a way through their shared and tangled history. 'I couldn't talk about it,' she said eventually. 'That's all.'

'I should have realised,' her stepmother said. 'I should have let you talk about it in your own time.'

Jamie shook her head. 'There was no *my own time*,' she said. 'What happened, it just happened and I don't think there were any magic words you could have said that would have made things any different.'

Her stepmother was about to speak, but then she shifted in her seat, her face creasing with pain.

'Are you all right?'

'My back.' The older woman's breathing was growing laboured and she started to scrabble at the arm of her chair. 'Can you help me? Jamie, please, I need to sit up a bit.'

Jamie slid a hand around her stepmother's back, not sure whether she was going to hurt her, and between the two of them they shuffled her up a little.

'That's fine, that's fine.' The older woman drew a rattling breath. 'Just give me a minute.'

'Are you okay?' Jamie was hovering, not sure what to do. 'Can I get you anything?'

'No.' Her stepmother's breathing was steadying, and she relaxed her grip on the arm of her chair. 'Sorry. If I don't get into the chair just right, my back spasms. I keep thinking I'm not going to be able to get back up again and I'm going to die here, stuck in the chair. Sorry. What were you saying? My memory's playing up a bit. I keep phasing out.'

'It doesn't matter,' Jamie said. 'I'm here. How have you managed on your own this long?'

'I haven't been alone. There are a couple of monks out at Lindisfarne. They've been making sure I'm all right.'

A voice spoke from the doorway. 'Jamie?'

She looked up to see Lowry.

'Hello again,' her stepmother said, and then added to Jamie, 'We met outside.'

'Finn's getting a bit restless,' Lowry said. 'I'm assuming you're not coming with us, so I wonder if it's worth getting settled in here, so he knows what's what.'

He'll be the only one who does then, Jamie thought. Aloud she said, 'I'll be there in a little bit.' Then a thought struck her. 'Who's with him? Callan?'

Lowry shook his head. 'He's gone with Gracie to check that hotel for a comms link. Rena's there.'

'You go.' Her stepmother reached up to touch Jamie's arm. 'I usually have a sleep around this time.' She leaned back and closed her eyes.

Jamie hesitated, then started towards the door. Just as she reached it, her stepmother spoke from behind her. 'You'll come back?'

'Yes. I'll come back.'

Lowry didn't ask Jamie what had passed between her and her stepmother, and Jamie didn't volunteer any information. It still felt unreal. All the vastness of space, and somehow they'd found their way back together.

As they walked down the slope to the beach Jamie scanned the shoreline. For a moment she couldn't see anyone at all, and then she caught sight of a figure sitting at the bottom of the dunes. Rena, with her knees drawn up to her chest and a distant expression on her face. The bags were piled beside her. But where was Finn? Had Rena let him wander off?

'Rena.' There was a tension in Lowry's voice that told her he'd had the same thought. 'Where's Finn?'

Rena kept her gaze fixed on the horizon, a tiny smile playing about her lips.

Jamie stared along the beach, shielding her eyes with her hand. She could feel the first stirrings of fear.

'Finn?'

Lowry grabbed her arm. 'There.' He pointed towards the harbour wall, just where Jamie knew it jutted out into the deeper water. There was a figure clinging to the wall, one hand reaching up to scrabble uselessly at the rough-cut stone.

Jamie ran to the water's edge and plunged in, wading deeper and deeper until the sand beneath her feet fell away, just a few metres from the wall. She swam the few strokes to his side and threw an arm around his shoulders. He twisted against her, his mouth gaping in a silent gasp of panic.

Drowning is quiet. She remembered someone telling her that.

'Finn. I'm here.'

He was flailing, and she was struggling to hold them both against the wall. She said his name a couple more times, but her voice didn't seem to be registering with him.

'Here.'

She looked up to see Callan above her, reaching down. Between the two of them they managed to haul Finn up onto the harbourside where he lay, clutching at the stones, still oddly silent.

Callan reached down again and helped Jamie to scramble up. She knelt beside Finn, her hand on his back, saying his name again and again until it seemed to penetrate. His breathing steadied, and after a moment he pushed himself up onto his knees and looked at her.

'Too deep,' he said.

Jamie fought back the urge to yell at him.

You could have drowned.

She took a deep breath. 'Yes, it's deep. You have to stay near the shore. You can't swim.'

He nodded. 'Okay.'

'You promise?' Jamie said. 'And not without me here?'

'I promise.'

When the three of them made their way back to the others, Rena hadn't moved. She looked up as they approached, her expression untroubled, as if they'd just been for a walk.

Jamie felt a surge of anger. 'Why didn't you stop him?'

Rena's gaze slid straight over Jamie, settling on Lowry.

'Are you ready?' she said. 'We have to keep going.'

Jamie took a step towards her, but Lowry gripped her arm in a surprisingly strong grasp. When she twisted round to glare at him, he shook his head sharply, before turning back to Rena.

'It's been a long day,' he said. 'Maybe we should stay here tonight.'

Rena's face was backlit with an unshakeable certainty as she climbed to her feet. 'No. We need to go on.'

Jamie opened her mouth, but Lowry shook his head at her again, his expression clearly readable.

No point.

'Do you really want to head straight off?' Callan said. 'It's another three miles.'

Lowry had his hand pressed to his ribs, and he looked tired. The kind of tired that isn't caused by just one day of hard activity, and won't be cured by just one day of rest.

'My stepmother must have a car,' Jamie said. 'You could drive.'

'No.' Rena's voice was calm and flat. 'We have to walk. Like the old pilgrims. We have to strip it all away. All the mess, all the things that get in the way.'

'It's three miles,' Jamie said again. 'And Lowry—'

'Is fine,' the old man interrupted. 'If that's what you want, Rena.'

'Pointless,' Gracie said abruptly. 'Pointless nonsense. Wearing yourself out because she's set on being some sort of martyr.'

There was an odd light in Rena's eyes as she turned to the engineer. Jamie felt her anger fall away, to be replaced by unease. 'It's all right,' Rena said. 'You don't understand yet. But you will. It took me a while too. There's a path, and we've all been on it for years now. Hundreds of years, maybe.' She frowned and rubbed at her eye, her serenity cracking for the first time. 'I can't quite see it.'

'Rena.' Lowry's voice was gentle, and Rena turned to him, her face clearing.

'It's all right, Marcus,' she said tenderly. Jamie thought she saw Lowry flinch. 'It doesn't matter how long this has been going on. It's where we're going that's important.'

'And where are we going?' Callan's tone was almost conversational, and Rena turned to him, her eyes bright with disclosure.

'To God,' she said. 'He's waiting for us, out there in the space between the stars.'

'So remind me.' Gracie was studying Rena with detached curiosity. 'Why are you going to Lindisfarne? If God's waiting somewhere else?'

Rena nodded, as though the engineer had confirmed something. 'It's a jumping-off point,' she said, and then chuckled, an odd, off-kilter little sound. 'A launch pad, you'd probably say.' She gave Gracie another unsettling smile, and then turned to Lowry. 'We should go. Time and tide, time and tide . . . you know.'

She bent and picked up her pack. When Lowry went to shoulder his own rucksack, Callan stuck out a hand to stop him.

'No need to carry all your stuff,' he said. 'Even if you're set on this damn fool pilgrimage, or whatever it is. We can bring it up tomorrow.'

Lowry hesitated, and then dropped the bag with a grunt of relief. 'Thank you.'

Rena shook her head, an odd, frightened look flitting across her face, as she clutched the straps. 'I need to carry it.'

Callan shrugged. 'Your choice.'

Rena turned away and started to walk down the lane. 'Time to go.'

As Lowry moved to follow her, Callan caught his arm. 'You sure about this? Just you and her stuck out there together?'

'There are some others,' Jamie suddenly remembered. 'Two monks.'

'Some of them made it then?' Lowry smiled. 'There's obviously something to be said for the religious lifestyle.'

'My point stands,' Callan said. 'She's not exactly firing on all cylinders. What if you need help?'

'This is about helping her,' Lowry said. 'I just need to get her away. Somewhere quiet, away from the things that set her off.'

'Why you?' Jamie said. 'What makes her your responsibility? You've got her here. Surely that's enough.'

The look Lowry turned on her was heavy with something that looked like regret. 'It's not enough. And I can't just walk away.'

'Why not?'

Lowry gave a slow, sad smile. 'Because some of it's my fault.'

'What do you mean?'

'Ask me another time,' he said, and turned to follow Rena along the lane.

It's summer and the world is ending in a long, drawn-out fade-to-grey.

No fire, no flood. Just a slow-settling silence, drifting in on the airwaves and spreading across their little frontier world.

They all know what's coming. It's in their blood, in their bones, in the air inside their lungs. Sometimes Jamie thinks she can feel it: a flutter behind her ribs, a quick stab of pain at the base of her spine. She's never been so aware of what lies beneath her skin. Not even when her body was stretching and reshaping itself around the baby.

She can feel the movement of blood through her veins, the soak of oxygen through the walls of her lungs. When she moves, it's with a clear picture in her mind of the way her bones shift against one another. There are so many hiding places inside her, so many dark corners where death might lurk like a piece of grit in the gut of an oyster. But there'll be no burgeoning pearl at the end of all this. There'll be nothing but dust.

When she thinks of it she finds it hard to breathe, as though that dust is already inside her, coating her throat and choking her lungs. But her reaction stops at the physical. She doesn't feel anything. It's as though her emotions have been quarantined.

If she'd ever imagined this, she'd have imagined panic, terror, people screaming and clawing at the world around them. Instead, the cattle station is still ticking over. Jim Cranwell still comes out in the morning and runs through the list of tasks for the day. The farmhands still feed and water the herd, and Jamie still takes blood samples and checks the results.

But they don't talk if they don't have to, and they don't look at one another. The syringe feels like it's the wrong shape in her hands, and when she rests her palm against the warm flank of one of the young steers she can't quite work out what she's doing there, in this place, in this moment.

The world is broken. It's cracked and splintered and numb and slow and muffled and lost. And it's ending. Long and silent and falling and fading and there's nothing beneath her feet and nothing around her and nothing in the sky and nothing inside her. Just some statistic she heard one of the farmhands say.

Nought point nought nought nought one.

CHAPTER TWENTY-SIX

Jamie stood with Callan, Gracie and Finn, and watched until Rena and Lowry were out of sight.

'Then there were four,' she said.

'You're assuming we're all staying,' Gracie said, turning to survey her surroundings. 'I'm not sure I'm ready for early retirement by the seaside. I might go see what the fuel situation is.'

Callan looked contemplative. 'The damage was pretty bad, but if we could get some fuel in, I might be able to limp it to a landing site. Get it patched up and flying again.'

'If the network's still up, you should be able to figure out fuel dump locations,' Gracie said. 'I might call in on Elsie and see if she can help.'

'How would you get the fuel to the ship?'

'Wherry?' Gracie said. 'If we can find a port, I may be able to override the codes. You want to come with me?'

The pause seemed to stretch out.

'No hurry,' Callan said eventually. 'A few days' downtime won't hurt.'

'Where will we sleep?' Finn asked suddenly.

Jamie glanced up the lane. 'You can stay . . .' She stopped. She didn't know how her stepmother's illness would progress. She pushed the thought away. She'd worry about it when it became an issue. 'You can stay with me. With my stepmother.'

'You sure?' Callan said. 'Lowry said she didn't look well.'

'Yes, I'm sure. What about you?'

He picked up his pack, nodding towards the row of holiday cottages by the lime kilns. 'I'll try one of these.' He glanced at Gracie. 'You want to take the place next door?'

Gracie swung her bag up onto her shoulders. 'I might head straight off. No point unpacking, then packing up again.'

Callan looked at her for a few seconds. 'Okay. You know where we are.'

Gracie nodded, and lifted her hand to Jamie and Finn. 'Take care.'

Callan watched her walk away. When she was out of sight, he gave a quick shake of his head and turned back to Jamie and Finn.

'Just like that?' Jamie said. 'No goodbyes, or anything.'

Callan smiled slightly. 'You did get a *take care*.'

'But after all we've been through, I thought . . .'

He grinned. 'Trust me. That was an outpouring of emotion as far as Gracie's concerned. And just because we crash-landed together, it doesn't make us all soulmates.' He started towards the cottages. 'I'm going to get settled in.

'Come on.' Jamie turned to Finn. 'Let's find somewhere for Emily.'

'Can't he stay with us?'

'I'm not sure he'd fit through the door.'

Finn gave her a narrow-eyed look.

'Sorry.' Jamie smiled at him. 'I knew what you meant. But probably not a good idea. It's not fenced and there's a fair drop from the garden down onto the shore. There's a field just down the lane.'

Finn was shivering a little, his wet clothes clinging to him. But she thought he'd probably settle better if he knew the horse was safe.

The field had a ramshackle shelter, and a lopsided notice,

saying *Please don't feed the pony. He's getting fat!* Finn walked around the edge while Jamie waited by the gate with Emily.

'Okay?' she said when he'd completed his circumnavigation.

He nodded. 'Okay.'

Back at the house, they found her stepmother asleep in her chair, with the dog snoring across her feet. Jamie took Finn upstairs and helped him unpack his few belongings into the chest of drawers in the spare room. By the time they'd both changed and headed back downstairs, Jamie's stepmother was stirring. When Jamie introduced Finn, the older woman gave him a quick, appraising look, and then smiled.

'Hello, Finn.'

'Hello.'

'It feels funny,' her stepmother said. 'Saying *hello*. It's one of those things you never really think about. When I first got back here I found myself talking to the seagulls.' She dropped her hand down, and the dog gave it a quick hard lick. 'And I had this one, of course. But no *good mornings* or *how are yous*.'

Her stepmother rubbed at her knuckle. Jamie had a quick flash of memory: that same gesture on younger hands. She'd never clocked it before. Did her stepmother have a catalogue of Jamie's own little tells and giveaways, that she'd never quite pieced together to find the truth that lay behind?

The older woman gave a quick shake of her head. 'But we're not alone any more. We're both here. And Finn.' She turned her gaze back to the young lad who was taking in his surroundings in a series of quick, furtive glances. 'Are you hungry?'

He shook his head.

'Why don't you take him along the headland?' her stepmother said. 'Show him the coves. I just need a few more minutes, then I'll make us some dinner. Maybe the others would like to join us. The gentleman I met said he and another lady were going on to Lindisfarne. But he mentioned a man – the captain of the ship, I think he said. And someone else. A lady. Grace?'

'She's gone,' Jamie said. 'Back to see someone we met on the way.'

'There's another survivor?'

'There are several.'

Her stepmother contemplated this. 'So they were wrong,' she said. 'That one-in-a-million statistic was wrong.'

'I think so,' Jamie said. 'In some places anyway.'

'Then the world might just go on. Beyond us, I mean.'

'Perhaps.' Jamie thought of telling her about the administration's fears, but it seemed wrong, talking about new life to a woman who had so little left of her own.

'Go on.' Her stepmother gestured towards the door. 'It's a beautiful evening, and the tide's almost out. Take him down to the coves.'

The lane ran parallel to the ocean, forging a straight line northwards, ignoring the tug of the headlands. Jamie kept up a running commentary, pointing out old landmarks. A rocky cove – *that's where I used to go to eat fish and chips*. The little path that followed the wandering line of the headland – *I used to race my sisters there*. The cottage where old Mrs Jameson lived – *she made the best muffins, but you had to keep on her good side*.

'What was on her bad side?'

Jamie laughed. 'Just an expression.'

They wound their way down a narrow track onto a rocky shore, where great tongues of black rock protruded far out to sea.

'There.' Jamie pointed along the shoreline, towards a cluster of humpbacked rocks, sheltering a network of shallow pools. 'That's where you find most of the sea glass and pottery.'

Finn took a few steps that way, glancing back at Jamie.

'It's okay,' she said. 'We've got time for a bit of a hunt around.'

At first Finn went too fast, eyes everywhere. Jamie kept having to call him back. She was moving in baby steps, nudging at mounds of pebbles, watching for the tell-tale glint of glass. Within a matter of minutes she had a fistful of fragments. The pieces were mostly clear, but there were a couple of tiny nubs of deep blue, and three pieces of china in faded rose-pink and off-white.

Finn kept glancing at her, his face twisting with frustration, but he gradually found a slower tempo, falling in beside her. When he caught sight of his first piece of glass, he stopped dead, his gaze fixed on the little fragment.

'That's a good piece.' Jamie bent down to pick it up. When she held it out, Finn took it reverently, cupping it in his palm. 'Nice and smooth.'

After about half an hour, they stopped, and spread the fragments out on the surface of a flat rock. Finn pushed the pieces around, his expression intent, but not as frustrated as when she'd first shown him the sea glass, back on the ship. He had a look of someone who was working something through.

'They'll never go back together,' he said.

'No.'

'But you like them.'

'Yes. I don't know why, but I like the feel of them, the patterns they make. They're not for anything. Maybe that's why I like them. They just *are*.' She stood up. 'Let's get back.'

Finn began to scrape the pieces together.

'Leave them here,' Jamie said. 'The tide won't come this high. We can come another time, bring a bag to take them home.'

'The tide?'

'It's what the sea does.' Jamie wafted a vague hand towards the horizon. 'It goes out, and then it comes back in again. Every few hours. That's what brings the sea glass in. We can only collect it at low tide.'

'Will it be . . .' He picked over the words carefully. '. . . *low tide* tomorrow?'

'There's a low tide every day,' Jamie said. 'Not at the same time, though.'

She felt as though she was shovelling information at him, but for some reason she wanted him to understand the rhythms of life here. She didn't want to be the only one who knew how everything worked. If he could fit in here, then maybe it would be like belonging. Maybe it would be like living again, not just surviving.

She reached down to brush sand off her knees. 'Come on.'

At the house, they found Jamie's stepmother in the kitchen, leaning heavily on the side as she stirred a pot on the old range cooker.

'You still get gas for this?' Jamie said.

'I had it converted to electricity a couple of years ago,' her stepmother said. 'The gas was getting too unreliable. Can you put this out?'

Jamie carried the heavy pot over to the table, and then opened a cupboard to find the familiar crackle-glazed plates. She laid three places, and then paused.

'I better see if Callan wants to join us.'

Round at the row of holiday cottages, the first door was locked, and the second, but the door of the final cottage opened when she pushed it. The lock was splintered, and the catch was loose.

'Callan?'

When Jamie stepped inside she saw his bag propped up on the sofa. She went to the foot of the spiral stairs.

'Callan?'

Perhaps he'd gone to look around the place. She went back outside, following the path down the side of the kilns. The sun was sinking towards the headland, and the beach was mottled with shadows, and trimmed here and there with a thin line of seafoam. The indefinable smell of the ocean was muted by the rising scent of night. She'd been right, back on Soltaire. The dark smelled the same everywhere.

There was no sign of Callan, and she turned back to the house.

The others were already at the table, her stepmother in a high-backed Ercol chair, wedged in with cushions. She saw Jamie looking and gave a wry smile.

'Trial and error,' she said. 'I know this set-up will let me get back on my feet again. Is your friend coming?'

Friend. That took her back to her teenage years, when her stepmother couldn't disguise her excitement on the rare occasions when Jamie passed through with a fellow youngster of the male persuasion.

Does your friend want a drink?

Can I get a snack for you and your friend?

Those sorts of euphemisms broke down when you grew up. Friends became friends. Lovers became lovers. In name, anyway. Even if you weren't entirely sure they fitted one of those narrow categories.

She sat down. 'He wasn't there.'

They didn't talk much. Finn kept rubbing his eyes, his fork sagging in his other hand, and her stepmother wasn't much better.

'Sorry,' she said, after an unsuccessful attempt to hide her third yawn. 'You must have so much to tell me, and here I am, barely able to keep my eyes open.'

'It's okay. Plenty of time.'

Her stepmother smiled sadly. 'Probably not. But some time, certainly. Maybe we should call it a night. Do you want to go to bed, Finn?'

He nodded, and put his fork down, balancing it across his empty plate at a precise forty-five-degree angle.

He followed Jamie upstairs, and she showed him the bathroom, leaving him to take himself off to bed, while she went back downstairs to help her stepmother up to bed. The older woman was breathing hard, and Jamie could feel her trembling.

'How have you managed so far?' Jamie asked, as they took a break on the landing.

'I just did.' Her stepmother leaned against the wall. 'Maybe what we can and can't do changes to fit in with what we have to do. I can manage from here.'

'Sure?'

'Yes, I'm sure. Are you turning in as well?'

Jamie glanced out through the hall window. 'I thought I might go down to the beach for a bit.'

Her stepmother tilted her head. 'You mean a swim?'

'Maybe.'

'I suppose there's no point telling you to be careful, not to get too cold, and to make sure you don't stay out too late?'

Jamie smiled briefly. 'Probably not.'

'If you look in Bella's old room, I think there are some swimming costumes in the bottom drawer.'

'Okay. Thanks.'

As she walked over to the door of the room her youngest half-sister had once occupied, she felt a pang of something like guilt. She was here, and they were gone.

'Jamie.'

She turned.

'Be careful,' her stepmother said. 'Don't get too cold and don't stay out too late.'

CHAPTER TWENTY-SEVEN

Jamie walked down to the beach wearing a cotton kaftan over a navy swimsuit, her feet shoved into a pair of old flip-flops. At the edge of the waves she pulled off the cover-up and threw it back up onto the dry sand. Then she kicked off the flip-flops and walked into the shallows. The cold wrapped about her and she clenched her teeth to stop them chattering. The chill had never bothered her before.

Asbestos skin, her mother once said when Jamie was little.

That's for heat, not cold, her father had replied, and then they'd argued and her mother had stormed off home. They'd found her asleep on the sofa, an empty glass beside her.

Jamie kept wading out until she was waist-deep. This was the tipping point, when you had to decide whether to turn back or take that final plunge. She breathed in hard, bent her knees and kicked off. For a moment she hung weightless, her whole body in a vice of cold, and then a faded memory sharpened into focus, and her body remembered how to take that cold and turn it into a hard, physical pleasure. She kicked out towards the open sea, head down, snatching quick mouthfuls of air in the furrows between the waves. It was harder than it used to be, and her lungs and legs were aching after just a couple of minutes. But it would come back.

After a few moments she stopped, tucking her legs underneath her and sculling on the spot. She was perhaps a hundred metres out. Past the harbour wall, past the sloping shallows, far past the invisible line that would have had parents scrambling to their feet to shout at their straying offspring, *Not so far, you're too far out*.

The tide was pushing at her, trying to shove her back towards the shore. *Not so far. Too far out*.

I'm fine.

And then she thought it might be true.

She was a speck of life, tiny and out of place in the vast cold of the ocean. What she'd lost, what she'd thrown away, it was all part of a world that was gone. And that was how it always was. Yesterday turned into memory, and the world remade itself, and there was never a moment when you looked at it and knew you had it right. Tomorrow she'd wake up and this moment would be just a memory, the world reshaping itself around her doubt and uncertainty. But there'd be other distinct moments, here and there, sharp and acute among the fug and muddle of it all.

To the north, the coast unfurled in a dark bulk, with the shoreline picked out in a shifting mix-media of surf and moonlight. You used to be able to see the lights on Lindisfarne from out here. Tonight there was nothing to indicate that this corner of the world was anything but empty.

The curve of the current was carrying her back towards the harbour, and she could see a figure sitting on the end of the wall. She swam a few strokes and caught hold of the slippery stones.

Callan looked down at her. 'Bit cold for swimming.'

'It's fine when you're in.'

He looked out across the dark surface of the sea. 'Why do I doubt that very much?'

'Why don't you join me and see for yourself?' His legs were hanging down, and she reached up to give his foot a shake. 'Might need to take your boots off first.'

He drew his legs out of reach. 'Nice offer, but I'm fine up here. And besides, I never learned to swim.'

'You can't swim?'

He shot her a narrow-eyed look. 'Not much call for it in the inner city. Or on board ship.'

'No. Sorry.' She turned in the water, still holding on to the wall. 'I was trying to get far enough out to see down the coast. There's a clear view for miles once you're past the headland.'

'You could take a boat out.' He nodded towards the harbour. 'There are a couple tied up. You know how to sail?'

She nodded. 'You?'

He gave her another hard look, and she raised a hand. 'Sorry, sorry. No boats in St Louis.'

'And despite the name, spaceships and the other sort don't have much in common.' He held his hand down. 'Let's go see what we can see.'

She braced her feet against the wall and reached up so that he could grab her hand and haul her up. The air was warmer than the sea, but she started shivering almost immediately, the faint breeze pricking goosebumps from her skin. She was very aware of how little she was wearing.

'Where's your towel?' he asked.

'I didn't bring one. My cover-up's on the beach.'

'Wait here.'

He jogged over to disappear along the path beside the kilns. Jamie followed more slowly, swinging her arms to keep the blood moving. She was almost at the gate when he reappeared with a towel. She rubbed herself as dry as she could, and then retrieved her kaftan and flip-flops.

'Better?' Callan said, as she rejoined him.

'Much better. Do you still want to go out?'

'If you do.' He looked at her. 'Might be colder out there. Don't you want to get dressed?'

She shook her head. There was an urgency to her need to see what lay beyond that headland.

'We're not going far out,' she said. 'And anyway, northerners are tough.'

'They seem to be,' Callan replied. 'A fair few of them have survived, anyway.' He looked out towards the horizon. 'I wonder if it's like this everywhere on Earth. Groups of survivors, I mean. If the ship wasn't grounded, we could have gone looking.'

'Do you think you can get it back in the air?'

'I don't know,' he said. 'It's got to be worth a shot. I went for a walk over to the hotel. They've got a working console. The network's in a bit of a state, obviously, but I found some info on fuel dump locations. There are a couple not that far from our landing site.'

Jamie had reached the first of the boats, a little blue coble with its name blazoned in perky gold script. *Northern Cross*. She bent down to loosen the painter, trying to keep her tone neutral. 'So you'll be heading off, then.'

'Not just yet. We've been dashing from pillar to post since it happened.' He looked out through the harbour mouth. 'I've been doing that for years now, come to think of it. A spell of staying put might be what I need.'

Is there nothing else you need? she thought, but, 'Sit down,' was all she said, as she cast off, and used an oar to steer out of the harbour. Once they were clear of the outer wall, she leaned over the stern and shipped the rudder. Then she raised the little sail, and eased them round, before reaching up to turn on the battery-operated hurricane lamp hanging from the mast.

'I've never quite understood sailing boats,' Callan said. 'How does it work when you want to go the opposite way to the wind?'

344

'You really want a lesson now?'

He shook his head. 'Plenty of time.'

Everyone always said that. And not long ago, the universe had given them all an abject lesson on just how untrue it could be.

Once they were out beyond the headland, Jamie lowered the sail.

'This should be far enough.'

Callan slid over to join her, setting the little boat rocking. He didn't say anything, but his knuckles whitened as he gripped the side.

'Don't worry,' she said. 'There'll be lifejackets in the locker.'

'They'll be useful,' he said, a little caustically. 'If we capsize, remind me not to drown before I put one on.'

'We're not going to capsize,' she said. 'Don't be a baby. You made less fuss over crash-landing a spaceship.'

As soon as the words were out, she regretted the flippant mention of his broken ship, but he just shook his head at her. 'I know how a spaceship works,' he said. 'And space, it's predictable. For the most part. No storms, no tidal waves, no great big beasts to take chunks out of you.'

'This is the North Sea. Not Shark Bay. And I don't think we're in much danger of a tidal wave on the Northumberland coast.'

'First time for everything.'

The coastline was an unbroken stretch of emptiness. She'd expected nothing else, but as she stared at that great dark expanse, with all the familiar clusters and pinpricks of light extinguished, she felt something clench inside her.

'Well.' She tried to keep her tone light. 'I guess now we know.'

As she turned away, reaching for the halyard, Callan leaned forward.

'Wait,' he said. 'What's that?'

She followed the line of his gaze, but she saw nothing.

'Turn the light off.'

She flicked the switch.

'Keep looking,' he said. 'Give your eyes time to adjust.'

As she stared into the darkness something glinted faintly in the corner of her eye, but when she turned to look at it, it winked out, like a too-distant star. But there was another, a few thumb-widths down the coast. And another – no, two, three – right down there on the very edge of their line of sight. And those weren't single lights. They were little patches of illumination in the dark sprawl of Tyneside.

'Can you see them?' Callan said.

Jamie nodded. It might not be people. Lights could have been left on, or there might be timers still running, like the last twitching nerves in the human race's old, shed skin. But somehow those little pricks of light changed everything.

She glanced at Callan and found him looking at her, his expression contemplative. Her breath caught in her chest. In an empty world, everything felt bigger. A glance. A touch. A silent sea beneath stars that were still just stars, despite it all.

He reached for her hand, sliding his palm under hers where it rested on the side of the boat, wrapping his fingers around it.

Just another moment.

His thumb began to draw tiny circles on the back of her hand. She didn't remember ever feeling so acutely *here*, in her skin, on this patch of the Earth – or sea. Gravity felt stronger than it should. She could feel the weight of her own body, of his hand, of the night air, making it hard to think beyond the next heartbeat.

Somewhere in the endlessness of the universe, another version of Jamie pulled her hand away and said, *It's late, let's go back*. Somewhere, another Jamie turned to another Callan and kissed him, bearing him down to the deck so that she could feel him moving on her, as the sea moved beneath her. Somewhere out there, for some other Jamie, the moment passed and did not come again.

But it seemed to her, in that moment, that those other selves could take care of themselves, along with all the possible futures they carried. And so she left her hand in his, and the two of them sat there beneath the stars, as the sea grew night-still, and those lights on the shoreline flickered through the dark.

When she woke in the morning, the night's events still felt immediate – from her sundown swim to the moment back on the harbourside, when she gently untangled her fingers from Callan's and stood on tiptoe to brush a goodnight kiss against the side of his mouth – but she couldn't recapture that feeling of the world narrowing to a single moment, and all other choices falling away. Whatever emotion and circumstance and time and place had come together to create that certainty, it was gone now. She felt a flutter of something like panic, that it might not come again. She knew what Lowry would say. He'd say the world wasn't powered on memories. It was powered on moments. It was powered on now. But still her unease persisted.

She got up and dressed in some old clothes one of her sisters must have left behind. Rifling through the drawers gave her a nip of pain, and she avoided the more distinctive items, sticking to a pair of cropped jeans and a plain white top. Her stepmother was still asleep when Jamie looked in. She was curled in on herself, the quilt clutched between her thin fingers, her face creased with lines of pain.

When she went to check on Finn she found his room

empty. He wasn't downstairs, or out in the garden, and the first flickers of anxiety made themselves felt. She walked to the end of the garden and looked over the edge. The tide had been in while she slept, leaving the stones bare and slippery with tangled nets of seaweed.

'Finn.' It was a wide, still morning, with no sea breeze to throw her voice back to her. 'Finn. Where are you?'

A cormorant regarded her disapprovingly, while overhead the gulls stepped up their heckling.

When she went round to the front of the house, the road was clear in both directions. Maybe he'd gone back up to the cove. That was probably it.

But there was an image stark in her mind: an arm coming up out of the deep water, to scrabble at the harbour wall.

Her breath was growing short, her thoughts crushing up against one another.

She'd brought him all this way.

She'd promised him a home.

She'd lost enough, surely. They'd all lost enough.

It doesn't work that way, a little mocking voice told her.

She swore out loud, sending the gulls into a frenzy of glee, and then she started to run down the lane.

There was no sign of him in the first cove, or the second. She turned off the road and out onto the headland. She'd be able to see the whole stretch of shoreline from there.

'Fuck's sake.' As she stumbled, a stopper of pent-up panic shook itself free, coming out as a volley of profanity. 'Fuck. Shit. *Shit*.' She scrambled to the edge of the cliffs, and stared along the shore.

'Finn.'

She shouted it again, conscious of the shrill leading edge of fear in her voice.

'Finn.'

She was suddenly very aware of the great expanse of open countryside around the village. Some roads would end at farms, with machinery lying about the place; other tracks would end at deep pools, or uncovered slurry pits. She might never even know what—

'Stop. Stop it. Stop it.'

She turned and ran back to the road.

When she reached the cottages, there was no sign of Callan.

The harbour.

As she rounded the kilns and emerged onto the harbour-side, her heart leaped at the sight of a tall figure standing on the curved wall, looking down onto the shore. And then her fear stepped in again.

A body on the sand.

Callan looking down, frozen in shock, trying to work out how to tell her she'd failed in a simple enough charge. Keep a cautious, quiet boy alive for a single night in a deserted village. But then she hadn't managed to keep the other one alive – not even wrapped up inside her where he should have been as safe as anyone in the universe.

When Callan turned at the sound of her footsteps, she saw that he was holding a mug in his hand. He wouldn't be standing there, drinking coffee, if Finn was lying down there on the rocks.

'Finn's been busy.' He jerked his head down towards the beach.

'He . . . what?' She stared at him.

Callan gave her a bemused look. 'What's wrong?'

'You've seen him? Where is he?'

Callan gestured again. 'Down there.'

Jamie lurched to the edge of the harbour. Finn was crouched on the shore, frowning in concentration. The wet sand in front of him was covered in fragments of glass and pottery, each one carefully placed equidistant from its neighbours.

'Finn.' Relief was ragged in her voice, and Callan gave her a sharp glance.

Finn looked up, his frown deepening. 'It's not finished.'

The fragments. There was a shape to them. They flowed in lines and curls, and wrapped round on themselves, like some hybrid of Celtic spirals and Roman mosaic.

'A horse,' she said. 'It's a horse.'

'It's for you. I went back for more pieces.'

Her fear was trying to reshape itself as anger. She could shout at Finn for frightening her, or at Callan, because he hadn't somehow read her mind and come to find her before she'd worked herself into a frenzy. But the shreds of her self-control had knitted back together just enough for her to recognise that it was so much easier to blame someone else, and so much harder to unravel your emotions and think, *It happened, that's all.*

'You okay?' Callan was still watching her.

She forced her fingers to uncurl.

'I couldn't find him. I was worried.'

His eyes searched her face, clearly finding more there than in her brief explanation.

'Finn.' The lad glanced up. 'Tell Jamie where you're going next time, won't you?'

Finn nodded.

Easy as that. Why was it never like that for her?

'Hey.' Callan's voice was gentle, and she looked up. 'It's okay. He's safe. You're all safe. You made it.'

'I know.' Down on the sand, Finn was adding another piece to the horse's tail. 'But it doesn't feel like we're safe, or finished. It feels like there's still something I should be doing.'

He gave her an amused look. 'That's the thing, isn't it? You're never done. Otherwise what's the point? If you woke up one day and realised you'd done everything you needed to do, you'd be finished, wouldn't you? Time to move on to whatever comes next.'

'Do you believe there's something that comes next?'

He shrugged. 'No idea. I'm kind of hoping it's a fair few years before I have to find out.'

'Is it really that easy for you?' There was a hint of resentment in her tone, and his eyebrows went up.

'Who said anything about easy? But it's all you can do, isn't it? Live today. Then the next day. And the one after that. Unless you're inclined to jump off the nearest cliff, of course, but surviving is fairly addictive. Do it once and you get more determined to keep on doing it.'

She shook her head slowly. If he'd said all this last night, she'd have looked up at the stars and thought, *Yes, that's it.* But now her old uncertainty was shouldering its way in again. Was this how it was for everyone? Little moments of being sure, of fitting into the world around you, all strung together on a flimsy thread of doubt and confusion and not belonging?

'So one step at a time,' she said.

'One step, one breath. For now, anyway. No point spending today worrying about tomorrow, because the big things tend to come crashing in with no warning.' He gave a small, ironic smile. 'End of the world, that sort of thing.' He took a sip of his coffee. 'And when something big does come out of left field, you need to take time to take stock. Someone's tipped the box up, and maybe some of the pieces are lost under the floor . . .'

Gracie told him about the jigsaw then.

'. . . and you're not going to get it all back together in one go. That's what they're trying to do, back on Alegria. They think it'll all be like it was before. But some of the pieces are missing. And the rest are scattered all over the place. It'll be centuries before we're back where we were. If that's even what we want.'

Jamie didn't look at him as she asked the next question. 'And where do you see yourself in all of that?'

He shrugged. 'Here.' Her heart leaped, and then steadied as he added, 'For a little while. And then, we'll see.'

We?

Finn was sitting back on his heels, surveying his work.

'Is it done?' she asked.

He frowned. 'It doesn't look like it did in my head.'

'It's beautiful,' she said. 'But you know the tide will come up.'

Finn nodded, apparently undisturbed. 'I can make it again.'

'So what now?' Callan took a sip of his coffee.

Jamie gave him a sharp look. 'I thought you just said—'

'Not that sort of *what now*. I just meant what are you going to do today?'

Jamie looked around. The sea was waiting, calm and cool beneath a clear sky. There were old paths to follow, beaches to comb. What would it be like to wake up every morning and ask that question? For every day to be something new, and not part of some pattern you were trying to weave with your life?

'I've still got Lowry's things,' she said. 'I should take them up there. I'll have to go by boat. The tide's on its way in.' She turned to Finn. 'Do you want to come with me to see Lowry?'

Finn nodded.

'What about you?' Jamie asked Callan. 'I could give you that sailing lesson.'

'Maybe later,' he said. 'I went for a walk first thing. Found some old sailing books in the harbour office. Looks as though boats are a bit more complicated than I thought. Figured I'd spend a bit of time learning the ropes.' He gave a brief smile. 'Literally. If we start off with you trying to show me what's what, I can pretty much guarantee we'll be yelling at each other before we're round the first headland. You go up to the island with Finn, and maybe I'll be ready for a practical when you get back.'

It was a perfectly reasonable suggestion, but there was a part of her that was trying to shape it into a rejection. Or she could take it at face value and not write a whole alternative *should be* out of whatever it was that had hung between them last night.

'Okay,' she said lightly, and turned back towards the house.

CHAPTER TWENTY-EIGHT

They took a motor launch that Jamie found tucked in between two of the larger sailing dinghies. When she checked the bio-oil tank, it was half full. More than enough for the trip there and back.

Finn sat quietly, trailing a hand over the side and snatching it back when a wave leaped up to catch at his fingers. Jamie kept them at a sedate pace, pointing out landmarks on the coastline and the great turbines mounted on manmade reefs a few hundred metres out beyond Lindisfarne.

They landed at an old wooden jetty, in the shallow inlet that formed a natural harbour. Ahead of them, the castle rose from its crag, solid and out of proportion with its setting, as though the long, low island must be right on the edge of upending and tipping into the sea. As she helped Finn out of the boat she cast a quick eye over the tideline, checking she'd left enough slack in the rope to allow for an hour or so of rise. She didn't want to be much longer than that. Her stepmother had been adamant that she'd be fine on her own, but she was so slight, her skin so thin, that Jamie could almost see the cancer tightening around her bones and vital organs.

They made their way through the odd little shanty town that edged the inlet. Beach huts, makeshift sheds made from old herring fifies sawn in half and turned upside down, doors fitted awkwardly into the curved ends, and window boxes of now-dead flowers nailed beneath recycled dormers. They skirted a couple of derelict skiffs, perched upside down on a row of bow-legged trestles. She was sure they were the same ones that had been sitting here untouched for as long as she'd been coming here. Somewhere, someone had always been thinking *later, another day* about them, until time had run out.

The island's religious community was at the far end of the village. It had been set up a few years before Jamie left for Alegria. The small group of monks had slipped into island life quietly and unobtrusively. After a while people had fallen into the habit of talking as though they'd always been there.

As they turned into the narrow lane leading to the abbey, Lowry emerged from a flint-walled cottage. Jamie unslung his bag from her shoulders.

'We thought you might need your things.'

'Thank you.' He gave a little grimace. 'I have to say, by the time we got here I was glad I wasn't carrying that thing. Rena set a fairly ambitious pace.'

'Where is she?'

'Praying.' Lowry's face was expressionless.

'Did you find the monks?'

Lowry nodded. 'Two of them. There were five, but when the virus struck the island they apparently agreed that the other three would tend the sick for as long as they could, while the youngest two isolated themselves so that the community could have a hope of surviving.'

'That's got to be hard to deal with,' Jamie said, trying to imagine how it would have felt to be on either side of that straw poll.

'They tell me they've spent a lot of time meditating and praying, and they're at peace with it. They see their survival as a heavenly endorsement of the decision they all made.'

Jamie thought she could detect a hint of envy in his tone.

'Did anyone else on the island make it?'

'One,' Lowry said. 'An old fisherman. He'd gone out on a

long trip around the time the virus must have been transmitted to the island. There's a pod of local dolphins that sometimes take themselves off for weeks at a time, and he was planning on following them to see where they went. He picked up some messages on his comm, and stayed out at sea until his provisions ran out.'

'He never caught it?'

Lowry nodded. 'He may well be the only one. The monks are sure it was God who saved him, but he seems to find that grimly amusing. He says the only god he's ever believed in is the sea.'

Something occurred to Jamie and she felt a little spike of fear-fuelled adrenaline. 'If he's never had it, could he—'

'It's okay.' Lowry cut across her. 'Same thing occurred to Rena when she got here. Turns out she's got a mobile lab kit in that bag of hers. She took samples and we're all virus free apparently. So it doesn't stay in the blood. It's gone for good.' His face darkened. 'No antibodies, though. If it did somehow come back, we'd have no protection. It seems wrong, going through all that and not even being rewarded with immunity.'

'No immunity?' Jamie felt a breathless rush of fear. She suddenly wanted to back away from Lowry, even from Finn. 'If it comes back . . .'

'It won't,' Lowry said. 'There's nothing left of the dead but dust, and Rena says the virus couldn't live in that.'

There was something unsettling about the thought of Rena crouching down, scooping the powdery remains of some unknown victim into one of her sterile test tubes.

'Why did she have a lab kit?' she asked.

'She picked it up on Alegria apparently.'

Jamie couldn't get a handle on the older woman. She was like one of those shapeshifters from mythology, slipping from your grasp just as you thought you'd figured her out. One minute she was rambling about God's will; the next moment she was in efficient lab assistant mode, analysing blood samples and collecting evidence. And for what? The virus was gone. It wasn't as though Rena was going to find a cure and bring back the dead. Jamie felt a flicker of anger. Mila had been shot, and they'd almost been caught for something that couldn't make any difference to anything.

'Are you staying for a while?' Lowry said, distracting Jamie from her thoughts.

'For a little bit,' Jamie replied. 'Not too long.'

'Come and have a cup of tea.'

Lowry led them to a wood-framed building that Jamie thought might have been a shop the last time she was here. Inside, there were little clusters of wooden chairs and tables scattered about a high-ceilinged space, with a stainless steel industrial kitchen behind a counter at the far end.

He went over to turn on the water boiler, before finding mugs and teabags. To Jamie's surprise, instead of milk powder, he pulled a jug out of the fridge.

'Brother Xavier has figured out how to milk a cow,' Lowry said with a grin. 'Not terribly efficiently, but it's a start.'

'Maybe he can hold classes.'

'I think that's exactly what he has in mind. They seem quietly sure they're founding members of what's going to be a growing community.'

'Why do they think people will come here?'

Lowry handed her a mug, and held a second out to Finn, handle first. 'The sea has always drawn people. There's something about the coast. It's an end, or a beginning.'

'So why did *you* come here?'

He shook his head. 'There's not a single answer to that.'

'So tell me the main reason.'

He swirled his tea around his mug. 'Because it's where Rena wanted to be.'

'You wanted to come here too.' Rena was standing in the doorway, wearing what looked like a makeshift monk's robe, belted with a piece of stiff, fraying rope. When she shifted her weight the fabric sagged open, exposing her bony clavicle and the top of one shallow breast. Her hair straggled loose over her thin shoulders, and she looked shrivelled and reduced, her unhealthy sheen reminding Jamie, with a stab of acute discomfort, of her stepmother.

'I did,' Lowry said. 'But if you'd wanted to go somewhere else, I'd have made sure you got there.'

'You always look after me.' The words should have been tender, but there was no softening of Rena's expression. 'But it's all right now. I'm going to set you free. Soon you won't have to worry about me.'

As she turned away, she collided with a man on his way in. He was no more than thirty, also robed, but his garb was neat and clean, and there was a discreet silver cross at his neck. He turned to Lowry, his brow creasing in concern.

'Still just the same,' Lowry said. 'I'll try and talk to her later. I thought she might settle down after she got here.'

'Give her time.' The young monk's voice was deep and resonant, with a clear line of serenity running through it. 'It will take a while for the dust and grime of the world to wear away.'

'Perhaps,' Lowry said. 'Brother Dominic, Jamie and Finn. Jamie is Laura's stepdaughter.'

'How is Laura?' the monk asked.

'Not great,' Jamie said. 'Thank you for keeping an eye on her.'

'We wanted to bring her here,' Brother Dominic said. 'But she didn't want to leave her home.' He smiled. 'Now I know what she was waiting for. Faith is a wonderful thing.'

Jamie felt a prickle of resentment. It wasn't God that had brought her here. It was a rambling line of mistakes and slow-forming desires, and a man who snapped his own life in two to give her what she'd told him she wanted.

'I have some things for you to take back,' the monk went on. 'Some vegetables, and I think we might find some eggs.' He glanced at Finn. 'Perhaps this young man would like to come help me look?'

Finn glanced at Jamie.

'It's okay,' she said.

Finn nodded and followed the monk out of the refectory.

When they'd gone, Jamie turned to Lowry. 'Rena's getting worse, isn't she?'

Lowry nodded. 'I don't know how to help her.'

'What happened? Between the two of you, I mean.'

Lowry looked down at his mug, his thumb rubbing the smooth curve of the handle. After a few seconds he looked up, a resigned expression on his face. 'Take a walk down to the shore with me.'

They passed the vegetable patch on their way. Finn was standing by the chicken run with Brother Dominic, who was pointing out different birds by name.

'He's young,' Jamie said. 'For a monk. You always think of them as old men.'

Lowry shot her an amused look. 'Like preachers?'

'I don't . . . I mean . . .'

Lowry raised a hand. 'I'm joking. Yes, he's young. He only converted a few years ago. You often find the most unwavering faith in those who come to it late. It's like falling in love, that first flush when all you need is to be with the object of your desire and everything will be all right.'

'You sound cynical.'

He shook his head. 'I'm not. Not really. I have no doubt that his faith is real. But it's not something I understand.'

'Was it not like that for you?'

He smiled. 'You mean when I found God?'

'Yes.'

'I didn't find him,' Lowry said, as they picked their way down a rocky path to the shore. 'I was brought up with him. Lost toy. Ask God to help. Cut knee. God will comfort you. The night too dark. God has his arms around you. He was always presented to me as though he was some sort of cosmic nanny crossed with an all-powerful bodyguard.' He gave another smile, this time edged with cynicism. 'It's a wonder my faith lasted beyond the first time a girl refused to give me a second glance, after I'd asked God to please make her notice me.'

They found a flattish rock, and sat down.

'You were going to tell me about Rena,' Jamie prompted.

'I'm getting there. By a roundabout way.' He drained the last of his tea and wedged his mug into a hollow in the shingle. 'My faith did last, and I went to Campion Hall in Oxford and became a priest. I never felt quite like I fitted in, even though I had the pedigree. Old Catholic family, educated by the Jesuits, a mother who did the church flowers every Sunday. I couldn't have been more soaked in the faith.' His voice twisted a little on that word. 'Maybe everyone felt like that. It was an odd time. The world was changing so fast. At Oxford we were surrounded by the brightest minds of our generation, the ones who were going to keep us all pushing into the future.' His smile turned ironic. 'Brave new world. I could never quite shake this image that kept popping into my head. The pope, sitting at his window in the Vatican, looking up at the sky as vapour trails shot straight up, heading for heaven – for the place he'd always been able to claim for his God – and thinking, *What now?*'

'The Church survived,' Jamie said. 'People were still packing out St Peter's Square, before the virus.'

'It was never quite the same. When heaven came within reach, faith found that it wasn't welcome after all. Very few people took their religion with them to other worlds.'

'But you were a priest on Alegria.'

'The capital had the only Catholic community of any size at all. No church, but there was a small circuit of private homes and rooms in institutions.'

'That's where you met Rena.'

She had a feeling that if she didn't keep nudging him he'd be quite happy to let the conversation wander off in some other direction.

'That's right.' Lowry picked up a handful of shingle, selecting a pebble and throwing it towards a pointed rock. It landed well short, splashing into the surf.

'And she was working for the administration.'

He tossed another pebble. This time it was closer, but still adrift by a good few centimetres. 'I never could throw,' he commented. 'Yes, she was already tangled up in it when I met her.' A third pebble bounced neatly off the pointed tip of the rock. 'Bingo.'

Jamie felt a surge of unfamiliar irritation with the old man. 'Lowry.' He turned, with clear reluctance, to look at her. 'What happened? You said it was your fault. Do you think you should have done more?'

Lowry gave a harsh bark of laughter. 'More? The opposite actually. I should have done less. Much less.' He turned his hand over and let the remaining pebbles fall back onto the shingle. When he spoke again his tone was brisk. 'I told you back on Alegria that Rena was bright and kind. What I didn't tell you is that she was so beautiful that it kept me awake at night, looking for any justification I could find for breaking my vows.'

'Breaking your . . .' Jamie's brain caught up with her. 'You and Rena?'

Lowry nodded. 'If I'd had an ounce of integrity, I'd have walked away and never looked back. Or maybe I should have left the priesthood for her. As it was, I tried to have the best of both worlds, and I nearly broke her in the process. I told you that her work at the department ripped her apart. Well, a good deal of the blame lies at their door, but not all of it. A large part was down to me. The deceit, the subterfuge, she wasn't cut out for it. I told myself that all her problems were down to her work. I tried to persuade her to leave the research programme, when I should have been persuading her to leave me. I was too selfish for that, of course. All that happened was that we swapped the privacy of the confessional for the intimacy of the pillow. She told me how she felt, and I made meaningless noises, the lover's equivalent of two Hail Marys and an act of contrition. And then, one night, she told me she thought she was pregnant. She was lit up from the inside. Not glowing, like they say pregnant women do. The kind of light that hurts to look at. She was manic, talking about us being a family. And all I could think was, *This is the end of everything*.'

'I thought you said she couldn't have children.' Jamie was reeling. She'd never dreamed that something like that lay between them.

'She'd been doing her own research, using herself as a test subject.' His lips twisted. 'And me as well, I suppose.'

'And it worked.'

'No,' Lowry said. 'It didn't work. I lay there beside her, all night, listening to her whispering in the dark, promises to her unborn child. And the very next day she bled. It was a false

362

alarm. It was like something inside her shattered. She barely seemed to register when I told her we couldn't be together any more.' He rubbed his face. 'I didn't leave her straight away. I stayed for a while, made a few attempts to get her some help, but the only thing she was interested in was her work. She spent hours in the lab, barely eating, barely sleeping. I couldn't reach her.' He picked up another handful of pebbles, but this time he just let them run through his fingers, back onto the shingle. 'So I left.' He gave Jamie a slow, heavy smile. 'I know what you must be thinking. Any name you can give me, I've already pinned it on myself, time and time again. Coward. User. Hypocrite. I can't even use the excuse of youth. I was forty when I met her. She was twenty-six.'

Jamie was silent for a moment, trying to superimpose this new picture of a young, fragile Rena over the sharp angles and edges of the middle-aged woman she knew. 'But she did leave the programme. Eventually. She came and found you on Soltaire.'

Lowry gave another humourless laugh. 'There's a whole load more to the middle of the story. We didn't see one another for a few years, although we exchanged the odd mail. I came back to Earth. My faith limped on for a while, but the cracks were already running all through it, and eventually the inevitable happened. I had a breakdown, left the priesthood and came here. I thought I might be able to shape some new beliefs out of the broken pieces of my faith.' He looked out to sea again. 'I used to walk on this beach and watch the sun going down, vast and red and perfect, and I'd almost remember how it felt to believe. *There it is*, I'd think. And then the sun would disappear behind the horizon and the moment would be gone. One sunset I saw one of those green flashes sailors talk about, the whole sky lit up in emerald, just for a split second. I stood here, looking out towards the horizon and I thought, *If that doesn't make me believe again, nothing will.'* He was silent for a moment, as though waiting for the sky to light up again, like it had all those years ago. 'Eventually I realised I could only rebuild by going out into the world and starting over. Figuring out what I believed, moment by moment. I worked in various projects all over the place. In between I'd come back here and try and piece together what I'd seen and done.'

'And then Rena came.' Jamie thought she could see the shape of the story. Rena had been so desperate to get here. Had it been the place where she'd rekindled an old love?

He nodded. 'Rena came. I'd thought she was broken when I left Alegria, but I hadn't realised how much of her was still left to be destroyed. She was gaunt and greying, and looked like she hadn't seen daylight in months. She wouldn't talk to me when she first came, and when she did say anything it didn't make much sense. After she'd been here a while, I put all those little pieces together and realised what she was telling me. She'd found a new faith, an obscure little sect that hadn't attracted many followers. It preached austerity, silence, space.'

'The space between the stars,' Jamie said.

Lowry nodded. 'I never really got to the bottom of how she fell in with the Pretergnostics, but she thought finding them was a sign. It fit with what she was doing in her work. Now it was God's work. Stopping the population from growing and growing, keeping the emptiness of space for his voice.'

'Why did she leave?' Jamie said. 'If she was so sure.'

'Because she wasn't sure. She had all the fervour of a convert, with none of the bricks and mortar of long-held faith. There was too much crowding around her. Her new faith, her old faith, her work, whatever she still felt for me, all pulling at her. But she seemed calmer after a few days here, and I thought I could see a few traces of the old Rena. I thought I might be able to save her.' His face twisted. 'I might have left the priesthood, but I still had all the arrogance of someone who's certain that God has his back.'

'What went wrong?'

'She got a message from the head of her department. She didn't tell me exactly what he'd said, just that they were close to some breakthrough and they needed her back.' He looked out across the waves again. 'I remember how her hand rested on her stomach. Her fingers were curved out in front, around the empty air, like there was something there that I couldn't see. She left that day, and it was nearly ten years before I heard from her again. I'd founded Longvale on Soltaire by then. Her mail was almost incoherent, full of ramblings about the gods of life and death. But she wanted to get away. She said there was something terrible coming. I arranged for her to come to Longvale. I wasn't sure I was doing the right thing, but I still felt responsible for her. She turned up just a few weeks before the virus hit.'

He stopped talking, and plucked at the edge of the rock, a quick, nervous gesture. Jamie's mind was turning over, trying to piece together everything he'd told her. There were gaps there, she was sure. Some of them were just little chinks of omission. Things too private to share. But there was something else. Something which was stopping the pattern from becoming clear.

There was something terrible coming.

Close to a breakthrough.

The space between the stars. The space between the stars.

And then, like a full-force punch to the stomach, she had it. She felt a lurch of nausea, and she clutched at the rock, the sharp edge digging painfully into her fingers.

'My God.'

Lowry lifted his head and gave her a long, level look. 'Not God. Just men.'

'The virus . . .' The way it had attacked the fertility of survi-vors. Its strange, self-destructive pattern. Its atypical lifespan. 'It wasn't something natural. It was them.'

'They couldn't have known what would happen,' Lowry said. 'They just got something terribly wrong. When it first started, Rena was hysterical, raving about Yama and Kali, the Hindu gods of death, and about Oppenheimer and Hitler. Later, when I put it all together, there was a terrible moment when I thought they'd decided it wasn't enough to limit the fertility of the people they didn't want. I thought they'd tried to wipe them out. But I think it just got away from them. They over-reached themselves, and unleashed Armageddon, when they'd been trying to create Utopia.'

'Why didn't you tell me?' Jamie stood up, looking down at him. 'Back on Alegria, you knew what had happened, and you didn't tell me.'

'Because you would have hated her,' Lowry said. 'And there are so few of us. I tried *not* to know. I never asked her outright. But knowing, it's not about logic and thinking things through. Callan was right. It's deeper than that.'

'But she was part of it.' Jamie thought she could taste dust in her mouth. Cranwell. Cathy and her children. Everyone on Soltaire. Her half-sisters too; they were out there drifting on some unknown wind because of Rena and the others like her.

'Don't.' Lowry stood up. 'It wasn't her fault. She didn't know—'

'That's not what you told me yesterday. You said we all have to take responsibility for our part in things. Or does that not apply to people you've slept with?'

'All right.' Lowry made a sharp gesture. 'It was her fault. Among others. But she didn't know what was going to happen. No one ever thinks they're doing the wrong thing. The choices we make, we're all just trying to muddle our way through. It's not a flowchart. *If this, then this.'*

The blood was thumping in Jamie's ears, and everything seemed to be receding around her. Maybe when it was small enough, she'd be able to see the pattern in all of this. Because there had to be a pattern. It couldn't all just be a scatter of moments, colliding and sparking off one another until one day you looked around and realised you'd been part of the end of everything.

She felt an odd little flicker of something that was almost relief. A hard, bitter relief. There was a pattern. There was a reason, an explanation. There was someone to blame.

'Don't.' Lowry said again, searching her face and seeing something there that made his own expression fold in on itself. He reached for her, but she turned and stumbled up the beach, not looking back.

CHAPTER TWENTY-NINE

Jamie found Rena kneeling on the grass amidst the broken-teeth pillars of the old abbey. She turned at the sound of Jamie's approach.

'You did this.' Jamie was surprised how calm she sounded. 'You killed them all.'

For a moment something raw and frightened looked out from behind Rena's bloodshot eyes. Then the older woman blinked and it was gone, her expression hardening.

'It was all part of the pattern,' she said. 'I can see it now. Soon you'll all see it too.' Her lip curled. 'Maybe not *you*. I should have realised sooner. Not everyone can be saved. You're only half a person. Deformed.' She looked past Jamie as Lowry approached. Father Dominic and Finn were just behind him. 'We're all deformed. A broken priest. A barren woman. An idiot boy. Don't you see?' Her voice was almost pleading now, and she scrambled to her feet. 'It has to end. God's breath on the wind. I am become Death.'

'Rena.' Lowry stepped forward, reaching for her, but she shrank back, hatred stark in her eyes.

'Don't touch me. You should never have touched me. God will punish us.' She rubbed her hand across her eyes. 'No. That god was never real. There was never just one. They are legion.'

'It was your fault,' Jamie said, but the heat of her anger was fading, leaving her cold and heavy. What was the point of raging at this broken shell of a woman? Whatever she threw at

Rena would be absorbed by her madness and sink without a trace.

'We were saving the world.' Rena's eyes blazed once more. 'We could have saved everyone.'

'Everyone?' Jamie said.

'The righteous.' Rena's face twisted again. 'Not the broken. Not the ones who should never have been. We could have made a new world.'

'Full of people like you.' Jamie's whole body felt as if it was curled tight, like a spring. 'Go forth and multiply.' She gave a harsh laugh. 'Not that you were exactly in a position to contribute to the new master race. You're broken too.'

She was about to turn away, but Rena suddenly took a step forward, her hands curling like claws. Then a body lurched in between them. Finn's own hands came up, fending her off.

Rena shoved at him, but Father Dominic stepped up to her side and threw an arm across her shoulders.

'Come.' His voice was calm and gentle. 'Come with me, sister.'

For a moment Rena resisted, and then she sagged in his hold. Jamie and the others stood frozen, a strange tableau against the backdrop of an ancient ruin, as the monk led Rena away towards the cottages, one halting step at a time.

Finn was standing stiff and very upright, fists wedged beneath his chin, like a child just learning to box. 'Are you all right?'

'You have to be brave,' he said. 'That's what she told me.'

'Who?'

'Emily,' he said. 'She said you have to be brave and look out for other people. Then they'll look out for you.'

Emily? Even in the middle of her turmoil, Jamie had time for a quick flick of curiosity. But that was a question for another time.

Her gaze fell on Lowry, but she didn't want to talk to him. She didn't want to talk to anyone. She needed time to process what he'd told her.

'Come on, Finn.' She turned away from Lowry, and started back towards the harbour.

When they reached the house, her stepmother asked if they'd had a nice trip and Jamie smiled and said, 'Yes, thank you.' Finn's brow creased in confusion, but he didn't question her.

For lunch she made omelettes with the eggs from the Lindisfarne chickens, stuffed with spring onions and fresh herbs from the box Finn had brought back.

Afterwards, they went down to the harbour, while Jamie's stepmother slept in her chair. The tide had come in, covering the sea glass horse. She left Finn hunting for shells while she took Callan out for a sailing lesson. He learned quickly, his hands deft and easy on the ropes and the helm. As they turned back he gave her a keen look, and asked her what had happened on Lindisfarne. When she told him about Lowry and Rena he was silent for a long moment, and then he said, 'Well, it's done. Knowing about it doesn't change it.'

'But how do we live with it?' Jamie said. 'How are we supposed to live with her?'

'You don't have to,' Callan said. 'She's one of a handful of people in an empty world.'

'I want her to go away.' Jamie knew she sounded like a petulant child. 'I just want her to disappear so that I never have to think about her again.'

'Life isn't usually that convenient,' Callan said, before changing the subject with a question about the ropes.

Jamie's edginess persisted throughout the day. Her thoughts wouldn't settle, picking and worrying at everything the other woman had said, everything Lowry had said about her. Her unease seemed to permeate the whole house. Finn was on edge too, all nervous gestures and quick glances. Her stepmother was restless, unable to get comfortable in her chair, pain holding her to wakefulness long after Finn had padded off to bed.

The headland had sunk into a shadowy backdrop behind the room's reflection in the window, where another Jamie sat with another stepmother. The faces of those mirror-selves were shadowed and vague, and Jamie could have been looking through the glass into any one of the many times she'd sat in this room. Perhaps she'd just told her stepmother that she was leaving, heading out to a new world, leaving her old one unresolved. Perhaps it was the night her mother died.

When her stepmother leaned back in her chair and quietly asked, 'What happened?' Jamie flailed for a moment, as though she'd lost her place in a book. That question could relate to this *now*, or to any one of the others that she'd glimpsed through the darkened glass.

What happened?

Why did you stop talking to us?

Why wouldn't you see your mother?

'On Lindisfarne,' her stepmother added. 'Something happened, didn't it?'

Jamie felt off balance, out of time. That perfectly straightforward question had thrown up a whole host of possible meanings. And most of them came back to one thing.

Perhaps everyone had some hard husk of a memory deep inside them, shifting and scratching with everything that happened. Perhaps that's how it was for Rena.

Jamie tried to push that thought away, but she could feel an odd, uncertain emotion. It certainly wasn't forgiveness, and it wasn't understanding, but it could have been the first stirrings of something that might one day grow into either or both.

She shook her head, answering the simplest version of that question. 'Just something from a long time ago. It's done.'

When Jamie woke in the night she couldn't work out what it was that had snapped her from sleep. She fumbled for awareness, her mind struggling to catch up with her senses. And then the sound came again, and she sat up, her tired fug falling away in an instant.

Gunshots. Distant, but unmistakable.

She got up and looked out of the window, her pulse thudding, dull and ominous.

Nothing.

She found Finn out in the hallway, clutching the neck of his pyjamas.

'It's okay,' she said. 'Go back to bed. I'm just going to the harbour.'

'It was a gun. They had guns on Pangaea. They shot birds.'

'Yes,' she said. 'That's probably it.'

She dressed and went down to the harbourside where she found Callan. The wind had blown up, and the stones were slippery from the hard leap of waves against the wall.

'It came from up the coast,' he said.

'Lindisfarne.' She voiced the thought that had been lurking in the back of her mind since she'd opened her eyes.

'I think so.'

'Maybe it wasn't a gun,' she said. 'Maybe it was something else.'

'Like what?'

'I don't know.'

'Get the boat ready.' Callan turned and walked back towards the cottage.

She was just unwinding the mooring rope of the launch when he returned, holding a couple of waterproof jackets, his face set in grim lines.

'My gun's gone.'

'What?'

He climbed down into the boat. 'It was in its holster in the side pocket of my rucksack. I didn't check before now. She must have taken it. Maybe it was when we stopped at Walton Hall.'

There it was. *She*.

Jamie pulled on the jacket Callan handed her, and fired up the motor. Just as she was about to kick it into gear, a figure came stumbling down the steps.

'Finn.' Callan stood up, setting the boat rocking. 'Go home.'

Finn sat down on the edge of the jetty, his mouth a stubborn pucker.

'You can't come,' Jamie said. 'We don't know what's going on.'

But he was already scrambling down into the boat, almost overbalancing in the process.

Callan swore and grabbed his arm, shoving him into a seat. 'Sit there and don't move.'

'He can't—' Jamie began, but Callan rounded on her.

'We don't have time to argue about it. Just go.'

Jamie opened the engine up for the first mile or so, battering them on into the wind and waves. As they drew closer they could see lights near the old abbey.

'How quietly does this thing run?' Callan asked.

'It's almost silent on its lowest speed.'

'Might be an idea to throttle back then.'

The reduced pace was torturous. Jamie found that she was drumming her fingers on the helm, echoing the rhythm of the *faster faster faster* that was running through her mind. She was so focused on their destination that she didn't notice the change in conditions until Callan said, 'Wind's dropping.' The spiky waves had smoothed to vague furrows. There was still the odd gust, but there was little conviction behind it, and she could already feel the settling calm that would greet the dawn.

They were approaching the end of the island, and Callan kept his voice low. 'Where do we land?'

Jamie hesitated, shifting her hands on the tiller. 'There's the harbour in the middle, but that'll take longer, and anyone looking out from the retreat will see us. Might be better to beach it here. It's a shallow slope, so we shouldn't damage the hull.'

'Okay.'

They were about a hundred metres out, and when she turned the engine off, the current drifted them towards the shore. Just as they ran up onto the shingle she thought she saw a shadow moving on the sea, a little distance away. When she tried to focus, it slid away into the darkness. She swiped her hand across her eyes which were stinging from the sea spray, and then swung her legs over the side, splashing down into the shallows to the rope around a spike of rock.

'Stay with the boat,' Callan said to Finn, as he joined Jamie on the shore.

They stepped carefully over the rocks and up to the cottages at the edge of the village, where Jamie tried to pick up the pace. Callan put his hand on her arm.

'Careful.'

As soon as they stepped into the lane it was clear that the moment for caution had passed. Lowry was lying in the road, his head cradled in the lap of a middle-aged, tonsured man. The monk – Brother Xavier she assumed – saw Jamie and raised his free hand in a weak gesture.

'Help us.'

Jamie stumbled across the distance between them and fell to her knees. Lowry's eyes were open, and he tried to smile when he saw her, but the attempt was shanghai-ed by pain. Blood was soaking through his shirt, staining his side red-black.

'What happened?'

'Rena.' It was Brother Xavier who answered. There was a patch of blood on his sleeve. 'I heard voices and I came out and found Lowry trying to stop her. She shot him, and when I shouted, she shot at me too.'

'Stop her doing what?'

Lowry shifted, as though he was going to try and sit up, but the monk pressed him down again. He groaned and clutched at his side. 'You have to stop her. I didn't realise. I thought she might harm herself, but I didn't think . . .' He gave another groan, his whole body convulsing around the bullet wound, his eyes closing.

Callan leaned down to grip the old man's hand. 'Lowry. Stay with us. What's she going to do?'

Lowry took a couple of rasping breaths, and opened his eyes again, staring up at the sky. For a horrible moment Jamie thought those breaths had been his last, and then he coughed and focused on Jamie.

'That pack from her lab. It wasn't just a test kit. I saw it. There are vials, serums.'

Realisation hit her hard in the stomach, as though Rena had left another bullet waiting for her. 'The virus.'

Lowry tried to speak, but his words were lost in another spasm of coughing. It was Brother Xavier who answered. 'She said she was going to finish what had been started. That God wanted everyone gone, so he could start again. She said . . .' His voice caught a little. '*I am become Death.*'

Jamie stood up, staring along the lane. A figure was jogging back from the direction of the harbour. For a moment she froze, and then her vision cleared and she saw the rangy frame of Brother Dominic. He was breathing hard, his robe caught up above his knees.

'I couldn't find her.' He turned to his brother monk. 'You're sure she was going to the boats?'

Brother Xavier nodded. 'She said she was going to be a fisher of souls.'

'Where's she going?' Callan said. 'Why didn't she just infect herself? Let things take their course?'

Jamie was replaying that confrontation earlier in the day, a cold understanding breaking over her.

'*God's breath on the wind.* It's not just us she wants to kill. She's trying to finish everyone. She's going out to the turbines.'

For a moment the low shiver of the waves was the only sound. The faces of the four men were frozen into silver-white masks, the shadows and hollows stark in the moonlight. Jamie's own face was numb, and she couldn't work out what expression she was wearing.

'The range isn't big enough.' There was a crack of doubt running through Callan's voice.

'We have to go after her.' Jamie's frozen inertia cracked, and she felt a surge of tight energy. She turned and set off back towards the path between the cottages.

Callan caught up with her as she reached the shore, the crunch of the shingle too loud beneath their feet. 'She's got a head start. She may be there already.'

'She must have taken a dinghy. There were no launches in the harbour. We can catch her.'

'And then what?' They'd reached the boat, and Callan threw his weight against the hull, shoving it out into the shallows as

Jamie scrambled in. 'She'll hear us coming, and she's got my gun.'

'I don't know.' Jamie lurched down the boat to pull the engine cord, and then stopped. 'Finn.'

He was crouched in the stern, his knuckles white as he clung to one of the gunwales. She'd forgotten he was even there, and they were already drifting clear of the shore.

'Shit.' She pulled the cord and the engine burred into life. 'Shit.'

'Focus,' Callan said.

As she turned them out to sea, the turbines were just visible in the distance, silver-white in the moonlight, their great blades stirring the darkness, soundless and steady.

'We don't know which one she's gone to,' Jamie said.

'Aim for the nearest,' Callan said. 'We'll see the boat when we get closer.'

After they'd been going for a couple of minutes he pointed to the base of the closest turbine where Jamie could just make out a blurred shadow. As she adjusted the tiller, the launch gave a sputtering groan, and then all engine noise fell away, leaving them drifting in near-silence.

The tank.

'We're out of oil.' Her voice sounded dull and flat.

Callan picked up the emergency paddle and slid it over the side. 'Then we row.'

'It'll take too long.'

'Do you have a better idea?'

Jamie stared out across the dark sea.

'Yes,' she said.

She stripped off her sailing jacket, shivering as the chill of the night air brushed her bare arms. Then she pulled off her boots and her jeans. Finn stared at her, wide-eyed.

'Stay with Callan,' she said unnecessarily, and then she swung herself over the side and into the sea.

It was colder than she expected, and she floundered, her face dipping below the surface. She'd never swum this far out, and she had a panicky image of the dark depths below her.

Full fathom five.

The fear twisted into a stab of adrenaline, and she kicked up and away from the boat, surfacing straight into the strongest front crawl she could summon up, snatching her breaths between the waves. As the turbine grew closer, looming over her, she kept her head down, terrified that she might see Rena staring back at her, gun poised.

Her leg scraped against something hard and sharp-edged, and she stopped, sculling on the spot, her hand going down to her shin. It didn't hurt, but she was fairly sure that was just the cold. She was right under the turbine, and when she felt cautiously around with her toes, she felt the rough foundations, slippery with weed. She stood up in the waist-deep water above the concrete base, barnacles crunching beneath her bare feet. Her wet hair dripped strings of seawater between her shoulder blades, and she clenched her teeth to stop them from chattering as she waded over to the steps, where Rena's boat was tied up. When she looked back, she could just about make out the boat, a darker patch of shadow against the sky, but she didn't dare risk a sign to Callan.

She scrambled up the steps and crouched down by the turbine's central frame, peering up the round metal staircase that disappeared up into the darkness. There was no sign of Rena. Perhaps she was already sliding a vial into the valves. Or maybe she was crouching on the stairs, bloodshot eyes flared wide in the darkness, gun pointing down. It took every bit of will Jamie possessed to move towards the staircase. She was racked tight with tension, waiting for the blaze of a gunshot, and the flare of agony as it entered her chest.

Nothing.

She stepped up onto the first steel-mesh step.

Nothing.

She climbed slowly, feeling for each step as she went. Every instinct was shrieking at her to *hurry, hurry, hurry* but she was terrified of slipping and sending a tell-tale clang up to the platform above. After the first turn of the stairs she couldn't see the water any more, and she had no idea whether Callan was close. She kept climbing, trying to remember the layout of the main platform. Was there any cover when you reached the top of the stairs?

The answer to that question came suddenly, when she rounded another turn and stumbled through a metal-framed doorway onto the platform. Her pulse spiked as she lurched backwards, almost toppling down into the dark stairwell below. She clutched at the railing with both hands as her breathing steadied. She'd seen little of the platform in that brief incursion.

A flash of glass on the other side of the space. The window of the control booth?

Something looming to her left.

A metal railing to the right.

'It's all right.' Rena's voice sliced through the silence. 'I know you're there. You can come out. Don't be afraid.'

Jamie froze, options running through her mind, soundbite swift as news tickers on a screen.

Rush out. Take her by surprise.

Engage her. Talk to her.

Distract her. Grab the gun.

She had to make herself move, or they were all dead. But she'd never been so aware of how breakable she was. All that exposed skin, too thin a layer over the parts of her that had to be kept safe.

She took a deep breath, and stepped round the side of the doorway.

Rena was crouched over a cluster of machinery to the left-hand side of the platform, looking grey and sickly in the artificial light. Above her head a heavy metal pipe rose to meet the central frame, just below the massive turning pin. The gun was in a loose grip in her right hand, while she used her left to turn a dial on the machine.

'Stay there,' she said. 'I'm nearly done. I'll be with you in just a second.'

'Rena.' Jamie's gaze darted around the platform. Had she loaded the vials yet? Was the virus already moving through the pipes, closer and closer to the distribution filters on the blades? No. The arms weren't turning. Was it worth rushing her? If she could just see the vial. 'You don't have to do this. I know you believe it's God's will, but what if you're wrong? What if we're supposed to live, build a new world, just like you said?'

Rena pressed something into place and then stood up, the gun hanging loose in her hand.

'You don't believe that,' she said, perfectly pleasantly. 'You don't believe in anything, do you?'

A footstep clanged on the stairs, as though someone had stumbled somewhere below them.

Rena peered past Jamie. 'Is that Marcus?' she said, a shy smile spreading across her face. 'Has Marcus come with you?'

'He's hurt.' The footsteps were closer, just a turn of the stairs away, or maybe that was a trick of the echoes. She hesitated before adding, 'You hurt him. Don't you remember?'

'We hurt each other.' Rena's voice sharpened. 'People do that, you know.'

'No,' Jamie said. 'You shot him. He's back on Lindisfarne, hurt.' An idea flicked a quick fin in her mind. 'He sent me to get you. He wants you with him.'

For a moment Rena stared at her, biting her lip, and then her expression darkened. 'He doesn't want me. He never did. But it's all right. It's meant to be like this. All the dispossessed, the lonely, the broken, they'll inherit the Earth.'

'They won't,' Jamie said. 'They'll be dead if you do this.'

'Then they'll have the void. The space between the stars.'

Her gaze snapped past Jamie as Callan stepped onto the platform. Jamie felt a surge of relief.

'You don't need the void,' he said. 'There's plenty of space for everyone now. You could go anywhere. You'd never have to see anyone else if you didn't want to.'

Rena shook her head. 'There'll never be enough space. There's too much filling it. All the stuff between us. All the words, all the hurt and broken things. We can't spread our wings. We can't stretch out. But in the void we'll be what we should be. In the void we'll all be angels.'

She took a step backwards, moving towards the control room. The gun was still slack in her hand. Behind Jamie, Callan shifted his weight, and she could feel him working through the same calculation she had. How long would it take to cross the space between them? How long would it take her to raise the gun and fire?

Jamie felt her spine tightening at the thought of the bullet tearing into him. *Don't*, she wanted to say, selfish and irrational. *Please*.

Rena was almost at the door of the booth.

'Rena.' Callan moved forwards, stopping as she tightened her grip on the gun and pointed it straight at his chest. 'It's okay, Rena. We can work this out.'

'I have worked it out,' she said. 'It's all part of a pattern. All those things I thought I got wrong, they weren't wrong at all. They were all part of it.'

It couldn't end like this. After everything they'd been through, it couldn't all end at the hands of a broken woman, high above the dark bulk of the North Sea.

A broken woman.

The thought rang a faint, off-beat bell in Jamie's memory. What was it Rena had said?

A broken priest. A barren woman.

Jamie put her hand on her stomach, an almost physical sense of her lost baby racking through her, with a more recent memory following hard on its heels. Rena stumbling towards her, just hours ago, arms outstretched and rage contorting her face.

She raised her voice. 'Why would God want you?'

'What?'

'If God has a plan, why would he choose you? You're broken. You're barren. God wouldn't even let you have a child when you had one of his priests to father it.'

'Jamie.' Callan's voice was low with warning. Jamie's heart was thudding. She knew the scale of the risk she was taking, but this was the only weapon she had.

There was a muscle twitching just below the other woman's eye, and she lifted her hand to swipe it away, as if it were a fly.

Jamie stiffened. Rena had used her gun hand.

She leaned into the attack. 'If there was anything right or good in you, God would have wanted to make more in your image. He'd have given you a child.'

'That's not true.' Rena's voice was shaking, that twitch growing more pronounced.

'No baby wanted you,' Jamie pressed on, vicious and reckless. 'You're empty. You're not real. If you were, you'd have had a child of your own. Someone would have loved you. No one ever did.'

As Rena plucked at her face again, Jamie opened her mouth to continue her attack. Just at that moment a voice spoke from behind her. 'Jamie?'

Oh Christ, no.

Rena's gun swung round, and Jamie turned, following the line that the bullet would take.

'Finn . . .'

He was pushing forwards, his brow furrowed and his hands upraised. She could almost hear the words echoing in his head.

Be brave.

'You don't belong here.' Even in the heat of the moment, Rena's voice was edged with contempt. 'Get away.'

But Finn was still moving forward, and, with a shock of fear, Jamie saw the other woman's finger tightening on the trigger.

No.

Jamie didn't remember moving. One moment she was frozen, her gaze locked on Rena's trigger finger. The next she was between Finn and the gun.

It was a funny thing, how long it took for the sound of the gunshot to make sense. Longer than when the same noise had broken her from sleep, just a little while ago.

Or maybe it was a long time ago.

She wasn't sure, but her shoulder was aching and there was fire spreading down her arm. Someone was shouting her name, but their voice was a long way away, so it couldn't be Callan, or Finn.

Finn.

Panic rose up, clawing at the base of her throat, making it hard to take a clear breath.

Rena had shot Finn. That was the noise. Jamie tried to turn, but there was something hard and cold against her back. She tried again, but a twist of pain went down through her shoulder and into her chest, like someone turning a corkscrew in her flesh. She shoved the side of her hand into her mouth, muffling the choked cry of pain. She had to be quiet. She couldn't remember why, but it had been important, just a moment ago.

There was another voice, scratching at the edge of her hearing, high and monotonous, hardly seeming to leave room for breathing. As she tried to focus, it started to rise and fall, like an imam calling the faithful to prayer. If she opened her eyes – *why are they closed?* – she'd be able to see the tower – *minaret, that's the word* – pointing up to heaven like a bony-knuckled finger. She forced her lids open. There was something looming above her, blocking out a great patch of stars.

Not a minaret. Too heavy.

The turbine.

Finn. The gun. Callan.

Rena. The gun. Rena. RENA.

With a lurch of disorientation, the world came back into focus. She was on the floor of the platform, pain raging through her shoulder. Finn hadn't been shot. She had. And somewhere out of sight, Rena was wailing that she'd failed.

Jamie shoved herself up, gritting her teeth against another shaft of pain. God, if she'd known it hurt this much, she'd have been more sympathetic to Callan.

Callan.

He was at the entrance to the booth, blocking it, the gun safely in his hand. Finn was crouched nearby, hands clutched over his head. And Rena was crouching too, clawing at the rail at the edge of the platform, her eyes wide and staring.

'Jamie.' Callan's voice was shot through with relief, but he kept the gun trained on Rena. 'Can you stand? The vial's still in the loader and I'm a bit tied up here.' He flicked the gun towards Rena whose wailing had sunk to a low, incessant mutter.

'I'm sorry . . . I'm sorry . . . I'm sorry . . .'

Bit late for sorry. But as Jamie clambered painfully to her knees, her shoulder burning, she could see that Rena had her head tilted back, her slack gaze aimed up at the stars. Her apology wasn't for what she'd done. It was for what she'd failed to do.

Getting onto her feet was going to be the thirteenth labour of Hercules, and Jamie couldn't face the attempt. She crawled over to the loading mechanism. A small vial of clear, innocuous-looking liquid was resting in a steel cradle.

The stopper was still in place.

Jamie waited for the leap of elation, but all that came was a dull-edged relief. A metal case lay on the ground beside the loader, lined with foam and holding three other vials.

'Is it sealed?' Callan's voice was tense.

'Yes.'

As she reached for it she had a flash of panicked certainty that it would slip from her fingers and smash on the platform, or that she might suddenly lose her own mind, and hurl it over the side to splinter on the base of the turbine. The world contracted, as if she was shrink-wrapped into the moment. Slowly, with shaking hands, she slid the vial into the empty slot in the case, and closed the lid.

'Got it?'

Jamie slumped back against the cold metal flank of the loader. 'Got it.'

She closed her eyes, thinking how comfortable the floor was. Really, she could just nod off right here. No one would mind.

'Jamie.'

Callan's yell yanked her back to herself.

Rena was crouched on top of the railing, balanced improbably, like a tightrope walker about to stand up, spread her arms and smile at her audience. No. She wasn't balanced. She was tipping sideways, almost rising to her feet as she fell, arms flung outwards, lips stretched around words that the wind whipped away.

Callan swore, lurching across to the edge.

'She can't swim,' Jamie said, and then remembered a more urgent danger. 'The rocks . . .' She scrabbled at the edge of the loader, and managed to get her feet under her, but Callan crossed the space between them in just a couple of steps.

'Don't,' he said, pushing her back down, gently but firmly. 'Don't look. It's over.'

It took Callan almost half an hour to get them down from the platform. Most of that time was spent trying to persuade Jamie to attempt the stairs. Her T-shirt was soaked with blood, and her dragging tiredness had given way to a bad-tempered truculence. She couldn't for the life of her work out why Callan couldn't just let her go to sleep. Finn stood looking back and forth between the two of them, like a child with bickering parents. Eventually, Callan's failing composure cracked, and he swore at her, before manhandling her to her feet.

A combination of fury at his high-handed method and pain from her shoulder pushed back the fug long enough for her to stagger to the stairs. Callan led the way down, with Finn bringing up the rear, and Jamie sandwiched between the two of them. When she snapped at Finn to give her room, Callan rounded on her.

'If we give you room, it's just more space for you to fall.'

They had to stop several times during the descent, as she bounced off the wall, or lurched heavily into Callan. At one point she found herself sitting down on the edge of a step, with no recollection as to how she'd got down there.

'Nearly there,' Callan said at least three times, but the stairwell kept twisting downwards until Jamie was gripped by a resigned certainty that they would never reach the bottom, that the world had rearranged itself while they'd been up on the platform, and the steps now plunged down into the bowels of the Earth. When he grunted and said, 'Last step, careful,' she felt nothing but a faint scepticism, until her foot jarred down onto the unyielding concrete, sending a jolt of agony through her.

Callan was at her side at once. 'Okay?'

'Hardly,' she bit back. 'I've got a bullet in my shoulder. Forgotten what it feels like?'

'Not the kind of thing you forget. Anyway, you don't have a bullet in there. It went straight through. Lucky for you, because I suspect my extraction skills aren't up to the standard of yours.'

'Great.' She leaned on him and let him help her down the steps to the boats. The sea was turning from black to silver-grey as the first thin cracks of dawn spread themselves across the sky. 'So I've got a hole right through me.'

'Could be worse.'

'How?' she said, teeth gritted against the pain.

'Sure you want me to answer that?' He nudged her towards Rena's dinghy.

Jamie clambered in and settled herself on the floor, with her back against the rowing thwart, and her eyes closed. 'Can you remember what you're doing?'

'I'll wake you up if we hit Norway,' he said, waiting for Finn to shuffle along the bench towards the bows before casting off.

CHAPTER THIRTY

Dominic came down to the harbour to meet them, catching the mooring rope and looping it through a ring on the little jetty. His face was calm, but Jamie could feel a tremor in his hand as he helped her off the boat.

'Rena's dead,' Callan said. 'We've got the vials.'

The monk made a quick, jerky gesture, as though he was thinking of crossing himself, but then he stopped. 'Thank God.'

'Lowry?' Callan asked.

Jamie felt a rush of cold, like she'd been plunged back into the dark ocean. She'd forgotten Lowry. The confrontation on the platform had blocked out everything else. She waited for the monk to say, *He's fine, he'll be fine*. The moment stretched out, and then Brother Dominic shook his head. Callan rubbed his face and said, 'Shit,' very quietly, and then, 'Sorry.'

There was a bitter edge of guilt to the grief that surged up around Jamie. She should have stayed, tried to save him. In the space of a couple of heartbeats a whole alternative scenario unwound. It was so full and clear that she felt a leap of hope. Lowry, carried by the monks into the refectory, laid out on the table. A trauma kit appearing from somewhere. No anaesthetic needed – he was unconscious. And anyway, she found the bullet on her first attempt, and the bleeding eased straight away. They all looked at one another and smiled in relief, and then Lowry opened his eyes and said, 'How long was I out?'

'You couldn't have done anything.' Brother Dominic was watching her. His voice was gentle. 'His heart stopped.'

She pressed the heels of her hands against her eyes. She'd never realised how close to hope regret really was. The hope that things might have been different, that somewhere else, in the vast, unfathomable universe, she'd saved Lowry, and still stopped Rena, and it hadn't been a choice of one or the other. This wasn't how stories like this were supposed to end.

End? The voice was so clear that she opened her eyes to see which of the men had spoken. And then she realised it had been Lowry's voice. *Nothing ever ends. There's always the next breath and the next.*

Her next breath was ragged and painful, but it still filled her lungs with cold, clear air, and he was right: another followed it, and another, all the way back to the refectory, where Brother Xavier was praying over Lowry's body. The old preacher looked peaceful enough, a not-quite-smile tugging at the corner of his mouth, but Jamie couldn't quite make herself believe that this slack, abandoned skin had once been filled with Lowry's wit and wisdom. And, as it had turned out, shame and regret.

She breathed through gritted teeth while Brother Dominic treated the bullet wound and covered it with a steri-dressing. She breathed all the way back to Belsley, Callan steering a cautious line along the coast. And when all the explanations were done, and a little of the colour had returned to her step-mother's grey, worried face, she sank into her bed and breathed her way down to a deep, troubled sleep, where dreams crowded close and Rena's voice said *sorry, sorry, sorry*, over and over again.

When she woke, the sun was already high in a clear blue sky.

Her stepmother looked a little brighter today. 'Needs must,' she said. Can't have two invalids in one house. Finn would be run ragged looking after us.'

'Where is Finn?' His name brought an echo of the fear Jamie had felt as he moved towards the gun.

No. That's over.

'Down on the shore with Callan. They've both been in and out, asking about you.' She smiled. 'He loves you, you know.'

Jamie's heart twisted hard.

'I don't know whether he'd understand it if you put it in those terms,' her stepmother continued. 'But don't make the mistake of thinking that his condition means he doesn't feel things every bit as strongly as the rest of us.'

'His condition . . .' She stopped. 'You mean Finn.'

Her stepmother gave her a concerned look. 'You don't look quite with it. Why don't you go back to bed?'

Jamie shook her head. 'I need some fresh air.'

Callan was on the harbourside, stirring a metal bucket with a stick.

'You're up,' he said. 'Took your time.' But she'd seen his quick glance, checking her over.

'What are you doing?' she asked.

'Mixing concrete. We can put the case in it, then sink it off the coast.'

Jamie nodded slowly, turning to look out at the sea. 'And what about next time?'

'Next time?' Callan gave her a faint smile. 'Next time I'd appreciate more warning if I'm expected to help save the world.'

She shook her head impatiently. 'I mean, what about all the other viruses and chemicals in labs all over the world?'

'Rena was a one-off,' Callan said. 'Most people don't wake up one day and realise they want to destroy the world. But you're right, I suppose. We're living from one deadly disease to the next, or from one god-bothering megalomaniac to the next, for that matter. But we always have been. We just weren't so aware of it. All we can do is get on with living and worry about things if they happen. Yes, the human race has left all sorts of deadly stuff scattered about the place. Biohazards, chemical poisons, radioactive waste. We can't erase those things from the world any more than Rena could pull down the turbines.'

Jamie nodded, thinking of her grandfather's plastic sculptures. 'I know. I just thought it would feel different. Safer.'

'What would?'

'Saving the world. Winning.'

'You don't save the world,' Callan said. 'You only ever buy more time.'

'You're upbeat,' she said with a small smile.

'More time,' he said. 'That's upbeat enough, isn't it? It's not so long since we all thought we were out of time. The next big thing could be a thousand years away, and we'll be long past worrying about it.' He gave her a lopsided smile. 'They can't expect us to be around to stop the apocalypse every time it comes calling.'

Was it really as simple as that? She wanted to believe him, but she had the sense of trailing ends, as though the thread of her life had frayed, and finally broken.

'Do you want to come with me later?' he said. 'To dump the vials?'

'Okay,' she said, and walked off towards the beach, where Finn was drawing pictures in the sand, the sea making little rushes towards him and pulling back just short.

The sun was setting by the time the concrete was hard. They took the boat out to a deep trench just off the coastal shelf. Callan wrestled the bucket over the side, and they watched it sink, faster than Jamie had expected, as though the sea was in a hurry to swallow it.

'It feels like someone should say something,' she said. 'Like a burial at sea.'

'Good riddance,' said Callan, and turned back to the helm.

As they headed back, the sky was growing heavy with a thick layer of cloud, and the air was ominously still and muggy.

'I might sit out for a while,' Jamie said.

He glanced up at the sky. 'Looks like it's going to rain.'

'You don't have to join me.'

'It was just an observation,' he said mildly, his eyebrows going up at her tone.

'Sorry.' She glanced away. 'I'm just . . .' She made an incoherent gesture.

'I know. Look, I brought some beers back from the pub. We could probably both do with a drink.'

'Are you asking me on a date?' she said, and immediately wished she hadn't. It was all that shock and stress draining out of her, and leaving her a little silly and reckless. 'I mean . . .'

He gave her a quick grin. 'Yes, you've caught me out. It's my best seduction technique. Get a girl shot, then offer her beer. And a patch of damp sand to sit on.'

'You didn't get me shot.'

His smile faded. 'I didn't do much to stop it. I should have just gone straight for the gun.'

'It's over.' Somehow saying that to him made her believe it more herself. 'You get the beers. I'll get the rug.'

Finn was in the kitchen with her stepmother who seemed to be giving him a cookery lesson. Jamie stepped lightly past the door, not sure why she felt the need to sneak about. She retrieved the sea blanket from her room, and went quietly back downstairs and out of the house.

When she got back to the harbour, Callan was holding a

couple of open bottles of beer. They went down to the band of smooth sand just clear of the waterline, and Jamie shook out the blanket, wincing as the movement pulled at her shoulder.

'Here.' Callan caught the corner and laid it out. 'It's heavy.'

'It was my grandfather's. We always used it on the beach. When it was blowing a gale we were the only ones who weren't hanging on to our picnic rug to stop it taking off.'

'Was I supposed to provide a picnic?' He sat down on the rug.

'The beers will do.' Jamie hesitated, not sure of the appropriate distance to put between them. That other night, out on the sea, being close had seemed right and natural, but neither of them had mentioned it the following day. Then events had intervened in the most dramatic of ways, and she wasn't sure if the moment had been knocked aside, never to return. Rena was dead. Lowry was dead. She didn't know what was left.

Callan glanced up at her with a questioning look, and she pushed away the crowding thoughts and sat down, leaving a few careful hands' breadths of space between them. They sat in silence for a while, swigging their beer and watching the sea. Then Callan leaned back on his elbow and looked at her.

'So do you think . . .' He broke off and held his hand out, palm up. 'Rain.'

A large drop landed on Jamie's arm, and she looked up to see the sky blurring and the surface of the sea beginning to blister.

'Picnic's over, I guess.' Callan drained the last of his beer and sat up.

Jamie wedged her bottle into the sand, and brushed her hand over the rough burr of the rug. 'My sisters and I used to flip the blanket over and get under it when it rained. With the oilskin side up. Everyone else would be running back to the caravan park and the cottages, and we'd be here, three humps under an oilskin rug. Everyone must have thought we were crazy.'

Callan gave her a long, unreadable look, then tossed his empty bottle onto the soft sand behind them. 'Here.' He caught hold of the edge of the rug and yanked it up over their heads. Their upper bodies were under cover, but their legs were sticking out. The rain was growing heavier, hammering down hard enough to leave round dents in the smooth sand. Jamie's jeans were growing stiff and heavy, and she made an unsuccessful attempt to tuck her legs up.

'I don't fit as well as I used to,' she said.

Callan looked up at the edge of the rug, considering. 'Okay,' he said, sliding in behind her, so that he was lying down in the fold of the rug. 'There you go.'

'Well, that works for you,' Jamie said.

'Plenty of room under here.' He nodded towards the patch of rug next to him.

Jamie hesitated for a long moment, and then let her breath out in a huff of resignation and lay down next to him, her injured shoulder uppermost. The top of the rug settled on top of them, leaving just a sliver of space through which she could see the rain flattening the surface of the sea. They were both lying on their sides, tucked together like spoons, and she felt him shift so that his chest was pressed against the curve of her back. A few drops of rain ricocheted under the edge of the rug, splashing onto her bare arms.

She reached over to tuck the rug down, but Callan's arm came over her, pulling her against him.

'Plenty of room,' he said again, quieter this time.

She lay still, breathing in the familiar musk of the old rug. She thought she could feel Callan's heart beating where his body was tight against hers. Then he lifted his head a little, leaning over her, his breath warm on her face. For a few heart-beats she lay still. All those moments when they'd glanced off one another, never quite finding a fit. She felt him breathe out again, and she knew all she had to do was turn her head. A small movement, but it didn't seem small.

The next breath.

As she turned and kissed him, the rug shifted, letting another flurry of rain whip in. She tried to roll around, to put her back to the gap so that she could keep on kissing him without worrying about the rain, but her shoulder jarred against him, and she breathed in sharply.

He pulled back and looked at her. 'You okay?'

She nodded. 'Just my shoulder.'

'You want to go inside?'

She shook her head. 'It's still raining.'

He searched her face for a moment, then nodded and leaned in to kiss her again, starting at her mouth and moving along her jaw and round to the back of her neck, lifting her hair so that he could work his way from vertebra to vertebra down the line of her spine until her shirt got in the way and he had to abandon that exploration in favour of another. One hand twined in her hair, while the other slid round to the front, drawing small circles over her ribs, each one drifting a little lower. When he reached the waistband of her jeans, she stiffened a little.

'Okay?' he said again.

She nodded, not trusting her voice. As he eased the button of her jeans undone, she lifted her hip slightly, trying to help him, but triggering an awkward moment of close-quarters wriggling, all colliding limbs and tangled clothing. Eventually she managed to kick free of her jeans, and somehow he extracted himself from his, and then there was that first shock of unfamiliar skin on skin, but it passed so swiftly that she almost forgot this was the first time they'd been here. As his leg slid in between hers, she took another slow breath in, and on the outbreath she leaned back into him, until they were pressed so close together that the next step seemed easy and inevitable.

Afterwards they lay quietly, his arms wrapped tight around her.

'The rain's stopping.' He lifted the edge of the rug to look out.

Jamie pulled his hand back. 'It might start again. Better stay here for a while.'

He kissed the back of her neck. 'Any idea what we could do?' She could feel the smile in his voice, and she felt her chest expanding, like some constricting bands of tension had fallen away.

'No clue,' she said. 'Game of I-spy? Quick round of—'

She broke off with a gasp of laughter as his hands created an instant distraction. Then he said her name, low and quiet, and she didn't feel like laughing any more.

The rain stopped, leaving only the sound of the sea as a low, insistent soundtrack.

Funny, she thought. All those millions of miles, all those worlds, and all she'd ever felt was *too much, too close*. And then it all spiralled and twisted down to just one moment, in one little corner of a world she'd tried to leave, her body wrapped so close around another that you couldn't have slid even a breath in between them.

She thought that if she didn't say it now, she might never say it at all. But the only word there was for this didn't seem right. Not for all the bits and pieces of him and of her and of the two of them together. So she told him slantwise, in fragments and snatches of words, in random moments and random thoughts. Seeing him for the first time. The bullet glinting in his side. When he spoke softly to Finn. When he'd said said, *No,* but he'd wanted her. His ship, falling from the sky. His hand on her hip in a night-sunk garden. No pattern, no conclusions, just *this is how it is.*

And when she was done, he smiled – she could feel the shape of it against her neck – and brushed the line of her body with his palm, the calluses snagging at her skin, and she thought, *Yes, that too.*

She often rides on the beach in the early morning, when the tide has washed the sand clean and no one has been out to break up that smooth expanse.

She's tried to persuade Callan to learn to ride, but he just says, Old dog, new tricks.

It's like flying, she once told him. It's not, he said and turned away. She thought he was angry, but that evening, when she took Emily up the beach to Bamburgh, he brought his dinghy and raced her along the shore.

The old man, he calls himself. But he feels younger to Jamie than he did before. Maybe it's because the life he lived has gone, and taken years with it. Being with him isn't what she thought it would be. There's more room in it than she remembers from those years with Daniel. Sometimes he goes off in his boat for days, alone, or with old Gray, the fisherman from Lindisfarne, and it never occurs to her to think that his going away has anything to do with her.

There are more people filtering in all the time, seeking the sea, just like Lowry said. They buried Lowry on Lindisfarne. Rena too. Their graves are next to one another, in the shadow of the ruined abbey, and when you sit there you can hear the sea. In those first days, Jamie felt like the world had lost some of its gravity. She hadn't realised how the old preacher had held them all together, keeping them in a loose orbit around one another. With him gone, it felt as though they were all just passing through, and for a while Jamie wondered if there was any reason to stay. There was her stepmother, of course, but they both knew that reason would fall away sometime.

As it turns out, the older woman is still with them. Her life is unravelling, growing thin and flimsy, but she still sits out on the patio overlooking the sea, wrapped in blankets and propped up with cushions. She's tired, she says. Almost ready to go. But not yet. Not quite yet.

A fortnight or so after the night on the turbine, a couple of hikers turned up and never left, and a week later a boatful of people who spoke no English. Brother Xavier set up a school on the island, and now they can talk, a little. Odd words, complicated gestures, and a lot of smiling and nodding.

Gracie came back after a few weeks. She'd met a woman who was trying to get an old steam engine working, and now it runs down the east coast line, bringing a surprisingly steady trickle of survivors into Alnwick. Whenever they turn up, Elsie mails Jamie on the network she set up, and someone goes down to meet them. If Jamie goes, she always gives Walton a wide berth, although she sometimes thinks they should go and check on the old people. But not yet. Not just yet.

It was a few weeks after Lowry and Rena died that Jamie saw the shuttle. It arced through the sky early one morning, dipping low as it disappeared to the west. That evening a group of people turned up, carrying few possessions and a story of a failed attempt to make the old world live again. When they started to disperse, a figure detached from the rear of the group, hanging back as though unsure she was welcome.

Mila was thinner than Jamie remembered her, and more nervous, her story emerging in short bursts. After each flurry of words she'd stop and bite her lip and look over her shoulder. After she'd been there a while, Jamie asked her, not sure she wanted to know the answer, if she'd seen Daniel.

'They all looked the same,' Mila said. 'The ones in charge. Most of them stayed, I think. The ones who were left.'

Mila went on to Lindisfarne with a couple of other survivors, but after a few days she returned. She said it was too quiet on the island. Jamie found her a cottage with a view of the sea, but she knew the girl didn't always sleep there. One night she knocked on Callan's door, when Jamie was with her stepmother. He didn't tell Jamie exactly what words were spoken, but she thought his No was probably a kind one. Afterwards Mila cried and told Jamie she was sorry, and Jamie found that it wasn't too much of a hardship to hold her until she was quiet.

There's a chill in the air this morning, and Emily is sluggish. He doesn't want to get his feet wet in the tongue of seawater lying across their path, and he sidesteps to avoid a line of marks on the sand. He never likes stepping in other hoof prints. Jamie doesn't know why.

She can always tell who's been out before her. There's a pattern and a language to the prints, but she doesn't recognise the shape of these ones. And they're coming from the far end of the beach, not from behind her. They end at the edge of a smooth round of sand, marked by a circle that looks like it was drawn with a stick. In the middle there's a name, one that she doesn't know. Beside the circle there's a scuff of human and equine prints, and then the regular line reasserts itself and heads off towards the dunes, as though something had attracted the unknown rider's attention.

Jamie looks down at the name. It seems like something a young person might do. There are a few youngsters here now. A couple of children who survived because they had no one to hold on to them, and a fifteen-year-old girl who doesn't talk about the time before. Mila sometimes plays with the children on the beach. They skim stones badly, collect sea glass with Finn, and build elaborate castles, their laughter an echo of all those summers from long ago.

The children were a double-edged blessing at first. Jamie couldn't look at them without performing an ever more complicated series of calculations, all circling round the same question. Which one would be left alone? Then one of the women from Alegria started to feel sick in the mornings, and suddenly the world was a different shape from what they'd thought, with a long line of possibility stretching out in front of them.

Not long after the Alegrian group arrived, Callan went off with Gracie to find their shuttle. The engineer came back full of plans to get fuel to the Phaeacian, but Callan was quiet and non-committal. Jamie tried to speak to him about it, but he snapped at her, before taking himself off on his boat. When he came back, he brought her a handful of sea glass as an oblique apology. One of the pieces of glass was rubbed to a smooth curve on one side, shot through with lines of amber and gold. On the other side there was a sharp break across the surface, the glass clear and unscuffed by the waves. She looked at it and thought, Yes, that's it. That's what we do to one another.

That night she tried to write a letter to Daniel. After an hour or so the page was covered with crossings-out and half-formed thoughts. In the end she just wrote, I'm sorry. We didn't fit. My fault, and yours, and other people's too. I did love you, but it wasn't what you needed it to be.

She wanted to say more. She wanted to tell him about all those other versions of themselves, all those other somewheres where things were different. The somewhere they kept trying till it broke them. The somewhere they never tried in the first place. The somewhere they got it right. And between all those somewheres, there were worlds being born and galaxies dying, and the two of them were just tiny fragments of something they'd never understand.

None of it sounded like something she'd ever say, so she left it alone, rolling the letter up and sliding it inside an old glass bottle which she took down to the headland.

She threw it into the outgoing tide, along with the amber sea glass. Perhaps they'd stay together, as some things did. Perhaps someone would find the bottle one day, with the piece of sea glass lying a few metres away, its crack smoothed away by the slow, patient grind of the ocean.

She looks at the name in the sand for a moment longer, wondering how it might fit into what they've made here. Then she hears her own name called, thin and faint across the waves. Callan is sailing close to the shore, and Emily pricks up his ears, anticipating a run. But today she smiles and shakes her head, waving Callan on. When he's gone, she puts her hand on her stomach, and nudges Emily back round towards home.

She'll tell Callan soon. Not quite yet. When she tells him, they'll both start trying to put the pieces together to find a pattern. They won't be able to help themselves. And there'll be all sorts of things that will have to be worked out and fitted in.

But for now it's just a possibility, just a fragment of what's left of them all, of that old nought point nought nought nought one statistic.

And it's enough. For now, it's enough, and so much more.